VULTURES

ALSO BY CHUCK WENDIG

THE MIRIAM BLACK SERIES
Blackbirds
Mockingbird
The Cormorant
Thunderbird
Interlude: Swallow (novella from Three Slices collection)
The Raptor & the Wren
Interlude: The Tanager (novella from Death & Honey collection)

STAR WARS: THE AFTERMATH TRILOGY
Star Wars: Aftermath
Star Wars: Life Debt
Star Wars: Empire's End

Zeroes
Invasive

ATLANTA BURNS SERIES
Atlanta Burns
The Hunt

THE HEARTLAND TRILOGY
Under the Empyrean Sky
Blightborn
The Harvest

NONFICTION
The Kick-Ass Writer: 1001 Ways to Write Great Fiction,
    Get Published, and Earn Your Audience
Damn Fine Story

CHUCK WENDIG

VULTURES

MIRIAM BLACK: SIX

SAGA PRESS

LONDON SYDNEY **NEW YORK** TORONTO NEW DELHI

AN IMPRINT OF SIMON & SCHUSTER, INC.

1230 AVENUE OF THE AMERICAS, NEW YORK, NEW YORK 10020

An imprint of Simon & Schuster, Inc. + 1230 Avenue of the Americas, New York, New York 10020 + This book is a work of fiction. Any references to historical events, real people, or real places are used fictitiously. Other names, characters, places, and events are products of the author's imagination, and any resemblance to actual events or places or persons, living or dead, is entirely coincidental. + Text copyright © 2019 by Chuck Wendig + Jacket illustration copyright © 2019 by Adam S. Doyle + All rights reserved, including the right to reproduce this book or portions thereof in any form whatsoever. For information, address Saga Press Subsidiary Rights Department, 1230 Avenue of the Americas, New York, NY 10020 + SAGA PRESS and colophon are trademarks of Simon & Schuster, Inc. + For information about special discounts for bulk purchases, please contact Simon & Schuster Special Sales at 1-866-506-1949 or business@simonandschuster.com. + The Simon & Schuster Speakers Bureau can bring authors to your live event. For more information or to book an event, contact the Simon & Schuster Speakers Bureau at 1-866-248-3049 or visit our website at www.simonspeakers.com. + Also available in a Saga Press paperback edition + The text for this book was set in New Caledonia LT. + Manufactured in the United States of America + First Saga Press hardcover edition January 2019 + 10 9 8 7 6 5 4 3 2 1 + Library of Congress Cataloging-in-Publication Data + Names: Wendig, Chuck, author. + Title: Vultures / Chuck Wendig. + Description: First Saga Press hardcover edition. | London ; New York : SAGA Press, 2019. | Series: Miriam Black ; 6 + Identifiers: LCCN 2018022465 (print) | LCCN 2018024534 (eBook) | ISBN 9781481448772 (hardcover) | ISBN 9781481448789 (paperback) | ISBN 9781481448796 (eBook) + Subjects: LCSH: Psychic ability—Fiction. | GSAFD: Fantasy fiction. | Occult fiction. | Horror fiction. | Suspense fiction. | LCGFT: Thrillers (Fiction) + Classification: LCC PS3623.E534 (eBook) | LCC PS3623.E534 V85 2019 (print) | DDC 813/.6—dc23 LC record available at https://lccn.loc.gov/2018022465

TO ALL THE UNCIVIL WOMEN WHO DON'T TAKE SHIT FROM SHITTY MEN

VULTURES

PART ONE

THE STARFUCKER

ONE

THE MISSING PIECE

Now.

This is what it feels like, six months into losing Louis:

It feels like someone has pushed a corkscrew through her middle. It is a comically large tool, this corkscrew, like a cartoon prop, but it feels cold and sharp as it pushes its way through her body every morning, every afternoon, every evening, every hour and minute and second of every fucking day and every fucking night, coiling deeper in her before it reaches her margins and then rips its way back out in one brutal yank, uncorking her insides, spilling her guts, hollowing her out from belly button to backbone. The vacancy is palpable, a ragged hole like a cannonball blast through a tall ship's sail, setting the craft adrift. It feels like her organs are exposed: her stomach, ripped out, unable to contain food; her heart ruptured and pouring blood; her lungs perforated, air whistling a mournful dirge through the ragged flaps of tissue with every miserable breath she pulls through them. Louis felt a part of her, once, and now he is gone. And she is reminded of that pain moment to moment—

Because she is carrying his child.

And that is the quite the ironic sensation, is it not? Louis is gone, and her middle feels ripped out—even as she experiences the opposite sensation of walking around with a squirming

3

fullness around her belly. It's as if the baby is not a baby but rather a black hole setting up shop inside her.

As she walks up to the Dead Mermaid Hideaway here in Hesperia, California, she feels the baby in there. Roiling around like a lone potato in a pot of boiling water. Little fucker won't stop moving. Like the baby wants to kung-fu-kick its way out of the womb. The doc they found for her in Beverly Hills, Dr. Shahini—with her enviable golden skin and those bold black eyelashes like the wings of a swallowtail butterfly—said that Miriam's body should release chemicals that make her welcome the presence of the child. The chemicals, she said, would help Miriam feel "at home" with the baby inside her, but Miriam told her, "Doc, my body doesn't make those chemicals." Because to this day, the baby feels like a parasite, an intruder—

(*A trespasser*)

—and mostly she just wants it gone. Gone because it reminds her of him. Gone because even in its fullness and agitation, it makes her feel hollow, empty, and painfully alone. And already she can hear Gabby chastising her inside her mind: *It is not an* it, *Miriam; she is a* her.

She's your daughter, not an end table.

"Feels like a fucking end table to me," Miriam grouses under her breath. "God, what a great mom I'm going to be." Like that matters. Right now, until she figures out a way forward, this child will barely be born before it dies—robbed from the world at the moment of birth. From darkness to a brief flash of light, and then taken away again. Returned to the formless chaos from whence all things come. Life gone too quickly to where it usually goes slow: unmade into death.

All part of fate's plan.

But Miriam is Fate's Foe. She is the Riverbreaker.

Fate will not write the end of this story. *She* will.

Miriam swears to herself now, then, always: she will figure

out how and why this kid—this parasite, this end table—is going to die, and she will save its life. Even if that means ending her own in the process. She owes that much to Louis. He is dead because she fucked up.

This baby will not suffer the same fate.

This baby will live.

Deep breath, Miriam. In. Out. The baby squirms inside her.

She takes out her cell and she texts **Gabby:** I'm here, Dead Mermaid Hideaway.

Gabby reponds: You're there early

Miriam: No traffic.

Gabby: Early is good

Gabby: See Taylor yet?

Taylor Bowman, the preening lackwit, and also the reason she's here. The doe-eyed pretty-boy is about to get himself murdered in the next—she checks her watch—37 minutes.

Miriam: I haven't gone in yet.

Gabby: I wish I was there with you

Miriam: I'll be fine. You've got a more important job. Any luck?

Gabby: None yet, will let you know

Gabby: What's the place look like?

Miriam looks up and describes what she sees: Awning has a fake mermaid skeleton draped across it. It's no lie. Someone has made a replica of a mermaid skeleton. It's a pretty good replica, too—still has some fish scale on its bony tail, some fake webbing between the fingerbones. The red wig is maybe a bridge too far, but the clamshell bra seems a nice touch. She doesn't bother describing the other signs plastered awkwardly around the doorway in: LADIES DRINKS = 50 CENTS OFF and LOOTERS GET DEAD and FAMOUS FOR OUR GHOST PEPPER MARGARITA, whatever the fuck that is.

Miriam adds: Shifty desert dive bar, except she doesn't

mean *shifty*, because autocorrect corrected *shitty*, so then she has to fix it in all caps: SHITTY desert dive bar duck you auto-correct, which just pisses her off more and leads her to type in thumb-punching rage, ducking motherducker fuck shift shit duck it.

Gabby: I told you, you should just put the profanity in your phone's dictionary.

Miriam: It's not my phone and that sounds like work. I'm going in. Will text you updates.

She slides the phone into her back pocket and heads inside the bar.

TWO

MERMAID CHUM

Inside, it looks like someone took a Gulf Coast dive bar out of Florida with a giant crane and carted it over to California, plonking it down here in the heat-fucked Mojave. Dollar bills are stapled to the ceiling. Various bits are covered in boat netting. The booths are old wood, and some of the tables are glass over ship's wheels. Then of course, you have all the assorted mermaid tchotchkes: sexy mermaid art, sexy mermaid lamps, and above the dead-ass jukebox in the back hangs a mermaid figurehead, like the kind that would point the way at the bow of an old pirate ship. Everything is dusty and dim. A little bit cracked. A little bit rotten. *Like me*, Miriam thinks, grimly cheerful. Or cheerfully grim.

The bar is pretty empty. It is, after all, noon on a Tuesday, and this bar is in the approximate epicenter of Satan's dusty asshole. She figures it probably lights up late in the day with bikers and truckers.

Right now, some old sunburned shriv sits in the back across from a trailer-trash blonde, asses hanging off their stools. The old dude is in some kind of man muumuu, and the lady wears a tie-dye halter-top and cut-off jeans *so* cut-off, they look like they want to crawl up the woman's butt like a teenage boy's jizz tissue hidden clumsily between two couch pillows. Other than that, the only person in here is the bartender: a gruff, butch woman whose pockmarked face looks time-scoured and worn, the gravity of a hundred thousand scowls having long dragged it down toward her buff-yet-paradoxically-bony shoulders. Her hair is short-cropped, dyed a pink that is less like the pink of a pretty heart or a My Little Pony and more the pink you'd get if you blended up a pack of hot dogs and poured the resultant slurry into a frosted glass.

Miriam sits.

The woman regards her the way one regards gum under one's shoe.

"'Sup?" the woman asks.

"Hello," Miriam says, drumming her fingers on the wooden bar top. "Lovely nautical theme you have going here."

"Thanks," the bartender says, but she doesn't *sound* thankful. She plants her arms out like a couple of kickstands, and Miriam regards how each is swaddled with ink—tattoos galore, all various animals, cats and wolves and birds and snakes. "Whaddya want?"

"That question, right there . . ." She clucks her tongue. "That is a tricky bitch, that question. What I want, what I want, whoo. Yeah. I want what every woman wants. Respect. Peace on Earth. Equality and justice. I want for nobody to give a shit that I don't shave my armpits. For good men to carry me around on a palanquin made of the bones of bad men. Mostly, I just wanna be left alone. To find somewhere at the ends of the Earth where I can go sit, be it a beach or a mountain, and stare out upon the horizon, where no one will bother me. Though, if we're being honest, really honest, *teen-girl-diary honest*, what I want is a fucking drink and a smoke."

The bartender sniffs. "You found the bona fide end of the Earth here, sweetheart. And I don't know what a . . . pelenguin is, so I can't help you there."

"Palanquin. It's like a—I dunno, like a bed or a cart you use to carry people. Don't you read trashy fantasy novels?"

"No."

"Not even with the mermaid shit going on here?"

"Still no." The bartender shrugs. "Can't help you there. But I can help you with the drink part. No smoking in here, though."

"You can't—what? You can't serve me alcohol."

"Why not?"

Miriam points theatrically to her middle.

"Maybe you're just fat."

"Uh, *rude*. Though—" She thinks about it. "Maybe that's not rude, you not making an assumption about me. Okay, I take it back. Not rude. Still, I'm telling you that I am *currently with baby on board*, so you can't serve me booze. Pregnant bitches can't drink. Even if what I want is a glass of your lowest-shelf tequila, tequila that has no lime in it but has perhaps once looked upon a lime."

"I can make you a ghost pepper margarita."

"I don't want that. I don't know what that even is."

"A margarita?"

"A *ghost pepper*. Is it a pepper that died?"

The bartender has reached the end of her rope in terms of patience, and she crosses her arms and gruffly asks, "Lady, you want a drink or not?"

And now it's Miriam's turn to reach the end of her patience, because she will not be out-impatiented by this gruff lump of pink-haired bison jerky. "You're missing my *point*, ma'am. It doesn't *matter* what I want. I don't get what I want. Nobody gets what they want. If I got what I wanted, I'd be on that beach with a hollow coconut full of blackstrap rum and no baby in my belly and no psychic gift in my head and no *Trespasser* fucking with my skull at every turn and did I mention that my head is broken and *did I mention* that the man I loved is dead now and *did I goddamn jolly well mention that*—" She hears herself talking faster and faster, louder and louder, and so she quickly swallows whatever nonsense was about to come out of her mouth, clamping her teeth so that no more words can easily escape. "Sorry. Point is, I can't drink. I mean, I can. But I shouldn't. I'm *responsible* now. So, no drink for me. What I *need* is information."

"I'm not your Google."

"I don't want to know the capital of Djibouti; I want to know if you've seen someone in here recently."

The woman arches an eyebrow to a near-perfect point. "I don't roll over on my customers."

Miriam slides a twenty-dollar bill across the wood. "And now?"

"What's her name?"

"Her name? Why her?"

The bartender grimaces. "Because it's a dyke bar."

"Is it?" She turns around and gestures toward the old dude. "What about him?"

"That's Sandra."

At hearing the name, the old man—woman?—turns and gives a little finger-waggling *toodle-oo* wave. "Oh," Miriam says.

"You want proof gender is a spectrum," the bartender says, "look no further than the very young and the very old."

Miriam shrugs. "Cool. Fine. *Regardless*, I'm curious if you've seen a certain *dude* in here. You might know him—a celebrity, Taylor Bowman. Kind of a young, hunky surfer-stud type, but with a guarded, vulnerable emo-hotness to him? Coiffed hair, soft lips, firm jaw. Dumb as a fence, this guy, a real ding-dong, he's like a . . . a human Applebee's. Mediocrity given form, like a monster made of dismembered boy band parts."

"I know him; he's on that rom-com cop show. But I ain't seen him in here. Biggest celebrity type we get is the cat lady, the one who had all the surgery, now she looks like a cat? She comes in once or twice a year trolling for, well—you know. Pussy."

"That's weird."

"Hunting for pussy?"

"No, turning yourself *into* a pussy."

"Ennh. People do what people do."

"Yeah." Miriam bites her fingernail in frustration. "So, no Taylor Bowman. Shit." She doesn't mention that she's pretty sure he's going to be here in about, ohhhh, twenty-two minutes, and when that happens, he's going to get dead. Thing is, what if she's wrong? The rules are the rules: when she touches someone, she sees *how* that poor fucker will die and *when*, but the *where* of it is left for her to figure out. In this case, she thought she had it figured out: the vision of death showed her a wood-paneled office, an old metal desk, and invoices from different vendors scattered around it, all addressed to *The Dead Mermaid Hideaway* in Hesperia, CA. But now she's questioning that. What if the room and desk she saw were somewhere else? An owner's room in a house somewhere. Maybe here in town, maybe miles away. Maybe in a whole other *state*. Panic cuts through her like an icicle stabbed in her chest.

"If you're not gonna drink anything—"

"You have a back room? An office?"

The bartender nods slowly. "Yeah. Why?"

"Can I see it?"

Miriam pushes another twenty across the bar top.

Tongue in the pocket of her cheek, the bartender shrugs. "Sure. C'mon." And then she gets up and heads to the back.

Miriam kicks the stool out from under her, then follows after.

THREE

PISS AND VINEGAR

The bartender pushes open a swinging door and walks to the back. Miriam follows, and as she does, the baby inside her flips and flops, punching her bladder before starting up another round of hiccups. Which trips Miriam out because, to reiterate, there is a *human being inside of her* and when this *little jerk* has hiccups, she can *totally feel it*. The hiccups arrive like the popping of champagne bubbles, an effervescence that both tickles her and makes her feel queasy all in one go.

The baby, she fears, is drunk. Even if Miriam can't be.

Worse, now she's gotta pee.

And now, the heartburn is kicking in again. The heartburn that comes with this kid is a hard vinegar burn that gushes up through her windpipe, forcing her throat to feel tight and summoning a taste to her tongue like she's licking nickels.

Pregnancy is a gift, they all say. *Blah blah blah, miracle of life, what a special time, cherish these moments, you're creating life.*

Well, creating life is a stupid shitshow, she decides. It is less a harmonic convergence of angels singing and more a tired, insane Dr. Frankenstein furiously cobbling ill-fitting body parts together in a fireworks show of lightning and hiccups and heartburn.

They pass a door. Gender-free bathroom that identifies

itself as a bathroom by the icon of a toilet crudely carved into a wooden placard.

"I gotta piss," Miriam says.

"Jesus, fine," the bartender says.

Miriam elbows open the door and shimmies her way inside, finding a cramped toilet-closet that smells of dry rot and urine ghosts. She maneuvers her burgeoning belly past the sink, grunting as she hikes down her jeans and panties before sitting. Ironically, it takes a few moments to conjure the urine to her, and she mumbles, "C'mon, c'mon, *c'mon*." The piss arrives suddenly, without much warning, a porcelain-polishing firehose blast that is deeply, irrationally satisfying. That is one thing, at least, that pregnancy has improved: peeing is now a sublime, even *divine* release.

From behind the door, the bartender asks, "You from LA?"

"Sure," Miriam calls back. "Well. Not *from*-from there, but I came from there today."

"What about that Starfucker thing, huh?"

That Starfucker thing.

She decides to go for it.

"That's why I'm here, actually," Miriam calls back, still pissing, still polishing porcelain, *pssshhhh*. She literally has to speak over the sound of her own vigorous peestream.

"You serious?"

"Serious as an In-n-Out Burger, double-double, animal-style." God, she loves In-n-Out Burger now. California can fuck itself right into the ocean (which would at least put out the wildfires), but it needs to leave behind that fast-food joint. Since being pregnant, she *craves* their burgers the way a clown craves the terror of children.

Finally, the waterfall of scalding urine ceases.

Wait, no—

Still a couple more blasts.

Psst. Psssh. Sshhhht.

There. Done.

Ahhhh.

Miriam stands, wipes, flushes, washes, and manages to shimmy her way back out of the room, where the bartender awaits.

"You some kind of detective?" the bartender asks. Maybe not an odd question, but an ill-timed one, given that Miriam emerges victorious from an epic pee session, and it rather takes her off guard.

"What? Do I *look* like a detective?"

"You said you're here because of the Starfucker. Taylor Bowman have something to do with that?" The lady's eyes narrow.

"I think so. I think he might be a victim."

"You think he's dead?"

"Going to die."

"Huh." The bartender resumes her walk toward the door at the end of the hall, but when she gets there, she pauses, hand on the knob. "What they say, is it true? About the Starfucker? With the faces?"

"True as the teeth marks in my bedposts." The bartender gives her a look at that; Miriam ignores it. "He cuts off their faces. While they're still alive, of course, so he can show the mask he's taken from them. That's what he calls it. *The mask.* Sometimes, he says some fancy-pants bullshit about vanity and narcissism and self-image as he removes the face, always with a skinning knife—a Ka-Bar blade with a gut hook at the top. He's meticulous and effective. He holds the face up like it's a . . . hot towel a barber might slap on the face of a freshly shaved fella. He shows it to the victim, always a celebrity, though also always some Z-grade celebrity or some young up-and-comer. Then he uses that gut hook to rip out their middle. One pull across, unzipping them like a suitcase. Their guts spill out. He gingerly pats the face back onto their wet, red skulls—*pat, pat, pat*, like he's slapping the sauce onto a circle of pizza dough. Then he walks away. They die slow."

The bartender blanches. "You seem to know a lot about this."

"Could be a hunch." She shrugs. "Or hey, maybe *I'm* the killer."

"Maybe you are. Or maybe I am."

Miriam elevates her eyebrows in a gesture of *yeah yeah, anything can be anything, whatever, can we just get on with this?* At least, that's the message she hopes her face conveys.

The bartender opens the door.

Miriam steps through, into darkness. The bartender reaches behind her, flips a light switch, but already in the half-dark Miriam sees a figure in the room, a man sitting bound to an office chair—a chair that looks familiar, in front of a familiar desk. The man, too, is familiar. . . .

Lights on. Taylor Bowman's panic-stricken face lights up like a spotlight as he sees her. Behind the swaddling of duct tape around his mouth, a scream lies trapped, muffled there behind the gag. He struggles in the chair, hands and feet similarly affixed with duct tape.

Oh, shit.

One of the bartender's arms wraps around her throat, closing tight as the woman's other arm braces it tighter—

Fifteen years from now, a different place. Cold, wet, pine trees standing around. The bartender is older, heavier, bundled up in layers of rain jacket. Hood, no umbrella. She stands in front of a gravestone in a cemetery, the rain going now from a pissy drizzle to a hammerfall, and she says to the grave, "Sorry, Dad. I miss you. I'll be seeing you soon, though. It's my time. And you can't change that." Then she peels off one layer of a coat, and then the sweater underneath, until her inked arms are revealed and bare to the rain. The tumors inside her are thick and fibrous, but they won't take her, not today, because the straight razor in her hand is eager to do its work, and it does— two lines slashed vertically, one down each arm, from the wrist to the bend of the elbow, fsshht, fsshht, each arm like a gutted fish, and the woman sits, leaning back against her father's head- stone, and the rain pulls the blood from her, washing it to the ground, as she dies.

—it's a blood choke, a carotid restraint, a mean-ass sleeper hold. It's a good one. Miriam's not ready for it. Her vision wobbles in and out, blackness spreading in from the edges of her vision like motor oil. She stomps a foot down, but the bartender, she's well placed and well braced. Miriam struggles like hell. She cranes her neck to the side, cheek against the tattooed arm—her mouth cranes open, her jaw crackling—

Chomp. She bites down hard. Teeth sinking into inked skin. Blood wells up around her mouth, down her chin, down the woman's arm. But *still* the woman is undeterred—

Miriam's heels begin to judder against the floor.

The baby, please—

She doesn't know what the resultant hypoxia would do to the child inside her, but already she wonders, could this be the thing that kills it in three more months? One bad injury now leading to a troubled birth? *If I can't get oxygen, the baby can't get oxygen . . .*

"Hold . . . still . . . ," the bartender says.

"Nnngh," Miriam grunts, the darkness now a living thing, reaching up and pulling her down, down, down. As it does, she sees something on the woman's arm—a familiar tattoo that had been lost amongst the others. Miriam didn't see it before, but now it's there, and she focuses on it—

A spider.

Black, with a white circle on its back, in the circle three lines spinning out from the center.

Once seen on a playing card handed to a man named Ethan Key as he died. Handed to him by his killer.

Destinare . . .

Nona, decima, morta . . .

"P-please," Miriam says.

But it's too late.

The blood choke does its job.

Her head is light as a balloon (*red balloon*), and it seems to float away from her, drifting higher and higher until suddenly it pops—*ploink!*—and down she plunges, down, down, down, falling fast into the black.

PART TWO

NO TRESPASSING

FOUR

Fuck Fuck Fuck Fuck

THEN.

The train of thought inside her head is long and fast, an iron beast black as the devil's own spit, traveling in circles and spirals, the lead locomotive passing its own caboose time and time again. *I can't be pregnant*, Miriam thinks as the ambulance drops a wheel into another pothole on its way to the highway. *I can't be pregnant. I can't be pregnant.* Choo-choo. Bang and judder, thump and shudder. The chain between the restraints binding her wrists rattles against the metal cuffs. *I can't be. The doctors told me my insides were ruined.* She envisions her innards like they've been run across a cheese grater: red, pulpy curls everywhere like blood-soaked pencil shavings. *I can't be pregnant. I can't be a mother. It's not physically possible, and it's not intellectually emotionally spiritually possible, either. If there is even a teeny-tiny modicum of justice in this universe, it cannot—will not—let me be a mother.*

But of course, that's where this train is heading, isn't it?

It pulls into the station of a single conclusion:

A modicum of justice? It doesn't exist. Not in a sliver, not in a splinter, not in a mote or molecule. The universe *is* unjust.

It is unfair as fuck.

There exists no cosmic balancing force, no great ledger where all the debts and credits are neatly squared, no scale in the hands of a blind lady.

And so, as the universe is a boldly unreasonable place, she decides that what she believes couldn't be real is in fact Very Goddamn Real:

Miriam Black is pregnant.

Louis gave her this child, and then he died. Shot by Wren in a cabin she once imagined was her escape from the world: a precious snow globe kept separate from the rest of life's uncomfortable grievances. Now Wren is gone, Louis is dead, so is his one-time bride, and so too is the vicious human carcinoma, Harriet—Harriet, who only died once Miriam cut open her chest and ate her heart. Because apparently, that's a thing.

And now, Miriam is pregnant.

It is the only explanation. She stood there under the shower spray in the police station here in backwater Pennsyltucky, and as she stepped out, she received a death vision like no other: a vision that swept up across her without ever having to touch another person. But she *is* touching someone, isn't she? A flicker of humanity inside her—not alive, not aware, not yet, not really, but for fate's purposes, that is enough, for the baby's fate is already signed, sealed, and delivered. All of time cast not in a line but balanced in a bundle of moments on the head of a pin, and in that bundle is a moment like any other, a moment she wouldn't or shouldn't give a hot red fuck about—a child dying upon birth, nine months after conception. Great, so what, that's life, that's the world, *infant mortality is a thing* and it's not her problem. Except it is. This is her circus, this is her monkey, her little baby monkey.

An impossible child, unable to be born.

Dead before it reaches the light.

Again, she thinks.

The cop here in the ambulance with her is Bootbrush—turns out, his name is Stuckey. Sergeant Abe Stuckey, in fact, though she still thinks of him as Bootbrush because of that black broom mustache hanging under his nose. He's watching her *not* like a hawk regarding its prey, but rather like a dog trying to understand an octopus. He regards her as if she's an alien: some otherworldly thing cast into his care for a short time.

The ambulance takes another bounce. She nearly falls off the white metal bench they have her seated upon. The ambulance driver is the only paramedic present. At this time of night, and so close to the holiday, they only had this one guy to spare. So, Bootbrush is along for the ride.

"I'm pregnant," she blurts out. Bootbrush looks at her, his face scrunching up so that his mouth is suddenly gone underneath the bristles of his mustache. He doesn't say anything, so she keeps filling the silence because what else is there to do? It's better than living inside her head, which is a toxic shitty pit if ever there was one. "I'm pregnant and I don't know what to do. I shouldn't be pregnant. I *can't* be."

Bootbrush just offers a conciliatory shrug. It's obvious this whole thing is making him uncomfortable. Finally he says, "I'm sure you'll figure it out." Even though he knows she won't. There's nothing to figure out. She's pregnant, handcuffed, and almost surely headed to prison for—well, for whatever it is she did and whatever it is they *think* she did.

Except—

What if that's why the baby dies?

What if the baby dies because she is going to jail, and the conditions in prison are deplorable enough to significantly up the chances of the baby's mortality? Or maybe they just rip the damn thing out of her on the eve of her execution, because they'll probably kill her, right? They think she beheaded an ex-FBI officer: her ally, Grosky. Not to mention the tally of Wren's crimes she's already loosely confessed to committing. *What have I done?*

But maybe it's the other way: maybe she slips this noose and *that's* why the baby dies. Out there, on the run, can't get care, only finds some backwoods veterinarian to deliver the baby—some hick used to castrating horses or expressing the anal glands of sheepdogs, and here he goes, rupturing the poor kid's brain-pan with a pair of ugly tongs usually used to grab a calf's head out of its mother's birth canal.

Though none of this matters anyway, does it? Because her powers work one way and one way only:

She sees death. A touch is all it takes, and the fate is revealed.

And that death happens irrevocably unless she counters it with another death—the life of the perpetrator, snuffed out. This is the one way in which the universe *does* let the scales be balanced: there's the victim of the murderer and the murderer himself, and if she kills the murderer, the victim is spared. It's clean and simple, pure as the smell of fresh sweat on a summer day. Lady gonna get pancaked by a car? Kill the driver before he can run her ass over. Drunk husband knocks his wife into a radiator, accidentally killing her? Drunk husband's gotta die; sorry, dickhead, but your wife gets to live at the cost of your demise.

But when there's no perpetrator, things get . . . *slippery*.

Like Gabby's suicide. It hasn't come yet. But time is tipping that way. And Miriam doesn't know how to stop it. There's no villain to stop. Ashley, the one who brutalized her face into a patchwork of scar tissue, is gone: eaten by a flock of gannets Miriam possessed. (Even now she can taste his blood, greasy and thick in her mouth. She can still taste Harriet's heart, too. That dark mineral tang of blood haunts the back of her tongue like the ghost of a meal past.) Will Gabby go through with her own suicide? Is there any way to dissuade fate without first giving it a tithing of death?

Miriam doesn't know. So far, the answer has always been *no*.

And this baby—

How would she save it?

Who would she kill? Is there a killer at all to dispatch?

Is it the doctor's fault? A nurse's?

Could it be *her* fault? Her body is a poisoned cistern. A rotten, ruined place, torn up and ragged. She's been pickling herself in a mash of liquor and nicotine and venomous self-disdain for a long time now, too long.

She speaks these thoughts aloud because her head is like a cup: all these thoughts are filling it up and spilling out the top.

"Maybe I don't *want* to save the baby," she blurts out. Again, Bootbrush looks at her cock-eyed. She keeps on, regardless: "It's not like I should be a mom. Me? A parent? You'd be better off handing a baby to a starving bear. Me as a mother would make *my* mother seem like a fucking saint—and let me tell you, despite what she may have thought, she was no saint." There, another pang of sorrow. Her mother, another soul lost on this journey of wreckage and ruination. *You're one broken cookie, Miriam. All the way down to the crumbs.* "I shouldn't have a kid."

"I got a kid," Bootbrush says, suddenly.

"Oh." Miriam frowns. "You like her?"

"Him. Cody. He's a good kid." Bootbrush shrugs. "Pain in my ass sometimes, but I was a pain in the ass to my dad, and he to his if you believe the stories, so I guess that's just the way things are."

It is what it is, her mother so often said.

"You're a good dad, though. I mean, probably."

"Eh."

"Eh?"

"Eh, I just mean, who knows what it is to be a good parent. Cody's alive and he's got his head on straight. That's less because of me and more in spite of me, I suspect. His mother deserves more of that credit. I don't beat on him or anything. I take him fishing, which if you ask him now, is more a punishment than a reward, though I think he liked it when he was younger. But I got problems. Chiefly, a hot temper and I drink too much."

She offers an awkward smile. "You and me both."

"It's hard," Bootbrush goes on to say. "But it's worth it. Just so you have a legacy. Everyone needs a legacy, I figure."

"I think I got one of those already, seeing as how I'm in police custody in an ambulance."

"You got a point there, miss."

"Also, I ate a woman's heart earlier tonight."

Bootbrush narrows his eyes. "I think we ought to stop talking now."

"That's probably fair."

She sits for a while.

But then, Bootbrush says something else: "You'll be okay. Things have a way of working out. Maybe not how you figure it, maybe never how you wanted it, but they do. Keep your head on a swivel and do what's right, and you and that baby will make it through however you need to."

However you need to.

She can do right by the child. Do right by Louis. She won't love it. Can she love it? Has she ever loved anything or anyone? She has; she knows she loved Louis. Maybe loves Gabby, too. She decides then and there she will save this baby. Even if it costs Miriam her own life. That's what Louis would have done. In a sense, that's what Louis *did*.

"Thanks," she says.

Bootbrush nods.

The ambulance bumps along down the road for a little while— until it stops short, forcing her to lurch forward, off-balance as the brakes whine against their pads. The vehicle sits still.

They look at each other after the ambulance comes to a halt.

Bootbrush frowns. "Deer, maybe."

"Uh-huh." But something feels off. The hairs on her neck stand up like good little soldiers. The ones on her arms, too. Miriam tells herself she's goofy—goofy from the pain, from the events of the night, from the grief that's got its chains wound around her. Doesn't help she's still got this wound under her left armpit where one of Harriet's bullets dug a ditch.

Bootbrush sits for a little bit, starts to look impatient. He sidles up past Miriam, pounds on the wall behind her, the one that would lead into the driver's side of the ambulance. "Jimmy. Got a deer up there?" he calls.

Nothing. No response.

Now Miriam's heart is starting to flip and flop in her chest. Her skin tingles and she starts to sweat. Some of it drips down into the bullet ditch. It burns as it does, like lime juice in a cut.

Bootbrush goes to the back door, pops it open. He gives her a cautioning glare. "You stay here."

"I'm in it to win it," she says, weary.

"Does that mean you're staying here?"

"Yeah."

"All right, then." He hops down, hooks around the corner, walking out of her sight. With the door open, a cold wind sweeps into the cul-de-sac that is the inside of the ambulance. It cups her like an icy hand, holds her tight. The stray thought ricochets and hits her full on: *Shit, it's almost Christmas.*

What did Santa bring you this year?

Oh, that fat-ass elf squeezed his red devil-trousers down the chimney, brought me a fiesta of delights: a bullet under the arm-pit, a prison sentence, and another dying baby. Merry fucking Christmas to all.

No sounds out there but the wind in the trees.

"Bootbrush?" she calls out. "Stuckey? Big guy?"

Nothing.

Huh.

She starts to stand up—

And then out of the darkness comes what she first thinks is Bootbrush.

But it isn't.

The breath is caught in her lungs like a miner in a collapsing shaft. Vertigo spirals up through her and drops her ass down on the bench again as Louis, *her* Louis, *dead* Louis, steps in through the back, filling the exit.

Already she sees that no, it's not her Louis at all. This one doesn't have the fake eye anymore—it's just that filthy X made of electrical tape ill patched over the ruined socket. And this Louis has a hole in the side of his head, where Wren's bullet entered his temple. Smoke drifts out of that hole, as if from a cigarette just stubbed out in an ashtray.

The Trespasser grins. Pill bugs crawl across the flats of his yellow teeth the way they would across a split log gone rotten. He licks them, chews them, *munch munch crunch.*

Her stomach roils with anger and fear.

"*You.*" That's all she can say right now. It's the only word she can muster. Anything more would have her rage-puking as she leapt for this ephemeral spirit, this entity that up until very recently she half-figured was just a figment of her own imagination. *The Trespasser.* She wants to wrap her hands around its throat, even though she has no idea if it *has* a throat.

"This is such a sad meeting," the Trespasser says. "I hear you've gone and done it. Got yourself knocked up with a little piglet. Oink, oink."

"You did this. All of this."

"Not that part." Not-Louis clucks his blue-black tongue. "You did *that* part yourself. But the rest of it, sure. I set up the dominoes and they fell . . . mostly where I wanted them." The spirit's one good eye casts toward her belly, and the disgust on the Trespasser's face deepens. "I'm glad you got my message, Miriam."

"That's what all that was?" she seethes. "A message?"

"A message, that's right."

"And tell me, you sick motherfucker, what was the message?

I'm a little *slow*. My head's been *knocked around* a few too many times so I'm not *picking up* what you're *putting down*."

Not-Louis sniffs, leans up against the doorframe like he's the cock of the walk. He says, "The message is, we aren't done, you and me. You got nine months left on this lease, and that's only if that little piggy doesn't die coming out of your fucked-up baby-maker, baby. Kid doesn't make it . . ." He takes a deep, satisfying breath. "Then you'll be stuck with me, Peaches."

Fresh anger surges through her—but that black, demonic geyser of rage is shot through with something else, too: hope. Because here, the demon is telling her something. He's telling her that what Mary Scissors said is true: if she can do this, if the child is born and if the child survives, then that's it. It's game over for the Trespasser. The curse is gone.

It would mean that she's free.

That puts a big smile on *her* face.

She stands, even as tentacles of shadow crawl into the ambulance like the tendrils of poison ivy vines set to fast-forward. Everything grows dark and the ambulance begins to rattle and bang, vibrating like there's an earthquake under their feet. Outside, the asphalt begins to fracture. Trees begin to shudder and split with thunderous cracks. She steps forward slow and steady, one foot at a time, handcuffed hands held in front of her as she meets the Trespasser nose to nose. From him emanates the smell of rot and ruin: a pickled vinegar smell, sickly sweet, wildly sour, like the smell of roadkill, like bad meat left too long in the kitchen trash.

"You sent her to me," Miriam hisses. "Samantha. Her and Harriet. You put all this in motion. You're trying to control me."

"I did some of that. I had to, killer. You've been trying to buck the leash. So, I'm trying a tighter collar." The eyepatch made of electrical tape bulges and strains as something behind it threatens to push out. Little feelers like centipede legs wriggle free and tickle the air. All around, the tectonic shaking worsens—

Trees begin to fall across the shattered road, only cratering the asphalt further. Dead leaves swing and swoon in the air. Her teeth clack. The sound is now a roar. The road begins to break and buckle.

She has to yell to be heard:

"I'm done with you. I'm almost *free*."

There. A spark of anger in the Trespasser's one good eye. His jaw tightens and the tendons pull taut. The next words he speaks, he does so through clenched, half-rotten teeth: "*Almost* isn't enough, you arrogant little bitch. I still got you. The message is that we still have work to do. Important work. *You will not shirk your duties*."

"I'm not doing your work anymore."

"What can I say? I have a few tricks left."

"Me too," she yells. It's a lie. She has nothing new, nothing to bring.

"Wanna see one of mine?" he asks.

"Bring it on," she says, bold and with as much fake-ass bravado as she can muster—even though the thought of the Trespasser pulling another dead rabbit out of his hat chills her down to the marrow.

Then, lickety-quick, Not-Louis is gone. One minute she's face-to-face with him, smelling his sour stink, and the next— he's vapor. The shadow tendrils disappear, too. The shaking has ended. The road behind is whole once more, as are the trees all around. None are broken. None have fallen.

Once more, all is silent and still.

A few lone flurries fall.

The silence ends as a gunshot fills the night.

Bang.

FIVE

SILLY RABBIT, TRICKS ARE FOR KIDS

The gunshot startles her. Even now, after all that's happened—it wasn't even eight hours ago that she was being chased through the woods by an unstoppable, unkillable Harriet Adams as gunshots zipped through the trees all around her—she can't help but feel jarred by it. Every part of her tenses, and a shrill tinnitus buzz fills her ears.

Swallowing hard, she reaches out with her handcuffed hands, balancing herself against the back door of the ambulance as she steps out onto the old road with unsteady legs. More flurries fall, fat flakes whirling about like white-winged moths. Shoulder against the back of the ambulance, she turns the corner toward the driver side and—

Bootbrush lies face up on the road. The wind ruffles that mustache as his dead eyes stare up at the stars. A hole in the middle of his head is like a third eye, an opened chakra, aware only of death.

His head rests on a pillow of his own brains.

Standing above him—striding his body lke a triumphant conqueror—is the paramedic, Jimmy. He's got a small snub-nose revolver in his hand. Bootbrush's own gun, a boxy pistol, remains in its holster. Jimmy must have his own gun—unsurprising up here in these parts, she guesses.

Jimmy is grinning like a fool. His eyes are wide and white.

31

Dark hair is tousled by the winter wind. Jimmy has a big awkward overbite, giving a sinister, clownish vibe to that fool's grin.

Miriam just stands there, unsure what this is or what to do.

"Why?" she asks, her voice a craggy, drawn-out croak.

"I told you I have new tricks."

That voice. It isn't Jimmy's. It comes out of him with a Southern drawl. It's Louis's voice. Slow, soft, comforting once. Corrupted, now.

It's him. It. The Trespasser.

The demon, the ghost, whatever the Trespasser is: it's inside the paramedic. It's taken him over.

"You again," she says. What hope she had is flagging now—like putting your hand over a flashlight to darken the beam that comes from it.

Jimmy shrugs. "Me again."

"This is what you did to Samantha, isn't it? You got inside her. You . . . made her do things."

"Took me a while with that one," Jimmy says with a playful shrug, his body language saying, *Nah, not a big deal.* "She was my first, if you're wondering. She had holes in her soul, and I was able to *sneak in* like a little skittering mouse." With his free hand, Not-Jimmy mimics a mouse running, the fingers wiggling like little legs. "*Dink, dink, dink!* Jimmy here was easier. *So* much easier. I was able to chew my own way in much faster. Jimmy has problems. His daddy beat him, abused him, then left him. Poor Jimmy. Hates himself so bad, it's worn holes in him, and now I'm in there, wriggling around. I'm wondering if I can do it with anyone. I guess we'll see, won't we?"

"Leave me alone. Leave them all alone."

"Not until we're done."

"We're done."

Jimmy brays with laughter—loud and obnoxious, filling the air, echoing off the trees. "I'll be seeing you, Miriam."

Then the paramedic puts the revolver under his chin.

Miriam cries out, reaching with her cuffed hands—

"Don't feel bad for ol' Jimmy!" the paramedic hoots.

The gun *pops*. Jimmy's head shakes like a coconut on a kicked tree. A small fountain of blood and gray matter sprays up from the top of his skull.

He drops. The gun clacks against the asphalt.

SIX

SPOILER WARNING: SHE SAYS FUCK IT AND RUNS

Miriam stands there for ten seconds.

Ten seconds in which no tears fall, because she has no more in her.

Ten seconds in which she regards the death of the two men in front of her, one sleeping on his own brains, the other staring up with dead eyes at a dripping red mess oozing down the side of the ambulance.

Ten seconds in which she wonders how long it'll take those brains and that blood to freeze solid.

Ten seconds in which she has to decide whether or not she's going to sit here and call this in and wait for the authorities— which is the smart thing to do, the path of least resistance, the path that will earn her none of the blame because it's not like her prints are on that gun—or whether or not she's going to say fuck it and run.

The eleventh second comes, and she has her decision.

She has a chance. The baby *is* her chance. This kid, whoever he or she is or will be, is her way out. The child is the key to a very stubborn lock.

The curse has to go. The Trespasser can get fucked.

Buy the ticket, take the ride.

She's going to run.

Miriam hurries over to Bootbrush and rifles through his

pockets until she finds the dead cop's keys—and with it, the key to the cuffs. She finds it, jingly-jangle, pops the lock, and the metal cuffs drop to the road, clickety-clack. Miriam gives her arms a little shake to stir the blood back into her hands. They tingle, pins and needles, as they come back to life.

Then, in his other pocket: a cell phone. It's a crummy clamshell model, beaten all to hell. On a lark, she tries the paramedic's pocket, and that's the way to go: he's got an iPhone. She's not really up on her technology, but she knows the iPhone beats the clamshell in a technology-based game of rock-paper-scissors, so she pockets that one, instead.

It's cold. The snow falling isn't covering the road yet, but it will soon enough. She shivers, realizing that she can't just hightail it out of here on foot. Which means—

"I'm going to have to steal an ambulance," she says to no one but whatever forest creatures slumber in the wintry dark.

It's a terrible idea, stealing an ambulance.

But it's pretty much the *only* idea, and it's better than freezing to death out here on this Pennsyltucky road to nowhere.

Miriam steals the ambulance.

SEVEN

COFFEE AND CIGARETTES

By sunup, she's in Maryland. She ditches the ambulance behind a closed-up gas station at the north end of a town called Manchester. The snow has stopped, but the wind has got teeth, and soon as she steps out of the vehicle, it takes a bite.

The ambulance is a worry. She has no idea if they LoJack these goddamn things or if they have some secret way to track them, but given that it looks like it's at least ten years old and it has 255,000 miles on it, she's hoping like hell nobody will find this thing for a good long while.

Miriam walks in the bitter, biting wind.

She wraps a blanket from inside the ambulance around her. Every step is painful. Pain from under her armpit. Pain from where Harriet beat her ass. Her skull throbs like it's about to come apart at the seams. Pain in her heart, too, because at this point she's lost near to everything and everyone.

Everyone except Gabby.

Gabby, who she hopes will be here soon.

She walks about a mile past gray clapboard houses that are part of the wreckage of what was fifty years ago a prosperous America, and farther down she spies a truck-stop diner. It'll do. She uses Bootbrush's phone to text Gabby the diner name. Then she turns the phone off and breaks it against the ragged metal corner of an old rusted dumpster behind the restaurant before tossing it in with the rest of the trash.

Inside, the diner is warm and spare. Everything is old lino-leum and cheap plastic. Country-bumpkin decor hangs on the walls, as do random household implements from days past: a slotted spoon, a sifter, a washboard. Interspersed is crab imag-ery: a crab in a chef's hat, a crab with fork and knife, a crab in a pot. Crabs happily eating crabs. Crabs happily being eaten by crabs. Whatever.

Miriam has no wallet, no ID, not any damn thing. But she goes in and lets them seat her anyway, even though they give her eyes like she's a vagrant. (Which is more or less true at this point.) She sits, orders coffee and a big plate of bacon and eggs, and eats like they just made breakfast illegal.

The coffee tastes like road tar thinned with battery acid, which is how she likes it. The bacon is salty, the eggs are good, and she eats both so fast, she barely tastes them. She orders more food after—near the counter they have one of those rotating glass cases of countless cakes and pies, so she asks for a slice of apple pie with some ice cream. The waitress is a young black woman with her hair done up in little braids, and as she leans in for a cof-fee refill, Miriam lets her hand brush the waitress's hand and—

—*in thirty years the woman's hand, now wrinkled, struggles while reaching for the oxygen tank she needs to get her air, but she can't quite reach the nose tubes from the hook near the night-stand. A pack of cigarettes sits nearby, the cigarettes spilling out like bones from broken fingers. The oxygen compressor hisses and hushes and gushes, and she can't breathe, not at all. Every part of her feels closed off: invisible hands around her throat, an imaginary box of books placed square on her chest. The blood pumps loud in her ears, louder than the compressor,* hiss hush gush, hiss hush gush, *and then she's thinking,* this is what it must be like to drown, *and that's it, she's done, dragged down by the undertow of her own failing lungs—*

Miriam shudders. The vision: it's not as good as a hit from a cigarette, but for the moment, it'll do. She clears her throat and says abruptly, "You should quit smoking. Sooner rather than later."

The waitress reels, suddenly taken aback. "You don't get to tell me that." A pause as she regards Miriam with (totally reasonable) suspicion. "And I don't smoke."

Miriam shrugs. "You do. I can smell the *ghost of nicotine* on your fingers, and lady, I gotta tell you, I'd drown a kitten for a smoke right now, but I had to quit, so I quit. I'm telling you this and you already know it, you already know it'll kill you someday, and maybe you care, maybe you don't, and truly, it probably doesn't matter what some crazy twat customer like me says. I'm just saying: quit smoking. Maybe you'll buy yourself some years."

The waitress stands there, scowling. "The worst years."

"I'm sorry?"

"The ones at the end are the worst. I'd rather smoke now and lose those, live my life how I like."

Miriam shrugs. "I get it. I do. I thought that way once too, and maybe sometimes *still* think that way. Thing is, it's bullshit. Everybody has their last years, whether they smoke or don't, whether they live to a hundred or live to twenty-one, and the last years, years of cancer or emphysema or drowning in your own lungs, they're gonna be worse for you than for other people. That's all I'm saying. Do what you want with it."

"I'll think about it," the waitress says, guardedly.

"Okay," Miriam says. And she believes the waitress. She *will* think about it. But she won't change. Because fate is fate.

"You're gonna give me a real tip and not this life-improvement bullshit, right?"

"Sure," Miriam lies, because she has *literally* no money.

As the waitress walks away, Miriam sees the front door of the diner open up, the little bell going *ding-da-ding*.

Miriam's heart rises in her chest like a bird.

It's her.

Seeing Gabby coming in through the front gives her a small island of peace in these turbulent seas—for just a moment, she can pretend that everything else that has happened and *is* happening does not matter. Gabby: her anchor, her port in the storm, her oasis. Gabby with the bleach-blond hair done up like it's a wave about to crest over her scarred-up face. Gabby with the puffy winter coat that goes *viiip voop zip* as she walks.

Miriam launches herself to standing—and the injury under her arm suddenly makes a sound like peeling masking tape, and as she lifts her arm way a bird holds up a busted wing, she sees Gabby's eyes go right to it.

"You're bleeding," Gabby says, sotto voce.

"Am I? Oh." Miriam looks, lifting her arm. Red spreads like spilled wine. "I like to think of it as a cleanse. I'm purging toxins. It's all the rage. Acai berry enemas and bloodletting yourself."

"Miriam, we should go."

"I have no money, and I bought food."

Gabby offers a stiff but sympathetic smile. Then, with the patience of a saint, Gabby lays down money on the table before coming back to put her arm around Miriam's shoulders. "C'mon, Miss Black, time to hit the road."

"I bought pie. Can we wait for the pie?"

"I don't think we can."

"Shit." She pouts. "Where we going?"

"Where else?"

"Oh, *please* say it's a cheap, shit-ass motel."

"It's a cheap, shit-ass motel."

Miriam gives her cheek a little kiss. "I've missed you, Gabs."

EIGHT

BEDSHEETS AND BLOODSTAINS

Here's the thing about cheap, shit-ass motels:

You go to a real hotel, a Holiday Inn or a Marriott-Hilton-Hyatt-whatever, everything is nice and tight and hermetically sealed: crisp sheets, soft carpets, minimal noise, and the plumbing works.

Hotels care about you, or pretend to. They want you to feel trapped in the isolation of their embrace, like you're in your own little *vacation pod* away from the world. Safe. Secure. A curated experience.

Motels don't give a cup of hot wet shit. They are as unpretentious as they come. No plate of cookies at the front desk. No turn-down service. No breakfast buffet. The decor is minimal—carpet from ten years ago, wood paneling from twenty, and somewhere along the way, someone said, "I don't know, put a flea market painting of a fucking lighthouse on the wall." The beds are usually hard as a rock. The TV gets good porn, and if the reception sucks, you can always listen to the people through the paper-thin walls: the fakey love-yowls of a road hooker giving the goods to a trucker, a family on vacation on the verge of divorce and destruction, two drunk forty-year-old brothers yelling at each other about some girl back in high school they each thought the other one fucked. You might find pubes on the sink. Old bloodstains on the carpet under the bed. Bedbugs hiding at the mattress margins. But the showers are hot. The rooms are cheap. Sometimes, you even get *theme*

motels: teepees or Victoriana or Americana. Miriam was in a
motel once in Kansas called the Maui Motel, pretended like it was
a slice of the island life in the middle of the cold, dead Midwest:
everything was coconuts and pineapples, ukulele music playing
over tinny speakers, and walls painted to look like the ocean (with
the paint peeling off to show the cinder block underneath). It
smelled like dust and the grotesque vanilla air freshener you use
to spray a bathroom after you've gone and shellacked the porcelain with whatever food poisoning you got from the pupu platter
at the "Hawaiian Grill" next door. It was horrible. Miriam hated it.

Which is to say, Miriam *loved* hating it.

Kitschy, crappy, don't-give-a-care motels.

They're authentic. That's why they matter.

(*Like me*, Miriam thinks, sometimes. Trashy but true to themselves.)

This one, though: goddamnit, it's disappointing. Why?

Because it's a *chain* motel. A Super 8, maybe once a real-deal
motel but now it's owned by a bigger hotel chain and the beds are
clean and the decor is hipster Americana (old cars, aspens, neon
signs in black and white, which dicks up the whole reason to take
a picture of a neon sign in the first place). As she steps into the
room, Gabby must see her scowl and responds accordingly: "Yeah,
I know, it's a Super 8."

"This is not a motel room where somebody died," Miriam says.

"And that disappoints you?"

"I mean, a little."

"Haven't you seen enough death?"

A shudder passes through her like a drifting shadow. "Probably."

She plonks down on the edge of the bed. Gabby stands there,
jacket still on. Sticking out like a sore thumb, like she doesn't
know what to do with herself, like she's not sure if she belongs
here. Miriam's face is down, but her eyes are up, watching Gabby.

"You're really pregnant?"

"That's what you want to ask me?"

"It's why you called me."

"Yeah, it is. And yeah, I am."

Gabby crosses her arms tight—again, her big puffy jacket *vips* and *vrrps* as fabric rubs on fabric. "How do you know?"

"I just—I just *know*. I had a vision. I can feel it."

"I thought . . . you couldn't get . . . that way."

That way. Like it's some kind of burden. Gabby sounds like a dude, the way she's talking about it. Of course, Miriam thinks about it the same way: pregnancy, uck, ick, nyah. It's a condition. A curse same as her other. "That's what they told me. Scar tissue in my derelict baby-bag."

"And yet—"

"And yet here we are. The times, they are a-changing."

She flops back on the bed.

Gabby sucks air between her teeth. "You're going to bleed on the bed."

"This room could use a couple bloodstains. Give it some character."

"You need to go to a hospital."

"I need to just . . . lay here for a while. No hospital."

"You need stitches."

"I need . . ."

Her words slip away from her and her eyes close. Her head's not even on a pillow. Her feet still dangle over the edge. Gabby's talking, and Miriam's hardly listening—she knows she left Gabby in the lurch. Didn't talk to her as much as she should've—or even could've. And here she is, to rescue her when she needs it most. But right now, she's tired. Every atom of her body feels like it's heavy as a piece of lead, and she's sinking like a handful of stray bullets tossed into water. Darkness comes up around her as exhaustion pushes her down, down, down, toward sleep—

NINE

DREAMLESS

She should dream. In the back of her mind, somewhere, she knows that—the only dream is the realization she is not dreaming. This would normally be a time for Miriam's own mind to haunt her way a ghost haunts the halls of a troubled house—or maybe it would be time for the Trespasser to make an appearance, to taunt her, to urge her. In the dreamless dark, she should hear a baby crying, she should feel the weight of a red snow shovel crashing down on her back, she should be chasing a small boy who is in turn chasing a red balloon across a busy highway. But none of that comes to her. In her exhaustion, she finds no specters. The demons that are uniquely hers remain quiet, exorcised or at least temporarily contained.

But in the stretch of rest, she becomes aware of one thing even in the bleak black of a formless and timeless void:

I'm not alone.

It's a presence. Not Gabby. A different sound. A different smell. A shape darker than the rest behind the curtain of her closed eyelids. *The baby?* she thinks, absurd because at this point, the baby is, what? The size of a little deer tick? No. Someone's here. *With* her.

Fuck.

Miriam gasps, and jolts awake.

Confirmed true: she is not alone.

A man sits on the other bed, facing her. He's in a black suit, black tie, like he's on his way to a funeral somewhere. His hands sit steepled in his lap, by his crotch. Dusky skin. Black hair mussed up, but in a purposeful way—like someone who likes chaos only when it's controlled.

"You're awake," he says, only a few feet away. He's troublingly close. He could hurt her. Maybe he wants to, maybe that's his plan. Behind him, sunshine through the blinds frames him like he's some kind of dark angel riding forth on rays of light.

Her mouth tastes like llama ass. Slowly she eases forward, sitting up so she's almost knee-to-knee with the stranger.

"I am," she says, her voice a croak. "You real?"

The man seems taken aback by that question. He gives himself a quick pat-down, as if to check. "I think so. Are you?"

"Real as a roller coaster, pal."

"Then hello, Miriam, let me introduce myself: I'm David Guerrero."

"Hey, David Guerrero," she says, her voice forced to an eerie stillness. "It's nice to meet you. Are you here to kill me?"

"No. I am not."

She urges a stiff smile to her face. "Lemme ask you, I had a friend here. Her name was Gabby. Is she around?"

"Nothing to worry about. She's just outside."

As if on cue, a shadow passes in front of the window.

Am I dreaming? Is this the dream rising up out of the dark?

"I want to see her. Make sure she's okay."

David hesitates for a moment, then nods. He stands up, goes to the door, cracks it open. Miriam hears murmuring back and forth. As he stands there, his jacket eases away from the pistol hanging in a holster at his hip.

Her muscles tense. So, he's a fed, not a pallbearer. Or a hitman pretending to be a fed. That's how Harriet and Frankie played it, once.

He is awfully clean, awfully crisp. Maybe too much so. Grosky was a fed, too, and he looked like a garbage bag.

A splinter of unexpected sorrow digs into her heart. She misses Grosky. He was all right, after all. Associating with her lost him his head—literally. *Everyone around me dies.* Her very presence is like a taste of slow poison. She's radioactive: a walking, talking, singing, dancing slice of Chernobyl. She thinks again of the little life inside her. A life guttering like a candle flame, put out by a pair of pinching fingers nine months later.

Guerrero comes back from the door, and Gabby follows him in. She's buttoned up in her big coat, shivering a little from standing outside. She's been smoking, and Miriam can smell it, and honestly, that hurts her.

A small but notable betrayal. It is not the only one, she realizes.

Miriam winces against the light. "Hey, Gabs."

"Hi, Miriam."

There, in Gabby's voice—clear as a rung bell—is guilt. Like a slightly mopey teenager who knows she just got caught doing something. Which means Gabby just got caught doing something. Not smoking. So—what?

Ah.

"You're a fed," Miriam says to Guerrero. Then to Gabby: "And *you* invited him here."

Gabby says nothing. Guerrero sits back down. "Miriam, that is correct. I am in fact an agent of the Federal Bureau of Investigation."

"So, you're here to arrest me." And to Gabby: "You sold me out."

"I didn't—" Gabby says, but Guerrero interrupts.

"I'm not here to arrest you. And Gabby didn't invite me here, not exactly. When you called her, I was listening in. I didn't give her much choice in the matter. I came because I need to talk to you."

Every part of her has gone pins-and-needles—an anxious

tingling, a heat rising through her. Miriam feels thrust to the edge and standing on the precipice while balancing on a single trembling toe. *I won't be trapped. I won't be caged.* Already she's planning her escape. Gabby dropped the keys to the car by the little desk near the door. If she can get past this dickhead, she can snap up the keys, grab the car, and get away fast as she can.

But she's injured. Can she manage it? Idly, she reaches up under her shirt to her armpit to feel the margins of the injury from Harriet's bullet—

And her fingers find only smooth skin there.

That tingling buzzes louder. Blood rushes in her ears.

It must be the other armpit.

She sends her other hand up under her alternate arm.

No injury there, either.

No wound on either side. No pain there, either—just an itch.

Vertigo assails her. The floor feels liquid underneath her. The air wobbles and the room doesn't spin so much as it shifts left, then right. *Get it together, get it together, this is fine, this is normal, don't worry about this shit right now. You're healed. Use it. Use it to get the fuck out of this room.*

Guerrero continues: "Miriam, I have a proposition for you—"

Her hand darts out, grabs the lamp by the bed, and flings it at his head. Or, rather, she *would*, but the damn thing is bolted to the nightstand.

She tries again. It won't move an inch. Guerrero watches her struggle through narrowed eyes. "You okay?"

This wouldn't happen if we were in a proper cheap-ass shit motel. In a real motel, she could throw the lamp. And when she did, she'd probably find an old condom or a human finger underneath it, as is motel tradition.

"I'm trying to throw a lamp at your head," she confesses.

"I think it's bolted down."

"Yeah, no duh, Agent Obvious."

"Are you done? Can we talk now?"

She sighs. "Sure."

He opens his mouth to speak—

And she punches it—

A burst of static in her head like a radio turned to a nowhere station, bits of voices garbled by the noise.

—his head rocks back and she knows she should be seizing this opportunity to mow over him, clambering her way to the door. But she doesn't. Even as Gabby gawps and Guerrero reaches up to wipe blood from his mouth on the back of his hand, Miriam doesn't move. She just stands there, fingers still coiled into a fist, her hand shaking.

"You're one of *them*," she says.

"You mean *us*," he answers. He pulls his hand away and his tongue licks blood at the split in his lip. "We play for the same team."

"You're a head-tweaker, too."

"I am."

"That doesn't say good things about you."

"And what's it say about you?"

Miriam, resigned, sits back down. Again, her hand idly returns to the now-missing injury under her arm. She should be finding a scabbed-over furrow, a stinging ditch in which her fingers could dip, but it's all healed.

"You're not here to arrest me?" she asks again.

He sniffs. "I should, after you hit me like that. Christ, you hit like a fastball. No pulling your punches, eh?"

"No."

Her hand throbs from the hit.

"I'm not here to arrest you. I'm here to make an offer."

"Make your offer. Then go."

He smiles, teeth smeared red. "Now we're talking."

TEN
THE OFFER

"I'm putting together a team, and I want you to work for me," Guerrero says.

"No."

He blinks. "You haven't even heard what it is yet."

"And I don't care. I got my own shit to worry about. I'm always sitting around here, worrying about other people's shit; meanwhile, my own emotional toilet is backing up so bad, it's going to go off like a porcelain bomb. So, my answer to your offer is *no*."

He stiffens. This is rankling him. The frustration bleeds off him like a body odor stink. "It's a team of people like you and me."

"Then my answer is Double-No with a side order of Nope-Nuh-Uh and a couple sauce packets of Extra-Zesty Fuck-No Dressing."

"That's it? Nothing I can do to convince you?"

"You could threaten me. You could tell me that if I don't help you, you'll arrest me. It's certainly your right, Mr. FBI."

He pauses like he's considering it. "I know you didn't even do half the things people think you may have done."

"It doesn't matter what I did or didn't do. My soul's got bills to pay; I know that. And if there is an afterlife, I expect I'll be servicing that debt till the Devil's asshole is *raw* from all the rim-jobs I will have to give him. But for now, I can't care about any of this. I can only care about what's in front of me." *And what's inside of me.*

He leans forward. Guerrero is eager. He's hungry for this, which scares her a little. It's also something she understands, because Miriam doesn't care much for being told *no* either. Meanwhile, Gabby stands off to the side, near the bathroom door. She's got her jacket on still.

"I can make the charges go away," he says.

"Miriam, listen to him," Gabby says, leaning in. "That's a real offer."

"And I don't want it. I'd rather *he* just go away, instead."

The agent chews on this for a while. A good minute passes, his facial expression wrestling with it, like he's trying to finagle a piece of gristle out from between his teeth—his handsome face twists up as he tries to wiggle and waggle his way through her unexpected denial.

He can't hack it. It's pissing him off.

Good. She likes pissing men like him off.

(Actually, just men in general.)

(Okay, *people* in general.)

But then, like that, he stands. "I won't threaten you. I could. But I won't. I'd rather you want to be a part of this thing. I am a man of honey, not vinegar." He sighs, and flips her a business card. It lands on her leg, and she brushes it off like it's a wayward corn chip.

"I'm sorry, I only do vinegar," she says.

"Call me if you change your mind."

"Have a nice day, sweet cheeks." She waggles her fingers in a sarcastically playful wave.

He nods, mouth pursed into a strained half-smile.

And with that, he's gone out the door. A swirling wind blows in as he exits. The wind is gone again when he is gone, too.

Gabby stares at her feet.

Miriam stares at Gabby.

"I feel you staring, so stop it," Gabby says.

"I'm imagining my eyes are laser beams." *Pyoo pyoo pyoo*.

"Yeah, I can feel that, too, *thanks*." Now Gabby meets her gaze, and there's a flint-scrape of sparks in the dark of her eye. Her face, intersected by scars as if seen through a broken mirror, tightens with anger. "You could be a little more appreciative. I didn't have to come. I didn't have to find my way back into the rabid raccoon orgy that is your life."

Miriam stands. "You also didn't have to bring that dickhead here."

"That *dickhead* was offering you something!" Gabby's hands are out, like she's trying to clutch reason and sanity from the very air. "Something *huge*. He had a way out. For you. For *us*. Don't you get it? A tunnel out through the mountain of bullshit you've heaped onto yourself, Miriam. You, you . . . you go through life like a tornado through an orphanage. It's wreckage and blood everywhere you turn, and *that* guy was giving you a way to get out of it. To get *above* it."

"Pfah, whatever. I had no idea what the cost would be. And don't think I didn't hear what you said—*for us*. You're looking out for you as much as you are for me, here. Don't pretend you're some angel."

"I never have! Of course I want to be okay. Who doesn't? I'm helping you out, but I'm tired of getting thrown under the tires of this bus you're driving. And as for the cost . . ." Gabby laughs, and it's a manic, mirthless squawk. "He was gonna *tell* you the cost of the deal if you just gave him thirty fucking seconds, Jesus Fucking Christ, Miriam."

"No. No! *No*. He would not have told me. He would have told me *part* of it. But it's like a used car salesman—that would be the upfront cost only. Nobody ever tells you the hidden fees because that's why they're fucking *hidden*. Because nobody wants to tell you the real costs you pay in this life. And I've paid them in spades, price after price, again and again. Fuck that. Fuck you. Fuck *all* of this." She sits back down on the bed, chest heaving. The sudden urge to have a good cigarette between her lips and a cheap, cold whiskey in her hand is like soft ground sucking her down into the inescapable mud. Quieter now, she says, "You could've at least ruined the surprise and told me he was coming."

"I was going to. But you were hurt."

I'm not hurt anymore. "I don't like surprises."

"And if I told you about him before we got here, you wouldn't ever have talked to him." Then, under her own breath, Gabby says, "Not that you gave him a chance anyway."

"You're mad."

"I'm not mad."

"You're pissed, you were literally just yelling at me."

"I'm . . . not, it's fine."

But it isn't fine.

Shit.

Miriam sighs. "You have every right to be pissed."

"What?"

"I ditched you. I went to Florida, you went your way with Isaiah, and I ditched your ass. I got back with Louis. I got into a world of shit, I got myself—ah-ha, miracle of miracles—knocked up again, and then I put it all on you. Here I am again, like a boat anchor chained to your ankle as we sink into the dark water together. I'm sorry. I don't say that enough, even though that saying it doesn't fix anything anyway." She sighs again. "I'm genuinely sorry, Gabs, for putting this all on you again, out of nowhere."

Gabby uncrosses her arms. She regards Miriam with a dubious up-and-down look. "Little Miriam's starting to grow up."

"Don't get too excited. I'm still asking for your help. And I'm still willing to bludgeon you for that cigarette you're pretending you didn't smoke out there."

"And I'll still give it to you. The help, not the smoke."

"Don't help me. You shouldn't. You should fuck off as fast as your feet will carry you. Go back to your sister. Go help her raise Isaiah. Go back to the Keys. Go find an island or a mountain or an underground volcanic lair as far away from me as you can."

Gabby comes and sits next to her. She takes Miriam's hand. Her hand is warm even as Miriam's is cold. "Let's agree to get past the point where you remind me how bad you are, then I remind you how good I am, and we dance around it back and forth until the next time. Maybe I'm a sucker. Maybe I need you as much as you need me. I don't know and I don't care. So let's skip ahead to the part where I agree to help you however you need me to help you."

"I need help."

"I know. That's why I brought the nice man from the FBI."

"He wasn't that nice."

"Well, if you don't want to work with them, I don't know what we're going to do."

"I don't know either. I have no money. I have no one. My mother is gone. I got Grosky killed. Louis is dead." *I only left Wren alive because I couldn't stand to lose someone else.* "I had an owl, and now the owl is gone. I don't know what to do, Gabby. I usually have a way forward, but now . . ."

That admission—with it, even as her eyes burn with the threat of fresh tears, it feels like a giant wooden beam across her shoulders is gone. A weight leaves her. She doesn't feel buoyant. She doesn't feel *happy*. But she feels somehow relieved. Somehow unburdened.

She lays her head on Gabby's shoulder.

Gabby strokes her hair. "We'll figure it out together."

I hope so, Miriam thinks. Gabby is a single bright tightrope hanging over a chasm of corpses and darkness. Miriam's hand, still holding Gabby's, goes to her middle and stays there for a while.

PART THREE

KEYS AND LOCKS

ELEVEN

SNOWBIRDS

THEN.

"It's hot," Miriam says, arm out the car door. Sweat drips down to her elbow and dangles there like a rock climber about to plunge to his death. They're pulled off, the car idling in an empty parking lot. On one side is the ocean. On the other is a small, run-down, sun-bleached office building, two-story. Above, gulls turn in the sky as if tethered to the clouds.

"It's Florida," Gabby says.

"I know, but it's winter."

"I know, but it's *Florida*."

"I fucking hate Florida."

"Then you should stop coming back here."

Gabs has a good point. It's been a week since the non-motel motel in Maryland. Miriam was lost, with no idea where to go or what to do. Gabby said: *I know people in the Keys*. People who can keep them off the radar for a while. Miriam said it sounded like a bad idea, though really that was just because Florida reminded her of her mother, and of Grosky, and also Florida is hotter and wetter than the foul sauna that is a pro wrestler's ass-crack.

So, they came down this way, and Gabby talked to a retired fisherman who knew her Uncle Charlie, and he got them a pretty cheap deal on a houseboat rental up in Key Largo. It's about the size of a shoebox (with the shoes still in it), and Miriam can barely sleep, what with the way the damn thing dips and bobs like the head of a blackout drunk, but . . .

(*It is what it is*, her mother's ghost says from the recesses of Miriam's memory. A grosser, sharper version of *Lord, give me the strength to accept the things I cannot change*.)

After they got settled in, Miriam said, "I need to see a doctor."

Gabby asked if it was about the injury under her arm, which Miriam said by way of a lie: "No, that's . . . um, healing up fine, it's not as bad as it looked." She's been sticking a couple bandages there to fake it, as right now she really doesn't want to broach the subject to Gabby. Mostly because she has no idea what to say, or if it's even real. She only has time right now for one bit of bizarre bullshit, and that ain't it. "I need to go to Tatooine, meet up with Obi-Gyn Kenobi, get these Skywalker twins checked out." She patted her belly. Then in a Yoda voice, she said, "Always two there are."

"Your pop culture game is on point today," Gabby said. "But if you're talking about getting a baby doctor to look at your . . ." Gabby gestured toward Miriam's stomach the way you might dismissively gesture at a knocked-over trash can or a dog licking its own parts. "Then I can't help you. A claustrophobic house-boat I can manage. Baby doctor, not so much."

Miriam thought going to the hospital wouldn't be a good idea, since, ohhh, she was maybe kinda sorta a fugitive from justice? Gabby reminded her: "We could still take the Fed job. We wouldn't have to do this dance."

"I don't trust them," Miriam reminded in a singsongy voice. "I haven't had a lot of luck with authority figures, let's remember. The Caldecott cop. Grosky and his partner on the first go-round. Harriet and Frankie *pretended* to be Feds. My trust levels here are at an all time low."

"Fine, but we need to find someone. You can't do this alone."

Miriam thought, *I need an off-the-books doctor. Maybe like a veterinarian or a boat mechanic who also happens to have studied the human uterus in his spare time. Or maybe a mob doctor.*

Mob doctor.

That was an interesting thought.

She knew someone who might know someone.

And with that, Miriam used a burner they bought outside of Miami to call her old neighbor, Rita Shermansky. Rita, who lived near Miriam's mother near Fort Lauderdale, maybe-sorta-half-ass confessed to being mobbed up once upon a time. Though maybe the Jewish mob, if that was a thing? Whatever. Point is, Rita was people who seemed to know people, and since she helped Miriam run a scam where they stole pills from old people (correction: *dead* old people) and sold them to other *living* old people. Rita answered the phone like no big deal: *Oh, it's you.*

"You back, doll?" Rita asked. "Didn't see you here. And I been watching."

"No, I'm not back. I'm . . . in some trouble."

"You ain't just *in* some trouble; you *are* some trouble." There's the crispy sound of her dragging on a Virginia Slim. "Explains why they had some people pokin' around your place. I told them to fuck off, chased one of them with a tiki torch."

"They didn't arrest you?"

Rita laughed a rheumy, phlegmatic laugh. "I'm just a crazy old cunt; they don't want to deal with *me* in handcuffs."

"I need your help."

"Say the word."

Miriam said she needed a doctor. Someone who could deal with a pregnancy.

"Like, deal-deal with it? Snip and flush?"

"No. A real doctor."

"You're knocked up?"

"I think I'm knocked up."

Another laugh. "Guess you can't run from life now, huh, doll?"

"I guess the fuck not."

"I'll make some calls. I'll get you a guy."

A day later, Rita gave her a name and address.

The name: Richard Beagle.

The address: off the Overseas Highway in Tavernier, here in the Keys.

"Dick Beagle," Miriam said to Gabby with a shrug. And, she noted, no MD, no OB-GYN. Just Dick Beagle. Like a guy who would sell you a 1998 Ford Escort without a VIN.

And now, that's where they are. In a dingy lot framed by the sea and by a sandblasted office building. A lone fast food cup rolls past.

"What's the plan?" Gabby asks.

"I dunno. Go in, see what Dick Beagle, Baby Doctor Extraordinaire, has to say about things."

"This is sketchy."

"Then it's right in line with the rest of my life."

"You okay?"

She forces a smile. "All peaches and cream."

Gabby cuts the engine.

And with that, they get out of the car.

TWELVE

THAT'S WHAT SHE SAID

The way in requires a buzzer. Miriam buzzes.

No one answers.

Miriam buzzes again.

And still, no one answers.

"Shit goddamnit shit," Miriam says.

"Maybe because it's—" Gabby starts to say, but then the door opens.

The man standing there looks like he's been awakened from a nap. He's got the air of an old hippie, but also like a shaggy sheepdog? Fuzzy long hair hangs in gray ringlets. Tired eyes sit pinched behind a pair of round spectacles. He scratches at the woolly beard framing his jowls.

"What?" he says, obviously irritated.

"Are you Dick Beagle?" Miriam asks.

"Richard. Or Rich. Or Richie." Irritated, he adds, "But *never* Dick."

Miriam snort-laughs and jerks a thumb toward Gabby. "That's what *she* said." Gabby frowns. Never-Dick frowns, too. "Because she's a lesbian. You know, a lady who likes ladies? So, 'never dick,' get it?"

"Whaddya want?" Never-Dick asks, his irritation rising.

"A friend of a friend referred me here. Said you're a doctor, or—" She says it again with vigorous air quotes. "A *doc-tor*. I have an, um, situation?"

She pats her belly, then winks.

"And you picked today to come see me," he says.

"Yeah, why?"

"It's Christmas."

She frowns. "It is *not*." Then, to Gabby: "Wait, is it Christmas?"

"I've told you like, three times already today."

"Oh. *Oh.*" She sighs. To Never-Dick she says, "I'm sorry. Shouldn't you be . . . out with your family or something?"

"No, I'm Jewish. Later today I'll screw off, go get some lo mein and beef with broccoli from Chang's Dynasty, maybe watch an old movie. And I don't have a family. At least none that talk to me, so thanks for that."

"I didn't screw up your family."

"No, but you had to bring it up, and now I'm sad."

"Go cry it out and then let's talk. If you don't have a family, I don't see the problem with me coming to see you today."

He shrugs. "It's still Christmas."

"Listen, it's hot out here; can you help me or not?"

"Five hundred."

"Five hundred what? Seashells? Bottlecaps?"

"*Dollars.* You want in, it's five hundo, lady."

"I don't have five hundred bucks."

"Then you don't have a way in this door." And he starts to close it—but Miriam sticks her off-brand Doc Marten through the gap, then nudge-kicks it back open. Never-Dick protests: "Hey!"

"We got like—" To Gabby: "What do we have? How much?"

"Maybe fifty bucks."

"We have fifty bucks. Ten percent. I can get you the rest later."

He scowls. "No. The price is the price. Whoever you talked to shoulda told you that. No negotiating. No wiggle room. None of this *ten percent down* business—I'm not a furniture store and you're not buying a mahogany nightstand."

"Rita didn't say anything about—"

"Rita. Rita who?"

"Rita, Rita Shermansky."

He stiffens. A bulge forms in his throat that he forcibly swallows. "Shermansky." Never-Dick waggles his tongue between the sides of his open mouth, his brow knitting into a cat's cradle of worry. "Shermansky. Okay. *Okay.* Come in."

"Come in?"

"Yeah, Merry Christmas, come on in."

THIRTEEN

A BAT IN THE CAVE

It's like if a doctor's office fucked a shitty studio apartment and this is the room that was born of such crass mating. It's got a desk and a pile of papers, but it's also obviously where Richard "Never-Dick" Beagle sleeps. There's a pull-out couch, a little hot plate, a TV on a small card table playing a *Price Is Right* rerun. A puppy pad sits nearby, with a freshly poured lake of urine slowly soaking in. The puppy that made it is nowhere to be found, so Miriam is left wondering if Beagle here doesn't have a bathroom and instead just chooses to piss on the floor like an animal.

He uses the heel of his foot—which she notices now is barely contained inside a bright-orange rubber Croc, easily the ugliest sandal to ever fit a human appendage—to drag out the chair. Gabby gestures for Miriam to sit before grabbing the second one.

Beagle sits down across from them and plants both elbows on his desk. He puts his hands together and sinks his chin into the hammock formed by his bent fingers. "So, whaddya got? You got a bat in the cave you want removed?" He must see her blank, slightly horrified stare. "I mean, you want an abortion? That's what you're here for, right?"

"No," Miriam says, grimacing.

"No," Gabby adds forcefully.

"No?" he asks. "Then why are you here? Usually, you come to me, you get an abortion, and not even because they're illegal—though the assholes who run this country sure want it back that way—it's just because I'm discreet and nobody needs to know. No lawsuits from abusive boyfriends, no problem with parents, nada. So, why me?"

Something slithers around Miriam's legs.

She jumps up out of her chair, yelping.

Beagle shrugs. "Sorry, that's Rex, probably."

A bald, wrinkled extraterrestrial rodent peeks out from under the chair in which Miriam was sitting. It's got a mouth full of heinous fuckery, with no one tooth pointing the same direction as any other individual tooth. Its top lip curls back, as if to give a greater look at those gnarly chompers. One eye is rheumy with a cataract—the eye looks like pondwater with a pale corpse hidden deep underneath the algae-scum surface. The other eye is . . . ennhhyeah, *fine*, except for the part where it bulges out like a marble, staring past a puff of Muppet hair coming off the top of its wrinkly scrotum head.

The rat-thing pants with a tongue far too long for its mouth. Like a businessman whose tie is far too wide and far too long.

"What the shit is that thing?" Miriam asks.

"It's a dog."

"It's so not a dog."

"It's a *dog*."

"It's a fucking horror movie is what it is."

"It's a Chinese crested. It's fine. He's friendly. Sit."

She sits back down, but the dog doesn't move. It just hangs out under her chair, staring off at nothing with that one "good" eye.

"You're pregnant and you want to have the kid," Beagle says.

"No, I don't want to have the kid."

"But you said no abortion."

"Right, no abortion."

He itches the top of his nose. "You want the kid, then."

"*No*," she says, flummoxed. "I don't *want* the kid, but I *need* the kid. I'm having the kid and I need to know that it's healthy and . . . Listen, I don't want an abortion, I'm having the kid, so—" She clamps her teeth together because all of this is very hard to say and even harder to think about at all and she'd much rather not have to worry about *any* of this thank-you-very-much but here she is and this is happening. "So help me."

"You know you're pregnant? For sure?"

"I peed on one of those plastic sticks. It gave me the double plus."

"And why not go to a real doctor, again?"

"Because I'm a criminal."

Not missing a beat, he says, "Whaddya do?"

"Nothing good."

He sighs. "All right. Time to get you in the stirrups."

"Wait, what?" Miriam panics, looks to Gabby. "I'm not—no, I'm not doing that. Not here. This is just a, a . . . whaddyacallit. A consult."

"Yeah, and that means getting you in the stirrups."

"You try to get me in the stirrups, I'll stick that Muppet rat-monster dog of yours right up your old hippie ass."

A soft touch from Gabby refocuses her. "Miriam. If you want to get checked out, this is the way. But if you want to leave, we can leave."

Her gaze flits from Gabby to Beagle, from Beagle to Gabby. Her heartbeat kicks up like hoofbeats. Even though it's cooler in here than it is outside, she finds herself sweating anew. "Fine," she says.

To the stirrups.

THE HOSPITAL

The doctor's voice drones on and on. He's not talking to Miriam. He's talking to Evelyn. Evelyn, prim Evelyn, buttoned-up Evelyn, Evelyn who's dressed like she's at a funeral (and in her mind, she is).

The doctor, a round man with hair that seems to have left the top of his head and migrated to his eyebrows and the inside of his nose, is going on and on about the consequences of miscarriage.

"The miscarriage was a bad one born of internal trauma," he's saying, his voice with a dog's gruffness, ruff-ruff.

Evelyn corrects: "*External* trauma. My daughter was attacked."

"Yes, yes," he says, still not looking at Miriam, not talking to her, either. "Caused excessive bleeding and a subsequent infection, and the result is . . . scar tissue has built up inside her." *Her*. Miriam screams inside her own head: *I'm right here, you can talk to me! Please talk to me!* "They call it Asherman's Syndrome. We did a hysteroscopy to determine the scope and severity of the scarring, and it's considerable. Difficult to know how considerable until she's a little older and her body sets into . . . more predictable rhythms, but it'll be a concern for her going forward."

"Can she conceive again?" Evelyn asks.

Miriam wants the doctor to stop talking to her mother and

start talking to her. She also knows something about him, something that can't be true: in seven years, he'll die from a heart attack in the parking lot of this very hospital on a cold winter's night. His death will be slow and nobody will help him, despite being so close to so many people who can.

"I'm right here," Miriam says in a small voice.

Her mother shushes her.

The doctor wets his lips. "Infertility is the likely outcome. If she *does* manage to get pregnant, her body isn't prepared to nourish the fetus, so a miscarriage remains a strong possibility."

"And the chances of her conceiving a child and bringing it to term?"

I'm right here I'm right here I'm right here.

"Ennnh. I want to be honest with you," he says. "It's a near-impossibility. A statistical impossibility."

Evelyn won't look at her. She just stares down at her own knees, her own feet. To the floor. *Through* the floor, to some faraway place where none of this is happening, where her daughter is not a shameful smear, a stain in the carpet that won't ever come out. Evelyn has ideas, Miriam knows, *ideas* about a woman's role in this world, in this life.

And Miriam does not fit them.

I should go. I should leave.

Those are the thoughts that repeat in her head like a mantra, even as the doctor gets up and goes, even as her mother sits simmering in silence.

FOURTEEN

THE SEED

She's weeping.

This is not like her.

Admittedly, it's happened more and more in the last year or so, but even still: it's way off-brand. Miriam sees herself as a take-no-shit, give-no-fucks kinda lady. She's all sneer and middle fingers. *I'm supposed to be impervious*, she thinks. Bulletproof. Bomb-proof. *Life*-proof. She's seen so much shit, so much blood, so many lives cut short by a merciless swipe of the reaper's blade that she has long believed herself to be comfortably and appropriately dead inside.

And yet, here she sits, blubbering like a little girl.

She's in Beagle's bathroom. Thankfully, he has one, and she's not required to pee on a puppy pad or squat over a litter box. It's clean, actually. Medicinally clean. So was the exam room, to her surprise—she figured it'd be as dirty as a barstool at a cheap Nevada brothel, but it looked how she expected a real exam room to look. All clean, all sterile. (When Beagle saw her shocked face, he said, "I'm a real doctor. Or was, once.")

Now she sits in the restroom, panties around her ankles. She peed like, ten minutes ago, and has been sitting here since, crying like an asshole and blowing her nose in so much toilet paper that the roll is almost bald.

The examination was, as examinations go, no fun. First came

the uncomfortable questions: "What was your period like?" (*Like the elevator from* The Shining.) "Do you drink or smoke?" (*I drink like a desert camel and used to smoke like a tire fire.*) "What do you do for a job?" (*Ha ha ha, "job," that's a good one, doc.*) "What type of birth control do you use?" (*Uh. Spray and pray?*) And then the real fun one: "Have you ever had a miscarriage?"

That's when she had to tell him—and Gabby, who was standing there.

She told them both how she was pregnant as a teen.

How the mother of the kid who got her knocked up attacked her with a snow shovel in a high school bathroom.

How she miscarried.

How something broke inside her, and how way too much blood came out of her for that to have been normal.

And how the doctor told her she had something called Asherman's, and that meant, at least in her case, a lifetime of infertility.

Hence, no birth control, because why bother?

(It was at that point Gabby reached for her, and Miriam flinched. Yet another thing to apologize for later, if she can muster it. For Miriam, apologizing is like passing a kidney stone. Necessary, sometimes, but hurts as bad as passing a LEGO brick through her urethra.)

After that came a blood test, a pee test, a pap smear.

And for the finale: a transvaginal ultrasound. (*Aren't you gonna buy me dinner first? Or at least put a song on the jukebox for me, sailor?*)

During the tests, she kept thinking that maybe she wasn't pregnant at all. *Maybe* this was all just a fluke. If she wasn't, then that meant she didn't have a way out of this curse that trapped her—a curse that so far had frustratingly failed to yield to her a vision of Beagle's death, because apparently "doctors" wear something called "gloves" to be all "doctor-like." Though she

wanted an escape from this power, if her body had once again chosen to be as inhospitable to life as a canyon on Mars, so be it. That wasn't her fault. That was life. That was fate. *It is what it is, Miriam.*

"You said you have Asherman's?" Beagle says, with some dubiousness.

"Yeah. Why?"

"No sign of it here."

"No sign—what? How is that even possible?"

"You have surgery to correct it?"

She frowned. "No."

"It doesn't usually heal on its own."

Heal on its own . . .

Like the wound under her arm. She was about to open her mouth again to protest his finding—

But that's when she saw it. She saw the seed.

"There it is," Beagle said. On the screen, a dot. Like a bug. "Bit bigger than a sesame seed right now," he said.

"What is it?"

"What *is* it?" he repeated, giving her an incredulous eyebrow.

Gabby's hand fell on her shoulder again, and this time, Miriam did not twitch or pull away. "Miriam, that's the baby."

"It's . . ." *Mine.* "So tiny."

"They don't start out fully formed," Beagle said, sounding irritated. "At this stage they're just a . . . a little bundle of cells dividing. Forming nerves and—there, see that?" In the sesame seed, a tiny fluttering pulse. Like a distant star winking. "That's the heartbeat."

That's the heartbeat.

Here, in the bathroom, that's what she keeps thinking about.

That's when it hit her. That little beating heart. It has a destiny now. It's like getting a social security number: that heart starts to beat, and now her baby is in the system. It has a fate, and the fate isn't long for this world. Hell, it never even *makes it* to this world. It dies on the way out. Born into death, still and cold. It never gets to make sense of the light. It never gets to see all the life around it. *All the life that will one day die,* she thinks.

She's been so inured to the realities of death, she has been left utterly defenseless to the light of life. It has blinded her with tears. She's left wracked and reeling, bewildered and utterly fucked.

She fumbles for the toilet paper roll, reminded suddenly that it's empty, and so she spins it fruitlessly as she grits her teeth and forces herself to shut up and stop crying.

A gentle knock comes to the door.

"Miriam."

Gabby's voice.

"I'm peeing, what."

"You've been in there a while."

"I've . . . got a lot of pee."

"Can I come in?"

"Ugh. Fine." Miriam reaches out, unlocks the door—it's a small bathroom, so she can reach it. Gabby slides in through the door, then gently closes it behind her. Now Miriam is in the uncomfortable position of sitting half-naked on the toilet while Gabby stands above her, knees-to-knees. Miriam sniffs. "Don't judge me. I see you judging me."

"I swear, I'm not judging you."

"I'm not really peeing. I haven't been peeing this whole time. I mean, like, a few drops here and there."

"I know." Gabby gives her a sad look. "You're upset."

"Yes. Yeah. Shit."

"You don't want to lose your baby."

"I don't give a shit about this baby because it's my baby. I give a shit because it's my way out. It's the key to my prison cell.

That's what Mary Stitch told me. I pop out this baby, it ends. I can shut it off and walk away."

Gabby stiffens a little. "But it's still a baby. A life."

Miriam wipes her eyes with the back of her hand. "Stop. Don't give me that speech. I've seen what constitutes *life*. Life is . . . not worth it, okay? It's here just to end. It's a slow walk into a wood chipper. Babies aren't special because they're babies; they're just weaker, doughier, poopier versions of actual people, and all people are stupid and *all people die.*" She sighs. "I'm overselling this, aren't I?"

Gabby holds her finger and thumb an inch apart. "Little bit."

"Fuck."

"Yeah."

"I care about the kid. The not-quite-a-kid. The *seed*. Okay? I care. I don't *want* to care but I *do* care."

"It'll be okay."

"It *won't*. The kid dies. That's what fate has in store. A death, and one that comes so early, it comes before life even really *begins*." She thinks of Louis now. And how happy this baby would make him. And how sad he would be to lose it. Worse, she can't help but feel sad at how she lost *him.*

Gabby starts to help her up. She says, "You've saved people before."

"This is different. I don't know how to save it. Just like I don't know how to . . . ." She doesn't finish that sentence. She doesn't have to.

Because Gabby finishes it for her:

"Just like you don't know how to save me."

"Yeah."

"I don't need saving."

"We all need saving."

"I'm not going to kill myself."

Oh, but you are. I saw it in my vision. Fate gets what fate wants, Gabs. And what fate wants is you swallowing an entire medicine cabinet full of pills and turning your heart off like it's a fucking stopwatch, cla-click.

Gabby shakes her head. "I don't buy it. I'll be okay. And this baby will be okay, too. Here—" Gabby eases down and helps Miriam get her panties back up. Miriam can feel her breath on her shins, her messy, spiky hair tickling her knees. It's an oddly intimate moment. Not sexual, not at all. Just *intimate.* A moment perfect for Miriam to ruin.

"This is not the time for oral sex," Miriam says.

"Miriam."

"Sorry. I can get my own panties up. I'm not some pregnant beast-blob who can't see her own toes. Not yet, anyway."

"I'm helping, so let me help."

Miriam lets her help. She stands, head craning back on her neck, staring up at the light above the toilet.

"Ugh. God. Fuck. I'm going to get pregnant. I mean, I know I'm *already* pregnant, but I'm going to get *pregnant*-pregnant. Swollen and wobbly. This little seed is going to turn into a giant watermelon."

But as she's saying that, Gabby is looking down. Studying something.

She stoops to pick something up.

It's a Band-Aid.

One from underneath Miriam's arm. Where the wound was before it . . . healed up and went away. It must've popped out of her sleeve.

"You lost a bandage," Gabby says.

"I don't think that's mine—Gabs, you shouldn't pick Band-Aids up off a bathroom floor. Pretty sure that's how Ebola starts."

But now Gabby is invested—like a mother monkey, she's grabbing Miriam's arm gently and giving a look down through the sleeve.

72

"I don't see any blood," Gabby says.

"I know— It's not—"

"Wait, is it this arm? This side?"

"Yeah, no, it's—"

"You should have the doctor look at it—I know he's not *that* kind of doctor, but he's still *a* doctor, so while we're here—" By now, Gabby's rolled up the bottom of Miriam's T-shirt, and Miriam thinks to fight it, but what's the point? It'll come out eventually. The truth is like a dead body: you can only hide it for so long before it pops back up somewhere.

It's then that Gabby says it:

"You're all healed."

". . . yes?"

"Yes? Yes. You're saying yes like you already know this."

"I . . . am maybe saying it that way, yeah."

"Miriam, that was a bullet wound."

"It was."

"A week ago, it looked like hell. You could've slotted a roll of quarters in that thing."

Miriam shrugs. "And now it's fine. Yay. Let's move on." But Gabby isn't satisfied. She's got Miriam's arm up. She's studying that area. Miriam says, "I didn't know you had an armpit thing. You could've told me. No shame here. We all have our sexual peccadillos, Gabs—"

"There's not even a scab. Or a *scar*."

"Yeah, I . . . noticed that."

"But you kept putting bandages on it."

Miriam winces like a guilty child. "I did."

"Why?"

"Because . . ." Miriam can't think of a lie.

"Because you wanted to fool me."

"Yes, to fool you. But wait, no, not to fool you, not exactly—"

"Not exactly?"

The explanation comes out in a gushing rush. "I thought it was weird and I didn't really wanna talk about it. I've got enough insanity on my mind right now to have to sit and contemplate the ramifications of healing a bullet hole in a few days—"

"A few days?"

"Maybe less. I woke up in the Super 8 and it was healed."

Gabby's eyes go wide. "That's fast."

Miriam sighs. "No shit, Nurse Ratched."

"That's *too* fast."

"I know! That's what I'm saying. I don't know what it means. I don't know why I have it. I don't know if I can do it again or if it was some kind of fluke or hey, shit, what if I can't even die and—"

The words are caught suddenly in her throat, trapped there like a rat in a tube sock. She replays the thought in her head: *What if I can't die?*

Like Harriet.

"I'm going to come for you now," Harriet says. *"And then I'm going to eat your precious heart. One animal eating the power of another."*

Miriam tastes heartsblood on her tongue.

Then she turns around and pukes in the toilet.

FIFTEEN

GROTESQUE REVIVIFICATION

The puke taste stains the back of her tongue like the ectoplasm of a passing poltergeist. Miriam staggers out of the bathroom, zombie-like, led by Gabby. Beagle asks her if she's all right and she mumbles something that, again, is zombified in its mush-mouthed meaninglessness. Gabby covers for her, says it's "just nerves."

Dr. Never-Dick is talking at her, but she's not listening. Instead, she's thinking about that night, not long ago now but one that feels like a lifetime before, where she cut out Harriet Adams' heart and ate it. She ate it because it was the only way to kill the bitch—a bitch who had risen from the dead on a mission to kill her. Raised from the dead perhaps by the Trespasser. Or, at least, possessed by her own version of one.

It was the only way to end her. Harriet couldn't be stopped. When Harriet came at her the first time back in Miriam's old house, she kicked in the witch's kneecap, attacked her with an owl, and yet the hag kept coming. Miriam went out the window to escape, and Harriet followed close behind, galloping down the roof on all fours like an animal. Harriet leapt off the roof but landed wrong—her arm snapped, breaking so bad the bone lanced through the skin like a spear-tip. And next time she saw that monster? Harriet was *A-OK*. Good to go without an injury in sight. Leg working fine. Bone back in her arm. No claw marks from Bird of Doom.

So, to kill her, Miriam removed, then ate, her heart.

But eating Harriet's heart, that wasn't Miriam's idea. Oh, no. That idea, she stole. She stole it from Harriet herself, because the undying bitch let that little tidbit slip. Harriet said to Miriam:

I'm going to cut off your head.

And then I'm going to take out your heart.

Your head I will leave behind so it can watch as I eat your heart. That is how I take your power. That is how I conquer.

Eat the heart. Take her power.

So, Miriam ate Harriet's heart instead. Not to take the power for herself but rather to take it *away* from Harriet.

Seems it worked both ways, though, didn't it? Yes, she robbed Harriet of her power to heal. Yes, it allowed Harriet to die, finally, there in the winter-struck forest, in the snow, in the cold.

But now Miriam wonders if she has that power, too. The power to heal all injuries. The power *not to die.*

And she has no idea what that means.

Miriam shuffles her way to the door. Walking out into the brutal bright vengeance of the angry Florida day-star, she hears the doctor say something to her. She offer a grumpy mammalian grunt, turning toward him—he's saying to her, "It'll be fine, you're healthy, the baby looks healthy, come back in a week for the results of the blood test, and—"

And then he does it. He reaches out.

He has no glove on.

He touches her forearm and

THE DEATH OF NEVER-DICK

Richard Beagle, Richie, Rich, Never-Dick, no longer a doctor, is in the stirrups. He's naked as a mole rat. His cock and his balls twitch and try desperately to hide inside his body. His asshole twitches too, like it's puckered from a lifetime of sucking lemons. He's mostly in the dark but for the spear of illumination coming from a halogen exam lamp angled in his direction—it's like he's the main event, the actor in the spotlight, the trapeze artist at the center of the circus stage.

Black electrical tape covers his mouth. A line of blood, now crusty, decorates his brow, drawing a squiggly zigzag line from an injury on the top of his head down between his eyes, down to the end of his nose. Those gray ringlets of hair are scabby with blood too, the ends matted and plastered to his cheeks and to his temples.

A shadow passes over Richard Richie Rich Beagle. Someone moves in front of the very bright desk lamp.

Beagle thrashes about. But his feet are bound to the stirrups by black Velcro straps. And his hands are flat against the padding of the table, wrists shackled with a long chain bound up under his flabby ass-cheeks.

His killer comes revealed.

It's a woman with a scarred-up face, like a vase that broke and was clumsily put back together again with pink puffy scar tissue instead of glue.

Gabby says to Beagle, "Miriam, I bet you can hear me in there. Miriam, darling, light of my life, I'm hoping you get this message. I'm going to kill him. I'm going to kill Never-Dick here. I'm going to—"

Gabby whoops and laughs madly, then crisscrosses a scalpel blade across Beagle's chest a few times—slice, slice, slice, erratic lines that immediately open up and drool blood. Beagle screams behind his gag. Sweat beads around the scabby crust on his brow.

"Yeah, I'm gonna kill him," she continues. "As you've figured out by now. This is his last day. His last few moments. I could torture him—"

She twirls the scalpel deftly in her hand, lets it tickle a path across his paunchy stomach, down past the sweat-slick line of gray hair, to the nest of his pubes, to the top of his dick. She gives the scalpel a little jab, like she's a kid trying to pop a balloon with a pin—Beagle shudders hard, moaning as a bead of red swells up from where the scalpel poked the end of his cock. She drags it down, down, down, occasionally stopping to do the same—little pin-pokes, little stitches, balloons of blood blowing up and going from beads to strings as they run down his manhood, down his sack, to the exposed tract of taint, to his puckered shithole. Stick, stick, stick. Thrash, thrash. Gabby chuckles as she gently encircles his asshole with the tip of the knife—not cutting in, not drawing blood, but scraping the skin there, kkkkk, kkkkkk.

"I should torture him, probably. He has holes his soul, too. I can feel them there. He's a bad man. Got shame coming off of him like steam off a pile of shit. You know how he lost his medical license? Well, darling Miriam, he was coked up out of his gourd, gonzo on the white stuff, and he tried to deliver a baby—key word: tried. The baby belonged to a nice lady named Paula, but boy, did he fuck up. Good news: he delivered that baby and that baby lived. The bad news? Oof. The mom didn't do so hot. *Baby came out in a c-section, which by the way you should know means they slit your belly open, vshht vshht—"* And here she slits Beagle's belly open with a long, vicious, dragging cut. He wails behind the gag as blood bubbles out and the gray shine of his guts bulges from the slit like earthworms from a frog's mouth. *"And then they lifted all those guts up and out of the way so they can grab the kid and rescue him from the womb. Only problem, Beagle nicked the bladder and didn't even realize it. Because, again: coked up out of his gourd. They stitched her up. Her insides bled like a stuck piglet. Postpartum hemorrhage led to sepsis led to oopsie-daisy, Dead Mommy."*

The next part comes fast. Gabby stabs the scalpel into his bulging bowels, then sticks it into him once, twice, three times, again and again—up his middle, to his chest, into his throat, and into his face. Stab, stab, stab. The pain radiates through him as he's punctured, perforated like he's a potato prior to baking, until one cut finally hits something vital—

A spray of blood gushes from a hole in his neck, spattering across Gabby's face. She leers into his own ghost-white visage with her own:

"I'm doing you a favor, because I'm sure you didn't want him delivering your little maggot baby anyway, did you? But better yet, consider this yet another message, this one from the future, dear Miriam. We have work to do. And until you decide to do it, I'll be here, rattling your chains, reminding you that you aren't off this leash yet."

SIXTEEN

RUNNING ON EMPTY

Miriam wants to puke, but there's nothing left. She wants to cry, but that well has gone dry too. So instead, she stands there for a few seconds, feeling disconnected from this life, this world, like she's the audience held fast by a horror movie unfolding on the screen in front of her. But this isn't a movie. This is real. This is happening—or, rather, it will happen.

It happens in three months.

"You okay?" Beagle asks her.

"Fine," she says, her voice hoarse from all the vomiting and crying. Gabby runs the flat of her hand across Miriam's back in gentle reassurance.

"It'll all work out in the end," he says.

Your ass is writing a check that reality won't cash, doc.

She doesn't say that, though. Instead she just nods.

"Thanks for seeing me. I'll make sure you get the rest of the money."

He waves her off. "Don't sweat it. I'll call you with the results of the tests. Maybe a couple weeks. I gotta send this stuff in under the radar, since, well. Not a legitimate practice anymore."

"It's fine. Lemme ask: why'd you lose your license? You did lose it?"

He hesitates. "I did."

"Something happen?"

She's expecting him to lie, because everybody lies. Nobody wants to cop to their own failures. It's one of the hallmarks of humanity. It's also one of the reasons most humans aren't worth a good goddamn.

But he surprises her.

"A lady died giving birth under my care."

Miriam shrugs. "People die. That's life. No reason to kick you out of Doctorland, right?"

"I was on drugs at the time. She died because I was out of my head."

"Oh."

"Yeah."

"You on drugs now?"

"Clean and sober since that day, eleven years ago."

"Good for you."

He frowns. "I guess. So, when the time comes, I can deliver yours, but maybe you wanna get back in the good graces of the law so someone with a steadier hand than mine can bring that kid into the light."

"I'll think about it. Thanks, doc."

"You'll hear from me."

"I know."

I'll hear you scream every time I close my eyes, doc. Every time Gabby—Gabby taken by the Trespasser—sticks you with that scalpel.

SEVENTEEN

THE LITTLE BOX

It is a struggle to seem normal.

Miriam is not feeling normal, not at all. Not that she *ever* feels particularly normal, of course, but right now she feels deeply disconnected from any sense of normalcy—she's an impostor, a stowaway, a castaway, flung far from any sense of ordinary. Her head feels like it's literally bursting with bad thoughts, like a mosquito who drank from the jugular. Louis is dead. He left her with a baby whose fate is to be born and then immediately die. She's a fugitive. The doctor she just met will one day be killed by Gabby, Gabby who can be taken by the Trespasser, Gabby who may yet kill herself because life is too hard *or now*, Miriam realizes, because she is vulnerable to being possessed by whatever the fuck the Trespasser is.

She's ants in a bottle. A colony of crawling ants desperate for escape.

The houseboat bobs and sways underneath her.

Gabby sidles up. In her hand is a present, wrapped. It's smaller than a breadbox, and in fact, fits in the palm of her upturned hand.

"So, it's Christmas," Gabby says.

Miriam's about to do the Miriam thing. She's about to go off on Gabby. *It's not Christmas to me. Christmas is just some bullshit holiday the hypocritical Christians stole from the pagans anyway, and I'm not really in the Yuletide Fucking Mood over here, and it's not like I got you anything anyway, and it's not like I deserve anything,* but then, the twinkling lights she hung earlier now twinkle and dance along the margins of her scars. And it's beautiful. It's innocent. It's perfect. And Miriam realizes she can't do it. She can't unload with both barrels. She has to grow up. Has to be better than this. *Turn it around,* she tells herself.

So, this time, she does.

She smiles a small smile and takes the box.

"I . . . didn't get you anything," she tells Gabby.

"I know. You've got a lot to deal with, and this isn't to make you feel bad. You can get me something later. And before you start, no, I'm not looking for a speech about how good I am and how bad you are. We're both as good as we can be, and as bad as we are. No speeches."

"You know me very well."

"I do. Or I think I do. We'll see when you open your gift."

"Let's get to it, then."

Miriam wants to do the childish thing and rip the paper off the box, tearing the thing open with the fury of a dozen badgers. But she doesn't. She is methodical and slow and takes her time with it. At first, she does this as a show for Gabby—*see, I can be better*—but as her fingers work the bow and gently unmoor the tape from the paper, she starts to enjoy it. No, she starts to *savor* it. Patience and care: two traits that are so far out of Miriam's wheelhouse, she may very well be seen as their opposite, but that suddenly manifest in her, and in a way that is oddly comforting to her.

The box reveals itself.

It is a jewelry box.

With the pad of her thumb she lifts the lid of the box and finds that inside, on a pillow of cotton, rests an owl. It is a shiny metal—"Silver," Gabby says as Miriam picks it up and regards it—and portrays not some adorable owl looking moon-eyed, but rather, an owl in flight, claws out, beak open, as if flying toward the one looking upon it.

"You said you had an owl," Gabby explains.

"Bird of Doom. I did. I miss it."

"Well, I know it's not the same thing as a real owl, but . . ."

Miriam kisses her on the cheek. "Thanks."

"The lady I bought it from—a little store down in Key West— said that the owl represents *seeing what others do not see*. She said it was a bird of chaos and change, and that the bird excelled at seeing through lies and through people's masks. Sounded a lot like you."

"I don't know about all that, but I am definitely Chaos Girl. And I *do* see shit that other people don't."

"You like it?"

"Fuck *like*. I *love it*."

"Merry Christmas, Miriam."

"Merry Christmas, Gabs."

They embrace. And for a time—a little while, at least— Miriam actually *does* feel normal, like it's not a sham, not some mask. Like she's someone else and her life is *not* in fact crazier than a coked-up chimpanzee.

EIGHTEEN

AWAKE IN THE DARK

Miriam is awake and alert even though the clock ticks over to midnight. The silver owl pendant sits cold and heavy against her chest, and sometimes her hand moves to it and presses it there so hard into her skin, it almost hurts. (But it also feels strangely satisfying, the way it feels when you tongue a bit cheek or poke at a loose tooth.) Outside she hears the gentle lapping of water against the houseboat. She tries to clear her head of all the ants that crawl there, all the spiders and all the snakes, and it works, for a time. She focuses on her breathing. (*God, I want a cigarette.*) She empties her mind. (*The Trespasser is out there and could be anyone, and holy hell, what is its game, who is it, why won't it just leave me the fuck alone.*) She cuts loose all her earthly ties and desires. (*I miss Louis, I want to fuck Gabby, I love my owl necklace, nobody will take my owl necklace or I will cut them with a broken whiskey bottle and drink their blood.*) None of that works, of course, and mostly she lies there, staring up at the dark.

Eventually, Gabby rolls over.

She's still awake, too.

"You can talk to me, you know," Gabby says.

"Yeah, no, I know."

"You miss him."

"Miss who?" she asks, even though she knows who.

"Louis."

She sighs. "Yeah. I mean . . . Yeah." Even though it's dark, Miriam presses the heels of her hands against her eyes hard enough that she sees a laser light show there in the dark behind her lids. "He was too good for me. He was too good for this world. I don't know what to do with him gone. I feel like a house without a front door."

"I'm sorry. You saved him, though. You did something good."

"Let's not congratulate me too hard," Miriam says. "Only reason I had to save him was because I brought evil to him. My version of saving him was hip-checking him off a cliff and then catching his hand before he fell to his death. Meeting me was the worst thing that ever happened to him. And I don't just mean that to be some kinda self-defeating boo-hoo woe-is-me thing—though, also, it is. I just mean, legit, that guy had a better life before I showed up and fucked it all up."

Gabby's hand found her bare shoulder and rested there. "You don't know that. Maybe fate had it in for him anyway. Maybe you bought him a couple extra years."

"That's a generous read, and I hope you're right."

"I won't get in the way, you know."

Miriam sits up. "In the way of what?"

"Of you and him."

"He's dead."

"But he's also not. He's still alive in your mind. In your heart."

"I just need time to deal with it all."

"I know." Still, Gabby sounds sad when she says it.

"It's nothing to do with you. It's just—this is hard. Okay? These are rough waters full of jagged rocks, and I don't want to drag you through those rocks with me." What she thinks but does not say is *And I don't want you to be one of those jagged rocks I have to navigate.*

"Okay. Yeah."

"You're mad."

"I'm not mad."

"You're hurt."

"I'm not hurt."

"People who say they're not mad or hurt are usually mad and hurt."

"And if I said I *was* mad and/or hurt?"

"Then I'd know you were."

Gabby sighs. "I can't win here."

"It's not about winning; I just don't want you to worry about this right now."

"You mean *you* don't want to worry about this now."

"Yes. No! Not exactly. But also, wait, yeah, yes, I don't wanna worry about this right now. My head's full-up on crazy."

"So, now I'm crazy."

"Gabs, c'mon—it's Christmas."

"It was. It's past midnight. Christmas is now officially over, and with it, the holiday cheer." She rolls over. "Good night, I need to sleep."

"Gabs—"

"Good night, Miriam."

Gabby pulls the blanket up over her head.

Miriam, meanwhile, lies awake in the dark, cursing herself, even though she knows she is already cursed in so many ways.

NINETEEN

BLOOD IN THE CUT

Later, after Gabby's gone to sleep, Miriam grabs a serrated steak knife from the kitchen drawer and heads out on what passes for the houseboat's front porch—really just an area with a couple beach chairs and a railing overlooking the moon-slick waters of the Gulf of Mexico. Or maybe up here it's Florida Bay, she's not sure.

As the boat bobs, she ponders where to cut.

In movies, idiots always cut into their palms. Why you'd ever do that, she has no idea, because that'll fuck up your hand. You need your hands.

The cut has to be somewhere out of sight. And it has to be somewhere that won't affect her very much. Fingers, toes, feet, face. Has to be out of the way, somewhere incidental.

Miriam decides that her left bicep can suffer the injury.

She rolls up her sleeve, pressing the knife against the skin.

She draws a breath. Sucks it in and holds it. Thinks idly how great it would be to smoke a whole pack of cigarettes right now.

In her head, she counts to three.

One.

The water laps at the boat.

Two.

The stars above watch and wink.

Three.

She pulls the knife across her arm. Miriam stifles a cry so as not to wake Gabby. The blood wells up and drips down her arm in streaks.

"Merry Christmas to me," Miriam says, singsongy, as she bleeds.

TWENTY
STITCH

By morning, the wound is gone. It leaves nothing behind but the stain of blood and the ghost of pain still haunting the skin.

TWENTY-ONE

THE GREAT UNBURDENING

It takes a week to spill her guts.

Not literally, of course. Not like poor old Dr. Never-Dick.

It's night and it's raining outside. It's a heavy Florida rain, which sounds like ball bearings pelting the houseboat on the top and on the sides. This rain, like all the rains here, will come and go, leaving humid air in place so thick you couldn't cut it with an axe. But for now, it's pouring down with the wrath of a drunken, vengeful god.

Since they talked that night after Christmas, things have been uncomfortable between them. Not knock-down drag-out throw-chairs-at-each-other uncomfortable, though Miriam would've preferred that, honestly. This was a subtler chill. A cold war. Gabby was acting like a cat, all slinking away and offering sideways stares. Miriam needs to escalate this thing, and she decides the way to do that is to tell Gabby the truth.

Lies are like lockpicks. A deft practitioner can use them to gently open a door and sneak through. Truth opens the door too, but it does so with the force of a rampaging bull. Miriam is gifted at both, but lies require work, and truth demands no such finesse.

All she needs is her opening.

That night, Gabby's on the couch, sipping a Corona, and as she does, the lime in the bottle releases the bubbles it's collected, fizzing to the top. The houseboat is cramped, but Miriam likes it that way. It's probably all this *preggo-talk*, but she can't help but feel the place is womblike. Lots of warm wood, tons of pillows, everything shoved just that much closer together. You wouldn't want to run laps around the place, but the whole house feels like a bed, like you could lie down and sleep anywhere. Like it would envelop you, swallow you up, bury you forgotten and deep.

"You could have one," Gabby says, after swigging from the bottle. "I read that beer is okay for pregnant women, long as they don't get drunk."

Miriam, sitting on a mustard-yellow recliner that came with the houseboat, has wrapped herself up into a bundle. Knees to her chest, arms around her knees. She knows she won't be able to make this shape forever, because soon she'll bulge with the shape of the growing parasite. Presently, she stares out from between the hills formed by her knees.

"Beer sucks," Miriam says. "It's like cat pee. I'd rather drink wine, and that's telling you something, because wine is really just sadness in a glass. Did you read anything about whiskey? Is whiskey good for a pregnant mom? Tequila? What if I mix orange juice with it, then is it healthy?"

Gabby gives her a quizzical look, like she's not sure if Miriam is being serious. (Miriam thinks: *I am being serious, give me whiskey, give me whiskey now.*) "The book didn't say anything about that."

"Book. What book?"

"*What to Expect When You're Expecting.*"

"You bought a book." Statement, not a question.

"Yeah. I bought a book." Her hackles were up. Good. "Why?"

"You're not the mom. Or my mom. Or *a* mom."

Gabby sits up straighter, an animal warned suddenly by the scent of a predator. "I know that. So what?"

"So what? I just mean—"

"You just mean I'm not involved in all this."

"Of course you're involved. You're right there. Look. There you are. *Here* you are. Involved."

"But not involved enough to buy a book. You want me to be here to help you but not be a parent to this kid."

"Yeah, right, exactly."

Gabby sits up all the way, now, and plunks the beer bottle down on the cheap-ass mid-century modern coffee table. It thuds. The Corona fizzes over, but Gabby doesn't seem to care.

"Nice," Gabby says. "Real nice."

"Why do you *want* to be a parent? This isn't about you. Gabs, I'm just not ready to . . . tag you in on this. It's not your kid and I don't want you to be responsible. I don't even know if it survives. Listen, there's something I need to tell you—" But Gabby doesn't hear her, and keeps on with this.

"I want to be involved. Like you said: I'm *here*, aren't I?"

"Why? Why are you here?"

"Because I *love* you, you stupid asshole!"

". . . oh."

"And I believe the baby will survive. You'll make it happen. I know you, Miriam."

"Like how my mother survived? Or Grosky? Or *Louis*?"

"Miriam—"

"Louis died. I didn't save *him*."

"I know, and I'm sorry, I just mean—"

"It's fine." She presses her face further into the valley formed by her own knees, cheeks to the bare skin of her legs, cold flesh on cold flesh. Darkness descends on her. Hands trying to pull her down into a bleak, unremitting despair. But she sneaks a peek, and the look on Gabby's face brings her back. It's a look of hope, contrary to all the rest of reality. A little glimmer of light in the black of each eye. Finally, the words come up out of Miriam unbidden—her face is smooshed between her knees, though, so the words come out, well, *smooshy*. "I need you. Okay? I need you to be there with me at the end of this."

"What?" Gabby leans in. "Sorry? Could you say that a little louder?"

Miriam repeats: "I need you to be there—"

"No, get your face out of your legs. It sounds like you're talking around a mouthful of mushy peas."

Miriam lifts her chin. "I'm going to resist making a sex joke about faces-between-legs because I respect you."

"Out with it."

"I. Need. You." Miriam enunciates each word like a fork tapped against a crystal goblet, *ting, ting, ting*. "I need you to be there with me at the end of this. And I mean that . . . no matter how this ends. With the baby alive or dead. With life being whatever life becomes. I need you."

"You got me. And I need you, too."

They sit in silence for a while. Gabby leans back and extends her leg out—with her bare foot she traces her wiggly toes up Miriam's calf. She leans over her bottle, a lascivious look on her face.

"First armpit stuff," Miriam says, "and now a foot fetish?"

"I'm not into feet *or* armpits." Her toes tickle up further, to Miriam's knee. Wiggle, wiggle, tickle, tickle. "But I *am* into *you*. We could hit the bunk. We could . . . mess around. What was that about a face between legs?"

Miriam reaches out and runs her fingers over the top of Gabby's naked foot—feeling the bones leading to her toes.

(*bones like bird bones*)

"I'm pregnant. You don't want me. I'm a hideous beast."

"You're not even ten weeks pregnant. The baby weighs an ounce."

"See? I'm huge already."

"So dramatic. Shut up." Gabby again sets the beer on the

table, right in the lake she formed the last time she put it down. She stands, and steps over, stooping down to press her mouth against Miriam's. Her lips are soft. Her tongue slides in, an intruder—

(*a trespasser*)

Hands slide around Miriam's middle. Fingers digging furrows across the flesh of her lower bag, meeting in the middle, pulling her up—

Miriam's own fingers find Gabby's face, cupping it—

(*a lacework of scar tissue*)

(*a broken mirror*)

(*a medicine cabinet*)

(*a suicide*)

Shit shit shit.

Miriam pulls away, gasping for air, a string of saliva connecting their two lips. The grin on Gabby's face is a wicked sickle. Her eyes flash with lust. But Miriam grits her teeth, moans, and says:

"I need to tell you something. Some*things*, actually."

"Now?"

"Now."

Gabby pulls away, sighing. She sits on the arm of the couch. "You could've waited until after we fucked like the last two bunnies on earth."

"No, I don't think I could."

"That serious, huh?"

"That serious."

"Lay it on me."

"All of it?"

Gabby makes a *bring it on* gesture. "All of it."

"I . . . am pretty sure I know how I'm pregnant. Pregnant when I'm not supposed to be."

"Okaaaaay."

"I . . . so, when I killed Harriet Adams, I may have taken some of her power. When I hurt her, she healed it, and now I . . ." She wrinkles up her brow, deciding that right now was *not* the best time to explain how she had to eat the other woman's heart. "I think I have that power too."

"The wound. Under your arm. Of course."

"Yeah." Miriam pulls back the sleeve of her tee, shows off her bicep. There, across it, is the ghost of an injury. "See this scar?"

"Uh-huh."

"I cut myself there last night. Fresh fucking cut, red blood, and now, it's this."

Gabby leans down, staring at it, fascinated. "It looks like a scar from . . . years ago. Childhood, maybe." She pokes at it. Miriam pulls away, not because it hurts, but because it tickles, and tickling sucks and nobody should tickle anybody ever, the end. "Sorry."

"So, I think . . . with Harriet's power, maybe it healed something inside of me. It let the pregnancy happen instead of miscarrying. I mean—assuming I don't still miscarry, but my vision says differently."

"Jesus, Mir. That's—that's good, right? A weird kind of miracle."

"If you say so. I'm still pregnant." Miriam hesitates. "And there's more."

"Do I want to know?"

Miriam shakes her head. "No. Which is why I have to tell you. You know the Trespasser? The . . . thing I see? The presence, the entity, the demon, whatever-the-fuck-it-is. It's gotten worse. More *powerful*. When I stole the ambulance and ran from the cops, the paramedic driving the ambulance killed the cop and then himself."

"Jesus. Miriam, you never told me that."

Miriam still tastes the Corona on her lips and tongue from

Gabby's kiss. It's a nice moment that breaks through the horrible memory, which only makes the whole story feel stranger as she tells is. "Thing is, he wasn't himself. He was . . . *possessed*. By the Trespasser, and I know because the Trespasser taunts me in its very special way. That demon is its own unique brand of motherfucker, and . . . I just know it was him. It. Whatever. And it's angry. Angry that I'm pregnant. Angry that maybe I have a way out, an escape."

"Okay . . . ," Gabby says, obviously not sure where this is going.

Deep breath, Miriam. Let it all out.

"The other day, at the doc's, I . . . the doctor reached out and touched my arm as we were leaving. And I saw how he dies."

"Is it bad?"

"It's bad."

"How bad?"

"You kill him."

Gabby snorts a laugh, but then furrows her brow when Miriam keeps a straight face. "Wait, you're not kidding. Why the hell would I kill him?"

"You . . . wouldn't. Especially like this. You carve into him with a scalpel, stabbing him. *Torturing* him. It's fucked up. But the thing is, it's not you doing it. It's the demon. It's the Trespasser."

"I . . . I don't understand."

"It possesses you."

She watches the realization cross Gabby's face—like a shadow darkening a bright day. "Like the ambulance driver. And the police officer. Oh, god."

"It gets worse."

"I can't imagine how," Gabby says, morose.

"I think I know how you die. You were right. You won't go into your house and eat a fistful of pills. Not on your own."

The look on Gabby's face says she gets it. "But if I were possessed . . ."

"Yeah."

Tears shine in Gabby's eyes. "I don't want to be possessed. I . . . I don't even think—maybe you're wrong, maybe this isn't real—"

"It's real. And I'm right. I know it."

"God. Fuck." The tears let loose, now—one by one, they roll down the topography that forms the map of Gabby's scar tissue. "*Fuck*."

"That's all the bad news."

"There can't possibly be *good* news."

"I think there is. Because if the Trespasser is the thing that kills you—if it possesses you and drives you to that point? Then I can stop it." She feels her heart hammering the inside of her chest like a punching fist. "I can keep you alive. All I have to do is kill it first."

"Kill the Trespasser?"

She nods. "Kill the motherfucking Trespasser."

TWENTY-TWO

BUNNIES THUMPING

They fuck like the last two bunnies on Earth.

And that is a very specific kind of coitus.

It's the kind of fucking that says, *We may be the last ones here, the rest of our kind may be gone, and we may be gone soon, too. No promises. No guarantees*. But it also says, *It's in us*. The potential. The *chance* to be alive and to make more of us. It's a desperate, insane kind of fucking—desperate and insane because despite what's come, and despite what's likely on the way, it thrives on a pulsating nucleus of *hope*, a pounding core of *possibility*. It's two people coiled and writhing around the axis of a single, defiant middle finger, defiant of everything that has gone wrong and may yet go awry, spiteful of what-yet-may-come.

This fucking is angry. It's *vengeful*. Not against each other, no—this anger is shared. The vengeance is a uniting element, not an agitating one, not one that separates them. It's skin slapping skin, it's teeth tugging on a lower lip, it's hands digging into the flesh of an ass-cheek in order to pull one another against each other, *into* each other, as if with enough heat and struggle, two could handily become one. Two phoenixes, rising together and fornicating in the consumptive conflagration of flame.

This fucking is like a song that goes slow, that goes quiet, and then that rises back up again like a spiraling resurrection of guitars and drums and cymbal crashes and cannons booming and buildings collapsing.

This fucking is intense. It's noise. It's sweat. It's mouths open and trailing saliva across open tracts of skin. The rain is a drumbeat, a heartbeat. The ocean is movement. They each come like a gun going off. The boom, the recoil, the quiet after but for the ears ringing.

They lay there for a while, each tangled in the serpent's embrace of arms, legs, sheets. Gabby is the one who breaks the silence.

She says, "We can do this."

"We can do this."

"But tell me, you have a plan, right?"

"I have a plan," Miriam says, still panting, still tasting Gabby on her tongue. She wipes a curl of damp hair from her face.

"What *is* the plan?"

"In the morning, I make a phone call. That's the plan."

TWENTY-THREE

COCKTAIL WEENIES AND SEAFOOD BOULDERS

Miriam's on the back patio of the Key Largo Conch House, leaning back as the waitress brings a plate of little deep-fried seafood boulders: conch fritters. It's her second plate. "I'm eating for two," she told the waitress—a forty-year-old woman who dies nine years from now after drunk-drowning in her own damn swimming pool.

The waitress drops the plate and asks if Miriam wants anything else, and she does: "Extra dipping sauce, please. This stuff is like liquid heroin. After today, I'm going to need to go to a meeting."

"Okay, hon," the waitress says, so obviously used to dealing with local randos that nothing could faze her. Her attitude is bulletproof. Miriam could kick off her shoes and eat the fritters with her monkeytoes and the waitress would just say *okay, hon*, like nothing about it was weird at all.

As the waitress recedes, the tide brings a new visitor:

FBI's own David Guerrero.

He's not in a suit, thankfully. He's got a short-sleeve button-down, tight on his muscular frame. A pair of khaki cargo shorts hangs beneath them. Sunglasses so dark, they might as well be black holes covering his eyes.

From under the table, Miriam kicks with her foot, pushing out the chair opposite her. "Sit," she says as she dips a fritter in the orange sauce and pops the whole thing in her mouth. "Thanksh for coming." Chew, chew.

"Florida, huh?" he says, taking a seat. "You keep coming back here."

She narrows her eyes. "That's right. You've been following me."

"Following your progress. Your . . . life, such as it is."

Cheek bulging with fritter, she spreads her arms wide. "And oh, what a life it is, Agent Guerrero. Magic and adventure every day. My existence is basically Disney World. I'm a Disney princess, tra-la-la, getting up every morning with songbirds helping me put on my clothes." And suddenly she realizes out loud: "Wait, I could actually do that. This changes everything." But then, a second, more disappointing epiphany: "Nah, you know what, birds crap on everything. Maybe they could help me get a T-shirt over my head, but they would shit in my hair."

"You seem awfully animated today."

"Animated. Good joke." Another fritter in her mouth, pop. She grins, with fritter smeared across the flats of her teeth. "Anyway. Get to know me and you'll soon realize: I'm just getting started, Guerrero."

"Conch fritters?" he asks.

"You bet. Want one?"

"Sure." With careful movement, he plucks one between thumb and forefinger and brings it over to him, bypassing the sauce. Gently he pulls it apart. Steam rises from the spongy fritter like little sea snail ghosts.

"The conch are tough, like little seafoody pencil erasers, and yet they're amazing? They almost make Florida worth it." She shrugs. "At least it's not brain-boilingly hot today." The view from the back patio is nice too: almost tropical. Shaded by an erratic ring of palm trees that look like they've gathered here as a cabal of friendly drunks, swoop-backed and bent over, leaning on one another for support and camaraderie.

Guerrero eats. Not in big gulps like her, but gently, slowly, methodically. A pull from a fritter goes into his mouth, and he chews, stiff-jawed, nodding as he does. "So," he says, finally done and pinch-wiping his fingers on the napkin there. "Why am I here?"

"In your pretty pink shirt?"

"Is there a problem with a man wearing pink?"

She thrusts up a finger. "To the contrary, my good man. A pink shirt is usually a sign of a big—or at least comfortably sized—dick. Not that the size of a dick is particularly significant—I'm no Size Queen—but a lotta guys certainly *think* it matters, and the ones who are self-conscious about their itty-bitty dinkle-doos are *also* the same ones who wouldn't be caught dead wearing a pink shirt because, I dunno, pink is the color of Strawberry Shortcake's vagina or some happy horseshit like that."

"Maybe I have a small penis, but I'm comfortable with it."

She sips on her iced tea, wishing like hell it had whiskey in it, or was just whiskey in its entirety. "Good point. But I'm looking at you—tall, lean, broad shoulders, long chin. I like the cut of your jib (whatever a jib is), and I think, nah. Solid dick. B+ at least."

"Maybe I'm gay."

"See, that's homophobic. Pink is not a gay thing."

"And yet here I am, a gay man wearing pink."

She narrows her eyes. "Huh. Gay. Okay."

"Pink used to be a boy color, anyway. In the 1920s, pink was considered a masculine color, and blue was the color for girls. Pink had connotations of strength, vibrancy, potency."

"Like blood. Watered-down blood, maybe."

"Maybe. Point is, gendered anything is nearly always non-sense. But on to the *real* point and my question once again: why am I here?"

Miriam sits up straight. "I'm ready to cut a deal."

"Cut a deal. You mean, come work for me."

"Come work *with* you. I don't work *for* anyone. Not you, not God, not—" She almost says *the Trespasser*, but she snips that off the end of the sentence with a pair of mental scissors. "Not anybody."

"Okay . . . ," he says, sounding dubious.

"I'm not done. I have conditions."

"And those are?"

"First, I'm pregnant."

"Oh."

"Yeah. Didn't know *that*, did you, Mr. Thinks-He-Knows-Everything. I've got a worm in this apple, so I need healthcare."

His lip curls into a small smile. "Okay. I can make that work."

"For life."

"That I dunno about, but I can offer it for the duration of your employment—"

"Partnership."

"Fine, *partnership*. Plus six months after you're done."

She clucks her tongue, thinking. "Fine. That'll do."

"What else?"

"I get a salary."

"That's already in the pipeline. I don't expect you to do this for free."

"Good. I don't need a lot, so I'm not asking for *beaucoup* bucks. I can do a lot with a little."

He nods. "Is there anything else?"

This one, it sticks in her throat a little. "A funeral."

"A funeral." He repeats the word like he doesn't understand. Because, of course, he doesn't.

"A man named Louis Darling died a handful of weeks ago in Pennsylvania. He died with his fiancée, Samantha. I figure he's been cremated by now. He has no family and I have no idea who will pay for his funeral, so I want the US government to pay for it. A nice funeral. North Carolina somewhere. A small town, a nice town, with a nice cemetery—I don't care if he's buried with her." *Samantha, who ruined everything. Samantha, who one day Louis would kill for reasons unknown*—though it wasn't her fault, was it? Miriam's anger was unfair; yes, Samantha was the other woman, but she was the ventriloquist's dummy to the Trespasser. It had picked her up, filled her spaces, urged her—even controlled her—to come and intersect with Miriam and Louis.

And one day, Louis would've killed her because of it.

But then—

The floor feels like it's dropping out from underneath her. Her head feels light as a balloon

(*a red balloon*)

as the thought hits her.

What if the Trespasser would have one day taken over Louis, too? Would that have been possible? Did Louis have, as the demon put it, *holes in his soul*? No. She refused to believe that. Him killing Samantha would've been because she forced him to. It was all part of a cruel chess game played by the Trespasser— that diabolical entity thinking a hundred moves ahead.

The only way to know will be to ask it. To find the Trespasser and to pin it to the wall and force the fucking monster to talk.

And so arrives her final condition.

She swallows hard, and Guerrero can see that she's visibly shaken. He's about to ask her something, but she cuts him off.

"You said you know others. Like us."

"I have a small team," he says.

"I need . . . help."

"Help?"

"I need someone who can see things. *Talk* to things."

He shifts uncomfortably. "I don't follow."

"Ghosts. Specters. Demons. Invisible fucking entities."

Now Guerrero looks *really* discomfited. He sits up even

straighter and shifts his gaze left and right to see if anyone is listening. Nobody is. It's 3 PM, for one thing, so it's not a heavy crowd. And the ones who sit nearby are paired off or in tables of groups—they're murmuring and chatting and laughing, not paying attention to the nutball bitch yammering on about ghosts and boogeymen. (Either that or they heard and just don't care. The Keys are chockablock with loons and kooks, so it would take some pretty wacky shit to get them to stand up and take notice.)

"I, ahh." He clears his throat. He wipes his mouth with the napkin. "I might know someone. Not on my team, though. But he's not far from where we'll be going. We have a list, and this person, he's on it."

She leans in. "And where will we be going?"

"City of Angels. Los Angeles, California."

"I've never been."

"From what I can tell, you'll either love it or you'll hate it." He shrugs. "Probably both."

PART FOUR

THE STARFUCKED

TWENTY-FOUR

IN THE DARK, ONCE AGAIN

Now.

Miriam awakens, groggy, in the dark. Her head feels like a fishbowl full of wet cement: a sign that after the choke hold, someone drugged her. A sleeper hold like the bartender did on her would've knocked her out for five, maybe ten minutes at most. She feels thick. Her every thought first has to surface through a mire of mud and clay. Whatever drug was in her, she prayed it was not hurting the baby. A distant realization lurks shadow-like in the back of her soggy brain, telling her that something so simple as a bad drug cocktail in her system could be the reason the kid dies on the day of its birth—and if that is so, then her chance to undo that turn of fate is now lost.

She can only hope that this newfound healing ability of hers will help the child as much as it is helping her. If she could mend a knife slash across her bicep after four or five hours of sleep, then maybe her body will metabolize the drug into harmlessness. And maybe, just maybe, the baby had her ability too, for as long as it lurked within her.

All this, though, is a problem for Future Miriam.

Current Miriam is trapped, bound in a cramped space.

Her hands are bound.

Not her feet.

She kicks. The margins of her confinement are close, cramped.

A vibration rides the space beneath her, thrumming up through her in a mechanical hum—uneven, too, a little dip here, a slight judder there.

I'm in a moving vehicle.

Probably in the trunk.

Her hands are bound behind her, so it's hard to maneuver and reach for anything, but one thing she knows from this life of hers that other people might not be so quick to realize:

All trunks in modern cars have an internal release lever or button.

That is literally a thing, she expects, because enough people are taken and locked in trunks that the car manufacturers had to put it into the design of their cars. It's like how if you see a warning on a product, DO NOT EAT THIS DISHWASHER DETERGENT, that's there because someone up and ate the dishwasher detergent. Maybe they were really high. Maybe they were dumb, or suicidal, or a four-year-old entranced by the pretty colors.

Doesn't matter. It happened, and so—*shoop*—on went a warning.

She rolls over, face mushed into the trunk carpet, ass in the air, fingers waggling above her in the dark—they trace the top of the trunk, the cool metal, and she has to shimmy herself around until she feels it with her near-bloodless finger: the latch release.

The baby is pissed now because she's awake and rolling around in positions that don't make any sense. So, the baby is tossing and turning. Which presses on her bladder. Which makes her want to pee.

She's tempted to do it. Just piss all over this trunk, let them deal with it, whoever *they* are. And it must be a *they*. She was expecting the Starfucker, and got . . . a tattooed bartender? It didn't add up. That, plus the spider tattoo, same as she once saw on a playing card in a vision, handed to Ethan Key by a cartel killer? No parts of this are coming together for her, which means there's a lot yet to learn. But she isn't going to learn it from the inside of a trunk, so—

Pop.

She pops the latch.

As she does, wind and daylight rush in to greet her.

Miriam expects to see the bleached, blanched, salt-fucked desert rushing past, but what she gets instead are green, rolling hills. On one side, she sees lines of snarling, tangled vines: grapevines in a vineyard. Old-growth, the vines thick and woody like the roots of an ancient tree.

Where the fuck am I?

How long was I out?

Again, problems that presently need no answer.

The only answer she needs know is how she gets out of here without dying. The easiest way would just be to roll out and hit the ground. Behind her isn't a highway but a long ribbon of back-road asphalt. No single or double lines, just the black-top receding fast. Emphasis on *fast*. The car is moving swiftly: a clumsy calculus says they're up over fifty MPH, easily.

I could just jump out.

That, once upon a time, would have been the end of the discussion. Miriam would have tucked and rolled out, hitting the road at an improper speed, probably cracking her head or fracturing a limb on the way out. It would have been fast and easy, not to mention it would have fulfilled what was for her a once-necessary condition: it brought her pain, maybe even the threat of death. Though she had sworn off actively ending her own life after her first encounter with the dreaded Harriet, nobody said anything about *passively* letting her existence in this world lapse.

Now, though, she's a bit older. A bit wiser.

And she's thinking for two.

She *does* recognize though that she seems to be healing

injuries these days at an improper rate. Harriet was able to mend grievous wounds—rendering her essentially indestructible.

Maybe I should *just jump out* . . .

No.

Because suddenly, she has a better idea.

The hairs on her neck stand up like electrified wires. She can feel it in every skin cell, every nerve, the presence of something above her, out of sight: she can feel the birds.

In this case, somewhere up ahead, she feels them. She closes her eyes for a moment and slips into the flock: speckled birds, gray and black, a hint of green shimmer behind the dull colors. Starlings. Hundreds of them. A murmuration: the swooping, amorphous shape pulsing and throbbing in the sky like a singular creature, a monoculture, a superorganism.

Miriam eases back into the trunk, pressing herself into the back of it—she extends a leg, catching the lip of the trunk with her foot.

With a quick pull of that leg, the trunk closes once more.

Then she closes her eyes and she becomes the birds.

TWENTY-FIVE

SHIMMER AND SHINE

Her mind enters one bird, then two, then four, then a dozen, then a hundred—soon it's in all of them, her consciousness blasted like grenade shrapnel and lodged in the avian minds across an entire murmuration of starlings. These birds are lost to the dance, thrown into a simple program: never be more than a few feet from one of your mates. Always be close. Wing-to-wing. Beak to tail. They each share the same rule, so they move and duck and fly together: no, not perfectly, but rather like a net stretching and warping one way, then another. The murmuration has no leader, no lone consciousness in the liquid swarm that guides and governs them; somewhere, they have been made aware of a predator—a peregrine falcon, Miriam divines—and so they move *en masse*, a perfect defense against a hunter like the peregrine.

There exists, as always, the desire for Miriam to remain here: though it is nowhere as enticing or as thrilling as being in the mind of an owl as it hunts, just the same, there is an elegant simplicity to life in the murmuration. But even now, Miriam's human mind cuts through and reminds her: this dance is not forever. Soon the murmuration will settle in trees and on power lines. They will break apart, some joining other flocks.

It is their way. Nothing is permanent. The dance must end.

And it must end now.

She will feel guilt about this forever, but it will also be quietly thrilling to her—because again, it fulfills a primal life-ending urge, a suicidal proxy that lets her experience the end of life without committing to it.

Miriam turns the murmuration down toward the ground.

Toward the road.

Toward, in fact, a silver Lexus speeding down that road.

They plunge swiftly—she must time it right, and time it right she does, for they dive not *exactly* toward the car but rather toward the space where it will be in three seconds, two seconds, one second—

TWENTY-SIX

BIRD STRIKE

It rocks the car like they're driving top-speed through a hail-storm, except in this case, the *hail* is a flock of soft, feathered, blood-filled things. The starlings pelt the car ten at a time, peppering it with a machine gun spackle. The car shudders and skids left. Miriam hears breaking of glass as she comes back to her own body—*voomp*—and she bears down against the back wall of the trunk, not sure what happens now. She half-expects the car to flip, to roll, but it doesn't—it slows but never stops. And Miriam thinks, *This is it, I can't wait anymore.* So again she puts herself ass up, face down, fingers wiggling—

Scooch, scooch, scooch.

They find the lever—

One—

Quick—

Pull!

The trunk pops, *kathunk*. Miriam maintains her balance as she scoots to the opening—the asphalt still whips out from underneath the car in a fast-moving conveyor belt of road rash, but the speed of the car has been cut in half, if not better. No better time will present itself, she decides.

Miriam rolls out of the car.

Her shoulder cracks hard. Followed by her head. She thinks she's going to be cool about it, doing some *maneuver* to help her land, but the impact coupled with her hands being bound behind her allow her no such athleticism. Instead, her body tumbles and rolls like a soup can that fell out the back of a garbage truck. And then, like that, it's over.

Panting, heart pounding in her chest like the leg of a flea-chewed dog, Miriam gets herself onto her knees once more. Blood drips into her eye. She looks to her shoulder, sees that the shirt has been rendered to threads, exposing the abraded, now-bleeding, stone-peppered flesh. Everything hurts. But the baby still moves inside her, so she says a small Hail Mary as the car speeds away through a cloud of still-falling starlings.

Groaning, Miriam gets one leg underneath her—

Then the other—

Wobbly as a spinning top, she stands.

Then she hears the shrieking of brakes.

The Lexus, now 500 yards off, shows off a set of red brake lights like the eyes of a waking demon as it skids to a complete halt. The road behind sits littered with hundreds of bird carcasses, the wings bent akimbo, beaks shattered amid glittering ice cubes of windshield glass.

The driver-side door pops open.

A man steps out. Broad, sharp shoulders sit tucked in a silver suit jacket. A slim waist circled by a black belt. And a mask he's currently pulling over his head: a black balaclava that suddenly shines in the light of the sun, gleaming in a hundred directions, eerily, freakishly bright. *Sequins*, she thinks. What a fucked-up, absurd thing: the front of the mask is stitched with a carpet of sequins, like a disco ball.

The other thing that shines is the knife in his hand.

The killer begins to stalk through the dead birds toward her.

Miriam looks up and down the road. No cars are coming to save her. The sky is big and blue and empty. No planes. No helicopters. Not even another bird that she can see. She is alone out here.

It's her, the open road, and an encroaching killer.

On one side of her, green hills and fields, on and on, endlessly anon.

On the other, the vineyard, and beyond, a fence row of tall trees.

She makes her choice. Miriam, hands behind her back, her one leg funky from the fall, limps toward the vineyard, toward the maze of vines.

PART FIVE

THE CITY OF LAST ANGELS

TWENTY-SEVEN

The Trash and the Glamour

THEN.

They have a home.

It's a temporary one; Miriam knows that. This apartment is a way station, nothing more. Still, she feels herself again slipping into that comfortable fantasy, the same fantasy she felt with Louis out there in the Pennsylvania woods: their precious little snow globe, settling in together away from the world, against the world, without the world. God, she misses him. She misses him like she misses a front tooth or a thumb. But she has Gabby now. Gabby, who comes up behind her on the balcony of their third-floor joint, overlooking the one palm tree, the pool, the pantsless sleeping guy in a Hawaiian shirt floating *in* the afore-mentioned pool.

She puts her hand on Miriam's back with one hand and with the other presents a steaming mug of the blackest, bleakest coffee. Miriam takes it and bathes in its bitter steam before supping a long, scalding sip.

"God, that's fucking good."

"Morning to you, too," Gabby says to her.

Outside, the orange fireglow of the sunrise is fading, soon extinguished under the blanket of acid-wash denim that will coat the sky.

"I feel like I should be hungover."

"Okay," Gabby says in that way that is both humoring her *and* waiting for the eventual explanation. *Okaaaaaay*.

"This city *feels* like a hangover. Like what happens after a raw bender. Cigarettes and cheap liquor, a long night with no sleep. Got this tawdry, slutty, *needy* vibe I'm totally into. Or I would be, if I had a drink in my hand to fight the hangover, and a cigarette in my mouth to fight the taste of last night's whiskey pukes." She sighs. "Fucking goddamnit, I wish I'd found this town ten years ago. Now I think I missed my opportunity. Can't drink. Can't smoke. Can't really enjoy all the . . ." Her hands gesticulate in the air like spiders swaddling a fly. "You know. The glorious, glamourous dumpster fire."

"I dunno," Gabby says. "I think West Hollywood is pretty quaint. And Beverly Hills and Bel Air were glitzy as shit. It's not Vegas."

"Yeah, but . . . all the quaintness, all the Richie-Richness is just a cover-up. It's plastic surgery on a drunken pig. You know what it is? It's a mask. At its heart, I can feel it—this city is shitty and mean, all its structures and industry built on a septic system overflowing with old, bad blood." She draws a deep breath. "I kinda *love* it."

"You're weird."

"Okay, I submit into evidence *this* guy." Miriam points down at the white dude on the pool raft. He's paunchy, his belly straining against his green Hawaiian shirt as his breath rises and falls. He's got no pants on, but he does have a pair of tighty-whiteys—*too* tighty, those whiteys. His hair is a mussy pompadour, and a thin little mustache decorates his upper lip, so thin it might as well be *gently manscaped calligraphy*. "This guy, he's, what? Is he homeless? Could be. An alcoholic? Why not! Male prostitute? Not impossible. But he could be a director, too. Famous, even. Shit, maybe that's Tom Cruise. Maybe he's *dead*. Maybe down there on that raft is a dead, bloated, homeless Tom Cruise. Do you know? I don't know."

From down below, the man calls out, eyes still closed:

"I am not Tom Cruise." Then, a second later: "Also, not dead."

"Go back to sleep," Miriam shouts back down at him.

He gives her the finger.

She gives it back, even though his eyes are still closed.

"See?" Miriam says. "How great is that?"

Gabby rubs some sleep out of her eye. "Okay, I can see why you like it. This is definitely a Miriam Black kind of town."

"This city doesn't give a shit. At the same time, it gives *all* the shit. It's like, I can't tell if it really cares but doesn't want you to think it cares, or that it doesn't care *at all*, but it's pretending that it does."

"The city is a giant narcissist?"

"There it is. The city is a giant narcissist."

"And you like that?"

Miriam shrugs. "We like what we like, baby. Don't yuck my yum."

"You liked that I yucked your yum last night." Gabby kisses the back of her neck, and Miriam shudders. She's not wrong. Miriam, now that she's on this hormonal roller coaster of pregnancy, runs the gamut of physical sensations. Mornings are normal. Midday, she gets the pukes. Midafternoon, she gets so hungry, she feels like she could *personally* slaughter and eat a herd of bison. And come evening, she's so fucking turned on, she's like the current running through an electric chair, all buzzy and voltaic, her every nerve ending crackling like lightning. She despises the word *horny*; it's like a fourteen-year-old's clumsy idea of what sex is like. And that one word is not enough, anyway. She doesn't get horny: she gets greedy and desirous, ecstatic and consumptive, feral and fuck-hungry. Especially these days.

Especially right now.

It's not evening, so she's off her usual schedule, but so what? She leans back and meets Gabby's mouth with her own. "I could yuck your yum for a little while. Go back in there on the futon and fuck like it's the end of the world . . ."

"You have work."

Miriam winces. "I have what?"

"Work. The job. Guerrero."

"Ugh. That's today. God. Fuck."

The job. She has a job to go to. That has traditionally never gone well, and she's entirely certain it won't go well today.

"It's your first day," Gabby says, with singsongy, overly saccharine sweetness.

"What if I don't go?"

"If you don't go, then Agent Guerrero will come and find you. And then he'll probably fire you. And if he fires you, we lose this apartment, which the FBI is paying for, and you probably get brought up on charges, and you will have that baby in jail. Worse, you won't find somebody to help you confront the Trespasser, and your pursuant demon spirit will probably end up possessing me, and I'll kill that doctor in Florida before swallowing a bottle of pills and killing myself."

"So, what you're saying is, I should go."

Gabby gives her a venomous little smile. "You should go."

"Fine. *Mom.*"

She heads inside, gulping down another mouthful of coffee. The inside of the apartment is boxy and spare, all white drywall and Pergo flooring. The furniture is all from a local West Hollywood antique joint, every piece mismatched in style, era, and color. She plonks herself down on their flumpy microfiber couch and hikes on a pair of jeans and a white T-shirt. Then, in the bathroom, she shakes a little mousse into her hair. It looks wild, unkempt, the hair of Frankenstein's Bride after a long night of ecstasy and fight-clubbing. Maybe, Miriam thinks, that's what she should do next for her coloring: right now, the hair is the blackest black, but a silver streak shot through it would be slick as fuck.

"Very professional," Gabby says, dryly.

"I am one professional motherfucker."

"Have a good day at school, dear."

"Uh-huh. What are you going to do today?"

"I think I'm going to try to get a job."

Miriam makes a face like she has an itchy butthole. "Why on this horrible planet we call Earth would you go and do something like that?"

"I like feeling needed."

"I need you."

Gabby shrugs. "Not while you're off playing federal agent."

"I'm not a federal agent; I'm just a *freelance psychic-for-hire*."

"You should put that on a business card."

"Seriously, don't get a job. Just be my concubine. Stay here at home, drinking mimosas and eating fondue chocolate, and then I'll come home and we can go eat Korean food and then we can make out like middle-schoolers until we fall asleep to the sound of sirens and helicopters."

"How positively domestic of you, but yeah, *no*, sorry, Miriam. I want to get a job. I want to contribute. I'm not just yours. I'm me. I'm mine. I gotta go be a part of the world too."

"Sounds gross, but you do you, lady."

"Go to work. You're going to be late."

"How do I get there?"

"What do you mean, how do you get there?" Gabby laughs. "You get in a car and go."

"We don't have a car."

"I told you last night, if you were listening: I put both Uber and Lyft on your phone."

Miriam frowns. "I don't know what either of those things are. Can't I just walk?"

"It's like seven miles down Wilshire. You cannot walk that. Besides, people don't walk in this city. People get in their cars to drive across the street to their neighbors' houses. The only people who walk are the homeless and serial killers."

"The FBI once had me classified as a serial killer."

"C'mon," Gabby says, holding her hand. "Let's go outside, and I will teach you *again* how to call a Lyft."

TWENTY-EIGHT

DRIVE

They stand out in front of their little condo complex, and Gabby holds out Miriam's phone and shows her the app. On it, a little Pac-Man screen of Los Angeles streets manifests, with a bunch of little cars swarming around like they're running from ghosts and gobbling dots. They pick a nearby car with a driver named "Steve," and then Gabby kisses Miriam on the cheek and heads back upstairs. Miriam calls after: "Fuck do I do now?" But Gabby is gone, and no answer is forthcoming.

She stands there. The car she has chosen, a four-door Kia sedan, does not seem to be moving. It sits nearby, apparently stalled.

Miriam shakes the phone.

It does not dislodge the car.

Technology is bullshit.

Behind her, she hears the security grate leading into the complex squeak and creak open. Someone pads out in flip-flops.

It is Tighty-Whitey Man, aka Probably-Not-Tom-Cruise.

"Hello, Tighty-Whitey Man," Miriam says, the way one might greet a regal bearer of kingly news.

Pool water puddles around his legs and flip-flops. He pulls a pair of sunglasses that are tucked around the side of his white underwear—because he still isn't wearing pants—and pops them on over his head.

"You call a car?" he asks. His voice is a little squeaky, like he's got a frog in his throat. A frog who drank a lot the night prior.

"Did you just pull sunglasses out of your underpants?"

"I'll be right back," he says with a sigh.

He pads around the corner, the flip-flops going *fwap fwap fwap*, once again leaving her alone. She looks at the phone, squinting at it.

Eventually, the car moves.

And when it moves on the screen, she sees it rounding the corner near her—and sure enough, here it comes in *real life*, too. Which isn't magic, she knows, but it damn sure *feels* like some kind of magic. Probably forbidden magic, too. Grim sorcery, enchanted fuckery. Technology is amazing and, she suddenly decides, will eventually ruin the world.

Tighty-Whitey Man rolls down the window. "Going down Wilshire?"

Miriam scowls.

"Who told you that?"

"You did."

"I fucking did not."

He rolls his eyes. "The phone, you put the address into the phone."

"I didn't do that." Gabby must've, though. "Okay, fine."

She gets in the car. The car is nice. Clean. In the back is a water bottle and a packet of gum. He pulls away before she's even got her seatbelt on.

"You keep your sunglasses in your underwear," she says. "Keys, too, I'm guessing? Were they up your ass?"

"No," he says, patting a chest pocket. "Here."

"Hm," she grunts.

The car drives. It winds its way through the sights of Los Angeles: palm trees, tourists, blowing trash, the tattoo parlors, the movie billboards. They round a corner and she sees a homeless guy fighting Captain America with a broken umbrella while Darth Vader and Elmo stand nearby, watching. She's sure there's a metaphor there but she can't quite peg it.

"So," she says, clearing her throat. "Do you normally just wait around in swimming pools till someone needs a ride?"

"I was on shift, and the phone told me I had a rider."

"Do you do everything your phone tells you?"

"When it makes me money."

"Where'd you get the car?"

"It's my car. I had it parked in the lot across from the complex."

"It's your car?"

He nods. "My car."

"This is fucking bizarre; so, this isn't a taxi?"

"No, it's my car, it's a Lyft."

"I'm sitting in the backseat of *your* car." A statement, not a question.

"Correct."

"Fuck that," she says, unbuckling her belt and spelunking across the middle valley between the seats. She crawls up over the center console, nearly kneeing Tighty-Whitey Man in the shoulder. He protests—"Hey!"—as she settles into the passenger seat, drawing the belt across her.

"What the hell are you doing?" he asks, his dry, droll tone stabbed by a spike of irritation.

"I'm not sitting back there. This isn't a taxi. It's not a limo. At this point you're just some dude giving me a ride; you're not my chauffeur."

"I'm not just some dude. You're *paying* me."

She frowns. "Gonna be honest: not sure I have any cash on me." She would feel bad about this, but somehow, she doesn't?

"You're not paying me cash; you're paying me with a credit card."

"Oh, I definitely don't have one of those." She laughs. "Yeah, I think the bank would probably give a credit card to a raccoon before they give one to me; sorry, Tighty-Whitey Man."

"My name is Steve."

"Agree to disagree."

He makes a frustrated sound, which is familiar to her—many people make it when she speaks to them. It's a primal exhortation of restrained disgust. Miriam has come to cherish the sound as a signal she's being true to herself and not changing who she is to suit someone's idea of pleasant interaction, because seriously, fuck all that right in the no-no hole.

"How do you not have a credit card?" he asks. "Is this a Bitcoin thing? We take Bitcoin. And Litecoin."

"What the fuck is a Bitcoin? Is that . . . chocolate money?"

"What? No. It's cryptocurrency!" He sighs. "So . . . *who* is paying for this ride, exactly?"

She shrugs. "Guessing Gabby, though really, it's the FBI."

"The FBI."

"Mm-hmm."

"Are you in witness protection?"

"No."

He seems really rattled now. His too-cool-for-school, hanging-out-in-my-underwear-so-what vibe is falling under the panic of being in her general presence. Good. Fuck him. "Are you some kind of extraterrestrial? Or an android? Who are you? How do you not have a credit card and not know what Lyft or Uber are, and—seriously, who are you and where did you come from?"

"Name's Miriam Black. Got a demon in my head who's trying to kill me and my baby. I'm also psychic and I can see how people are going to die. I control birds and I *might* be invulnerable to harm."

He stares at her.

But a strange thing happens. He's no longer rattled. It's almost like he's *relieved*. "See, there you go. Now I know who you are."

"You do?" she asks.

"Yep. You're LA."

"What's that supposed to mean?"

"I mean, that gonzo bullshit that just came out of your mouth is typical Los Angeles. I drive all kinds of people around this town, and half of them are either out of their gourd or pretending to be. It's the sun, the wildfire smoke, the pharmaceuticals in the water supply, maybe. Live here long enough and it starts to rot your pumpkin."

"Look at you, you're not even wearing pants."

"Exactly," he says. "Couple days ago, I drove around a guy who swore to high heaven that he was the reincarnation of Ringo Starr. I tried to explain to him that Ringo Starr is neither dead nor somebody particularly worthy of reincarnation, but he wouldn't hear it. He didn't have an accent. He didn't look like Ringo Starr. Didn't appear to have a musical bone in his body—though, ha ha, neither did Ringo, *zing*—but it was all he talked about. That and his cats. Seven cats. All named Micky Dolenz."

She stares at him.

"Drummer for the Monkees," he explains.

"I don't care. I'm still trying to figure out if the shit you said about me is a compliment or what."

"Not a compliment, not an insult. It's just a thing."

"Just a thing."

"Uh-huh. LA is a thing, and it gets in people. It's in you."

"I haven't even been here a week."

He dips his sunglasses and stares at her over their margins. "Then honey, Los Angeles has been inside you a lot longer than that."

TWENTY-NINE
DESTINATION

The drive down LA roads bears the sense of endless reiteration. It's like being on a loop in a movie set, like the city doesn't have enough money or land to deliver new sites, so it keeps parading the same stuff past in the hopes you don't notice. Every corner is a little strip mall, and in each is a similar set of locations: a nail place, a sushi joint, a taco place, a massage parlor, a tattoo parlor. Korean food, Thai food, check cashing, hipster donut place, emergency clinic, and then shake the dice cup and roll them out for a remix of the same, again and again, on and on. On Wilshire, the scenario changes a little: bigger buildings, hotels, a golf course, and eventually, the Federal Bureau of Investigation building: a tall, austere brick that has all the personality of a roll of paper towels.

"You weren't kidding," Tighty-Whitey Steve says. "This is really the FBI building." He eases the car into the lot, at the drop-off point before the guard gate. "You don't look like FBI. So, what's your deal?"

"Friends in strange places," she says.

"You're really not from LA, either?"

"Nope. Pennsylvania originally, though been all around. Never here."

"Well," he says, pulling out a business card. He flips his sunglasses up over his broad forehead and looks upon her with

132

tiny, bloodshot eyes. "Listen, there's no way with the car app to request a specific driver, but this is my card. You ever need a ride, call me. I'll show up. We'll work something out. Cool?"

"And you'd offer this why? I told you I have no money and you called me an extraterrestrial."

"I like extraterrestrials. I feel like an alien myself sometimes."

"Good sales pitch." She takes the card. On it, his full name. "Thanks, Steve Wiebe. Maybe I'll talk to you again."

"Have fun with the FBI."

"Job's a job," she says, even though that's totally not true. This is about the furthest thing from a real job that you can get, she wagers. *What do you do for a living? Oh, you know, I'm an FBI psychic. You?*

She watches the Kia sedan pull away, its pantsless driver with one oddly pale arm out the window. There comes a moment when she thinks, maybe she doesn't have to do this. She could just fuck off. Go find one of those Thai joints, drink a Thai iced tea, and never actually go to work, but again Gabby's reminder slithers into her ear like a nibbling brain-worm: there's a lot riding on this gig. Not least of all, she needs Guerrero to identify for her a fellow psychic who can help her identify the Trespasser. That, in order for her to *kill* the Trespasser. To slay her demon, to save Gabby, she's gotta play ball. And then maybe she can save this baby, too.

The pressure builds so fast and so furious, it's like her breastbone is suddenly being stepped on by a brontosaurus. The anxiety of it feels like the air is being crushed out of her, like her heart will soon be pulped like a tomato. Vertigo makes her head spin even though she's standing still.

Get it together, Miriam.

You have work to do.

Internally, she summons strength and gathers to her all the broken parts of her mind the way one might collect a pack of biting rats in a bucket. It works. She can breathe again. She can stand again.

She walks forward to the guard booth.

"Hi," she says to the bald man with neck fat behind the gate. "My name is Miriam Black, I'm here to see superstar FBI Agent David Guerrero. I'm here to—" *Say the word, say the word, no matter how horrible it sounds, say the goddamn word.* "Work."

The guard mumbles and flips through a list on a clipboard.

"I'm not seeing you here."

"And yet here I am."

"Hold on."

He grabs another clipboard.

"Right," he says finally. "You're not in this building."

"I was directed to this address, dude."

"You're across the street." With a hot-dog finger he flags her past this building. "Go that way. Cross Veteran Ave. You'll see a little trailer in the lot under the 405 overpass. That's where you go."

"A trailer. In a parking lot. Under an underpass."

"You got it."

"Really rolling out the red carpet for me."

He stares at her, saying nothing.

"Okay," she says. "Good talk."

Then she proceeds to do as commanded: she heads down the sidewalk before crossing the busy Veteran Avenue and stepping into the cracked, fractured lot. The shadow of the highway above darkens the ground ahead of her, blotting out the sun. A hundred feet away, a portable work trailer sits, gray as a winter day, nestled amongst the cracked and fractured lot.

Miriam steps to the door, gives it a *shave-and-a-haircut* knock.

A tall woman in a gray suit answers. She looks past a set of rich, dark curls, down a hawk's-beak nose. "Miriam?" she asks, businesslike.

"The one and only."

"Come on in. David's inside." She steps out of the way, and as Miriam sidles past, the woman says, "I'm Julie Anaya."

"Nice to meet you, I guess," Miriam says, feeling suddenly awkward, like she's the New Kid in Class who has to walk to a far desk across the room as all eyes stare at her. That, even though the trailer is only home to three people, including herself. But the feeling of being an impostor, of starting a new job and not knowing anything about anything, rings clear in her head like a broken bell. *Clonnnng.* Inside, David Guerrero stands over a folding table, papers spread out before him.

"Miriam," he says. "Glad you could make it."

"Kinda have no choice."

"You always have a choice. This isn't prison."

"But prison is prison, and this gets me out of that."

He shrugs. "Fair point. Like our office?"

She takes it in. All 300 square feet of it. The three desks, the file cabinets, the little air conditioner in the window, chugging away. "It's about as inspiring as a telemarketer's cubicle."

"It's not flashy," Julie says. "But it's the job."

Miriam eyes her up. "Are you . . . " To David she reiterates the question. "Is she . . ."

"A psychic?" he asks.

"No," Julie answers.

"Are you a believer in all this psychic stuff?" Miriam asks.

"I am a believer in results."

"You want coffee?" David asks, pointing to a glass carafe next to a little swan-neck water kettle. A kettle that appears to be electric, since it's plugged into the wall. "It's pour-over."

"I don't know what that means, but sure, long as it's black as the Devil's asshole." At that, neither startle, nor do they give her alarmed looks, so she either figures she's dealing with a couple A-grade professionals *or* the two of them have gone suddenly deaf. Usually, shocking people is easy—you curse a little, start talking about sex and death and buttholes, everybody gets their tender nipples in a quick pinch. But these two are un-flummoxed.

David then performs what could only be described as a meditative act. Hand-grinding beans. Pouring those ground beans into a metal filter. Boiling water and then gently pouring the water atop the grounds in an easy, languid spiral. Steam rises like a couple of coffee phantoms, and with them come a coffee smell like Miriam has never before taken in. She nearly passes out.

He hands her the cup.

She takes a taste.

"It tastes like coffee smells," she says.

"I make a good cup," Guerrero says.

"I want to fuck this coffee."

"You should probably let it cool down first."

"Fair point."

"Shall we get to work?"

Miriam takes another long, noisy sip of the black brew, savoring it with her eyes closed. When she opens them again, she asks:

"Where do we begin?"

THIRTY

WE BEGIN WITH THE STARFUCKER

They sit around the small folding table, and Guerrero shuffles the papers present into a neat pile in front of him.

Julie hands him a folder.

From it he pulls three crime scene photos, and slides them across the table toward Miriam.

Were she a different person, these photos might make her blanch. Upon seeing them, she would tremble and clench up to stem the tide of nausea; worse, she would likely fail at that, and thus, she'd probably puke like a sorority girl after too much jungle juice or hunch punch.

But she is Miriam Black. She's seen a thing or two. She has the emotional constitution and the iron stomach of an autopsy-room technician. The kind who can eat a sandwich over a corpse's open chest cavity. The kind who might say, *Sorry, I dropped a little mayo inside the rib cage, hold on, let me get that*, before dipping a gloved finger into the mayo-plop and then popping it back into her mouth.

Miriam Black has seen a knife through an eye, a face cross-stitched with scars, a man lose his foot to a hacksaw in the back of an SUV.

She has herself eaten a fresh human heart.

Even still, these photos are something to see.

In each, a dead body. A dude. Young, but not a kid—mid-twenties, early thirties. Two white guys, one black guy, all of them on a floor, a white sheet covering all but their faces. Or, rather, their total lack of faces.

Someone has taken their faces.

Their skulls have been skinned. The muscles gleam, wet and red. Teeth are exposed like polished marble fixtures. The contours of the skull are there, present without the covering of the face to remind everyone that humans are, in fact, just skeletons lined with layers of meat and leather. The eyeballs of the victims stare up in dead panic, as if witnessing the most horrific thing they can possibly imagine—that, of course, because the face has no skin and the eyes have no lids, and so those big bold peepers cannot be given any mood *other* than pants-shitting fear. Still, they probably did witness something pretty terrible, which is to say, someone cutting off their faces. And with that thought, Guerrero slides across three more pictures.

Their missing faces have been found.

"The faces were next to the bodies," Guerrero says, "displayed there, pinned carefully to the wall or near them. As if to make them see."

In the photos, the faces are less faces and more masks, appearing so precisely because they are eyeless. *Eyes*, she thinks, *really are the windows of the soul*. The spark of life lurks there, and without it, the skinned faces look more like gory props than anything else. Their margins sit crusted with the puckered ridgeline of black scab. But the removal of the faces, while crude and hardly surgical, was still performed with a steady hand. The edges aren't jagged. The cuts are clean enough. There aren't many mistakes.

"This isn't what killed them," Miriam says, sipping coffee.

Guerrero nods. *Another* three photos.

In these, the plastic sheets have been peeled back to show that they have been unzipped like a backpack, their guts bulging and spilling out.

"He guts them after," Guerrero says. "Though that may not be what kills them either. We found in their bloodstream the presence of a drug: succinylcholine chloride, brand name, Anectine. A paralytic—neuromuscular inhibitor. The injection site is in the side of the neck. We aren't yet clear if the drug is meant to paralyze them so that the Starfucker can do his work without much interruption, or if it is the thing that ultimately kills them—"

"Or both," Julie says, chiming in.

"I'm sorry, did you say *Starfucker*?"

Guerrero nods. "The serial killer has been given that nickname."

"He gave it to himself?"

"Why do you assume it's a man?" Julie asks.

"Aren't most serial killers men? White dudes, actually?"

Julie stiffens. "Not necessarily. Women commit ten percent of all homicides, but 17 percent of all *serial* murders. Which means they're likelier to be serial killers than killers of opportunity or passion." The way she's looking at Miriam, suddenly Miriam gets the sense there's some other nasty business going on here: Julie, who seemed cold and businesslike at the outset, has the vicious stare of a praying mantis, and she's pointed that predatory gaze right at Miriam. The gaze of a hunter fixing intent upon its prey.

"You're accusing me of being a serial killer," Miriam says.

"Not accusing. But I am suggesting you might be deflecting. Or projecting. Perhaps women are more often serial killers— they're just too smart, too capable, to get caught."

"Or *maybe*," Miriam seethes, "men swim in a septic pool of bad ideas about tough guys and big dicks, and they float there, soaking in it, gulping down *mouthfuls* of that shit, and it gets inside them, *infects* them, makes their blood go black and sour. Fathers take their sons and shove their heads down under the water, too, just to make sure they all get a taste. Maybe men are fucking broken. You ever think that?"

"You say fathers but classically, it's *not* their fathers, is it? It's their mothers. Missing fathers and bad mothers." Julie's gaze narrows down to a laser focus: eyes like a pair of nail guns trying to stick Miriam to the wall. "Know anybody who fits that description? A bad mother? A missing father?"

"I don't like where this is going. And you're a sexist twat."

Wham.

Guerrero slams the flat of his hand down upon the table.

"We are not here to discuss toxic masculinity, nor are we discussing whether or not Miriam Black is a serial killer. That is not our purview today. Our purview is catching a real serial killer who, yes, has been called the Starfucker, and he has been called such because he preys upon young up-and-coming actors in Hollywood. We did not give him this nickname, but rather, a producer did: Jack Ellison. He said, and I quote, *Probably some aggrieved starfucker did this; Hollywood's thick with failed actors and spurned fans.*" Guerrero reads from a page in front of him when he says that quote. "Around the Bureau, the name stuck. I wish it hadn't, but every serial killer is in want of a catchy name, so here we are."

Miriam keeps her stink-eye pointed right toward Julie even as she responds to Guerrero: "Is the news having a field day over this?"

"So far, the news hasn't found out. But they will. They always do."

"How long has this been going on?"

"Three months. One victim per month. Always on the same day: the eleventh. And January eleventh is in three days."

"So, we've got three days to catch the Starfucker."

He nods. "Or he kills again. Potentially."

"That certainly sounds like a Miriam Black situation," she says.

"Yes, which means we need to get to work."

She holds up a finger. "Before we do, I want to know some things."

Julie crosses her arms in defiance, but Guerrero shrugs. "Go ahead."

"Three things, actually." With each item, she holds up a finger, one two three. "First, I want the name of the psychic who you said could help me. Someone who can help me contact a . . . spirit. You said you knew someone, a medium; I want to know who that is and how I contact them. Second, I want to know who you are. You, David Guerrero, have a psychic power too, and I want to know what it is. Third and final? I want to shake *her* hand." Miriam points all three fingers at Julie. "I want to see how you die, Agent Julie."

Guerrero leans across the table.

In a quiet voice, he says, "No, no, and no."

Miriam laughs.

"You're fucking with me."

"I am not fucking with you, Miriam."

"You need me. I want these things."

"You've made your demands, and we've given them. Money, healthcare, an apartment. You'll also be free from any charges related to the many deaths that have been left in your wake, including a one-time FBI agent, not to mention your ex-lover and his fiancée."

She snarls, "Then I walk."

"So walk. Your apartment is paid up till the end of the month, though it won't matter. We'll have you and your girlfriend in custody by nightfall."

"Fuck you."

"Think carefully, Miriam."

"Eat shit carefully, Guerrero." She stands up, knocking her knee in the table on purpose—it rattles and lifts, sending papers sliding to the floor. As Julie struggles to catch them and pick them up, Miriam heads for the door, kicks it open, and escapes this shitty job.

THIRTY-ONE

THE GREAT EGRESS

Outside, though she stands in shadow, the sun in the distance thumbs her square in the eye, and she winces against its hot, spearing light. She wishes she had a pair of sunglasses in her panties the way Tighty-Whitey Steve did. But she doesn't, and so she steps down from the FBI trailer with her arm up over her eyes to shield them.

Shortest time on a job ever, she thinks with pride so smug, it might as well be vegan.

A sense of freedom blooms inside her. It's like watching a rocket go up, up, up, punching through a layer of clouds toward the blissful void of space beyond, a glittering eternity of stars:

I can go anywhere.

I can do anything.

I am not bound by—

And the rocket sputters. It tilts and spirals. It drops back down through the cloud layer like a brick. Because the reality again hits her that she has to be responsible. She's routinely run reckless and roughshod through everyone else's existence, doing whatever feels best and most fuck-you-ish at that particular moment in time. Now, though, Gabby's life is once again in her hands. The *baby's* life is in her hands. Louis's legacy is with her, too. And, selfishly, so too is her ability to escape this curse and to maybe, *just maybe*, be a better person. A different person.

But she only gets that if she plays ball.

And what if *this* is what the Trespasser wants? Her working with Guerrero and the FBI? Is she doing the demon's bidding even now?

"Fuck!" she yells out loud.

It startles a crow, who had been poking at a Carl's, Jr. fast food bag. The bird takes flight, squawking angrily. Miriam can feel, for a moment, its irritation at her. Crows, she knows, are smarter than people think. They can remember things about you. They can remember your face. That crow will remember her face as the shitty bitch who startled it.

Behind her, the door to the office opens.

Julie Anaya steps out.

"We will concede on one of your points."

Miriam gives her a look.

"You can see how I die," Julie says.

"Really?"

"Really."

"That's something, at least."

"Will you come back inside?"

"I want to do it now. You. Your death."

Julie pauses. "How does it work again?"

"You know."

And she does know. Because Julie puts out her hand.

And Miriam takes it.

HOW JULIE DIES

Julie Anaya looks upon herself in the mirror of the makeup table at which she currently sits. She marvels darkly at how she looks: whittled-down, carved away. It's not her age: at sixty, time has taken its expected toll, leaving behind the furrows and divots, the dings and dents, the liver spots and the amplified imperfections. It's the cancer. Breast cancer has taken parts of her away, piece by piece. One breast, then the other. Then her hair, twice—this time, it's started to grow back again, her scalp a peak of salt-and-pepper stubble. The radiation stent in her too has left its mark. And the cancer has done its deeper work, too: her bones ache, she can't sleep well, she feels tired all the time. This has been a ten-year journey for her.

And it ends here today.

On the makeup table sits a gun.

She just received a call an hour before where Dr. Tranh told her that the cancer was not only back, but it had metastasized. It was all throughout her now, insidious, like the roots of an invasive weed. He said they would need to operate on her abdomen, because she had a tumor in her pelvis, and also they'd need to do the standard run of chemo and radiation and—

And it was too much. She didn't tell Tranh that. She made the proper mouth noises, mm-hmm, yes, yes, we can fight this, mm-hmm.

But she didn't mean them.

She can't fight it.

They often say that cancer is a battle, and that is true, she supposes: though the truth of it is more complicated than she understood at first. Once, she believed in that battle she was one of the fighters: as if she and cancer were neatly matched up in gladiatorial combat, and whoever had the most diligence and vigor would win. She merely had to outlast the disease.

But that's not the truth.

The truth wasn't that she was a fighter, but rather that she was the battlefield. She was the town that would endure bombing. She was the field whose trenches would be run through with craters and corpses. Her body and her mind would be the poisoned sand, the shelled earth, the houses burned out through endless sweeping fires.

And she just can't do it anymore.

Her fields are fallow. Nothing more will grow here. There have been greater, deeper costs, too. Her husband left her, because of course he did. She can't do her job anymore. She had to move out of California because the smoke from the never-ending forest fires makes it hard to breathe.

She takes the gun, an old Glock she'd been keeping in the closet. Julie checks it. Makes sure that it's loaded. Then she thumbs the safety off, puts it under her chin, and

THIRTY-TWO

THE OTHER GREAT EGRESS

Julie pulls her hand away, and Miriam feels her piercing stare. The sound of the gun going off still echoes in Miriam's ear, even though it didn't happen—not yet, anyway.

Miriam, for her part, simply breathes. In, out. In, out. The echo of the future gunshot fades, replaced by the sound of traffic all around her: the roar of the highway above, of the boulevard just beyond, of all the city's endless automation. Somewhere, the crow squawks again: an unfriendly dismissal.

"Well?" Julie asks.

"Do you want to know? How it happens? When?"

Julie doesn't stop to think about it. "No."

"Okay. Cool."

"Did you get what you wanted from it?"

"I don't think so."

"Why did you want to see how I'd die, then?"

"I sometimes get an illicit thrill out of it. Sometimes, it tells me a thing about a person. Sometimes, it gives me a secret. Other times, it connects. It connects to a killer, or some plot, some vicious thread. But mostly, I decided I didn't like you and I wanted to see how you bit it. I wanted *satisfaction*."

Julie nods, like this is fine. "And did you get it? Satisfaction, I mean."

"No."

"I'm sorry."

"I am too."

And with that, they get to work.

THIRTY-THREE

PRESSING FLESH

Three hours later, she's on a backlot film-set in Culver City, which she's told is its own city inside Los Angeles, as if that makes any sense. But she goes with it because far as she can tell, nothing really makes sense out here on the Left Coast, and maybe she likes it that way.

Presently, she has been left alone with the industry at work. She has no idea what's happening, though it's becoming increasingly clear that making movies is one of the grandest illusions mankind has ever conjured. Miriam knows that what will end up on a screen is there, in that little box made to look like the front stoop of a Brooklyn apartment: it's like an unframed, unbordered square of illusion, and that small slice of cinema is supported by infinite infrastructure. Big camera rigs, tracks on the ground, microphones hanging everywhere, monitors here, monitors there, people in headphones monitoring the monitors, star trailers, green screens, craft services tables, cables, wires, boom stands, and who knows what else she isn't seeing? Somewhere nearby there's probably an antechamber full of emotional therapy dogs, bags of fancy cocaine, and a cabal of cock fluffers.

All *this* to create two minutes of *that*.

(*That* being a trio of millennial actors made to look like they're having some melodramatic argument on the steps of their apartment building.)

So much effort to craft a glitzy lie.

Though, she thinks, that's the thing about lies, isn't it? The truth requires only itself, but a lie always needs infrastructure. It needs support. It needs other lies to hold it up, a realm of artifice to keep it running. It's why lying is so much goddamn work: you often have to craft an entire fantasy realm just to convince somebody of a single untrue thing.

Truth can be truth alone. But a lie always needs architecture.

Eventually, they break from filming, and Guerrero wanders over with another man who he introduces as Jack Ellison.

Ellison looks unlike what she expected—Miriam's opinion of Hollywood is that it contains an endless stable of upgraded car-salesman types, all schmaltzy and schmoozy, all boozy and blustery, each greasier than a glazed donut, calling everyone *babe* and *chief* and other nonsense bro-type nicknames. Ellison, though, has a small sweater vest on, and big clear-frame eyeglasses above an arrowhead nose and pinched, pursed lips.

"Miss Black," he says, his voice not so much nasal but rather living somewhere in the back of his throat—not in a dorky way, but in a dismissive, overly aloof manner. He enunciates everything, too: putting a fine point on every syllable. "Jack Ellison. Producer here at Pyroclasm Pictures."

He doesn't offer to shake her hand, but boy, she wants to see how this guy dies. How does a Hollywood producer bite it? *God*, she wants it to be exciting—gored by a supermodel dressed up as a rubber-clad bull, replete with platinum horns! overdose on a fancy new smart drug with a weird name like *Robot* or *Permanent Marker* or *Dave*! trampled to death in a Santa Monica orgy dungeon!—but she's also afraid that he dies like everyone else. Heart disease, butt cancer, car crash on the 405, blah blah blah.

Nothing is so disappointing as a mundane death, Miriam decides.

"Hi," she says. "I'm Miriam."

"David here says you know how people die."

"I do."

"You know how I die?"

"Not yet. Rule is, I need skin-on-skin contact. A handshake. A kiss. A straight punch to the mouth."

Ellison shrugs. "Sounds like my last marriage. Shall we get down to business?"

Miriam notes: *He didn't want me to see how he dies, then.* Interesting.

Guerrero explains how this is going to work: "Miriam, we have a number of actors here on set or on adjacent sets. Their agents or managers are going to bring them by, and you're going to shake their hands. One by one. You'll see what you can see. Maybe we'll get a vision that will lead us to the killer. Maybe not."

"And what do these people think they're doing, just lining up like that? I'm not handing out new iPhones. Not to be too on-the-nose with this shit, but what exactly is their motivation?"

Ellison does this thing where he sticks out his lower lip—it's almost a pout, but she realizes it's him doing a kind of condescending *let-me-explain-the-world-to-you* thing. "Miss Black, actors are basically cats. And before you try to tell me that you can't herd cats, let me tell you that all it takes is a can of open tuna. You wave it around and they come this way and that, like you're Moses and they're the tides of the Red Sea. The actors think you're Somebody, which is better than Nobody, and it means that one day, you might be able to give them a job. They don't know what Somebody you are; we're keeping that story mysterious, because mystery breeds interest, and Hollywood breeds desperation, and desperate interest is an added value here. They will question who you are and what you can do for them, and a question mark is shaped like a hook for a reason. With it, you'll snag them, reel them in, see how they meet the Grim Reaper."

He looks her up and down, narrowing his gaze. The scrutiny has with it the feel of scissors snipping her to pieces.

"What is it?" she asks. "Coffee stain?"

"Your outfit. It's sloppy."

"Fuck you," she says.

"No, that's good. We can't sell you as a producer or an agent—we dress well. But you can be a creative."

"A what?"

"A director. Or a writer. Creatives dress like . . ." He gestures toward her with splayed-out fingers. "You."

"I feel judged."

"Welcome to Los Angeles. Here, come on."

He walks off. She gives Guerrero a *what the fuck is this shit* look, and he returns it with a faint smirk and a shrug. Ellison heads over to craft services and waves his hands toward it like he's a wizard casting a spell. "You need something to eat? Now's the time. We've got vegan treats, gluten-free pasta, seaweed salad, *poke* bowls, and next table down we've got Armanda Glix, a smoothie chef from Vancouver—I recommend mangosteen, maca powder, chlorella, spirulina, and cordyceps. Plus, zhe can make it all black with activated charcoal, so that's something."

"Yeah, I'm fine," Miriam says. Her stomach roils at the thought. Her stomach *also* roils at the just-on-time midday morning sickness. Sudden nausea sits in her stomach like a sponge soaking up a septic spill.

Still, she follows after.

Ellison steps into a small trailer, one that's decorated sparsely—it has a little kitchenette with an espresso machine, and a few pieces of furniture that look like they belong in the tiny apartment of an Icelandic architect: the chairs alone possess a Scandinavian severity, brushed aluminum and pale wood. Ellison gives her one such chair, and it is about as comfortable as sitting on a stump in the woods. "Sit here. I'll wave the tuna.

That'll bring the cats. One by one, shake their hands; we'll see what we can see."

"Great," she says. Queasiness makes every molecule in her body feel like it's on a different boat, rocking this way and that on the unsteady waves of this pregnancy she's enduring. "Yay. Woo. Let's do it."

The parade of death begins.

THIRTY-FOUR

AUDITION

First up, a doe-eyed stud who introduces himself as Caleb van der Wald. He's blonde, with a purposefully messy mop-top of blond hair casting its shadow on his otherwise cherubic baby-face. He launches right into his pitch, "I'm playing Hank Spears next season on the CW's adaptation of the young adult novel, *The Brickhouse Boys*, but I'm *mos def* looking for the next big thing, you know?" His California accent runs rampant through his every word, and though he never says the word *brah*, Miriam feels that it's pretty much implicit every time he takes a breath. "Like, I don't want to be typecast or *fenced in,* if you know what I mean, and I can play the good boys, right, but I can *also* totally play the *bad* boys, and—"

"Uh-huh," she says, her guts churning. She *urps* into her hand and then, as if passing the tiny belch onward, uses that hand to grab his and—

It's 10:30 AM on a Tuesday and Caleb is on a snowy hill, talking to a young boy with a mop of blond hair and a set of ice-blue eyes, and Caleb says to this boy—who is his son—"You wanna see how Daddy kicks it on a sled, check this out, little dude," and then he gets on the wooden sled, lowers his sunglasses, and rockets down the slope, hooting and wooing and laughing, but then the sled lifts up and he veers a little left, then farther, then farther still, until he's no longer heading down the clear path but rather toward a set of evergreens and he's still laughing thinking, Oh shit, I'm gonna crash, *and then that thought is gone from his head as he smacks face-forward into the base of a pine tree, his skull cracking like a egg, the brain bleed spreading fast like red wine from a broken bottle—*

She winces with the tree strike.

Caleb stares at her like a lost puppy looking for love.

"Just be sure to name the sled *Rosebud*," she says.

"Okay," he says, obviously bewildered but not wanting to offend her, the Creative Talent, in this thing that may or may not be an audition.

Ellison comes up behind Caleb and ushers him away with a dry-as-tinder "Good job, van der Wald."

After, it's a parade of young, mostly white men. Some are hunky stallions, others thin wisps of hipster meat. They have names like Dorian and Dashiell, Malcolm and Logan, and in her head she plays them out like Rudolph the Red-Nosed Reindeer: *You know Dashiell and Dorian and Malcolm and Logan, you know Connor and Spencer and Brickley and Dickhead—but do you recall, the wealthiest prick of them all, oh it's Chandler, the Trust-Fund Baby, had a very shiny Porsche, and if you ever saw it, it's probably because he was drunk and ran you over while speeding down Santa Monica Boulevard.* (She admits, that Christmas carol probably went a little off the rails at the end.)

Their deaths are as predictable as they are dull.

A late-night cocktail of Oxy, Ambien and, well, actual cocktails means vomiting inside your own lungs, yet somehow peacefully—

A raging case of antibiotic-resistant gonorrhea spreads through his body like a brushfire on the Fourth of July, shutting down organs like the lights after a stage play—

The Porsche hits a skid of scree while driving too damn fast along the cliffside highway, swerving hard away from the sweaty man on one bicycle only to crash head-on into another, and together—as the liquor bottles take flight inside the fast car—they fly off the highway, tumbling down the cliff, not exploding as happens so often in the movies but simply crashing and crumpling there like a microwave thrown off a rooftop before finally making one last lazy roll into the sea—

(Hey, she didn't make that Christmas carol up out of thin air.)

They don't all die from the expected causes, of course. You get your expected culprits, too: the cancers, the heart diseases, the suicides.

As each death hits her, as she shakes each hand, her stomach feels loosier and goosier, like it's not attached to anything inside her and is just . . . sloshing around, her middle a bag of unpinned guts.

That's when she meets Taylor Bowman.

She's just gotten off of seeing a young black actor die—fifteen years later, after getting his first SAG Award, by tripping and falling in front of a speeding limousine and getting his head crushed like a sat-on birthday cake—when Bowman walks up, with his porcelain anime-boy skin and his coffee-colored hair. He's all looking at his phone, slurping at a Batman-black smoothie (there's that activated charcoal), and as he steps up, she catches a whiff of whatever it is he put in that smoothie. It stinks. It smells like fucking feet. She wrinkles her nose and looks up at him.

"It's durian," he says.

"I already met Dorian."

"No, *durian*. It's a fruit? From Asia? It's a superfood. Want a sip?"

"No. What? No." She feels her throat shudder. "It smells like someone shoved a half-rotten onion up the ass of a waterlogged corpse."

"That's kinda rude," he says. Then, to some even younger man behind him, and to Ellison, he mutters: "I don't need this job, whatever it is. I'm good at CBS right now. I don't need to look at the horizon, like, because I *am* the horizon, I think? If that makes sense. Does that make sense? It makes sense to me, anyway." He offers an insecure little chuckle, like he's not actually sure if it makes sense or not but he's just gonna speed past it and hope nobody calls him on it. "Anyway, so—"

Miriam vomits on him.

There's ample warning, probably. She can taste that pukey taste on the back of her tongue. Like a sick dog, she does that thing where she's tasting what's to come, her tongue licking the roof of her mouth. She can feel her throat tighten, her stomach loosen. And then it comes. No dry-heaving warning, no time to turn away. Or maybe there is and she chooses not to take that luxury. Either way, she opens up, her jaw feeling like it's practically unhinging, and then she pukes. Hard. Hot. Fast. A projectile spray full of what-was-once-coffee geysers Bowman in the chest and phone. He juggles the phone and drops it. The screen cracks.

He yelps like a kicked terrier.

Miriam doesn't miss a step. As he backpedals, she spits puke out of her mouth and lurches up out of the chair. "No, you don't, Tay-Tay."

And then she grabs him by the wrist and

INTERLUDE

THE MAN WITH THE SHINING FACE

Slap.

A hard, open-handed hit wakes Taylor Bowman up. He's bound to a chair. Still bound. Been bound so long, his hands and feet are numb, so numb they're less like limbs and more like hunks of dead meat hanging there, bloodless and raw. It's dark here but he can still see the margins of the room he's in—a desk, wood paneling, the smell of dry rot and desert sand. He sees an old poster on the wall: got no name on it, though, it just shows a mermaid drawn up like the St. Pauli Girl, drinking a tall seafoam lager. Papers too lie scattered about the room.

A shadow emerges from the corner of this room. The person who slapped him. Who brought him here. Tall. Lean. Mask over his head. Something gleams and glimmers across the face—a shimmer and shine that make no earthly sense, but Bowman is tired and scared and not sure what the fuck is going on here. "Where is she? I saw her. There in the doorway. Where am I? I just . . . I just wanted . . ." *What was it he wanted? Why was he here? How did he even get here? Was something he wanted . . .*

Drugs. He wanted drugs.

And he got them. Someone injected something into him . . .

Made his muscles feel like sandbags . . .

He struggles. The tall man in black, the man with the shining face, comes closer. The man has a knife. A hunting knife with a hooked tip.

"I have a mask. And you have a mask."

When he speaks, his voice is deep and rich, a baritone timbre.

"What?" Taylor says, mush-mouthed. "I don't—please, let me go, I'm rich, I got a show, a show on TV, I can pay anything—"

"You are an icon of vanity. You are a beacon of the narcissistic fire threatening to consume this country. The Me-Me-Me Generation. While the common people starve and die, you traipse about, tra-la-la, chasing Instagram food trends and getting injections of toxins into your skin to keep everything high and tight. You sleep on a bed of money and fame. You got yours, and nobody else matters. Isn't that right?"

"No, no, man, it's not like that—I'm not—"

"You don't believe me. I will show you your mask."

"Please. Sir. No, no, no, no—"

"This will take a while. I will need you to hold still."

A flash of a needle. The plunging sting in the side of Taylor's neck and then everything goes slippery and sideways. But he remains awake. The dose is just right. His body feels disconnected from his brain—but his eyes are still open and still seeing, even if he can't say much except drool-mush gabble in response. He feels something tugging at the side of his face, a tug-tug-tug, a pull-pull-prod, and slowly the vision in his left eye is obscured by something, like a flap of curtain pulled over a window—then the blood runs into his eye. It happens again with the right eye, and slowly, surely, something peels away from his face, and he thinks, What is that? Is that plastic wrap? Is that a mask? He said it was a mask. . . .

The man with the shining face now holds something up like a dishtowel, and Taylor wants to laugh and say, Why are you showing me this? It has holes in it. Three holes, by the look of it, and he tries to close his eyes and go to sleep but he can't. His lids won't respond.

And then it dawns on him what he's seeing.

The light through the eyeholes.

Through the hole where the mouth once was.

The margins of the lips.

That faint little mole on the left cheek.

It is his face.

He is staring at his own face.

The man gently sets it upon the desk so that it's draped over the edge, so its hollow empty eyes can continue to regard Bowman.

Then there is a hard, stubborn feeling that ripples across Taylor's middle—a body-shuddering line pulled from left to right, and then he feels suddenly, strangely lighter even as his lap feels heavier.

He looks down and sees that the man with the shining face has put something in his lap, something gray and gleaming, something big and blobby, an asymmetrical tangle like a bundle of serpents . . .

My guts, *Taylor thinks.*

Those are my guts.

The man with the knife takes Taylor's face and gently puts it back onto his skull with a ginger pat. "Usually I put the mask on display so that you may see it as you die," the man says. "But here in the half-dark of this back room, I think this is a better display, don't you?"

"Muhh. Mmmm. Iiiiii. Whh."

"Your mask is gone. You are primed now for your final performance, Mr. Bowman. The cameras will come. They will capture you at your most authentic—this is your rawest, most honest performance yet. . . ."

As he speaks, the blackness descends upon Taylor Bowman, but in the back of his mind, he hopes that the man in the shining face is right: he hopes he really pulls off this role, that they never forget his performance.

THIRTY-FIVE

MOURNING SICKNESS

It's later. Miriam sits alone in Ellison's trailer. Turns out, there's a shower in there—admittedly a shower big enough for a human hat rack, but given that she's only a *leetle* bit preggo right now, she fits just fine as she washed off the coffee puke from her middle.

Now she sits on one of the uncomfortable chairs, trying to navigate the mystery of what she saw in Taylor Bowman's death vision *and* her own emotions about it. Or, rather, her total lack of emotions.

Because that's the thing. Miriam doesn't care.

She should care. Someone is going to get murdered. But she's having a hard time conjuring much compassion for a smug little prick like Taylor Bowman. Every murder isn't hers to solve before it happens. The Trespasser would want her to fix it, because that is what the Trespasser always wants. It *wants* her involved. It *needs* her to stop these deaths before they arrive, and why it needs that, she has no earthly idea. To answer that question, she needs to screw that fucker to the wall so it—or he, or she—will hold still long enough for her to demand truth from its spectral lips. But there's the twist of the knife, innit? Because to find someone who can help her talk to the Trespasser, she has to first secure Guerrero's help, and to secure Guerrero's help, she has to solve this murder. A murder she cares nothing about.

But she cares about Gabby.

She cares about this baby.

She cares about getting free.

Her mother's voice floats up out of the void:

It is what it is, Miriam.

So, she goes through it, replaying the vision in her head again and again. When Guerrero and Ellison come in through the trailer door once more, she's *still* replaying it, trying to see what she can see.

"Bowman is mad," Ellison says, sipping a smoothie the color of mustard. He licks a blop of it off his lips. "But he's a turd, and a little turd in a big bowl at that. I got him an invite to a party I'm throwing."

"Great," Miriam says, her voice an acid-chewed croak.

"You saw something," Guerrero says. "With Bowman."

"I did. The Starfucker kills him."

"He's our next victim."

And here's the part where she disappoints them.

"What?"

"He's not the next killing. If these keep going, he'll be the sixth."

Guerrero's fists ball up at his side. "Fuck." He points an accusing finger at her. "You need to do better."

"Me? I did what you asked. You put me in front of a line of vapid fuckboy actors, and I got results." She lurches up out of the chair, feral as a cornered coyote. "Way I see it, that means you owe me a little something, tit-for-goddamn-tat. You owe me a name. I want to meet your medium."

"No. Uh-uh. Not yet, you haven't even told me the details—"

She gives him the details. "Bowman dies in a dark room. I saw . . . a mermaid poster? I dunno. Looked like an office: desk, papers, stapler, that sort of thing. It happens in four months, like I said. The Starfucker is a tall, thin man. Wearing all black.

His face was . . . shining, somehow. Like you figured, he cuts off the face after injecting some kind of drug, then disembowels Bowman with the same knife. This time, he won't put the face on display, though—he just pops it back on Taylor's red skull."

Guerrero paces. Ellison just stands coolly off to the side, regarding all this like a voyeuristic bystander, slurping his smoothie.

"This isn't enough," Guerrero snaps. "I need more."

"Don't you have, like, actual FBI agents on this shit? Why am I alone your savior? Have you seen me? I'm nobody's savior, asshole."

"Yes, we have a whole investigation."

But it's then she understands.

"You're trying to prove something," she says.

"No." But the way he says it, it's defensive, like he's got his guard up. It's how she knows she's right. She found his tender spot.

"It's why we're working out of a fucking trailer in a parking lot under the 405, isn't it? You're not in the Big Boy Building because you're not wearing the Big Boy Bureau Pants." She laughs, incredulous. "Grosky's theories were marginal and you picked them up and don't have any support, so you need a win, real bad. And you're pinning your hopes on me. Oh, Jesus, dude, do you know what a bad idea that is? It's like handing a bag of money to a compulsive gambler and trusting him to invest your money, safe and sound. Spoiler warning: he's gonna blow it all at the craps table."

"You are far from my only hope."

"Horseshit. I'm your fucking Obi-Wan and you know it." She cranes her head back on her neck and grits her teeth. "God, do you even *have* a team? Is there really a medium or are you just stringing me along?"

Guerrero is up on her now, in her face, and she can smell mint on his breath and sweat under his arms. His voice is restrained, but he can't contain the tension and anger there. "You are not the only one I have. There *is* a medium. You will find out his name when we stop the Starfucker. Then and only then. Until then, you shut up. You do the job. Or you go to jail."

Her mouth stiffens into a plastic smile. "You got it, boss."

It was a lie. She would betray him. She just didn't know how yet.

THIRTY-SIX

END OF DAY

Guerrero parades her from backlot to studio and back again, from Culver City to Century City, all the way up to Burbank. That means she's stuck in LA traffic all the way there and all the way back. The highways are parking lots. Each car like a glob of cholesterol stuck in a thickening artery. She meets a batch of actors at every location, and in each she sees the deaths, the slip-and-falls, the liver failures, the drug overdoses, the car crashes, the deaths of the young-and-wealthy, but in none of them does she glimpse the man with the shining face. The Starfucker is a ghost once more. And all the way, Guerrero keeps quiet, saying nothing to her. He simmers in his own thoughts. She can see the look of consternation and rage on his face; it's contained, but poorly, like a demon in a box. No matter how thick the walls of that box, no matter how strongly you reinforce them, you can still hear the demon scrabbling to get out. Claws scraping. Teeth chattering.

For a time, Guerrero had seemed so put together. So buttoned up. But he, she realizes, is a man repressed. Whether he has some darker specter that haunts him—his own emotional, traumatic version of the Trespasser—or whether he's just your classic everyday control freak dude, she can't say. And it doesn't matter. Because she's going to have to fuck him over in the end before he fucks her over. It is the way of the things.

Eat or get eaten.

Kill or be killed.

Fuck before you get fucked.

He drives her back to the apartment instead of the trailer. By now, it's late, almost 10 PM. As he eases his car—an electric Toyota Mirai—up to the front of her condo complex, he says, "I apologize."

"I don't need your apologies."

"You were right."

She leans back, certain that *you were right* are the three sexiest words in the human language. "Okay, go on."

"I do need proof of concept with what I'm trying to accomplish in the Bureau. The pressure is on. I have no formal team. I do have others like us in this city and state that have worked for me in a freelance capacity; you're the first that I've brought on in a more official framework."

"Do you really have a medium? Someone to help me."

"I do. I keep a whole spreadsheet of people like you. He is here in Los Angeles."

"Tell me his name."

Guerrero reaches up and grabs the steering wheel. He grips and flexes, like he's revving the throttle on a motorcycle. His nostrils flare when he says, "I can't do that. I know what happens when I do that. I tell you a name, and you're vapor. I get a sense of who you are. You've told me who you are. The moment I give you that name, I lose all my leverage with you."

"So, you're going to fucking hold out on me."

"For now. Until . . . until we get more results. It's only the first day."

"Fine." She goes to open the door but it's locked. "Unlock the fucking door or I put my head through the glass."

He does as she asks. *Kathunk*. The door pops.

She's out, and he drives off.

Miriam resists giving him the finger as he goes.

She takes it as a sign she's growing up.

With that in mind, she heads inside and plods up the stairs and unlocks the door, finding herself in a dark condo. Gabby is in the bedroom, face down in a pillow, not snoring so much as she is breathing that loud, slumbering sleep-breath. Miriam contemplates jumping up and down on the bed, singing *wake up wake up wake up*, because she's oddly weirdly awake all of a sudden. But she doesn't.

Again, she's growing up.

She ponders her options. Option one: kick off her clothes, get into bed, lie awake staring at the dark abyss of the ceiling. Option two: sneak out into the living room and, like, what? They don't have a TV. She could go out on the balcony and . . . Okay, the usual answer here would be *smoke and drink*, but she doesn't do either of those things right now. What would she do? Stare creepily at the pool? Sip some mint tea? God, being preggo is the fucking worst. It turns you into the most boring person ever.

This explains why some pregnant women talk only about being pregnant. It's all they know. It's their whole world. They've been reprogrammed by the human tapeworm they've chosen to host in their body. The parasite makes itself the most interesting thing. I mean, here she is, right now, *thinking about being pregnant*. It's just—ugh.

Miriam chooses to do different.

She heads back downstairs, fishes out Steve Wiebe's card, and gives him a call. He answers, mumbling into the phone: "Wuzza."

"Put on some pants, Tighty-Whitey Man. It's time to—" Time to what? "Time to go . . . do something."

"What? Who is this. I'm off the—" He pauses. "Oh. It's *you*."

"It's me."

"All right. Where are you?"

"Here in the condo complex. In my lovely Palm Coast villa. Waiting for you to put on pants and bring the car."

"I'll see you in twenty out front."

"Make it fifteen."

"Fine."

She makes kissy sounds into the phone and heads back outside.

THIRTY-SEVEN

A MOCKERY OF JUSTICE

"This is just fruit juice," she says, staring over a tall tiki glass that looks like some angry island monster frozen in the moment of a vicious bowel movement. "It's just—" She looks into it, dispirited. "Fruit juice."

"It's a mocktail," Steve says, taking a sip from his own tiki drink, which is very much *not* a mocktail. His hair is in a similar pompadour, and he's got on a different Hawaiian shirt: this one blue, with a shitload of green parrots all over it. He is wearing pants this time: baggy khakis that end on a pair of Birkenstock sandals. Occasionally, he fidgets with his narrow little mustache, like he's very proud of it.

"It has no alcohol in it."

He licks his pencil-thin mustache. "Yes, because you said you were pregnant and couldn't drink alcohol."

"But this is just fruit juice."

"It's not just fruit juice. It's got orgeat in it." Orgeat, which he pronounces with the extra flourish: *or-zhaaaaa.*

"The fuck is orgeat."

"It's . . ." He laughs. "I don't know."

He flags down a waitress, a bored goth girl who has discarded some but not all of her gothiness for a kitschy grass skirt and coconut bra. "What?" she asks, irritated. Miriam likes her.

"What is orgeat?"

"It's almond syrup, with a little orange flower water and rose water. And a lot of sugar."

"Thank you," he says, and she zips away.

"So, it's fruit-and-nut juice," she says.

"And flower water."

She sighs. All around her, a dark tiki bar in the Hollywood Hills: place called Tonga No-No. Everything is bamboo and palm fronds, tiki torches and pineapples. It's cheesier than a yeast infection. Worse, it suddenly calls to mind the events of that day down in the Florida Keys. The tiki bar where Ashley Gaynes found her. He shot everyone in that bar that day—well, almost everyone. One of the survivors was Samantha, a young woman so affected by the trauma, it let the Trespasser in. It urged her. She met Louis. Got engaged. And where did that end? Oh, that's right. Both of them dead, Louis by Wren's hand.

God, everything I touch turns to blood and shit.

"We should go," she says, frowning into her glass of fruit juice, almond nonsense, and flower urine. "I don't want to be here anymore."

"I just got my zombie. You'll have to walk home."

"Yours has like forty-seven kinds of rum in it."

"Four, actually. White rum, dark rum, golden rum, and—" He scrunches up his nose, which leaves a series of V-shaped dents in his forehead. "Some other kind of rum." He hums, giddily. "It's good."

"Oh, I bet. I'll be over here drinking this ball-less scrotum of a drink, this sad specter of a cocktail, this whimpering cup of impotent tiki jizz."

"You *do* have a way with words."

She groans. "Being sober is bad, Steve. I see now why I never did it. It's no fun. You're exposed to—" She gestures toward *everything*. "All this. People. Objects. All the world and its endless disappointments."

"Sorry you're pregnant. Is that a thing? Is that rude? I know that being pregnant is supposed to be a special thing, so . . ." His voice trails off.

"It's fine. It's not rude. I mean, it *is* rude, but my threshold for rudeness is so high, you'd probably have to hit me over the head with a"—*red snow shovel*—"baseball bat before I thought it rude."

"How'd you get pregnant?"

She stares at him, incredulous. "Well, Steve, when a man and a woman love each other very much, the man sticks his wangle-rod into her fleshy love-puddle and fills her with—"

"No, I mean—you and your girlfriend—or wife? Is she your wife?"

"Gabby?"

"Sure."

"No, she's not my—" Miriam laughs. "Wife? Wife. Oh, I don't think anybody would ever want to be married to me." In her head, she sees the peaceful solace of a snowglobe, gently shook up . . . "I mean, c'mon."

"So, girlfriend."

"Ahhh. Well." She leans back. Is Gabby her girlfriend? No, of course not. Right? Wait. No? She hasn't stopped to really think about that. They *are* fucking again. And it's not like she's getting sexy with anyone else. She stammers her only possible reply: "We don't like to put labels on it."

"Is the baby a mutual decision?"

"Oh, no. It wasn't even my decision." She sips the mocktail mai-tai and scowls like she just licked a subway turnstile. "I, uhh, thought my baby-maker had been ruined. Doctors told me it was done for, too much scar tissue from a violent miscarriage, and so I . . . did not expect this. But here we are. With me sipping from a cold glass of mockery-of-justice mai-tai."

"Who's the father? If you don't mind me asking."

She leans forward, planting both elbows on the table and staring over her two fists. "I met a man named Louis Darling. He was a truck driver. He was a big fella, a real sexy Andre the Giant type, and once upon a time, I saved him from a batshit Eurotrash drug dealer named Ingersoll—though he lost an eye in the process, earning him a pirate-like eyepatch, at least until he got a fake eyeball later on. Thing is, I didn't really save him. I just . . . extended his time on Earth a little bit, which is maybe a favor or a curse, depending on how you view this world of ours, because before Christmas this past year, he got shot in the head by . . . a young woman I was mentoring, a girl named Wren who mistook him for something that he wasn't. In a fit of confusion, she killed him, but only after he had put a baby inside of me. He's dead. Wren is gone, escaped, in the wind—because I let her, which I probably shouldn't have, but even now I realize she was caught up in something bigger than the both of us, and she was as much a puppet in that situation as I was. Not to say I'm not still mad. If I saw her today, I'd probably fucking kill her for taking Louis away from me. But at least he left something of himself behind, I guess. Now I just have to get this little fucker over the finish line and into the world safely. No easy task, if you're me."

Steve stares at her.

Paralyzed.

He says nothing, though it looks like he wants to.

Finally, he says, "I'm sorry."

"I'm sorry, too."

"That's . . ." He blinks. "I'm sorry, but it's all real? What you said?"

"It's all real."

"You also told me you were psychic. That was just a joke, right?"

She offers a sad smile. "Not a joke. I am cursed with a power to see how people are going to die. I gained this power when I had the aforementioned violent miscarriage back when I was in high school. The father of that child killed himself, and his mother attacked me in the bathroom, beating me half to death with a snow shovel. I lost the baby and gained the sight of death."

"Jesus."

"Yeah."

She can see it in his eyes—it's like a light-switch flipping. He went from not believing her story to believing it, click. She can see in his eyes that he sees the truth in *her* eyes. And they stare at each other like that for a while. Sharing this strange moment.

"The baby," he says. "Will you keep it?"

"I don't know," she says honestly.

"You can see how people are going to die?"

A slow nod. "I can."

"That's pretty fucked up."

"It is. What's more fucked up is how it's become background noise for me. I guess surgeons are like that too. Death is just a part of life to them. It's just a part of it to me, too. Can't have a snake without a head and a tail."

He hesitates. She knows what he's going to ask. Finally, he's out with it, spoken in a hushed voice across the table, as if he's speaking some kind of heresy, some forbidden question of a fallen and forgotten god. "Do you . . . know how *I* die?"

"I haven't touched you yet. I need skin-on-skin contact." She gives him a long, hard look. "Do you wanna know?"

"Not yet," he says, answering quickly.

"Let me know if you change your mind."

"With your life, you really *do* need a stiff drink."

"You're not wrong." She finishes her Betrayal Juice and then says, "Enough of me oversharing. Time for *you* to overshare, young man."

He puffs out his cheeks. "Hold on." He slams back the tiki

drink and then summons the waitress for another zombie. "Okay, I am ready. You may begin your interrogation at your leisure."

"So, what's your deal?"

He makes a frowny face. "That's your question? What's my deal?"

"Everybody's got a deal. I gave you my deal. What's yours? What're your peccadillos, who are your demons, what's your bag, your jam, who the hell are you?"

"Peccadillos. Good word, peccadillos." He eagerly takes the next cocktail when the waitress brings it. "Hold on." He takes a drink. "Okay. My deal. My deal, my deal, my deal. My . . . family hates me. That's something. And it's maybe a big something since I think about it . . . every day? And multiple times every day."

"That's a bummer. Why do they hate you?"

"A lot of reasons. But three—I think, three big ones."

"Let's hear them."

"Number one, I'm a Democrat."

"Like, the political party."

"Yes, the—how do you not know that?"

"I know that; I just wondered if that was maybe a new slang term for like *guy who fucks cats* or something. They just—they don't like that you're a Democrat?"

"I'm from a part of Ohio which is basically Kentucky, and being conservative is, I think, a part of our actual *genetic makeup*, so—yeah, it was a problem. But it's probably the shortest leg on their stool of criticism."

She nods. "Go on."

"Also, I'm asexual."

"What?"

"Asexual."

"Like, you . . . reproduce by . . . cellularly dividing?"

"No, being ace means I have no sexual *thing* toward people.

No attraction toward them. Intellectual, sure, romantic, okay, but like, I don't feel a physical, visceral attraction to men or women."

She leans forward, brow furrowed with the scrutiny of a scientist discovering a new physical force in the universe. "You don't have sex?"

"I have, but don't usually."

"Do you like sex?"

"It's . . . okay. I like eating hamburgers, too, but I don't wanna fuck 'em. If that makes sense."

She *hmms*. "Not really? But it doesn't have to, because I'm me and you're you, and honestly, you do what you like, Steve Wiebe. PS, I would totally fuck a really good hamburger."

"Have you had In-N-Out yet?"

"No, wuzzat?"

His mouth opens wide, and his eyes open wide to join his mouth, as the light of pure joy emanates from him in nearly tangible crepuscular beams. "Ohhh, ho ho ho, ohh, oh man. Miriam. Oh. *Oh*. It's good."

"It's just what, fast food?"

"We're going. After this, we're going."

"Is it just going to disappoint me? Do I need to be drunk?"

"This isn't just drunk food. This is just—the best fast-food hamburger you will ever have. I mean, maybe there are more *refined* hamburgers, but none as satisfying as this."

"I'm dubious, but okay. So, what's the third thing?"

"Oh. The third thing."

"Out with it."

"Ahhh."

"C'mon."

"Unhhh."

"Spit. It. Out."

"I'm trans."

"Trans what?"

"I was . . . born a woman. I'm a trans man. Assigned female at birth."

Miriam puckers her lips, then shrugs. "Okay."

"Okay? Just okay?"

"Yeah. Okay."

"Some people get weird when I tell them. Like, my family."

"I just told you I'm a psychic who can see how people are going to die and I'm impregnated by a dude who got shot in the head. You rolled with the punches on that one, so I kinda feel like I should be cool with whoever you are and whoever you wanna be."

"Cool."

"Cool."

"*Cool.*"

THIRTY-EIGHT

WAIT WAIT DON'T TELL ME

In the car, on the way to In-N-Out. All around, the smear of Hollywood lights, the press of crowds, the claustrophobia of cars after cars after cars. She says, "Wait, so, what bits do you have?"

"You're not supposed to ask me about my bits. Besides," he says, "it's not about the fiddly bits. It's about who I am."

"Everything is about the fiddly bits," Miriam says. "But I'm basically a twelve-year-old, so I think a lot about fiddly bits."

He pauses. "I think a lot about poop," he says, earnestly.

"Oh my god, me too. We all poop. It's one of life's unifying bonds. Frankly, I think it's weird when people *don't* think about poop."

"Right?!"

They sit in silence for a while, contemplating this deep, sacred reality.

Finally she says, "By the way, I can also become birds—er, sorta—and I think I can heal injuries faster than the average individual. Maybe really fast. Maybe really grievous injuries too; I'm not sure yet. Jury's still out."

"You're the queen of oversharing," he says.

Miriam nods. "And all shall be serfs in my kingdom."

THIRTY-NINE

TRUTH IN ADVERTISING

"Jesus fuck," she says, chewing.

Together, the two of them sit on the hood of Steve Wiebe's Kia sedan at the back of the In-N-Out parking lot, finishing their burgers. Except, for Miriam, it is no mere burger. Steve told it true: this was a truly sublime hamburger. He told her to order it "animal-style," whatever the fuck that meant, and she took his suggestion. Soon as she took a bite, the beef angels did sing. A moo-cow chorus of beatific deliciousness. Greasy and meaty and fatty and burgery and cheesy and saucy in *all the perfect proportions*. The Greeks would have spawned entire schools of philosophy about this burger. This burger should have a cult.

Miriam contemplates starting one.

"Maybe it's queendom," Steve says, suddenly.

"What?"

"Sorry. I do that sometimes? I continue a conversation that has long been over without warning the other person. Earlier, in the car, I said you were the queen of oversharing. And you said, *all shall be serfs in my kingdom*, but maybe it's queendom. Because queens, not kings."

She shrugs, cheeks bulging with burger-flesh. "Whatever, dude."

"The burger's good, right?"

"The burger's not good, Steve. The burger is the kind of

burger that could start a war. Or end one. This burger might be the one good thing God above has given us, or it might be the most tempting artifact dangled before us by the Devil himself. This burger would be the thing I would give to an extraterrestrial invader to prove that we were worthy not only of saving, but of uplifting to a greater state of cosmic evolution. This is no mere burger, Steve, nor is it merely good. It is awesome in the truest sense of that word."

He nods, dabbing at his mouth with a napkin.

Moments pass.

"But the fries kinda suck," he adds.

"*Totally* not great fries," she says in vigorous agreement. "I mean, how do you make a burger that amazing but then kinda fuck up the fries?"

"Maybe it's like," he says, swallowing one last bit, "they could choose to make one thing truly amazing, or two things just really good."

"So, the mediocre fries are the price we pay for divine burgerfood."

"Could be. Just a thought."

"Thanks for this, Steve."

"It's been fun. And I got a burger out of it."

"I guess I should go home now."

He puts out his hand. "I'm ready."

"Ready for what?"

"To see how I . . . *you know*."

"Bite it."

"Yeah."

"Suck the pipe."

He nods. "Right."

"Take the big ol' dirt-nap, ride the bone-coaster to Reapertown, tap-dance off the end of Death's naughty parts—"

"Yes." He thrusts his hand out farther. "Let's do this."

But Miriam hesitates.

Her chest tightens.

"What?" he asks her.

"I don't know that I wanna."

"Why?"

She makes a face. "I don't know! This has never happened to me before. I always wanna see. I kinda get off on it—like, in a spiritual way, not in a *soggy-panties* way. But I'm starting to like you and I'm afraid that you're going to die in a bad way, and soon, and it'll be my fault."

Steve looks wary. "Why would it be your fault?"

Because it's always my fault, Steve-o.

"I just—I'm not ready."

"Oh."

He retracts his hand.

The disappointment comes off him in waves like stink lines off a cartoon skunk. She rolls her eyes. "Fine."

"No, don't worry about it, it's—"

She pinches his cheek and—

FORTY

THE HEART WANTS WHAT THE HEART WANTS

"—it's cool," he finishes saying.

She pulls her hand away. It feels cold, suddenly.

A bit of trash blows across the parking lot. A car pulls through, rocking heavy bass. Someone yells something to someone else: a friendly shout. An airliner overhead. All while Steve's death replays in her head.

The good news is, it isn't her fault.

For once.

"What is it?" he asks.

"Do you," she starts, but then she has to clear her throat because it's suddenly tight. "Do you have a heart condition?"

He blinks.

"Yeah."

"A heart valve problem," she clarifies.

His face goes ashen. "Yeah. It's fixed. I had surgery when I was little—and I take beta-blockers and vasodilators and—"

"And it kills you."

"Oh." He laughs it off, nervously. "At least I have time—"

"You have three years."

"What? Three years? Three? That's it?"

"That's it."

"I'm only twenty-seven. I'll be thirty. I'll die at thirty."

"Yes. That math is accurate."

He says, "That can't be right."

"It's right."

"I can—I'll get it fixed, get surgery again. I'll be okay. Thanks for the warning."

She looks upon him with sad eyes. She forces a smile, though it damn sure ain't a happy one. "It doesn't work like that. You can try to bend fate and twist out of its grip, but you'll just end up making it happen. Fate gets what fate wants. I can stop it sometimes, but only when someone else causes it. If there's a killer, I can kill them before they get you. I can balance those books. Without that, it just . . . happens." Her own blood goes to slush as she thinks about Louis's baby inside her. She knows of no killer, has no sense of how to save the child. Hopelessness sucks at her like hungry mud. She has to willfully not be drawn down into that mire of despair. "I'm sorry."

"Three years."

He looks off in the distance, toward the fast-food joint, but he's not looking *at* it. He's staring *through* it.

"Do I just . . . die? Like, on the toilet or something?"

"No. You die in a hospital. You have some warning, it seems."

"Is anybody there? At my bedside?" Idly, Steve cracks his knuckles one by one: an anxious, nervous habit. "Or am I alone?"

"Bunch of people there," she tells him, and it's not a lie. "I don't know who they all are. They don't . . . introduce themselves in the vision. Only one I know is someone named Emily. You say her name, holding her hand as you go into tachycardia and . . . pass on." She hates that phrase so bad, but she feels the need suddenly to soften all this for him.

"Emily? Seriously?"

"Emily."

"Black hair? Long-ish? Little scar on her chin?"

"That's the one."

He smiles. "That's my sister."

"Oh."

"We're not talking right now."

"Well, you'll be talking then."

His eyes shine with tears that threaten to fall but never do. "When I stopped talking to my family, she was part of the fallout. Maybe I can reach out to her. Maybe we can reconnect."

"Sure."

"Three years. That's not a long time."

"No. But also, it can be. Life is short, but life can be long, too."

"Maybe this is a gift, you know? A really . . . fucked-up gift. You tell me I have three years, maybe I can fill those years with some meaning."

"See, there you go."

"I should probably stop eating In-N-Out burgers, though."

"I wouldn't go that far, shit."

"This burger tonight may be the thing that kills me in three years."

She shrugs. "I'd say it was worth it."

He takes a moment, then licks his fingers, one by one.

"You might be right."

FORTY-ONE

THE WORM IN THE APPLE

Home. Or what passes for it. Their half-ass condo in this crazy-ass city. Miriam, sober as a Sunday morning, full of mocktails and burger meat, climbs her way back up to the condo and plods into the bedroom, realizing that she's going to have to be awake in four hours to go do the thing again with Guerrero. Because they have to. Because they have three days.

No.

Two days now.

Two days until the eleventh.

Two days until the Starfucker kills again, absolving some dipshit prettyboy of his face and of his bowels.

Once again, Miriam Black is on the clock. Not for the Trespasser this time, but for the Federal Bureau of Investigation. Does this appease the Trespasser, though? Is this just what that demon wants of her? To once again step in, to slam her rock down and break the river in twain, to divert the course of fate and save the lives of others while her own hangs in the balance? For a long time, she thought the Trespasser just wanted to fuck with her. Then she thought, maybe the Trespasser, in its fucked up way, is trying to right some wrong. Now she's not sure about any of it. She feels again and again like she's playing into the Trespasser's hands. Or worse, like his hand is up her ass: she, its destiny-killing puppet.

But why? Why does the Trespasser want this?
What is it? *Who* is it?

She doesn't know, but she intends to find out.

Stop the Starfucker. Get the name of the medium from Guerrero. Find the Trespasser and kill it, however she's gotta.

Into bed she goes. Cuddling up next to Gabby. Though she is the smaller of the two in Actual Size, she curls up to Gabby's back as the Big Spoon. She presses her cheek to Gabby's T-shirted back and starts to drift off. But Gabby must know she's here. The other woman moans a little and rolls over, and in the half-dark of the early morning room, Gabby's eyelids flutter. She smiles a little and says, in a whisper:

"Don't feel bad for ol' Jimmy!"

Gabby's eyes flash with manic glee.

Miriam gasps, pushing herself backward, tumbling off the bed, the sheets tangled in the closed scissor of her legs. Her head cracks hard against the floor, but she takes no time to get her bearings—already she's launching herself unsteadily to her feet, hands clenched into fists.

There sits Gabby, blinking wearily. One eyebrow up in total bewilderment. "Wha? What are you doing?"

"I . . . Gabby?"

"Yyyyyeah."

Miriam lets out a breath.

"Sorry, I . . ." She winces. "Just had a bad dream."

But she knows it wasn't. It was no dream. It was real.

It was a *warning*. The Trespasser: letting her know what's to come. Letting her know that he can flex his powers over her, and worse, over Gabby. Maybe not all the way. Maybe not yet. But soon.

"Come back to bed," Gabby says.

And Miriam does.

But she does not sleep.

PART SIX

BLOOD MAKES THE VINES GROW

FORTY-TWO

The Falcon and the Field Mouse

Now.

Miriam runs through the vineyard. Her leg is aching. Her collarbone, too, pulses with hot fire every time she takes a rough and ragged step. She winds her way through gnarled vines, each as thick as her arm, twisted and bulging with fat grapes. At the end of each row is a mystery: roses planted in a half a barrel, red as cartoon blood, thrust up in an ostentatious spray.

She has no time to dwell on why one would plant roses here in the vineyard, away from the eyes who would see and appreciate.

All she can do—all she *must* do—is run.

Like a shark: *swim forward or die*.

It occurs to her how often this is the life she has led: on the run from bona fide fucking maniacs. This is what her curse and the Trespasser have done to her time and time again: running from Harriet and Frankie at the behest of Ingersoll; running from the Mockingbird killer again and again, not realizing that the Mockingbird was not one killer but rather a whole *family* of them; running from Ashley Gaynes, who knew her every move; fleeing the Coming Storm's militia camp in the sun-fucked desert; again escaping the resurrected Harriet as the seemingly unstoppable witch-bitch pursued her doggedly.

But that last one, that one was different, wasn't it?

Because at the end of things, Miriam stopped running.

Miriam started *hunting*.

She pursued Harriet. Caught her. Cut out her heart and ate it like a raw filet. And from there, it seemed that some of Harriet's voodoo passed to Miriam now. Reigniting her candle, so to speak, by healing her womb and letting her once again become pregnant. And letting her heal whatever damage came her way. She did not know how much of that carried to the child in her belly—the kid wasn't necessarily afforded that same pre-ternatural protection—but it did mean she could take a beating.

Even now, as she limps—

She feels the leg straighten.

The soreness in her shoulder and collarbone—she hears a *click* as something moves back into place of its own volition.

The pain moves from being a sharp needle to a dull, prodding throb.

She winds her way past the roses, to the line of trees above them, and there she stops and scans the horizon. She spies no pursuer.

Time, then, to change the game. No longer the field mouse, she will now be the falcon. Or maybe the hawk. Because that is what she finds there, soaring above her: the humble red-tailed hawk, one of North America's ubiquitous raptors. Not as fancy as a peregrine or osprey, not as beloved as the sky-raccoon known as the bald eagle, the red-tailed hawk is a utility player, a common bird with unparalleled skill. It's a bird you find everywhere, wheeling in the sky above, or perched on a telephone pole waiting to grab a vole and fuck back off into the blue. Miriam crouches there by the trees, dipping her chin to her chest and—

The rush hits her. The feeling of being *up, up, up,* and away: a swift lateral wind hits her as the heat from below buoys her like a lifting hand. She's up there now. In the hawk. Her talons contain wretched, alarming power—two are so large, so hooked, that she can use them to grab struggling prey and secure it firmly as she carries it away. But she also knows that their power is used in mating, too—a gentler use, two birds crashing together, talons grasping one another as they cease flying and fall toward earth, fucking and screaming and spiraling ever downward, and Miriam thinks, *Like Louis and me*, or maybe *Like Gabby, too*, except then for a moment, she doesn't know who Louis is, or Gabby, or even Miriam—

But this is not new to her. She knows what it is to be lost there in the sky, in the hunt. Miriam exerts her will. She forces her identity forward, thrusting her presence into the present. *I am me. I am not this bird.*

And I am looking for someone.

She is looking for the Starfucker. The man in the shining mask: a cheap black balaclava studded with sequins—a gaudy façade, a visage made perhaps to mock those the Starfucker kills, or maybe just because the Starfucker like shiny things. Whatever the reason, it makes him all the easier to see, and the gleam of sunlight on those hundreds of little sequins is like light on a solar array. The bird sees it easily, gleaming. He's on the other side of the vineyard now. Approaching the line of trees but at the opposing side of this field. He must've thought Miriam went that way.

Soon, he'll come around.

He'll find her.

But she has found him first.

She resists letting the hawk scream—red-tailed hawks have an amazing, sky-piercing shriek. Everyone thinks it's the bald eagle that screams that way, so majestic is their vision of the bald eagle. But the bald eagle is a scavenger half the time. It doesn't shriek. It simpers and coos. The scream belongs to the hawk, and it is a *power move*, a black-metal bird-cry, but she doesn't want to alert her prey to what's about to happen.

The hawk descends.

Relatively speaking, the hawk descends slower than its other raptor ilk: a kestrel is like a bullet, while the red-tailed's descent is almost slow, almost lazy. And yet, at the same time, it is inevitable. The talons tighten into something resembling bird fists. The bird does not plunge so much as it settles ineluctably downward, like a plane landing on a short runway. Then, as it closes in—nearing the man in the shining mask—its feet thrust out and down. Its talons open, hooked and ready—

"*¿Quién eres?*"

Miriam gasps, jostled. She experiences a hard deceleration, a sudden release of pressure—she nearly falls over, pulled out of the mind of the hawk. Someone stands near her, *over* her: a migrant worker, an older man, his face carved with so many lines and crevices, his skin carries the look of sunbaked driftwood. He has a knee-high sprayer tank plonked next to him in the grass. He looks upon Miriam with some concern.

"*¿Estás bien?*" he asks.

"I don't—I don't speak—" She swallows hard, lurching to her feet. "Where are we?"

"*¿Qué?*"

God, I need to learn to speak some fucking Spanish.

"Where are we? What city? What state?" Frustrated, she hisses: "What. Planet. Is. This." *New tactic*, she thinks. She holds her hand up to her ear, miming a phone call. "Do you have a phone? A phone. Cell phone. Cellular, mobile." *Fuck fuck fuck what is the word for phone in Spanish?* Then it hits her, the word floating up out of the ether. "*Teléfono!*"

He hesitates, so she barks the word again at him, putting as much of a heartfelt plea into it as she can without seeming like a crazy lady.

The field worker looks down at his hip and reaches around to his back pocket—and there he pulls out a cell phone. An old one, a flip phone.

He hands it to her.

Soon as it touches her hand—

Bang.

A gunshot.

Blood flecks her face. His eye is gone. His mouth hangs open, as if confused. And then he falls face-forward—she has to juggle her feet backward to avoid what is now the man's corpse.

There, stalking toward her, from a hundred feet away—

Black mask. Shining face. Silver suit.

Knife in one hand, and now a gun in the other.

He raises the gun and fires again.

FORTY-THREE

NOW I HAVE A CELL PHONE, HO HO HO

She staggers, her heel caught on a root—

The air around her feels alive, hot, as something cuts the air by her cheek, like a pebble thrown at a thousand feet per second.

A tickle at the base of her brain, firing her synapses—

The masked man stalks toward her, the gun still up—

About to fire—

Miriam closes her eyes, finds the cause of that brain-base tickle, and then her mind is filled with the flutter of wings and the startled coos as she sends a turtledove flapping down from a nearby tree—

Right into the man's hand. The gun fires, but its aim is knocked off center—the bullet thrashes through the old, gnarled vines as the bird flies up in his face, fluttering there as he swats at it.

Miriam pulls herself back *to* herself, and then takes a hard left into the tree line. Head down, she ducks through the brush, thorns snagging her arm and raking across her like little talons. The tree line is thin, so in half a minute, she's back out among another vineyard, this one with vines that are newer, thinner, the plants bulging with fat, green grapes. She skids to a halt in front of a barrel-trunked tree. Miriam drops to the ground, scooting to the far side of it to hide.

There, she pulls out the cell phone.

Which, miracle of miracles, she's still holding *and* it has power *and* it isn't locked by any kind of password, *thank what-ever gods exist*. She flips it open, is about to call 911 and—

No. She can't. Last time she met a cop, he was possessed by the Trespasser and killed himself. And she's gone rogue from Guerrero. No. She has to call someone she trusts.

Shit.

What the *fuck* is Gabby's number?

Miriam has zero memory of any phone number right now. Really, does she know *any* phone numbers? They're always . . . what? Programmed into her phone. She doesn't conjure them from memory. Christ, does anybody remember fucking phone numbers anymore? If only she can conjure one, *just one*, from the ether. . . .

Wait.

She slides the flat of her hand into her pocket.

There, crumpled up, is a business card.

Steve Wiebe.

Gritting her teeth, she fumbles with the phone—every number she pushes makes an obnoxious *boop*, which she's pretty sure is loud enough that someone could hear it on the surface of Mars, and that's confirmed when she hears the crackle of brush headed her way.

She punches in the number and dials it—

C'mon, c'mon, c'mon.

Ring.

Ring.

Fucking hell, answer the phone, Steve.

Ring.

Ring.

The footsteps close in.

Ring.

Ring.

Voicemail.

Shit.

Steve's voicemail message plays: "Hey, this is Steve. If you're getting this, I'm either busy or I don't want to talk to you. Love you!"

Beep.

Miriam winces before breaking from cover, sprinting toward the next field, toward the vines. As she runs, she breathlessly yells into the phone: "Steve, it's me, Miriam, I don't know where the fuck I am, but I'm being chased by a killer, there are vines and shit and—"

Bang.

A gunshot digs a spray of grass and dirt up at her feet.

"And I need you to contact Gabby and—"

Bang.

Another gunshot cracks through the vineyard brush—grapes hop off the vine in a little spray of juice.

"And tell her—"

Bang.

Her hand jerks away from her ear as a lancing pain scorches through the meat of her bicep. The phone spirals away, disappearing under a tangle of grapevines. Miriam cries out, her right hand moving to her left arm as she stumbles forward, the hand coming away wet with red.

She hits the ground where the phone disappeared, pawing the underbrush for it but not finding it—she finds stones, pebbles, roots. Ants crawl on her hand as blood snakes down her arm. She looks over her shoulder, and here comes the man with the shining mask, the Starfucker, the glitterface killa. She closes her eyes and tries to feel for any birds nearby—even a single fucking nuthatch would give her a beak to stick in this fucker's neck, but there's nary a single winged thing within her mind's reach.

"Hey! Who are you?"

What? It's an absurd question, and at first, she thinks the
Starfucker is calling to her—but the shining-faced bastard turns
away from her, in the other direction. She sees someone there.
Another worker, dark-skinned, a migrant working the field.
Younger. Jeans, a sweaty T-shirt. This one speaks English.

His eyes go wide when he sees the mask, the gun.

Starfucker points and shoots.

Miriam doesn't stick around to see what happens. She springs
to her feet, ducking under one set of vines, then the next, then
the row after. Onward she goes, up an aisle, then underneath,
then up another. She winds her way to another tree line, and into
another field, and to another line of trees beyond that. Forget
being the predator. Being prey is all she can be right now, with
her only choice to run, rabbit, run.

FORTY-FOUR

THE SAFE HOUSE

Time has lost meaning.

That happens, when you're on the run. The adrenaline chews through her like locusts. It rends any mooring she has to place and time. The best she can do is move. Not stop to think. Not stop to consider. Just move.

(And bleed.)

For a while, she's felt alone. She's crossed how many fields of grapevines now? A half-dozen at least. Probably more. Through the vines she wanders, ducking low and staying hidden. She thinks she's lost the killer; she hasn't heard any footsteps. No twigs breaking, no leaves rustling. No gunshots, either. And now she visits with a circling vulture above, a vulture whose eyes are keen and sharp (the better to see dead things with, my dear), and she does a quick scan of the vineyard—

Nothing.

Nobody.

No one.

Except: a house.

A big house, too. Modern. Sprawling. A Range Rover parked outside. A small blue-tile fountain in the circular cobblestone drive.

Someone lives there. The owner of these fields, she guesses. And now, some sense returns to her: *I must be in wine country.*

That's north of Los Angeles, right? Maybe even north of San
Francisco? She wishes like hell she had the presence of mind to
tell Steve that when she left a message on his voicemail.

She does what she can do. She heads down the slope of
well-manicured grass, toward the house ahead of her.

Miriam stops for a moment by the Range Rover and looks at
herself in the passenger-side mirror. Predictably, she looks like
roadkill. She has a zombie-like vibe going on: she's pale, crusted
with blood, her shirt filthy, her clothes ragged. The swell of her
pregnant belly only adds to the ghoulish veneer: *preggo zombie
lady here, don't worry, she's eating for two now!*

She knows that marching up to the house will not instill the
homeowner with the *finest impression*, but what choice does she
have? Not like she can spend time to freshen up.

Staggering across the paver-stone driveway, she concocts
her story, and as usual, cleaving to the truth is the easiest: *I've
been attacked; I need to use your phone.* She won't have to feign
desperation and fear, because she's got those in spades, baby.
If they give her shit, she'll push past. She'll kick and scream.
She'll throat-punch. Let them call the police. Guerrero will
straighten this all out.

At the door, now. She thumbs the doorbell. She hears it,
muffled, inside the house: not a bell but a simple, clean *tone*. Is
it possible for a rich person to have a rich-person doorbell? This
is that.

From inside, gentle footfalls approach.

A quick click of a lock, and a man opens the door. He's older,
maybe mid-sixties. Average in nearly every way: five-eight, balding, narrow shoulders, a slight-but-expected paunch. He's white
like balsa wood. Only thing not average about him is the moneyed
haze that hovers around him like a miasma of tiny dollar signs.
His cardigan looks tailored, soft yet crisply fitting. His eyeglasses
are clear plastic. A smartwatch hangs on his wrist, smooth and

black, shiny as chipped obsidian. He smells like sandalwood.

(Miriam doesn't even know what sandalwood smells like, only that he smells like it.)

The man's face wrinkles softly, like a tissue gently crumpled: "Miss. Are you all right?"

She bites back the snarky answer of *Do I look all right? Are you fucking daft? I'm bleeding from my arm. I look like I was thrown out of a car because, oh, just spitballing here, I was thrown out of a car. I am filthy and thorn-torn and leaf-strewn. That seem all right to you?*

Instead, she says, as politely as she can muster:

"I'm hurt. Someone is chasing me. I need your phone."

"Come on, yes, of course, come in."

He ushers her inside a long foyer: inside is something best described as modern yet rustic, or rustic yet modern. Like somebody made a barn and a skyscraper fuck and have a house-baby. A flat waterfall gently eases over granite so dark, it eats the light. The floor is the opposite: pale, unfinished oak, blonder than a Nazi girl eating a sugar cookie. He eases past her, saying, "Come in, come in, please, let's get you to a phone. Then we can see about that arm of yours, miss."

And she thinks: *This guy is a fucking rube.* People with money can be so deeply stupid sometimes. She could be here to rip him off. Or worse, kill him. This could be a con, a trap. And here he is, the goodness of his dumb, money-stuffed heart making him blind to the realities. Some rich people are vicious, venomous fuckers. Most of them are, because too much money becomes a drug that makes you do bad, bad shit—all in search of the next monetary high. But then you get the subset, like this guy: mooncalves, knock-kneed fawns, who buy expensive art and play the stock market but have literally no idea how bad the world really is.

Good. His wealth-fatted naiveté helps her here.

He leads her through a door—of course it's not just a *door*, no, but rather a sliding door that hangs on a track with a couple of old pulleys, and he eases it aside with a squeak and rattle. Beyond are a kitchen and a small dining nook: white cabinets meet butcherblock. He urges her into the dining nook, where she stands in front of a table artfully piled with books. The table looks like someone just cut it out of a massive tree—still has the bark on it. Past that is a massive square window overlooking the cobblestone driveway—past the Range Rover she sees the driveway forming a long, bumpy ribbon laid between more grapevines and framed by trees.

"Wait here and I'll get the phone. Do you need anything?"

"Just the phone, *please*," she says, again biting back bitter rage.

"Of course." He goes to the kitchen, and she hears him mutter, somewhat flustered: "It's not—it's not in the cradle, it's a cordless and Esmerelda must not have put it back in its . . ." His voice dies off and he leaves the kitchen, heading off to god-knows-where in this massive house. Miriam's chest tightens. She calls after him:

"I can just use your cell—do you have a cell phone?"

But he doesn't answer. He's off on his mission.

Her gut turns sour. The longer he's gone, the greater the chance she'll be found. The killer will come. He'll kill the man. He'll kill her.

He'll kill her baby.

She turns to the kitchen, thinking, *I'll grab a knife. Just in case.*

But no. That'll scare her mooncalf savior off. He comes back with a phone and there she is with a big-ass knife? Wouldn't play well, would it?

So, back to the window she goes. Agitated. Pacing. She cracks her knuckles. Tries to ignore the pain sizzling there in her bicep. (And she wonders, idly, how long will it take to heal? It will heal, won't it? That little gift from Harriet Adams and her raw, still-beating heart . . .)

Then something catches her eye.

Way down the driveway, movement.

A car.

A silver car.

A silver *Lexus*.

She needs that knife, and she needs it *now*.

Miriam spins around and starts to make a beeline for the kitchen. There stands her savior, the good man with the open door, and she starts to say: "He's coming, the killer is—" But then she sees he's not holding a phone. Rather, he's holding a gun. A small, boxy pistol.

Leveled at her middle.

"You fucker," she says. He wasn't being nice. It was a trap.

"I told him," the man says, softly. "I explained that we did not have to come for you, that eventually you would come to us."

"You're with him. You're with the Starfucker."

"Rather, he is with me." He rolls his eyes, almost playfully, like he's feigning embarrassment. "Where are my manners? Welcome, Miriam Black. Welcome to my home. I apologize for my rudeness. I won't be getting you a phone, but I can offer you something to eat and drink."

"I don't understand. . . ."

"You will."

"Fuck you."

"There's that fighting spirit."

Outside, an engine cuts off.

"My friend is here," the man says. "Would you like to meet him? I know he'd very much like to meet you. We've all wanted to meet you, Miriam Black. We have *much* to discuss."

PART SEVEN

THE ONLY WAY OUT IS THROUGH

FORTY-FIVE

THE GIFT

THEN.

They have a car now. Gabby and Miriam. It's not an exciting car by any stretch: a late-nineties Mazda Miata, cherry red, with an engine that sounds like a lawnmower orgy under the hood. They were told, unabashedly, that you cannot live in Los Angeles without having a car. No, no, no, oh no. They could be expelled without a car. Sent to live in the wastelands of Barstow or the Salton Sea or, worst of all, Orange County. Miriam has tried walking places, and though it's doable, people gave her looks like she was a serial killer on the prowl for fresh meat. You get a car, or you don't belong. *One of us, one of us*, the car freaks chant.

So, they expended the least amount of money and, honestly, got the least amount of car. This thing is like a sporty go-cart. Children could own and drive this car. But it's fine. It's clean. It smells like Pine-Sol, for some fucking reason. Probably to cover up the deeper, more secret scent: cigarette smoke. It's still here, an olfactory memory. Miriam catches whiffs of the nicotine and tar from time to time, and it makes her teeth ache with pure, unmitigated *want*. People who lose limbs experience phantom itches. People who quit smoking experience phantom cigarettes—she smells that smell in the car, and she can *feel* the airy, crisp cancer stick betwixt her fingers.

Now, though, she can't smell the smell. They have the

windows down. The wind slides through the car like a serpent. They're in a parking lot, Gabby in the driver's seat, Miriam in the passenger seat. The car too means they don't necessarily use the services of one Mr. Steve Wiebe anymore—though with only one car between the two of them, they still call on him from time to time. And they hang out with him, too, a few times a week because . . . well, they don't know many people here. Gabby has friends now from waitressing, but Miriam does not share those friends because, at least as Miriam tells it, Miriam does not like people. (In more honest moments, she knows she admits to herself that she's really afraid of connecting with people—*new* people in particular. Because people are fragile. Relationships are doomed. People up and fucking die on you, or they betray you, or they just stop caring. In less-honest moments, Miriam tells herself it's because she's a rebel, Dottie. A loner. And that's cool, isn't it? Aren't all the cool kids aloof and standoffish and smart-assed?)

Presently, the car is off. They sit parked on a side street in Beverly Hills. Nearby sits a little boutique hotel, and she can see a pool through the bougainvillea, and she catches the movement of bikini girls and surf-short boys and waitresses serving fancy-ass small-batch locally sourced artisanal cocktails, because people around here can't just drink a shot of tequila or put some tonic in some gin and call it a fucking day. No, here they drink, like, weird shit some fey mustachioed lad made up: *It's got three bitter liquors you've never heard of, plus barrel-aged suntan lotion, saffron, muddled sumac, roasted celery, and the fermented semen of a Tibetan yak who was manually mastur-bated as he died from a slow bleed with a sacred knife. The rim is crusted with dried, sugared salmon roe. I call it an Enlightened Gosling. That'll be $54. Namaste.*

But they're not here for that.

They're here for what's across the street.

The OB/GYN office.

It's her next visit with Dr. Dita Shahini.

"We can go in," Gabby says. "Sit down."

"I'd rather sit in the car. We're a bit early."

"But they have magazines in there. Good ones, too. And they give out bottles of coconut water."

"Coconut water tastes like tree jizz."

Gabby gives her a look.

"No, really," Miriam says, protesting. "Coconut water tastes at least a little bit like jizz. It is *redolent* with jizz. Reminiscent of tropical spunk. And besides, the doctor's waiting room always smells like . . . a doctor's waiting room. I know, I know, it's a rich person's doctor, which is new for me? I expect I deserve a doctor operating out of an alley dumpster, à la Oscar the Grouch, but no matter how shiny and fancy her office is, with the waterfall and the coconut water and those fancy cookies she has sitting around—the place always smells like a doctor's office. Antiseptic scent covered over with a Glade plug-in." Miriam pauses. "What do you think they use to *make* Glade plug-ins? I bet it's people. *Soylent Glade.*"

"You're doing that thing again."

"What thing?"

"That thing where you talk a lot because you're nervous."

"I'm not nervous."

"You're totally nervous."

"Okay, *fine,* I'm totally nervous."

Gabby reaches over, puts a stabilizing hand on her knee. "Is it the baby? Is that what's worrying you?"

"It's everything. Everything is worrying me. I've got anxiety pouring out of my ears like panicked ants pouring out of a kicked over anthill. It's the baby. It's the Trespasser. It's this . . . this Star-fucker. I just . . ." She bites down willfully on the inside of her cheek, enough to draw blood. (It'll heal soon enough, she knows.)

"You'll catch him."

"Two people are now dead. Two. And more will be on the way." Two more months have passed since she began working with David Guerrero. Which means two more actors—young, handsome actors who are vehicles for good cheekbones more than any kind of thespian skill—have been killed. Faces sliced off. Guts spilled into their laps. Last month, the Starfucker murdered Roderick Goynes, both a model and a background player on a ton of shows and movies. Killed him in his own house. Pinned his face to the drywall with shards of broken mirror. And just last week, the Starfucker slayed Kago Demarco, an actor on some lawyer show on ABC—played some scheming paralegal. He was on his way to catch a flight to head home to South Africa for a week to be with his family after the loss of a parent, but instead of a rendezvous with his driver, he had a date with the Starfucker instead. He thought he was getting in a car to take him to the airport, but the only place he went to was Hell— slaughtered in that car, in a parking garage. Face stuck on the steering wheel, bowels bundled at his feet.

That one, nobody could hide.

Media caught wind of it.

And now it was a proper story. Which put the pressure on. So far, she hasn't delivered for Guerrero. Which means he hasn't delivered anything to her—she doesn't have the name of any medium, doesn't have any idea how to move forward. He's got her on a hook. And Miriam doesn't like being on a hook. But what other choice does she have?

"You'll make it happen," Gabby says. "I believe in you."

"What do you want from me, Gabs?"

Gabby, taken aback, asks, "What?"

"I mean—what are you doing with me, exactly? What's your point? Your . . . goal, your plans, your dreams?"

"God, more of this. Really? We're doing this now?"

"No, I'm not saying—"

"You are saying it, and I hear you loud and clear. You think I'm just some sucker along for the ride, some bit player in your big life. I'm not you. I don't have some insane gift or some crazy purpose. I'm like everybody else out there—I just want to live my life, pay my bills, have a bed under me every night. I want to eat tacos and ice cream and go to the beach. I want a life. I want a life with you. That's it. Not everybody is the ringleader of the circus, Miriam. Some people are just happy to see the show."

"This show is a shitshow."

Gabby thunks her head against the steering wheel. "Ugh. Talking to you is literally the worst sometimes."

Miriam thinks but does not say, *I think when Ashley Gaynes cut up your face, it broke you. It broke you like a mirror, and now all you see are shattered versions of me instead of yourself.* It makes her feel equally loved and saddened and angry all at once. Like, here's this woman who has given her so much but taken little for herself. All just to be a—how'd Gabby put it? A bit player in Miriam's big life.

Gabby goes on: "This is what normal life feels like, Miriam. Not solving murders, not talking to . . . fucking birds or mind-demons or whatever it is you've got going on. It's not about death; it's about life. Regular life. Not bloody, terrifying adventures, just regular adventures. Like sitting in a car, or having a baby, or snuggling under a blanket to watch goofy stuff on Netflix. I'm not *weak* just because I'm with you. I'm not *weak* just because I want . . . *something normal* for us."

"I didn't say you were weak."

"But you thought it."

I did think it.

"I also think if you want normal, you need to look elsewhere."

Gabby scowled. "But isn't that the point of all this? To get clear of the Trespasser? To put aside the gift? To get *normal*?"

"This isn't how I thought this conversation would go."

Silence.

Gabby pauses.

She leans back.

Blinks a few times.

"Oh, my fucking god," she says. "You're breaking up with me."

"What? No."

"You are."

"I'm not, shut up. God. I'm fucking—" Miriam draws a deep breath, exhales it. "I bought you something."

Now, Gabby looks *really* confused. "You bought me something."

"Yes. Yeah. Yes."

"Why? And what is it? Is it something mean?"

"No! It's not mean. I just thought—Christmas came and went while we were in Florida and you got me something." As if to demonstrate, she hooks her finger and pulls down the collar of her white T-shirt so that the owl necklace can be fully seen against the pale expanse of her chest. "And I thought of something I wanted to get you."

With that, she hauls her bookbag from between her legs, up onto her lap. She unzips it with a *vvviiiip* and roots around inside until she finds the thing, then pulls it out.

It's not wrapped. It's just surrounded in the crinkly brown boulder of a cheap paper bag.

"Is it heroin?" Gabby asks. "Did you buy me a brick of heroin?"

"It's not heroin, stop it. Just . . . just open it or whatever."

A dubious look plasters itself on Gabby's face as she unwraps the bag.

In a few moments, she is holding a snow globe.

She holds it up. The sun shines through it, casting prismatic light on the rough, scrapwork scars of her beautiful face. Inside the snow globe: the Hollywood sign. She turns it upside down and fake snow glitters, swimming through the water. It makes no sound, but in Miriam's mind, it does: a light, fairy-like piano tinkly-winkle.

"It's glass," Miriam says. "Not some cheapy plastic one. I mean, it's still cheapy, because it's a snow globe. But at least you can use it to smash in somebody's head if you have to."

"A multipurpose gift," Gabby says, wryly.

"See, there you go."

Gabby squints. "Why a snow globe?"

"Do you hate it? You hate it."

"No. I love it." Her face, scars and all, softens. Her eyes seem to glitter a little. She *does* love it. "I just want to know why."

Miriam thinks back to the cabin. Her and Louis. Snow falling. A slice of life captured in time, away from everything. Encased in a frozen bubble.

"I just thought it was pretty" is all she says.

"Thanks. I love you."

"I love you, too. I'm sorry I'm such a hot mess."

"Good news for you," Gabby says, reaching over the middle console to kiss Miriam's cheek. "I kinda *like* hot messes. Now, let's get inside and get you in the stirrups."

"You just want some coconut water."

"I really do!"

FORTY-SIX

SEX PARTY

"You're having a little girl," Dr. Shahini says. The obstetrician blinks. Her dark, fringed eyelashes are so big, so ostentatious, it looks as if they're coyly waving at Miriam. *Hello, hello.* In contrast, Dr. Shahini's voice is mostly steely and flat, like she's reading numbers off a spreadsheet, except that she always injects a lift when she says the last word, as she does here with "Congratulations."

Miriam can't tell if it's sarcasm or delight. Or, somehow, both.

On the screen of the ultrasound, the baby curls in on itself—*her*self. Little hands search strange fluid. A bundle of umbilicus strays from the child, wandering off into the dark of Miriam's body, like a tether, keeping it bound—but also keeping it safe. But now Miriam wonders: will that cord one day work its way around the child's neck? Will it cut off her baby's airway? Is that why it's born only to die? Can she stop that? How? Saving a life means ending one, and whose can end to preserve the baby's? Her own? Maybe. But would that even be possible now that she seems unable to suffer much harm for long? Harriet, when *shot in the head*, still began her crass reconstruction, emerging once more from the intimacy of near-death.

And now Miriam thinks, *The baby looks like a ghost.* A pale specter, diaphanous like a bedsheet held up against a moonlit window. The ultrasound paints it in the strangled blue-corpse color.

Miriam shudders.

Gabby gives her hand a little squeeze. It helps.

"A girl," Gabby says. Her voice is hopeful and light. Maybe this really is something for her.

"I don't want a girl," Miriam says, suddenly.

Eyes turn to her.

Even the baby's eyes seem to flick toward the screen, as if it—*she*—knows. *I'm watching you, Mama.*

"I don't want a daughter. I'd rather have a son."

"I apologize," Shahini says, the eerie flatness of her voice casting her sincerity in deep question. "But in this, you do not get to *choose*."

"I was told gender is a spectrum."

"Gender, yes. Gender is largely a social construct. Sex is not."

"But some people choose if they're boys or girls, and—"

"And your child can one day make that choice for herself. That is not your choice to make, and today is not that day. Today, I am telling you that you are having a daughter. What you do with that information is up to you."

The baby on the screen floats in the void. When it—oops, *she*—turns, Miriam can feel that movement inside her.

It's disconcerting, and she says so.

"You will grow comfortable with it," the doctor says. "The brain releases chemicals that help you respond pleasantly to the sensation."

A parasite has hijacked my body and has tricked it into liking it.

To her credit, Miriam does not say this out loud.

Though she still thinks this, and she reminds herself right now that it's probably high time to stop thinking of the baby as a parasite. It's just too weird. A *tinier human* has taken up residence inside her, the *larger human*. And it (she!) grew there from the size of a raspberry seed, swelling and swelling, and already now it's (she's!) got a fluttering heart and wiggling fingers and kicking feet (only two of them, but it honestly feels like a whole karate tournament in there). The baby is the size of a banana. One day, it will be the size of a cantaloupe, and then it will kung-fu kick its (*her her her*) way out of Miriam's vagina, probably—tearing the tract of skin leading up to her butthole along the way, because as it turns out, passing a cantaloupe through your vagina is naturally unnatural.

Oh! And maybe, just maybe, she'll shit herself.

Shahini explained that on their first visit to her. That, along with every other bit of body horror that will slowly unfold. All the heartburn and cramping, the bladder weakness and the hiccups and how the baby is in there gulping down amniotic fluid—which the child will then eventually poop out in some kind of rotten-seaweed, road-tar spread. Miriam's supposed to want this. She's supposed to love it.

And she's supposed to *save* it.

FORTY-SEVEN

The Deluge

Miriam cries forever. That's how it feels, anyway. She sobs on the way home. She weeps in the condo. She cries on the balcony *of* the condo. She spills tears in the bathroom because she has to pee, again, always again, always with the peeing. Crying while peeing, dehydrating her double-time.

Gabby, to her credit, lets it go. She doesn't push. Doesn't try to stop it or dam up the flow. She either knows that it needs to happen or she's figured out she can't cork that bottle.

Either way, she stays near.

Anxiety tears at Miriam like a starving animal. It feels like she's standing in a dark tunnel. A train is coming—one that is traveling far faster than she can run. Except here's the Shyamalan twist: it's not one train but two—even if she could outrun it, another one is rushing toward her from the other direction, and the two trains will crash, a sandwich of screaming metal. She, and her baby, and Gabby, are the meat. Somewhere, maybe there's a doorway hidden in the dark, an exit. Or maybe a lever she can pull to switch tracks and send one train screaming past the other. But she can't find them. She doesn't know where they are. She's lost. She's bleeding time.

You're the Riverbreaker. You can change the course of the river.

But it's not a river, she tells herself. *In this metaphor, it's a*

215

pair of fucking trains on the train track; keep up, you daffy bitch.

So, break the trains.

Shear the tracks.

Be so big, so fucking impossible, that even two screaming banshees of iron and steel cannot touch you even as they collide.

Change fate.

That's it.

Miriam blows her nose, throws open the door. She nearly runs into Gabby, who was clearly waiting by said door.

"You okay?" Gabby asks.

"Better than okay. I have a plan." She frowns. "Okay, I have no plan, but I'm starting to think there needs to *be* a plan. But first I need food. I need protein and carbs and fat and sugar. I need an In-N-Out burger. If I can't have a cigarette, if I can't have a jug of liquor, then I need *that*."

"I'll get the car."

"And we will dine like queens. Thrifty, meat-loving queens."

FORTY-EIGHT

THRIFTY, MEAT-LOVING QUEENS

They hit the In-N-Out on Sunset and Orange, across from the IHOP and near those storage units with all the cartoon faces graffitied all over them. It's the middle of the day, and on the corner there's a black drag queen yelling at a little old Vietnamese guy—just knock-down, drag-out screaming, their fists in the air, everybody frothing.

Miriam loves this city.

They sit outside at one of the two-tops.

With a mouthful of burger-meat, Miriam says, "I've been playing defense. I'm tired of playing defense. It's time to play offense." She narrows her gaze and pauses chewing. "That's a sports thing, right?"

"Sports and war," Gabby says with a shrug. Gabby, too, eats the burger with great vigor, which only makes Miriam more enamored.

"Like, I'm just sitting here, *waiting* for something to happen. I go into the trailer, I meet with Guerrero, we go out, I shake hands, I see how these vapid little fuckboys are going to die, and I'm no closer to finding the Starfucker. Which means I'm no closer to Guerrero giving me the name of that medium, which means I'm *no closer* to getting in touch with the Trespasser and saving your life, my life, and hopefully, the baby's life." That last part, she knows, is a little wifty. The Trespasser may not know

217

anything that can help her, but, her intrusive demon also told her, point-blank, that it would try to stop that child from being born. So maybe, just maybe, killing the Trespasser will save their future.

"How are you going to go after the Starfucker?"

"I'm not," she says, swallowing an unctuous wad of delicious grease, cheese, and cow. "Fuck the Starfucker. I don't care. He's killing actors in Los Angeles—cutting off faces, emptying their guts, it's gross, it's twisted, and it's not my problem. I'm not here to save the world, and it's not like these dudes are sad kittens or lost puppies. Half of them are venal, trustafarian idiots. The other half will become that way. Who cares?"

"But that's what you need to do to get the name from Guerrero."

"Maybe. Or *maybe* I just steal the name."

Gabby pauses in eating. She looks worried. "What does that mean?"

"He's got to have the name somewhere. He said he had a . . . a whaddyacallit, a spreadsheet. It *has* to be on his work computer, right?"

"Miriam, I don't know. You know that the Starfucker is going to try to kill that Bowman guy in two months. That's not a long time. Instead, just bide your time. Wait for the opportunity. Be patient and we'll get there."

"I've *been* patient. I don't *do* patient. Being patient has just left me frustrated, with time bleeding out on the floor like a throat-slit dog."

"You know I'm eating, right?"

Miriam shrugs. "Sorry. I'm just saying I want to handle this. I want to go after it. Fuck Guerrero if he thinks he can dangle this over me."

"This is dangerous. He can take all of what we have away. He can throw you in jail!"

"Ah, but only if he finds out. I don't intend to tell him. Do you?"

"You'll steal the name and keep playing along? Miriam, you didn't even know how to call a Lyft. How are you going to crack his computer?"

"Uhhh. Answer unclear, ask again later? I'll figure it out. I *need* that name." She wipes a smear of ketchup and mustard from her mouth. "Are you with me?"

But Gabby *isn't* with her.

She can see it in Gabby's eyes—hesitation flashing like light on the blade of a knife. Gabby hesitates. Looks away. Miriam follows her gaze and sees that on the corner, the drag queen and the little Asian guy are now hugging and swaying back and forth like late night bar-drunks lost to the rapture of Journey on the jukebox. Finally, Gabby groans and says, "I don't know. This sounds risky as hell."

"I need you with me on this. We can do this. Tell me you have my back if I need it."

"You don't need me. You . . . do what you want, when you want." Gabby pushes her burger aside.

"And I'm *tired* of doing that. You say you're with me? Well, reverse it. I'm with you. You tell me not to do it, then I won't do it. I'm done with running off, half-cocked, doing the thing without asking anyone else. I'm asking you. I'm *begging* you for your permission."

A narrowed gaze meets her. "What if I don't give it?"

"Then I . . . throw a tantrum?"

"*Miriam.*"

"Then I don't do it. End of story."

And here's the thing—

It's true. Miriam is floored by that internal revelation. Because, truth be told, she's the type to make this kind of promise and immediately break it. She won't be saddled, bridled, led around the yard like a show pony. She's Miriam Black. Fate's Foe, Riverbreaker, Kicker of the Grim Reaper's Skeletal Testes. She doesn't just *not* do the insane shit she proposes she do. That would be, well—

That would be very un-Miriam.

And yet she says it.

And she *means* it.

Two things that for her are usually very different.

That's when she realizes Gabby's going to tell her no. She's going to say to play it safe, play it easy, and that'll be that. But maybe, Miriam tells herself, that's the right call. It's not like running off half-cocked has really been the good decision, mmm, *ever*. She's a cat chasing a laser pointer into the mouth of a wood-chipper, every time, right? Wouldn't it be smart to do the opposite for once? *Just* once? Gabby's going to tell her no, and that would be for the best, really, it would be the smartest decis—

"Let's do it," Gabby says, a wicked grin forming on her face.

"For real?"

"For real."

"Oh, shit."

"You should really come up with a plan."

Miriam agrees: "I should *really* come up with a motherfuck-ing plan. One more burger, though. You know. For *brain energy*. And I'm eating for two now, I hear."

FORTY-NINE

THE MOTHERFUCKING PLAN IS...

"What?" Steve Wiebe asks.

He's at the condo pool again. Not in the pool this time, but rather, on a patio chair, sprawled out with a Laura Lippman paperback tented on his chest. He does that quintessential 1980s move where he dips his white-rim sunglasses down over his nose so he can stare out over the top. Miriam casts her shadow upon him, blocking the midday sun.

"Yeah, I'm not getting it either," Gabby says, arms crossed. "And I'd like to get it real soon, because otherwise, I'm gonna be late for work."

"Steve," Miriam begins, "*knows* shit about shit. He can help us *hack into* Guerrero's computer."

Steve stares. "I can?"

"You can."

"I . . . don't think I can."

"But you said all the fancy words. In our first cab ride, you talked about *cryptocurrency* and *eight-bit-coins*—"

"Bitcoins. And it was a Lyft, not a cab." Under his breath he says, "We've been over this like six times."

"Whatever. I'm just saying, that stuff you said, that's hacker shit."

"It's not hacker shit, it's just . . . millennial internet shit."

"But you *know* hackers."

"I . . . don't think I do? I mean, I might, but they don't advertise it."

Miriam is growing frustrated. "You drive all these people around, and you don't know a single hacker who can help me hack a computer."

"Again, maybe; people are chatty. But I don't have their private information. I can't . . . just find them and say, *I need you to hack the FBI for me, cool hacker guy.*"

"And you're sure *you're* not a hacker."

Steve's mouth purses into a dubious pucker. "Do I look like a hacker? I don't see a black hoodie and a sickly pallor. I'm colorful. I'm at the pool."

Miriam growls and petulantly steps aside, letting the sun's angry rays punch him right in the eyes. Steve swats at the light as if it's a swarm of biting flies before pushing his sunglasses back up into his face.

But the rage doesn't last long. Strange, in a way, because for Miriam, rage is a kind of fuel, long-burning like an underground coal fire. Her rage has sustained her. Suddenly, though, as fast as it arrived, it's gone again. And in its wake is a special kind of despair. She can feel those two trains bearing down on her and all that she loves.

She doesn't bother kicking off her boots when she sits down at the edge of the pool and dunks both feet into the water.

Gabby comes up on one side. Steve on the other.

"It'll be all right; we'll figure something out," Gabby says.

But we won't.

I won't.

You won't.

Steve says, "Besides, I'm not sure hacking the FBI is . . . advisable? They have to have pretty intense security. That building looks like an uncrackable rock. Cameras everywhere, a secure network—"

"I don't work in that building," she says, bleakly.

"Where do you work?"

"In a trailer. In a parking lot. Across the street."

Steve half-snorts a laugh. "Wait, what? You work in a trailer?"

"We're kinda off the books."

"Is the computer you want to access right there in the trailer?"

She shrugs. "Yeah."

"Can't you just . . . access it when he's off taking a whiz?"

"I don't know that Guerrero *does* piss. And the only time Julie leaves the trailer is to, I dunno, change her fucking robot batteries."

"Is that it? You work with two other people? Gimme all the deets."

So, she does. She tells Steve and Gabby the ins and outs of her days: most of the time, they're off-site, on sets, shaking the hands of actors and witnessing the unfolding array of overdoses and car crashes that end their precious, preening lives. All in search of the elusive Starfucker. When they're in the trailer, it's the three of them. It's Guerrero, so tense that she can see his heartbeat pulsing in his jaw, looking through papers, or on his phone, or on his laptop. It's Julie, who floats in and out between the trailer and the big building, apparently working cases that don't intersect with this one, at least as far as Miriam can tell.

"Does he lock the computer when he walks away from it?"

"Like with a fucking padlock?"

"No, I mean—does he close the laptop, does it go back to a black screen? Do you need to re-enter a password to get back into it?"

She tries to think back. "Shit, I don't know. I don't think so."

A shadow passes over Steve's face. "Oh, no."

"*Oh, no* what?"

"Oh, *no*."

Gabby and Miriam share a quizzical look.

"What's your prob, dude?" Miriam asks.

"I have an idea." But the way he says it, it's like the idea is pure ash in his mouth. Like he's somehow simultaneously sad about the world and disappointed in himself. "I can't believe I'm saying this, but I think I can help you."

"Seriously?"

"I'm going to regret this."

"Probably," Miriam says. "But you have a plan?"

"I think I have a plan."

"Is it a motherfucking plan?"

"I don't . . . I don't know what that means."

Miriam slaps her hands together. The despair she felt is suddenly golden, glowing with the renewed flames of hope and chaos. "Sounds like we got ourselves a brand new *motherfucking plan*. We're gonna do this."

"Ugh."

FIFTY

RED WREN

It's late. Or it's early. Miriam's awake, standing in their little galley kitchen, drinking a glass of milk. It seems to help the heartburn, which presently feels like someone ran her throat over a citrus zester. It's so bad, her trachea flutters, like a spasming snake.

So, there she stands, drinking milk in the dark.

Fear pushes through her like fingers in dirt. Grabbing whole clumps of her, roots and stones and earth, and flinging it into the void. And every time a part of her is ripped away, more fear slithers into that wound.

Tomorrow is the big day. The Motherfucking Plan, Part Two. And it could go very poorly. If she gets caught, that's it. It's game over for them.

Someone steps into the kitchen with her. A familiar shape.

"Hey, Gabs," she does not say so much as she croaks.

"Miriam," says Wren.

A sliver of half-light from the microwave confirms it:

It *is* Wren. Still looking like Miriam. White T-shirt, knife-slashed jeans, big black boots. Her hair is dyed red like Louis's blood, and the bangs are ratty and uneven. Miriam moves fast, her hand darting out like an eel to seize its prey—and in an instant, she's got a chef's knife in her hand, the angular blade slashing the air: less a threat, more a promise.

"I *told* you," Miriam seethes, "that if I ever saw you again, I'd kill you. You little fucker."

Then Wren laughs. It is a wretched sound: wet and splashing, like it's gabbling up through the water and mud of an old, algae-slick pond. Miriam can see black water pushing through the girl's mouth, forcing over her lips like high tide over a rotten boardwalk. It spatters on the linoleum.

It's not Gabby.

And it's not Wren, either.

"You," Miriam says to the Trespasser.

It has been some time since she's seen the demon. Not since that night nearly two months ago, when Gabby spoke with its voice here in their bedroom. Miriam still holds the knife, now as less of a threat and more of an accusing finger. She knows she cannot kill this thing. Not here.

Not yet.

"Haven't caught the Starfucker yet," Not-Wren hisses. "*Tsk-tsk.* Those pretty boys, dying with their faces sliced like fancy ham."

The Trespasser takes a step into the kitchen. Toward the knife.

"That what you want from me? To solve that case? Catch yet another killer? Too bad, fuckhead. I've already given up. I don't care about it."

Wren laughs, shaking her head. "No, no, no, you just think you've given up. Like so many times before. You don't see it, do you? I don't make you do these things. You do them because you're you. I'm the gun. You're the one that points me and pulls the trigger. You can't *help* doing what needs to be done, because I chose you well."

"Oh, so now you *chose* me."

Another laugh. "I did."

"I thought you were on the side of free will."

"Oh," Not-Wren says, feigning innocence. "I am. I am the

avatar of free will—*you're* the one choosing the path, Miriam. Sometimes, I . . . plant signs along the way to help you through the dark, though."

Another step forward. The tip of the knife blade is only inches away from Wren's chest.

"I choose the path away from you. I'm getting closer. Closer to shutting you out. To closing the door."

"Are you, though? You think you're walking into the light, but you could just be walking into the fire. You're fumbling with your clumsy fingers, thinking you're *untying the knot,* when really you're just pulling the rope tighter."

Again, Not-Wren steps forward.

Now, the tip of the blade is just against her middle. Against the soft middle, underneath the gentle V of her ribcage.

Miriam knows it's not real. No—that's not it.

It's real, just not tangible.

The Trespasser is an intrusive phantom. A creature of lies. Insubstantial as a bad dream. But right now, the way the knife presses against Not-Wren's skin—it has pushback, it has presence, she can feel the subtle, springy bounce of the blade not-yet-sinking into the flesh. Flesh that isn't real but that damn sure *feels* real.

"You want to know the trick?" Not-Wren asks.

"Fuck you."

"The trick is, you are the architect of your own undoing, Miriam. You stand there, saying *never again* as you set up another winding trail of dominoes, saying *I won't knock them over this time,* and then you do—and it's not an accident, you don't nudge the dominoes with a heel, you don't bump into them with your elbow as you're setting them up. You line them all up, nice and neat, thinking that *this time* you'll keep them standing, and then off you go again! To the front of the line, where you put out your hand, tuck back your finger, and *flick* the lead domino once again, and there they go, *clickety-clack*ing against one another—"

Fuck this.

Miriam stabs forward with the knife.

Her elbow urges the blade forth, and it sinks in deep—the sensation is grotesquely satisfying, like pushing her thumb into soft, warm bread; like easing a foot down into cool clay; like urging her finger deep into Gabby's wetness, a delicious, penetrative thrust—

She looks up to meet Not-Wren's eyes.

But that's not whose eyes she sees.

It's her own.

She's standing there, arm out, blade buried into her own middle. Miriam—no, Not-Miriam—opens her mouth, agape, and all that emerges is a mousy, panicked squeak.

"Wh . . . why?" Not-Miriam begs.

"I . . . I don't . . ."

Then Not-Miriam smiles. "And the dominoes fall."

Then the Trespasser is gone.

And for a moment, Miriam is alone in the darkness, with only herself and the silence and the gleam of the blade in her hand. But then something twists up in her middle: a knot tightening so hard, the thread begins to fray. Then whatever it is, it breaks—like a twig snapping, like a snow globe breaking and spilling out all that was inside it.

"No," she says, her voice small.

She feels the wetness down there, spreading. *I pissed myself,* she thinks, but when her hand falls to the space between her legs and returns, it's slick with red. Her limbs start to wobble, gone weak.

"No, no, no," she says, pleading with whoever will listen.

The knife falls from her hands.

She cries out for Gabby as she falls to the kitchen floor.

FIFTY-ONE

ANOTHER BROKEN SNOW GLOBE

She keeps saying it again and again: "It's dead. The baby is dead. I can't feel it. *I can't feel her in there.*" Miriam lies there in the hospital bed, hands holding on to the cold metal bedrails so hard, her fingertips buzz with encroaching numbness. Gabby soothes her, brushing hair out of her face, rubbing her arms and her shoulders. She's telling her that it'll be okay, that Dr. Shahini is on her way, but Miriam already knows what's coming:

The baby is dead.

The Trespasser killed it.

She says this: "The demon did it. It killed my baby."

"You don't know that. Your little girl is supposed to live—your vision should tell you that." Gabby does not further that thought, but Miriam understands: her vision of the child's demise comes upon birth, roughly nineteen weeks from now. But Gabby doesn't get it.

"The Trespasser isn't like people. It's like me. It can *change* fate, I think. It can kill my baby early. It can take you from me early, too."

"You don't know that," Gabby says in a lowered voice, as if recognizing how absurd all of this sounds. "If the Trespasser could change fate, it wouldn't need you."

"It's gaining power, though. It's . . . changing."

"We'll figure it out, for now—"

The door to the room opens, and in walks Shahini with a resident.

Shahini stares down with her dour, severe face and says:

"Subchorionic hematoma."

"What does that mean? Is my baby okay? What happened to the—"

"The baby is fine." The resident wheels in an ultrasound machine. The goop goes on the belly. The wand presses there, rolling against the growing roundness of Miriam's middle. And then Shahini shows her: sure enough, there is her little girl, curled up around her own body, a human cashew.

She's sucking her thumb.

Miriam almost laughs. A mad sense of relief fills her. She didn't want this baby at first. Then she wanted her, just to escape the shackles of the Trespasser and to honor Louis—her desire to see the child live was unabashedly selfish. But in this moment, she wants the child to live. Not for any other reason than because the baby is hers, and she loves her daughter.

Shahini points out pockets of dark matter on the screen. "This is blood. You had a mild placental hemorrhage. It . . . happens. Sometimes, it's a sign of a larger problem, potentially an infection or injury, but—whatever it was, your body has already healed it."

A mad thought skitters through Miriam's mind:

Thank you, Harriet Adams.

"You may," Shahini continues, "experience some more bleeding or spotting for the next week or two, but nothing serious, I don't expect."

"You'll be there, right?" Miriam asks.

Shahini raises one of her considerable eyebrows. Her lashes flutter with a kind of dubious confusion. "Be where, and when?"

"You're the one who will deliver this baby."

"I will, for as long as you remain my patient."

"Good." *Because*, Miriam thinks, *I trust you.* It's an odd feeling, because truly, she trusts almost no one in this world, especially now with the life of her baby. Gabby, yes. Steve, maybe, okay. Guerrero and Anaya, not at all, not anymore. Shahini, definitely.

And Wren, too—

That is a puzzling thought. One she does not invite, but there it is, like a vampire waltzing into her house anyway.

Wren, who killed Louis.

Wren, who was a pawn of the Trespasser too.

Wren, who has killed so many.

Why would she trust her? A part of her misses her, though. It was seeing the Trespasser appear as Wren. *Maybe Wren is like the daughter you fucked up. Maybe this one, the one in your belly right now, can be the one you save. The one who stays good. Who doesn't turn into* you.

"Thanks," Miriam says to Shahini, lost suddenly in her own mind.

"Go home, get some rest," the doctor advises. Then she turns, heel to toe, and walks out.

FIFTY-TWO
ACCELERATING TOWARD DISASTER

Back at the condo. It's 4 AM. Neither of them are sleeping. Miriam sits propped up against the headboard with a lot of pillows. Gabby brings in a glass of water, urges her to drink it, which she does.

"Maybe we need to call off the plan," Gabby says.

"No. I don't know. Shit."

"You probably shouldn't even go *in* tomorrow."

"I'm going in."

"Miriam, after today—"

"I said I'm going in. And the plan is still on."

Gabby sits next to her. "Listen. You heard Shahini. She's your OB, long as you stay her patient. If you . . . mess with Guerrero, if he drops you from that plan, she's gone. You'll end up with whatever ER doctor is on duty, and . . . then what?"

"The Trespasser was sending me a message, Gabby. It came to me. It looked like Wren. And then it . . . *did* something to me. I don't think it was going to kill the baby; I think it was letting me know it can. Or it could. When this kid is born, when she comes into the world, I think it's the Trespasser that kills her. Just as I think it'll be the Trespasser that kills you." Her hands ball up into fists. "That fucker told me that I have free will, that it just . . .

points me toward the path. I think it burns down all the paths it doesn't want me to take so I go where it wants. And I'm tired of doing that. I need the name of that medium. I need to know what I'm dealing with."

"There have to be other mediums in this town. Christ, I bet they have Yelp reviews and everything—"

"And they're not the real deal. None of them are like me. I need *real* psychics, not a bunch of greedy little fuckbabies who are fleecing Beverly Hills housewives. They're all going to pretend to be real, but not a one of them will be."

Gabby nods. She's not on board; Miriam can see that. But she must know not to push. Miriam's heels are dug so far in, she's up to her neck.

"The plan is on," Miriam says again, saying it louder this time as if to make it sound like a good decision and not the very bad one it probably is.

FIFTY-THREE

THE CLOCKWATCHER

THE NEXT DAY.

Miriam's queasy and tired. She sits in the trailer, at a desk. What little sleep she got before coming into work today was plagued by nightmares: not the living nightmares of the Trespasser but garden-variety anxieties, unsheathed and ripped from their cocoons, a parade of crawling worms and snakes. Gabby, dead, her face broken into pieces like a shattered clay pot. Her daughter, pulled from her womb and dropped into a trash bin as a red Mylar balloon floated over Miriam's body. Louis, a gunshot cratering his temple, suddenly looking up with one eye gone yellow and sickly, the other staying white because it's fake, and he whispers her name and asks her why she let him die. Then there's Wren. Standing astride it all. The gun still in her hand. She says she's sorry even as she points the gun at Miriam.

So, she's not just bone-weary from the events of the night before, but she's *soul-tired*, too. Like her body and her soul were both dragged behind a speeding car over a rough and ragged road.

She glances at her watch: a calculator watch she's worn on and off since the old days, the scavenger days, her vulture days. It's beat to hell, the watch. So scratched and chipped you can barely read the time on it. Those days of seeing how people were going to die, then ripping off their corpses and running for the hills, pockets flush with cash and credit cards and whatever else she could steal from the carcass. The watch was one such plunder.

T-minus thirty-seven minutes.

In thirty-seven minutes, the Motherfucking Plan begins.

It ain't much of a plan, but it's what they have.

In the meantime, it's a day of treading water. She knew this going in: it's a Monday, and Guerrero explained that today meant forming a new plan, setting up more meetings, more handshakes. Which more or less means *he's* doing it—the man is on a tear, buoyed by the anger and desperation born of having suffered another dead actor just last week. Today being a day of treading water is essential, in fact, for the Motherfucking Plan.

It means, though, that the minutes crawl by like a gut-shot old man dragging himself across broken glass.

Guerrero sits on his computer. Then he's up again and looking at crime scene photos. Then back at the computer, and his phone, and up again to the table. He's agitated. It's like watching a fish in a fish tank go back and forth, picking up pebbles and moving them from one end to the other. All the while, he keeps throwing her these *looks*.

Little, flitting glances.

Eyes narrowed.

Lips in a firm, conservative line.

She knows the look. Her mother used to make it.

"You're disappointed in me," she says out loud.

He halts his reiterative movement and stiffens. "Excuse me?"

"I see the looks you're giving me. I know your deal. You're disappointed in me, David Guerrero."

At that, the door to the trailer opens, and in walks Julie Anaya. She's got a latte. She doesn't do Guerrero's "pour-over" nonsense, she said; she likes steamed milk and espresso. Miriam did her old line then: *I like my coffee like I like my men, hot, black, and coming down my throat*, but that didn't earn her any favors. She didn't even get a tiny little smirk. Just disdain and silence. No fun, these people. No fun at all.

Guerrero continues, even as Julie gives him a curious side-eye. "To be honest, I am disappointed. We've lost two more on your watch."

"My watch? It's your watch. It's the whole FBI's watch. I'm just a consultant, big guy. I consulted. I've given you actionable information that, in two months, that vapid piss-boy Taylor Bowman will get his face sliced off in some office back room."

"And where is this back room? Where's the office?"

"I don't know. You're supposed to be Sherlock. Don't you have other psychics to help you out?"

He says nothing. Worry scratches at the back of her head like rats in the wall: *Does he have other psychics? Does he really have a name to give you? Or is he just dangling a lie as bait to get you on the hook?*

Finally, he says, "Nobody with any skill in this regard."

"Fine, so, that day, you just put a detail on Taylor Bowman. You follow him. He'll lead you right to the killer."

"That's in two months. That means we still lose another. *And* we lost two already."

"Because of me. That's what you're not saying, but I still hear you saying it. Like a *whisper* between your words."

He nods, hands on hips. "I place a little responsibility on you."

"But none on yourself, of course."

"More on myself. Because I don't have anything to go on. I have you. I'm relying on you. Which, you know, no, that's not your fault, and maybe it's not mine. Maybe it's just supposed to shake out that way. But I can't help feeling disappointed in myself and in you because neither of us are saving lives. We're just sitting *here*—" He extends his arms, as if to regard the whole wide world. "In this terrible little box. Waiting. Just . . . waiting.

Waiting for a day to come where maybe we can catch this predator and end his reign of terror."

"*Reign of terror* is a little extreme. He's killing actors."

"Actors are still people."

Miriam gives a half-hearted shrug. "Ennnh."

She gives her watch a passing glance. Still got twenty-three
minutes left.

Tick-tock, tick-tock.

"Sorry, am I boring you?" he asks.

Shit, he must've seen her looking at the watch.

Might as well lean into it, she figures.

"*To be honest*," she says, aping his voice. "I am bored."

"I'm not. I'm fired up. I'm ready to get this done."

She shakes her head, incredulous. "Why *are* you so fired up?
You're intense. You're like a fucking laser beam right in my eye."

Julie watches the exchange with detached curiosity.

Guerrero grabs his office chair and wheels it over to Miriam's
seat. He sits right in front of her, knee-to-knee. His intensity
doesn't dwindle; it only ratchets up tighter. He's like a star about
to go supernova.

"We're real. You and me and Julie over there? We're the real
deal. These things we can do—" And here Miriam thinks: *But
I still don't know what you and Julie can do, David Guerrero.*
"They're legit. But they come at a cost, and you know that. We
paid the price. So, we need to make some good come of it. We
need to get our money's worth."

And that's when she gets it.

"I see," she says, nodding. "I got your number now. Some bad
shit happened to you, gave you whatever curse you're carrying
on your back like Jesus with his cross, and now you think you're
a martyr. Or worse, a *crusader*. You want to make sense out of
what happened to you, so at least it gave you some kind of purpose, some goal, some power that takes the curse and convinces

you—and apparently, the world—it's a gift instead."

He leans back. Quietly, he says, "So, you do know."

"Know what?"

"How we're made. How we get our . . ." He taps his head. "Tricks."

Miriam nods. "A woman named Sugar explained it to me. It's trauma. Bad things happen, and it snaps something inside us like little wishbones." *You're one broken cookie, Miriam. . . .* "And then we are reborn with . . . whatever terrible power grows inside our *wound.*"

"That's right. Trauma." He steeples his fingers together. "You ever hear of a moonflower?"

"Sounds like the name some celebrity gives to their spoiled kid."

"A moonflower is really just a flower—it's a pretty flower, grows on a snaking vine. It blooms in the darkness. That's what I want for myself and others, like you. To bloom in the darkness."

"That's poetic. What's your darkness, Dave?"

He hesitates. He gives Julie a look. Does Julie know his story? She's about to, if not.

"I was ten years old," he begins. "I was taken."

Here, Guerrero slips off his suit jacket.

"It was winter in Oregon. A man drove up as I was walking home from school, and he chased me down, put a bag over my head, threw me in the trunk of his car, and drove off."

He undoes his tie.

"I was not the only child he abducted. I was with seven others. We were kept in a pen outside like animals. Tall fences. Coils of barbed wire at the top. We had our jackets and we huddled together at night for warmth as the temperature dropped. Then two days later, he took one of us out of the pen, kicking and screaming. Another boy—Jeremy. We were all boys. He liked boys. We heard the boy screaming inside the man's farmhouse."

Guerrero begins to unbutton his white, starchy shirt.

"The next day, we saw him dragging the boy out by one heel. Jeremy was dead. Bloody, too. Dragged out through the icy, slushy mud. The man moved aside a piece of half-rotten plywood under a dead willow tree and tossed the boy down into what turned out to be an old, disused well."

He finishes unbuttoning his shirt. His chest is bare, mostly hairless.

"This happened again a couple days later—this time, a boy named Carlos. Same situation. Screaming inside the house. The screaming cut short. Next morning, Carlos was dead, tossed into the well. We tried to escape, tried to dig out under the fence. But the ground was cold, nearly frozen, and we were young. Our hands were bruised and bloody just from trying, and he sank the fenceposts and the chain link deep. We screamed, too, shrieking into the woods, across the fields—but we couldn't see any other houses, any signs of anything. And no one came."

He slips off his shirt.

"I said, *I'm leaving*. And the other boys said, *How?* I said, *I'm going to climb one of those fenceposts. I'm going to take off my shoes and get a toe hold on the chain link, and haul myself up*. I was always climbing trees at home, and I thought, *I could do this*. So, up I went. Even as it started to rain a cold, nasty rain, I went. Then I slipped and fell, hurt my ankle, but I tried again, because I thought, *I'm not going to be like Jeremy. I'm not going out like Carlos. I want to live*. So, I climbed up. Inch by inch. The fence, wavering back and forth. When I got to the coils of razor wire . . ."

He pivoted himself to reveal his bare back.

It was laced with puffy, pale scar tissue. Not as boldly scarred as Gabby's face, but worse overall—so many slices, each crossing the other. He didn't have to explain how he crawled out—he went under the wire. Shimmying back and forth. The blades of the wire cutting him this way and that as he went. It was plain to see: a roadmap of his pain.

"I was going to climb back down," he continues, "but the blood slicked my hands and I fell the ten feet. Broke my left collarbone—"

He rotates his left arm. She can hear a palpable popping.

"Still clicks when I move it. Hurts a little, too."

"What happened?"

"I passed out for a little while but then woke up as the rain intensified. And then I left. I walked across a field at midnight. I wandered into the woods. At some point, I was so cold and in such pain I just . . . fell over and passed out. I would've died if a local farmer—a pot farmer, if we're being honest—found me, took me to the police. I helped them catch him, the man who took me. John Samuel Solomon was his name. He got the death penalty for it." He pauses. "They found the other boys, too. Of the four remaining, three were still alive. They found the bodies of the others in the well—alongside six boys who had gone missing the previous winter. All sexually assaulted. All murdered with a claw hammer. That would've been my fate had I not escaped. Violated and executed by Solomon."

"And after that, you awoke with a new curse."

He smiles. "I consider it a gift."

"And what is your gift?"

But he doesn't answer. Which makes her suspect: why isn't he telling her? After that whole story, *why*? It's something he explicitly does not want her to know. It's not incidental. It's willful.

What he *does* say is: "So, that's why I have such intensity for catching this killer. These young male actors, they may be vapid, they may be rich little pricks, but they still don't deserve the torment. They deserve someone trying to save them from their fates."

It's at this moment that Miriam feels a pang of empathy for him.

She understands him. She doesn't feel bad for him, not really—but she gets it. He really does have a cross to bear. Just as she has hers.

It makes her feel guilty that she's about to pull one over on him.

But she doesn't have any choice. His story was harrowing, and his purpose may be true. He's still keeping her at arm's length. She still needs that name, and he still has it. It is what it is.

As he's putting his shirt back on, it affords her the chance to take a surreptitious glance at her watch.

Eleven minutes.

So, it shocks her when he, after slipping on his jacket, grabs the keys to his car. "C'mon, let's take a ride."

"What?" she asks.

"I'm tired of sitting here. Julie can watch the shop. You and I are going back out. We're going to . . . do something. I'm tired of sitting here, and I see that you are too. I'll make some calls on the way; we'll get on a location shoot or a lot or something. I think HBO is doing a casting call today in Santa Monica. Maybe that'll turn something up."

Shit. She needs to be *here* for this to work.

Stall him.

"I . . . don't feel so good."

"What?"

"I—you know, I've got the blahs."

"The what?"

"The blahs. The ughs. The pukes. I don't—" She makes a Mr. Yuk face and pats her stomach. "It's the baby. Morning sickness."

"I thought you were over that."

"I *was* until you told me a story about child rape and murder. Take a moment to think about how that affects a mother-to-be."

His nostrils flare. "I would *think* it would help motivate you." But then he wilts a little. "Okay. I see your point, though. You need to use the bathroom?" He points toward their little bathroom with a thumb.

"I do; I'll be out in a few."

"All right. Make it quick—if you can. I'm done blaming you and I'm done feeling bad. I'm ready to work if you are."

"You got it, boss."

And then she slides mopishly into the bathroom.

FIFTY-FOUR

THUMP-BUMP

She sits.

She waits.

She checks her watch.

Occasionally, she fakes some high-quality pukey noises.

She pees, because, c'mon, she pretty much always has to pee.

She imagines what that must've been like, to be Little Davey Guerrero, trapped in a pen like an animal with a bunch of other kids, kids you know are about to get killed and dumped unceremoniously into a well—kids you only later find out were *raped* before they were *clubbed to death with a hammer*. That miserable crawl up a fence in the freezing rain. The razors at your back. The fall. The escape, not certain if the boogeyman is coming after you, in the dark, in the cold.

No wonder it scarred him. Physically and psychically, it seems.

He probably still wakes up with nightmares. She wonders now if he too has a Trespasser. Wren seemed to. (Though Miriam still thinks that Wren's specter may have just been her own, playing the game from another angle.) Still, Trespasser or no, he must be a haunted man. She has to forgive him his attitude, at least a little. He's a dick, but now she knows why.

Of course, Miriam is still going to betray him. Because she has no other choice. He had to make his choice and she has to make hers now.

He knocks on the door. "You ready?"

"Almost. Just washing up."

Idly, she spins the faucet, lets it run, *pshhhh*. She splashes some on her hands, more for the auditory effect than anything.

Three minutes left.

C'mon, Steve Wiebe, don't fail me now. They synchronized their watches and everything, like kiddie superspies.

She steps out of the bathroom.

"Let's go," he says, headed to the door.

His computer screen is dark. Panic stabs her in the heart like an icicle. That won't work. It has to be on. Not password-locked. But screen on and open. She improvises:

"Hey, can you pull up your computer real quick? I want to show you something."

"It can wait."

"No, it's important."

He's suspicious. "What is it?"

"A cat video. It's a cat who uses a toilet *and then flushes.* It's . . . pretty amazing."

"Miriam—"

"Settle down. It's related to the vision. The Taylor Bowman one. I haven't figured out where he dies yet, but I've gone over the memory and—c'mon, I just need Google Maps."

He sighs.

He's not going for it, she realizes—

Until he does. He shakes his head, awakens the laptop by lifting the screen. Guerrero quick-types in a long string of characters. What opens is his desktop, revealing an image of a black sand beach framed by lush greenery and a palm tree bulging with coconuts. David is in the picture, wearing a yellow Hawaiian shirt, holding up his hand in a gesture with the thumb and pinky out, but the other three fingers tucked to the palm.

"Where is that?" Miriam asks.

"Maui. Place called Hana. Ever been?"

"I'm not exactly a Hawaii type of girl."

"Hana, though—you'd like it. Away from everything. Hard to access. It's peaceful. It's like . . . the end of the world. But in the best way."

"Cool," she says, feigning interest. "All right, just pull up the maps thingy," she says, trying like hell not to sound impatient.

He reaches for the keyboard.

And then, like clockwork—

Thump-bump.

The entire trailer judders with an impact.

Something has hit their trailer. And Miriam knows exactly what.

Or, rather, *who.*

Guerrero curses under his breath and then stands, alarmed. He and Julie and Miriam all head toward the door—

And as those two go out, Miriam remains inside. And she gently nudges the door shut. And then she gently locks it.

She figures she's got about three minutes. Outside the trailer, right now, Steve Wiebe has backed his car into the corner of the trailer. Gently, so as not to do much or any damage to his car or the structure—but just enough to kick over this anthill and make the bugs come running.

Through the walls, she can hear the muffled murmurs of Steve and Guerrero talking: Wiebe's tone is plaintive, apologetic. Guerrero's voice sounds stiff, steely, and angry.

Good.

Miriam pulls the laptop up, now open.

She doesn't know a hot hunk of shit about how to actually *use* a computer in the way that she needs to, but Gabby gave her some instructions—the computer is a Mac, so she goes to something called the Finder and pulls that open. She clicks over to the documents and scans the list—it's hundreds of

CHUCK WENDIG

files, various documents and spreadsheets and—

Panic hits her.

I don't know what I'm looking for.

I have no idea why I thought this would work.

She scrolls, faster and faster, more and more anxious, as names of files zip past at breakneck, whiplash pace—

But then—

Team_personnel.xls

Bingo.

There it is. That's gotta be it. She clicks it open and—

It asks for a password.

She cannot continue until she enters in a password.

She knows she should stop here. Let go. Give in, give up. This plan isn't working. But she's *so fucking close*. Try, she must, so try, she does.

She types in:

password

Nope.

password1234

And, no.

She tries three more: *qwerty, 1234567890*, and, finally, *fuckyoufuckyoufuckyou*.

Unsurprisingly, none are the key to the kingdom.

She sits there. Chest heaving in panic. The baby chooses *now* to remind Miriam of her presence, stabbing out with a hard kick, hard enough to make Miriam think the baby is literally trying to escape—just the same, after last night's hospital visit, she's happy to feel the kid in there at all. She doesn't know what she'd do now if she lost her.

Lost her.

Losing a child.

Trauma, terror, pain—

That's it.

She types in:

JohnEdwardSolomon

Aaaaaand—

No.

"Shit!"

Wait.

What about . . .

Solomon.

One word. Just the last name. That's how Guerrero referred to him the last time. Right? *Violated and executed by Solomon.* A name as much as a title. Almost mythic and biblical. She types it in.

The file opens.

And the angels did sing.

Miriam lets out a mad half-laugh, half-sigh. She almost wants to cry.

It's a list of five names. Miriam's is one. The rest, in order, are:

Juliet Anaya | Clairsentience (Abhijñā?)

Samira Abbar | Hypnosis?

Abraham Lukauskis | Mediumship / Manifestation

Lizzie Priest | "Bloodstopper" (folk practice)

Each comes with a phone number and address. Two of them are here in Los Angeles: Juliet, aka Julie, obviously. And the other is Abraham Lukauskis. Abraham is the medium, and so Miriam thinks, *He's the one.* Quickly, she scrambles around for a Post-it note and a pen, and scribbles down his deets. She thinks, *What about the others?* Fuck it; she writes those down, too. Not that she has any idea what a Bloodstopper is, or what clairsentience—Abhijñā?—even means, but information is power, she tells herself, even if that information leads to fewer exclamation points and more question marks. Quickly, she folds up the note and shoves it into her pocket, and—

That's when the door to the office rattles against the lock.   **247**

Shit! She rushes to close the windows she has open even as she hears his keys jangling, the lock turning. Miriam starts to pull away from the computer, but the wheel of the office chair is caught—the laptop pulls toward the edge of the desk as the power cable is tugged taut. The laptop clatters to the floor, the screen splitting with a hard crack—

Just as the door opens.

There stands David Guerrero.

He's surprisingly fast, taking advantage of her shock. He's already up to his desk, grabbing the laptop off the floor even as she backs away. The screen is bright, but now bleeding weird colors behind the crack. She can feel the rage bleeding off of him like the acrid tang of expended gunpowder—and, before she knows it, he has his pistol pointed at her head.

"You set this all up," he says, his voice cold but trembling with the threat of boiling over. "That shit outside right now? That's you, isn't it?"

"I . . . I can explain," she says.

The pistol does not waver. "So, explain."

At that, Julie comes back inside. She watches this unfold with little emotion registering on her face. Like it's an idle curiosity to her.

"I . . . I've waited long enough for you to give me the name of the medium," Miriam says through clenched teeth. "I've helped you with the case. I deserve to get what's owed to me. I started to wonder if you even *had* a name to give me. So, I did what I did. I set up a friend to back into the trailer so I could try to find the name on your computer."

"Looks like you found it."

"I did."

"You're under arrest."

Tears burn at the corners of her eyes. "Don't. Please."

"Miriam, we had a deal. You broke the deal."

"*You* broke the deal," she growls.

"Stand up."

Wincing, she stands. She stares down the black eye socket of his Glock. His finger hovers just outside the trigger guard.

She tries to imagine how she's going to play this. She can't go to jail. *Won't* go to jail. That course of action could be exactly what leads her to the place where her daughter dies upon entering this world. She needs to be out here. She needs to pursue the Trespasser, which means finding the medium.

So, what's the play, then? She can't compete with a gun held only seven inches from her head. Harriet's strange, heart-given gift thrums through her, vibrating with secret power and promise, and maybe, just maybe, she can risk taking the bullet if she can get away—but even still, a bullet to the head will knock her flat, give them plenty of time to either put handcuffs on her or stick her in a body bag, thinking she's dead.

If she can just distract him, for just a moment, she can get his arms, raise the gun—but Julie is an outlier and—

Suddenly, Julie is in the game.

And all Miriam's uncertainties are uncertainly answered.

Julie draws her own weapon—a small, blunt-barreled bulldog of a revolver. She points it—

At Guerrero.

(Miriam did *not* see that coming.)

"Let her go," Julie says.

David sighs—this does not surprise him as much as it should. Something about this is something he expects, or at least understands.

"Julie, now is not the time or the place to assert yourself."

"David, you know how this works. Let her go."

Guerrero takes what seems like a deep, cleansing breath before lowering his pistol. "Fine. Go."

She gives Julie a quizzical look. "What is happening right now?" **249**

"I have a hunch and I am making a play," Julie says. And that's when Miriam sees: Julie, who usually seems to demonstrate little emotion, if any, seems to be welling up. Tears gently crawl down her cheeks.

"Why?"

"I don't know," Julie says, honestly. "That's just how it is."

That's just how it is. Spoken like someone with a curse. With a power that they do not entirely understand. Miriam feels that feeling on the daily.

"Are you going to be okay?" Miriam asks.

"You know I will be. Now leave while you can."

"You can't run anywhere I can't catch you," Guerrero warns as she skirts past, out the door, and into Steve Wiebe's car.

FIFTY-FIVE

STEVE WIEBE, TRUTH-TELLER

It's five minutes into the drive—a very normal drive, Steve using his blinker, stopping at lights, merging lanes with professional confidence and also relative gentleness—before he speaks.

"That didn't seem to go well," he says.

"No," Miriam answers. She is balled up in his passenger seat. No seatbelt. Just hugging her knees to her chest. Then she thinks: *Shit! The baby.* Clumsily, she struggles against the belt and clicks it across her burgeoning lap.

"I thought I saw a gun through the door. Did I see a gun?"

"Yes."

"Did I just commit a felony?"

"I don't know."

"Did you just commit a felony?"

"Also don't know."

"Are we going to jail?"

"Uhhhh."

And that is all they say on the drive back to her condo.

FIFTY-SIX

BOILOVER

Nighttime in Los Angeles. Miriam and Gabby sit in their car. It's parked in Boyle Heights, south of downtown, sandwiched between a row of little ranch-style houses and a small park near the freeway entrance—in the park sits a messy sprawl of tents, boxes, blankets, and crates. Homes on one side, homeless on the other: an encampment, in fact. They've no streetlight to shine on them, so all Miriam can see of them are shadows shuffling around in the city's half-dark, like ghouls unable to reach their final slumber, kept from the satisfaction of the grave. Poor fuckers.

Gabby has not spoken to her very much since Miriam called her earlier in the day, after the Motherfucking Plan went Motherfucking Tits Up. They had little time to do much, since Gabby was at work. So, Miriam grabbed everything she counted as essential, chucked it in a couple bags, chucked *those* into Steve Wiebe's trunk, and they took off to grab Gabs.

From there, they transferred those bags to the Miata.

And now, here they sit, across the street from what Miriam believes to be Abraham Lukauskis's house. It is not a nice house. Garbage lines the narrow cement walkway, and more garbage is mounded on the porch. It's entirely dark too. A few black cats slink around the low chain link fence that surrounds the property. There's no car in the driveway.

"Maybe he's not home," Miriam says.

Gabby says nothing.

It's like sitting next to a simmering pot. Eventually, it's going to boil over. So, Miriam just stokes the flames to get it over with.

"Go on; say it."

"I'm not saying anything," Gabby says.

"You're mad."

"I'm not mad."

"Oh, god, don't pull the *I'm not mad, I'm disappointed* line, because I really can't hack that kind of condescending bullshit right now."

Silence. It stretches out like a multiplicative void—emptiness feeding on emptiness, the chasm between them becoming positively consumptive.

"You *do* get it, don't you?" Gabby says, shattering the silence.

"Get what?"

"How badly you fucked this up. We had . . . everything. Everything we needed, at least. We had a place to live, you had a paycheck, we had health insurance, we had a *life*. Or the promise of one."

Miriam rolls her eyes so hard, she's pretty sure she catches a glimpse of her own brain. "See, that's the thing. You want a life, a normal life. The job, the house, the car, probably a cat or some shit. And you chose the literally worst person in the world—the most abnormal human you know—to try to have a normal life with."

"But now we have nothing."

"I've had nothing before. We can do this."

Even as she says it, she knows it's a lie. Usually, she says something like this, she means it whether it's right or wrong. But now it comes out hollow: a kind of bloated bravado, a balloon filled with nothing but her own hot air. She *can't* do this. They just lost access to their doctor, their apartment, their income.

She was getting *used* to those things. No, their shitty little condo in West Hollywood is no magical snow globe: they weren't away from it all in a snow-speckled, owl-possessed forest on the edge of nowhere. They were in the thick of it, sweating it out alongside the failed screenwriters and Oxy addicts and that drunk guy who dresses like Disney characters down by the Chinese Theater. But it was real.

And it was theirs.

And now it's gone.

Guerrero will come for her. He knows where she's headed. Truthfully, Miriam is surprised he isn't already here.

Shit, maybe he is. Waiting there in the dark of that house.

"We should go in," Miriam says, "maybe have a look around—"

"I didn't choose you to do this adventure. We chose each other."

"Oh, whatever. At the end of the day, the number one problem is you think I'm something I'm not. And you're trying to change who I am!"

"*You're* trying to change who you are, and I'm trying to fucking help! Was that all a lie? Were you just telling me that bullshit to string me along so I can drive you places and massage your feet at night? You're a *barely functioning adult* and you are on the cusp of having a baby—a human baby, a real, crying, flesh-and-blood-and-poopy-diapers baby."

"*You're* a flesh-and-blood-and-poopy-diapers baby."

Gabby stares.

Miriam stares back.

Gabby cracks. She snorts a small, eruptive laugh.

Miriam laughs too.

Then they're both doing it. Cracking up so hard, they can't catch their breath. Miriam has to brace herself against the dashboard. Gabby has to wipe her eyes. They both make that sound for when you're going off a laughing jag, a kind of happy deflation—*OHHhhhhhh.*

"Fuck," Miriam says.

"Fuck," Gabby agrees.

"You're right about it all."

Gabby raises an eyebrow. "What did you just say?"

"I said you're right. Does that get you wet?"

"It kinda does, a little?"

"Listen. You were right. You *are* right. I have a habit of acting first and then thinking second. Or maybe third. Maybe I don't think at all. Point is, I do things, and this time, I thought I could make it work—I could pull one over on Guerrero and get the name and be a tricky little bitch and sneak away with all the cookies. You warned me, and I didn't listen. And now, here we are. About to be eaten by an encampment of homeless people."

"We're homeless too now; have a little sympathy."

"I'm sorry."

"I'm sorry too." Gabby sighs. "We'll be fine. We'll figure it out. But next time, let *me* do the packing? You grabbed the most asinine shit."

"Shush, I packed fine."

"You brought three packages of cookies and left our toothbrushes."

"I'm a work in progress." She chews on her lower lip. "We should probably . . . I dunno, see if this freakshow is home, whoever he is. Guessing he's a hoarder, or just a fan of garbage?"

"I'm coming with you."

"Stay here."

"No, we're not separating. Not again."

"You sure?"

"I'm sure."

They share a quick kiss, and out of the car they go.

FIFTY-SEVEN

THE HOUSE OF ABRAHAM LUKAUSKIS

They wind their way up the cement path, slaloming between bags of trash. There's little smell—this doesn't appear to be food waste, or worse, dead rats or human body parts. Miriam gives one a little nudge with the side of her boot; something inside crinkles and whispers, like paper. The next one does the same. Are they all filled with crumpled paper?

Why?

Dangling from the overhang over the front door are—

"Dead birds," Gabby says, making a face.

Miriam recognizes them. They're just skeletons—a little dry skin and feathery bits still cling to the delicate bones. "I knew a guy in Florida who was really into wind chimes, but this is a whole other level." Miriam looks upon these dead creatures and knows, intuitively, what they are:

They're blackbirds.

They duck the dead birds gently rotating on strings, and Gabby goes for the front door—but, unsurprisingly, it's locked.

"C'mon," Miriam says. "Around back."

She takes a step off the concrete porch and sidles around the back of the house, using a narrow dirt path through the scrubby weeds that threads the space between the clapboard house and the chain link fence. The backyard, if it can even be called that, is about the size of a postcard—and half of it is just more concrete.

And half of *that* is mounded again with more bags of trash. More dead birds hang back here. Mostly blackbirds, but some sparrows, too. A word rises from the mists of Miriam's memory:

Psychopomps. In folklore, birds as vehicles, shuttling the souls of the living to the land of the dead. *And maybe*, she wonders with a shudder, *back the other way, too.*

They go to the back-patio door. That is also locked.

Next to it is a window—big enough for the both of them to fit through, Miriam thinks. She tries it. Locked. But *flimsily* locked: looks like this place was built in the 1950s and hasn't seen many updates since.

Miriam has, in her back pocket, a small-blade knife. She flips it out, slides it under the window, and jimmies it around in there a bit.

"So, now we're adding breaking and entering to our rap sheet?" Gabby hisses in the jaundiced, sodium-lit dark of Los Angeles.

"You bet."

The lock pops. The window opens.

"*Et voilà*," Miriam says. "Ladies first."

"Does that mean you or me?"

"I didn't really think that far. I better go in first, just in case."

"In case of what?"

"I don't know. Rats, roaches, bear trap, a slick-walled pit."

Gabby winces. "Then shouldn't I go in first? You're pregnant."

"And hardly helpless. Oops, here I go." With that, Miriam does a practiced move (that she is admittedly a bit out of practice with), hopping up and pulling herself through the open window.

She does it nimbly and quietly—though she nearly knocks over a stack of unwashed plates sitting in a sink. She has to *sidle* sideways and drop into the small, dank kitchen. It smells of weaponized mildew and food that has turned bad not once, not twice, but three times: not so much rotten but utterly forgotten. Has anyone even been here in a while?

Her hope begins to sink like an injured boat.

Maybe Abraham Lukauskis is not here.

Maybe he hasn't been here in a long time.

No time to worry about that now—Miriam helps Gabby through the space. Gabby is not practiced in this and never has been, so it takes some doing to make sure they don't both end up on the peeling, ruined linoleum.

They each check that the other is all right. "Hope you had your tetanus shot," Miriam says to Gabby. *She* sure had one; having a baby, they make you get the DPT vaccine. Shahini was insistent on that point.

Miriam plucks her phone from her pocket, flips it open, and uses the meager screen as a flashlight.

Slowly, she turns.

This isn't a hoarder's house, not exactly. It's something else. The counters are piled with baskets of herbs, polished stones, strange poultices, little piles of bones. A dream catcher hangs in front of the fridge. On the opposite counter, little glass jars line the back—Miriam gets closer, sees that they're more spices: turmeric, cinnamon, clove, but some of them too contain little bones, or white pebbles, or what look to be rust flakes.

In what counts for the living room, they find the same thing, only more so: statues of the Virgin Mary, several candles featuring the Virgin of Guadalupe, arrowheads dangling from strings, a round bowl filled with dead rose petals floating in brackish water—

Gabby suddenly gasps, staggering backward—she makes a low, keening sound, a sudden whine of fear as she balls up her fists and hugs them to her chest. Miriam rushes to her. "What is it?"

"Cats. Dead cats. *Dead cats, Miriam.*"

Sure enough, she's right.

There, on a coffee table, three dead adult cats.

And two kittens.

So dead, they're practically mummified. Black as road tar. Brittle as autumn leaves. Crispy like deeply fried chicken. Their mouths are all open, the tiny teeth like needle tips. Eyes long gone, desiccated to nothing.

"I touched one, I touched one," Gabby repeats, again and again. "Ew, ew, ew, ew." Her fingers waggle in the air like the legs of a panicked spider.

"Lighten up, Francis."

"Miriam. Why are there dead cats in here?"

Miriam does not answer at first. Instead, she moves over to a side table next to a leather couch that has lost most of its shape and turned more into a moldering pile of forgotten cow—there, she leans in and sniffs at a Mason jar, which contains some manner of liquid. The jar is painted with black, clumsily scrawled symbols.

The sniff is quick and tells Miriam all she needs to know.

Wincing at the acrid smell, she retreats and says, "The dead cats are probably here for the same reason those jars of piss are."

"Cat piss?"

"I think human, but I'm not exactly a *piss sommelier*."

"You really do take me to the finest places," Gabby says.

"What can I say? Only the best for my gal."

Onward she pushes throughout the first and only floor of the house. There's a small anteroom—not really fancy enough for the *foyer* moniker, unless you say it less like the French (foy-*yay*) and more like a Midwest hotdish housewife (foy-URR). Piled by the door is a bunch of old mail—plus more trash bags. Miriam creeps along and takes a left into the bathroom—in here, she finds more of the same. No trash, but more candles and statues. Another bird skeleton hangs over the mirror.

(It's a cuckoo.)

(Again, she's not exactly sure *how* she knows that.)

It's then she looks into the mirror.

Which, as it turns out, is a mistake. A moment replays in her head—

There, in another house, in Florida. It was her in a bathroom, Mervin's bathroom, an old guy who died. She and Rita Shermansky were robbing the place. Bathroom was about the same size as this one. She was going through his medications, and then when she closed the mirror—

She saw then what she saw now.

Someone is standing right behind her.

Then, it turned out to be the Trespasser—who slammed her head face-forward into the mirror. Or, at least, that's what she hallucinated.

Now, she has no fucking idea.

No idea if it's real.

Or if it's the Trespasser.

She spins around, ready to kick, punch, bite—

A dark shape, shaggy and baggy, like a mound of rags and writhing ants, stands there in the shower stall. Hidden in the dark of the bathroom. Miriam's about to say something, to reach forward and grab whoever it is—real or delusion—when she sees something rise up in its hands.

She realizes a half-second too late—

It's a shotgun.

It goes off, right into her chest.

ON A BEACH, WITH A BOOK, WITH EVELYN

The wind hits her.

It comes off the gray, foam-topped waves and rides across the beach like invisible horsemen. They gallop over her. They surprise her, steal her breath. She knows this place. Miriam has been here before.

She's in a two-piece. Black. Simple. Her toes play like mice in the sand. Next to her sits her mother, Evelyn Black. She's in a black one-piece, with a floppy beach hat over her too-big bug-eye sunglasses.

Evelyn reads a book: a Harlan Coben thriller.

"Am I dead?" Miriam asks. She knows the answer when her mother says it out loud:

"No, Miriam. You're not dead."

"Should I be dead?"

At that, her mother seems noncommittal. A halfhearted shrug is her only retort. "Life is strange" is all she says. "All is not as it seems."

"Someone shot me. With a . . ."

"Shotgun."

"Yeah."

Her mother gently takes off her sunglasses. With slowness and precision, she folds in the arms of each with a little *click*, *click*, and then sets the sunglasses down next to her in the sand. Gulls shriek above.

Evelyn regards Miriam.

"You're pregnant."

"I am." Miriam tensed up. "You always wanted me to have that kid in high school, but that got all fucked up. Here we go, second chance. It's what you want, right? Does it make you happy?"

"It does. Of course it does." Evelyn sighs dramatically. "It kills me, though, that I may never get to meet the little tyke." Her mother's eyes twinkle with mischief. "Get it? Kills me? Wokka, wokka, wokka."

"You're not usually one for the jokes."

"The afterlife is rich with time to cultivate new habits."

Miriam rolls her eyes. "That's nice to know. Maybe you can learn to cook for once."

"My cooking was very good."

"Uh-huh." She looks down at her belly. Only a faint roundness has begun to show, easier to see now in the two-piece. "You know, I should be more to you than just a baby-maker."

"And yet, to you, that's what I was—the someone who made you."

"Yeah, but you made me in different ways. You popped me out of your body—"

"That's a rude way to put it."

"That's literally the *least* rude way for me to have put it, Mother."

"Eh."

"Point is, what you were to me wasn't just a mechanism for my . . . entry into the world. You were the person who made me who I am. And you know that's not necessarily a good thing, right?"

At this, her mother shrugs as pelicans now fly low and slow over the shore, now zooming out over the water where they casually—like crashing planes—dive-bomb the churning surf to bring fish into their bucketed beaks.

"I know I wasn't a good mother to you, Miriam. But maybe I wasn't all bad, because you turned out okay."

"I turned out terrible. I'm a baby in a stroller barreling downhill toward an alligator farm. I'm a rat drowning in the sewer. I'm a nuclear accident at the Macy's Thanksgiving Day parade."

"You got a good heart."

"I ate a heart."

"I saw. So foul. You're a very strange girl."

"Thanks."

"You should go. It's time to go back."

Miriam sighs. "Okay." Then she says, "Is this really the afterlife? Some kind of heaven-hell combo pack? Limbo, Purgatory, some middling, in-between place? Are you really Evelyn? I know you're not the Trespasser. Tell me the truth. Tell me who you are, what this is."

"I'm whatever you need me to be. But no, I'm not that other thing. That other thing, it's very angry, Miriam. It's the angriest, most spiteful thing you've ever known. And it wants you very badly. It has orchestrated all the world to come for you and that child of yours—but I sense there's something else, too. Some grander, stranger plan it has. Some tricks up its sleeve that I can't see."

"The other thing. You mean the Trespasser."

"Yes, but that's not what we call it here."

"What do you call it here?"

"The Ghost of All-Dead."

FIFTY-EIGHT

SHOTGUN GOES BOO-YA

Her ears ring.

The air reeks of expended powder: that eggy, infernal stink.

In the darkness of Lukauskis's house, Miriam gasps, lurching to consciousness—the pain in her chest alternates between scorching hot and arctic cold, and she claws at her shirt, knowing what she's about to find: a ragged crater where shotgun pellets rent her chest asunder. A breastbone blasted open like a kicked-in door. Blood and bone. The wind whistling through her exposed heart—and with it, one thought running through her bad brain like a sacred mantra: *please heal, please heal, please heal.*

And now, here comes Harriet. Her face, moonlike and pale, looms into view over her. Hands pressing down on her shoulders. Mouth leering, bisecting her face into a crocodilian grin, all teeth, *all sharp little teeth*—

"Miriam, are you all right?" Harriet asks.

Correction: Harriet asks, in Gabby's voice.

And then Miriam blinks, and Harriet is gone. The darkness resolves and it's not Harriet Adams but Gabby, who hovers over her.

Miriam tries to say *I'm not all right, I've been shot.* But the words come out a squeak-and-whistle. Gabby helps her sit up and she resists, because she knows if she sits up, more blood will pour out of her, and her heart might just fall out of her chest like worms out of a kicked-over bait-bucket. But she doesn't resist enough and now she's sitting up. . . .

Her hands, still searching her chest, find no hole.

No crater.

No splintered bone or ruined flesh. No blooming blood flower in which sits her still-beating heart.

All the skin, all the bone, seems to be where it needs to be.

It hurts, though, to the touch—tender as a broken jaw. She gasps sharply at her own searching fingers. *I healed*, she thinks. *I healed fast*.

But then Gabby holds something up: a square something-or-other, like a little pillow. "A beanbag," she says.

That's when Miriam gets it: whoever shot her didn't shoot her with buckshot or birdshot or a slug from a shotgun. It nailed her in the chest with a beanbag—admittedly, a beanbag that punched her chest traveling several hundred feet per second. Which explains the pain.

"Fuck," she wheezes, tears in her eyes.

"A little lower," Gabby says, "and I don't know . . ."

Miriam touches her belly. She doesn't feel anything . . . broken.

Gabby helps her stand up. "I saw someone run out of here—a man, big beard, the gun in his hand. He ran out the back."

"We can . . . nngh, catch him."

"I don't know, Miriam; it's been a few minutes already—"

Outside, the *woop-woop* of a police siren. Miriam's pulse throttles. Maybe it's Guerrero. Maybe it's just that they heard a weapon discharge.

Either way, they can't stick around. "Shit. We have to go."

"C'mon, we'll sneak out the back," Gabby says. "See if we can't make it back to the car. You okay to walk?"

"I'm okay," Miriam says, but she's about the furthest fucking thing from okay. If that was their medium, then their one good chance of soliciting his help may have just run out the back door with a shotgun in his hand. He's either in the wind, or he'll be in the back of a cop car soon enough. Miriam has overplayed every hand she's been dealt and re-dealt.

Despair sings a grim dirge as they flee his house, into the bleak yellow night of the City of Angels.

FIFTY-NINE

THE TRAIL OF THE DEAD

Time passes, as it must. As it wants. For time knows no other desire than to move ineluctably forward, though to Miriam, it is less an act of forward momentum and more a downward one— it winnows and dwindles, like a supply of food that cannot be reclaimed, like money you spend but never get back, like age that piles up while life slips away.

Time is ticking down on what feels like a countless array of clocks and alarms and hourglasses: Taylor Bowman, killed; Miriam's daughter born only to die; Gabby, too, dead by her own hand, or rather, likely by the hand of the Trespasser. All this is made worse by the fear that these clocks can be changed: the hour and minute hands wind sooner and sooner, moving their flashpoints of fate far closer, because with the Trespasser involved, and with the intervention of other psychics like David Guerrero, fate is no longer quite so elegantly fixed, is it? She and others like her are fate-changers. They move the needle. They can change the path of the river.

It occurs to her only after their encounter with the man in Abraham Lukauskis's house that, if that man *were* Lukauskis, he could've very easily ended her child's life then and there. Because he, like her, breaks fate. He's not bound by those chains. He shatters those chains.

Her baby is destined to die upon birth, but the hand of a **277** psychic could change that. And the Trespasser could change that too. Once upon a time, the Trespasser needed her to change fate. Now it's learning to do it all its own—though it must still need her for now.

And perhaps she shouldn't even be calling it the Trespasser anymore.

Because her mother, or the spirit of her mother, gave it a new name:

The Ghost of All-Dead.

That's a name she doesn't understand. She cannot say how to take it: is it literally a ghost? What does All-Dead mean? Most of all . . .

Does it even matter?

Whatever the case, they need to find Abraham Lukauskis.

But they also must remain safe.

So, they do as time does: they move forward.

She and Gabby flee the city. They know that Los Angeles is David Guerrero's domain, and they don't want to be in it. Bad enough that they're on the run, but being caught in whatever snares he has waiting for them will do neither of them any favors, so they drive out, into the desert.

Miriam makes a call to Rita Shermansky, hoping like hell that old bat (and her former, if brief, cohort in crime) can help her get a place to stay, but Rita doesn't know anybody out on the West Coast who can help her ("not anybody that's still alive, anyway, doll," Rita explains), so instead they drive and drive, looking up ads in local free newspapers for some place to stay.

They end up in a place called Twentynine Palms, about 150 miles due east of Los Angeles. It's right on the edge of the Joshua Tree National Park, which also puts it on the cusp of the Mojave Desert. They rent a little one-bedroom shithole—painted blue as a robin's egg—in the middle of some defunct ranchland for two hundred a month. They rent it from an old Paiute named

Walter, and the last of their money goes toward the security deposit and a load of meager groceries.

Gabby gets another waitress job. A diner out by the park entrance. They pay her under the table, and the tips from tourists are good.

Miriam lets the dye in her hair lapse; she wants to color it red, but Gabby is all, blah blah blah, you'll have to bleach the hell out of it, you're probably ruining your hair follicles, and that can't be good for the baby, so instead Miriam just chops it short, forms it into a kind of stiff peaky faux-hawk.

The days are hot as a blister. The nights are cool, sometimes cold. They can see the sunset from their front door, and it always looks like firelight on a full-body bruise.

While Gabby works, Miriam works, too.

She works at trying to find Abraham Lukauskis. Who remains her only chance, she believes, at understanding the greater picture. She's tried to find other mediums—she called around, and sure enough, like she thought, they're all fake-ass phonies. It's charlatans all the way down. And it's not like there's some other way to find a real-deal medium; Lukauskis is the first she's ever heard of, and likely, the last. Psychic powers don't seem to see a lot of duplication.

It's Gabby, though, who has the idea one night as they're sitting around, staring out over the desert (because they have little else do to): "He had a bunch of weird shit around that house." Miriam agrees he did, yes, including dead cats and symbol-marked jars of human piss. "But some of it," Gabby continues, "was like real occult-type stuff. Maybe he shops at those kinds of stores. Might be worth calling around."

So, that's where Miriam starts.

She doesn't have the Magical Internet on her phone anymore—because she ditched her phone and bought a cheapy burner from a convenience store—so instead, she heads to a library northwest of them, back toward civilization, in Hesperia. There she accesses the Net and uses it to gather a list of New Age stores, occult shops, Santeria botanicas, and the like. She starts calling them, first calling the ones that were near to Lukauskis's house.

On the second call, she already hits paydirt.

A man, quiet-voiced and serious, says, "Yes, we know Abe. Is he all right?" Which, already, is a red flag. That's a strange question to lead with.

Miriam says as much.

The man explains: "Abe hasn't been around in a few weeks. Maybe even a couple months. He always seemed . . . troubled."

Miriam lies: "I'm a friend, and I was hoping you'd seen him."

"No, sorry."

"You know where he might've gone?"

A long pause. "You say you're a friend?"

"I am. I went to his house in Boyle Heights; I saw signs of a scuffle." She neglects to mention that she helped cause the scuffle.

Another long pause. "He's been known to hang out with some of the witch circles in Henderson, Nevada. He grew up in San Francisco, I think, so maybe he went to be with family—though I don't think they're around anymore. Sometimes, he takes trips to Lone Pine; I think he communes with some of the natives up there. Shoshone or such."

It's a start.

Miriam heads back to the rental in Twentynine Palms.

On the way, she sees something interesting.

SIXTY

THE SIGN OF THE MERMAID

"It was the fucking mermaid poster," Miriam says.

Gabby sits across from her on a ratty pull-out couch—same one they've been sleeping on every night, since this dingy little desert box came furnished, just without an actual bed. She plugs away at a Corona as Miriam explains what she saw:

"I was driving out of Hesperia and I saw a bar."

"You didn't drink," Gabby says, direly.

"Says the woman currently drinking—which, to me, is really just a cruel taunt, you know that, right?"

Gabby makes a sheepish smile over the lip of her bottle. "Sorry?"

"Ugh. It's fine. No, I did not have a drink. But . . . this bung-hole of a bar had a poster outside, on the wall. Ratty, fraying. But in a frame, almost like you'd see a movie poster displayed at an old movie house. It was the fucking mermaid poster. The one from my vision, where Taylor Bowman gets got by the Star-fucker." The vision replays in her head—

A hard, open-handed hit wakes Taylor Bowman up. He's bound to a chair. Still bound. Been bound so long, his hands and feet are numb, so numb they're less like limbs and more like hunks of dead meat hanging there, bloodless and raw. It's dark here but he can still see the margins of the room he's in—a desk, wood paneling, the smell of dry rot and desert sand. He sees an old poster on the wall: got no name on it, though, it just shows a mermaid drawn up like the St. Pauli Girl, drinking a tall seafoam lager. Papers too lay scattered about the room. . . .

"You think that's where he dies."

"Could be. It's literally the only lead I have."

"What are you going to do about it?"

Miriam nibbles a thumbnail. "Nothing."

". . . nothing?"

"Not a thing. It's not my fucking problem."

"No, I know but—maybe you can use the information anyway."

"How's that?"

Gabby leans in, almost conspiratorially. "It's currency. Give it to Guerrero. A peace offering. He wanted actionable information, so give him some actionable information. Maybe it gets you back in."

Miriam doesn't think about it for long.

"No," she says.

"Miriam—"

"I know! I know, but hear me out. It's a huge risk. I call him, and that just lets Guerrero zero in on where we are, *and* it gives him a theoretical win. Or the info I give him is wrong and it just pisses him off more."

"But it could get you back to Shahini as your doctor."

"Yeah. I know." She bites her thumbnail down to the quick. It starts to bleed, so she pops it into her mouth like a lollipop. "We'll blow up that bridge when we get to it."

"Maybe you're right, though; maybe Guerrero isn't trustworthy."

"He was keeping things from me."

"*And* he was ready to arrest you at the drop of the hat. He never really made the charges go away."

"Fuck that guy. He doesn't deserve the win."

"So," Gabby says, "what will you do? About Taylor Bowman."

"I . . . don't think anything."

That seems to stun Gabby. "You're just going to let him die?"

"Gabby, people die. I dunno if you've noticed that, but it's a recurring problem, people dying left and fucking right, almost like none of us are immortal, almost like death is a part of life. It's not my job to correct that. I've been treating it like it's some kind of mistake, but maybe it's not my business. I don't know that I've ever made anything better by meddling."

"You saved Louis."

"But his death would've been my fault."

"You now have his daughter."

"That's . . . something, but I remind you that she dies too."

"You saved me."

"Not yet, I haven't."

They sit in silence for a while. Gabby doesn't have anything more to say, it seems. Maybe she's realizing that what Miriam said was true. But finally, she seems once again to get her back up, and she leans forward and, while gesturing with the beer bottle, says:

"No. I *don't* believe it. You've made lives better. You've killed killers, which means there are victims you don't even know about who get to live because of you. You've given closure to people, too. Like that teacher you told me about, the one who had pancreatic cancer—you gave her a chance to live out her life on her terms. Steve, too."

"Steve Wiebe. Shit. We should call him."

"You think they'd arrest him?"

Miriam *hmm*s. "I don't think so. But they might watch him."

"We shouldn't call."

"Nope."

"Fuck."

"Fuck."

"So, Bowman just dies?"

"Bowman just dies."

"And Guerrero gets nothing?"

Miriam nods. "If I had a drink, I'd clink it against yours."

"So, we just hunker down, focus our energies on finding Lukauskis."

"That is exactly it."

Miriam goes to suck her bloodied thumb again—but the blood is dry and the nail is not only healed, it has grown once more over the quick.

SIXTY-ONE

REMNANTS

Halloran Springs, California.

It's about forty miles from the Nevada border, on the highway toward Vegas. The highway is littered with homespun grave markers: the signs of those who died, probably half-drunk and mostly broke, on the way back from Las Vegas at four o'clock in the morning.

The Miata sits marked outside an abandoned gas station, above which towers a skeletal, arrow-shaped sign that says:

NED'S GAS.

Underneath in letters of pure rust:

GIFTS, 24-HR TOWING, EAT.

Miriam gets out of the car. Her belly is now bulging. They have been out here, in exile from Guerrero and Los Angeles, for over six weeks now. Long enough for the Starfucker to have claimed another young actor—the newspaper identified the victim as Ostin Cole, some up-and-comer producer's kid. That was a month ago.

A month ago to the day.

Today is the 11th.

Today is when Taylor Bowman dies.

Miriam knows this as Gabby follows her into the abandoned gas station. She tries not to think about it.

The gas station seems eerily preserved. Dust-swept, wind-worn. **275**

Windows long broken. The chrome on stools and counters has corroded. It's like the ghost of a gas station, lingering on long after death to haunt the desert highway where it once stood.

"This is it?" Gabby asks.

"Yeah."

For weeks, they've been following up false leads on Abraham Lukauskis, their medium. It's been one dead end after the other. People *knew* him. He shopped at their weird stores: he bought crystals and peace pipes and dreamcatchers, he bought saint candles and chicken's-foot amulets and collections of bird and lizard bones. They heard he might be in Henderson, so they took a drive out there, met a witchy goth chick who told them who his weed dealer was. They heard he was in Lone Pine, so they went to Lone Pine to meet his weed dealer, a dude who called himself Red Boy, but Red Boy hadn't seen him (information they only learned by buying a considerable bag of weed, which neither of them smoke, so Gabby parceled it out to the other waitresses at the diner, thus earning her the temporary role of "weed dealer"). Then Red Boy called them, told them he'd heard from an old white mystic living down in Halloran Springs that sure enough, Lukauskis was haunting the area. And that he'd set up shop here.

In this abandoned gas station.

He's not here. She can see that much.

Miriam goes over to the counter and sits down on a squeaky, ancient stool. The upholstery on it is so brittle, it's gone full saltine cracker. It crunches as she sits on it, like she's sitting on a carton of eggs.

The counter contains an endless line of names and initials, so she takes out her knife and adds:

MIRIAM <3 GABBY

It feels twee and stupid, but fuck it, she loves it.

(She'll take any measure of momentary solace she can manage.)

Gabby calls her over, so she hops off the stool. Gabby is toward the back, near busted-out freezer cases and behind a couple of toppled aisle racks. There they find a discarded, dirty mattress, plus a ton of blankets and rags. Not to mention: a few saint candles, a small ceramic Virgin Mary statue, and a plate full of bird bones. (A mix, Miriam sees: blackbird, crow, and even the bones of a single mountain bluebird.)

"He was here," Gabby says.

"And he's not now," Miriam answers, defeated, deflated, destroyed. "I feel like we've been chasing shadows."

"Here, hold on."

Gabby stoops, picks up something that's half-stuck under the mattress. A ratty, fraying envelope. Not letter-size but larger: big enough for a portrait-style page. Gabby pops the flap, pulls out a couple twenty-dollar bills, some takeout menus, and—

A map.

On it, he's got several places in the state marked with scribbled handwriting: *The Methuselah Tree, The Integratron, Los Feliz Murder Mansion, Zzyzx Mineral Springs*, but they're all crossed out.

All but one:

Black Star Canyon, just southeast of Los Angeles.

That one remains uncrossed.

"Why's he crossing them off?" Gabby asks.

"I don't know. He's taking a tour. Either visiting them for a reason or ruling them out. Maybe both." She squints. "He must have a car. Or someone's driving his raggedy ass around."

"We could go here. It's a couple-hour drive."

Miriam winces.

"Why are you making that face?" Gabby asks.

"It's today."

"Today is always today; that's why they call it *today*."

"No, I mean—today is the eleventh."

"I don't know wh . . . Ohh. *Oh*."

"Yeah. Oh."

Gabby gets it. Today's the day Taylor Bowman dies.

"You said you're just letting it happen," Gabby says.

"I know."

"But you're not going to, are you?"

"I should. I really should. I don't . . . I don't fucking like this douchebag actor, he was drinking some shitty milkshake smoothie thing that smelled like rotten onion and overripe banana and I puked on him, and I don't really care if he lives or he dies, but . . . I can stop it. I can stop him from dying. Today. In three hours, I can maybe go and stand in the Starfucker's way. And I don't even have anything against the Starfucker. I don't care. That's what I tell myself. Go kill people; what shit do I give? And yet . . ."

"You need to go."

"It's like a—" Miriam grits her teeth as she forms her right hand into a fist and holds it against her middle. "It's this feeling deep down inside that I gotta handle this. I can't just have this kid be born and tell her, *Yeah, I let some actor prick get his face sliced off because I couldn't be bothered to do anything about it. Life's hard, kid; nobody's gonna be there to save you.* I don't want her to feel that way."

Miriam thinks but does not say:

I don't want her to feel the way I feel.

"You're going to stand in the way of a serial killer."

"I think I am."

"That's dangerous. Maybe just call Guerrero, let him handle it."

"It's not his job. It's mine. He's fucked it all up already. And the last time I saw him, he pointed a gun at me. I don't trust him."

"Jesus, Miriam. Don't do this. Not today, we're close—I bet Abraham is going to whatever this . . . Black Star Canyon is. Let's go. Together. We'll find him."

"You go. I'll . . . catch up."

"You're not just stopping for milk. You're stopping a serial killer."

"Hopefully stopping a serial killer."

Gabby paces. Because she knows. Miriam *knows* that she knows.

"I should go with you," Gabby says, walking back and forth.

"No. You go . . . find the medium. I'll do this. It'll be fine."

"Famous last words."

"Yeah. Well. Let's hope not."

"You be careful," Gabby says.

"You be careful, too. Last time we met ol' Abe the Spirit Guide, he blasted a goddamn beanbag into my chest with a shotgun."

"I love you. Don't die."

"Back atcha, babe. Back fuckin' atcha."

PART EIGHT

THE SPIDER AND THE FLY

SIXTY-TWO

THE WHITE ROOM

Now.

Miriam is bound to an exam table. She is clothed. Her feet are in stirrups, bound there with a cruel swaddling of duct tape, the ankles elevated above her head. Her hands are fixed to a set of bedrails, also with tape—so much tape, it bulges, like a nodule, a tumor. Her arm, where the bullet cut through her, is already starting to heal up.

(And it itches something fierce. As if the injury is stuffed with crawling ants struggling to dig a colony in the meat of her body.)

The walls of this room are white and padded.

The floor is black, smooth, rubbery.

The ceiling is industrial, its beams, ducts, and conduits artfully and purposefully exposed.

A black padded bench sits along the far wall. A closet is open nearby, next to a bathroom, and in the closet hang what look to be a variety of outfits: a lab coat, a geisha dress, something gold and glitzy, something black and rubbery. On the opposing wall, a flat, red table with a red rubber sheet upon it; above it is constructed a skeletal architecture of metal rods—a framework on which hang various metal rings and poseable shackles.

All it is smeared with garish, bold, neon-blue light.

They have not gagged her, so she screams.

(And even if they did gag her, she tells herself she'd chew through it and scream anyway.)

A little part of her wonders if this is what it felt like to be David Guerrero—trapped by someone with murderous intent, unsure how you'll escape. It is a feeling she is sadly all too familiar with, isn't it? Harriet Adams and Hairless Fucker. The Mockingbird. Ashley Gaynes. Ethan Key and his Arizona militia. Go after the killers, and the killers come for you.

She fell into this trap, and she's kicking herself for it.

Upstairs, gun to her belly, she contemplated how to escape— kick, punch, grab something, throw something, run. But that gun, pointed right at her middle, and the Man with the Shining Mask stepping in through the door, the sequins of his black balaclava gleaming and glittery? Where to go? She could risk herself easily—especially now that she knew she could potentially heal her injuries. (Certainly, Harriet could—that cuckoo bitch dropped off a roof, broke her limbs, and kept coming like a shattered automaton whose motherboard brain failed to acknowledge the damage. And next time Miriam saw her, she was back to normal, limbs stiff, bones back in her skin.) But the child inside her gave her some pause: if she ran, and they shot her, what if the bullet struck the kid? Her daughter is scheduled to be born to die, yes, but maybe, just *maybe*, Miriam can avert that fate.

She can't avert a bullet.

They brought her down here, each wearing gloves so that she was never afforded the chance to see how they die. They brought her here, to this basement, to what the older man called his *playspace*. They put her here, in this humiliating position.

And now she waits.

She hears them upstairs. Murmurs. The gentle thumping and creaking of footsteps back and forth. Is it just the two of them? Or are there others?

Miriam can't tell.

But now, she hears something down *here*, too. A rustling of fabric. A clatter of hangers. From the corner of her eye, she sees it:

Something moves in the closet.

She's *sure* of it.

But when she stares, she sees nothing. No movement. Nothing. Nobody. Until—

A dark shape steps out from the curtain of hanging clothes.

A big, dark shape.

Louis.

Not-Louis.

"Miriaaaaaam," he says, his voice deep and rich but distorted too, as he sings her name as a warped and warbling song. "Wicked Miriam."

"Go fuck yourself."

But as he emerges from that room, stepping closer and closer with slow, ginger steps—like a comical thief sneaking into a room with overdramatic tiptoes, *dink dink dink*—he sings another song:

Your counsels I have slighted all
My carnal appetite shall fall
When I am dead, remember well
Your wicked Polly groans in Hell.

The Mockingbird's song.

"Fuck you," she spits.

"Such venom," Not-Louis says. As he gets closer, she sees that his one eye socket is plugged shut with a golf ball painted crudely with an eye: iris, cornea, and all. Like a child painted it. "It's sad how you find yourself in this situation again and again. Oh, how history repeats itself. Like you're a broken record, sk-sk-skipping. A broken brain, replaying the greatest hits."

"Isn't this where you want me?" she snarls. "Here, in the nest of the killers? Isn't this the path you want me on?"

He chuckles. Wet and diseased. A throat full of stagnant water.

"It is. You're still doing my work. You still choose this path."

"So, fine. Let me out. Do some magic, motherfucker."

"I am not God."

"No, but you're learning to possess people, right? You're *evolving*. So, evolve your boogeyman ass upstairs, possess one of those awful bastards, and do what needs doing. You don't even *need* me anymore."

Not-Louis shakes his head. He grins, and as he opens his mouth to speak, a fat-bellied camel cricket leaps out of his mouth and drops against the floor, hopping away.

"It doesn't work that way. I can only possess those without purpose—with holes chewed in their souls. Those men upstairs have great, grave purpose. They are assured of their place in this universe, and so they are closed to me." His grin grows wider, nearly splitting his face in two. "Besides, what fun would that be? I always love to see how you get out of these things. You have such an imagination."

"Go away. Haunt someone else, Ghost of All-Dead."

At that, the Trespasser straightens up. His teeth clamp together.

"Who told you that?"

"I've hit a nerve."

"You have work to do, Miriam. I suggest you get to doing it, because they're going to want to cut that baby out of you and take your heart as a prize. Get it done. Save yourself. Kill the killers. Break the cycle."

She screams at the demon, but it's already gone.

SIXTY-THREE

UNMASKED

Minutes give birth to hours, and time multiplies endlessly, infinitely. It loses meaning. Miriam struggles. She screams. At some point, she even sleeps—a restive, electric sleep, earned in unwanted fits and starts. Her legs are numb. Her hands are numb. Her cheeks feel flushed. The baby kicks her bladder, and at some point, she pisses herself. It is a thing she does willfully, with wanton disregard, because she knows they're going to have to deal with it. She can hear it drip against the table, and off it, onto the floor. *Too bad this room is designed for easy cleanup*, she thinks. She wishes like hell she was pissing on a carpet right now or in between some fancy floorboards. If they're going to kill her, at least let the rank stink of her urine haunt this place—a nose-curdling *pisstergeist*.

And then, at one moment, she opens her eyes and discovers again she is not alone. Two men stand there. Each wearing black gloves.

One, the owner of this house. Cardigan, smartwatch, and pistol.

The other, a man in a silver suit. In one hand, he holds a familiar knife with a hooked blade. In the other, he holds a black balaclava.

The Starfucker, unmasked.

And Miriam recognizes him.

The vision of Ethan Key's death plays out once more inside her mind, with the leader of the Arizona militia dangling naked from a pipe.

His killer, that day, is the same man who stands here now.

He showed Ethan Key a playing card, but all that was on it was a spider, inked there in the center of what might be its web, a circle on its back. He asked Ethan Key: *"Is this your card?"*

In that vision, the killer explained that he was from the cartel before he said something that Miriam considered then—and considers now—strange to come from of the mouth of a common assassin:

Life. Existence. Presence. It is decided at the moment of inception. A length of string carefully meted and measured out, then cut. All things, predetermined. Destiny: from the Latin, destinare. *Meaning to make something firm. To establish its permanence. As if carving it in stone. Fate: a thing ordained. Fate. Fatal. Death. Nona, Decima, Morta. You established your fate when you built your little town.*

Creation is thought to be a gift, but it is not. It is not a thing given but rather a thing bought. Purchased. A debt incurred at the moment of becoming. All things must end. It is not just a person's life that incurs this debt. All things that exist must make the purchase and owe the payment. Everything that exists will one day not exist. That can be troubling for some, but I find it freeing. Our presence here is given margins. A start and an end. Everything in this way has a story; some stories are long and boring. Others? Short and exciting. Yours was exciting, I think. And good for you. But it will be shorter than you like.

Then he killed Ethan Key. Drove a blade up under his chin. Pushed it deeper and deeper until it found the brain.

That would have happened by now, except Miriam knows

that it didn't. Ethan Key was dead by the hand of a young boy—a psychic—named Isaiah. A boy with a psychic touch, now living with Gabby's sister.

This man never killed Ethan Key.

But he would have, had they not intervened.

When Miriam sees him, she can't help it. She says:

"*Nona, Decima, Morta.*"

It works. The two men seem taken aback. They look to one another, and for a moment a spark of actual panic passes between them, like a bit of lightning juggled from one dark cloud to the next.

It gives her some small, cold pleasure.

"You are quite surprising," the man in the cardigan says. "You are trickier than we imagined you to be. Our mistake, I see."

"I don't know you," Miriam says. But she looks to the unmasked Starfucker. "*You*, though. I know you."

His eyes pinch to uncertain slits. "Do you?"

"You were going to kill Ethan Key."

"Ethan Key. And his wife, Karen. Yes." His voice now, as it was then in the vision, conjures burned, smoky caramel. He raises a dark eyebrow and says, with some curiosity, "You stole that kill from me."

She declines to correct him, that it was Isaiah who did that.

"You bet," she says.

The man in the cardigan says, "You see, Alejandro? This one has been violating the tapestry for a long time. I told you that if we put out the right bait, eventually one of them would come along and get caught in our web."

"Yes, Emerson. You were right."

"But this one," the man called Emerson says as he takes a step forward, "is a prize, indeed. I don't know that we've ever caught one that's with child."

"Don't think about it."

"What? We could keep her. Bring the child to term. See what happens. Think of it as an experiment."

Alejandro sneers. "You cannot domesticate this little untethered beast. The moment you reach for her, she'll bite your hand clean off at the wrist. Her destiny will be to destroy us, if we aren't careful. I say we just open her up, cut the baby out, and choke them both with the umbilicus."

Miriam growls back at him: "Destiny: from the Latin, destinare. Meaning to make something firm. To establish its permanence. As if carving it in stone." Again she sees the man flinch.

"Who told you this?" Alejandro asks.

"You did. In the future where you kill Ethan Key."

He smiles. "That *is* something I say when I . . . do my job. You are good. You do see things." His gaze drifts to the space around her. "You aren't tethered to the rest of us. Only one comes off you. One that connects to something. Someone. But who, or what?" Then, to his cardiganed cohort: "We should kill her now. Sever that tether. Stop her from disrupting the rest of the pattern."

Emerson takes another step forward. "I am undecided. My scientific mind, my doctor's curiosity, begs me to choose differently."

Now Alejandro looks angry. His brow creases so deeply, the lines form little, bitter canyons. "You foolish old man—"

"Hey!" Miriam barks.

They both turn toward her, equal parts stunned and irritated.

"Who the fuck *are* you people?" she asks.

So, the man, Emerson, explains.

THE FUCK THESE PEOPLE ARE

Yes, I suppose this is all strange to you.

It shouldn't be, perhaps. We've whispered past each other now and again, our threads running parallel, if never quite . . . tangling together.

Alejandro and I belong to a small, intimate organization. The Organization. Our formal name is the Chelicerae, but generally, that name goes unused—the Organization is name enough for us.

We are . . . or represent . . . a legacy. The Parcae. The Moirai. The Fates. Nona, Decima, Morta. Or in the Greek: Clotho, Lachesis, Atropos. More to the point, we are the children of the latter: Atropos. Clotho spins the thread, Lachesis measures it, and Atropos—

(here he makes a scissor-snip with his fingers)

—cuts it.

Everyone, every human alive, dead, and not yet born, gets a thread. And that thread is woven neatly into a tapestry. Individually, each thread is . . . chaos. It's just a line of color and shape and texture. When you look closely, that thread intertwines with and is tied to other threads, and they form lines and knots that only seem to . . . create more chaos. Colors clashing, knots snarling in the skein. But if you pull back . . .

Back, back, back, farther and farther, an interesting thing happens.

An image starts to emerge.

A pattern. From the chaos of individuals, the order of the pattern is made. The tapestry is seen to be a thing of design.

It is as all should be.

But then there are aberrations.

Then there's you.

Not you specifically. But those with power. The untethered, we say, sometimes, but what we mean are those, like you, who are afforded the gift of seeing the pattern that so few others can see—but are also cursed with the ability to change the pattern. And you do so wantonly, without regard for the shape of things, without a sense of how it all comes together. You're a fool in the kitchen, fire in the forest, someone throwing paint on a master-piece just because they like the sound of the paint hitting the canvas.

You are ruinous.

And you help to destroy the pattern. We believe that if you keep destroying and disrupting the pattern, then it will not only fray . . . but it will fall apart completely. Life, death, the universe . . .

All in tatters.

Scraps on the floor.

Like you: you save people whose deaths have been ordained. Fate has chosen them to die: their threads end. To fix this, you cut another thread that was expected to go on—but one thread does not replace another. The pattern was sound. Until you, and others, ruin it.

So, we find your kind.

And we stop you from ruining the pattern.

Your thread must end.

SIXTY-FOUR

HYPOCRISY

For a time, she just stares at them. Her face wears a mask of utter incredulity—a face that bears not fear so much as the face of someone completely, unabashedly, unreservedly fed up with their bullshit.

They seem to find this uncomfortable. They look to one another.

Miriam finally asks, "You're not the Starfucker; that was just . . . like you said, bait. Really, you're cartel." That, she says to Alejandro.

"That is correct."

"Like, Colombian drug cartel?"

"The one and only."

"And you," she says to the man named Emerson. "All this that you have, the vineyard, your *playspace*, it isn't aboveboard, is it? You're a criminal."

"All wealthy men are criminals."

She snarls, "You're ducking. You're not Silicon Valley. You're the fucking Underworld. I can smell it on you, sure as I can smell my own piss."

The man, Emerson, pulls the gun closer, pressing the flat of it against his middle. A threat, she thinks. But he concedes: "Yes, I operate in that space."

"*I operate in that space,*" she says, mocking him. She snorts a laugh. "You pretentious fuckos. Here, let me give you my read of that twat-waffle you just gave me: you and the rest of your so-called Organization are a bunch of buttfuck buddies in crime. You all go out. You do crime. But, oh, *heavens forfend* you just go out and, like, do bad shit without reservation. No, you've gotta create this wild mythology around it. This *story* that somehow you're serving a larger pattern when in reality, all you're doing is the act of common evil. You pretend like you have some grand purpose, some higher mind, blah blah blah *Nona, Decima, Morta, Clotho, Lachesis, Atroposuck my dick*. But all you are is common."

Emerson purses his lips. The gun twitches in his hand.

To Alejandro, he says, "Cut her open."

The cartel assassin drops his mask and flashes his hooked skinner knife. He takes a step toward her, and panic throttles through her body like she's sitting on an electric chair and someone just flipped the switch. He gets between her legs, knife out—he rips the shirt over the swell of her belly. The blade flashes—

She screams.

She screams out loud and in her own head: *Think of something, think of something, they're going to take your daughter and dash her against the wall, they'll cut her to pieces, think of something—*

The blade is cold against her skin—

In that moment, she sees Alejandro, leaning forward, a viciousness upon his face as the blade begins its cut, and she knows it'll happen fast, because she's seen the death of Taylor Bowman and saw how quickly his bowels were piled into his lap—

She sees the man named Emerson, arms folded limply together, the fingers dangling next to each elbow like fringe of an ugly jacket. He has a cold, clinical stare as he watches all this unfold—

And then she sees a third member of the audience.

Just behind Emerson stands a tall, broad shadow. Not-Louis. His one grotesquely painted golf-ball eye is rotated the wrong direction, but the one *good* eye is fixated pointedly at her, and he wears a strange, mad smile—it's not a Louis smile, not at all, it's broad and deranged, a curl to the lips that brings to his face a Joker's flair—

That's it.

She hurriedly screams, "Wait, wait, wait, I have—I have an offer."

The knife stops.

She feels blood trickling down the side of her stomach.

Alejandro looks to Emerson and Emerson looks to Alejandro. The older man makes a face that says he's considering it. Then holds up his hand.

Alejandro takes a step away. She sees her blood drip from the blade.

"Offer?" Emerson asks. "I can't imagine what it is, but I'll hear it."

So, she tells them.

SIXTY-FIVE

MIRIAM'S VERY KIND OFFER

"I'll give you the demon," she says, breathlessly. The pain in her stomach throbs with every beat of her heart. She can see that he didn't cut deep—he didn't get below her muscle layer, not yet. Just the same, she can see the ridge of skin opening up like a steam-peeled envelope.

Neither seems to understand her offer.

"Demon?" Emerson asks.

Not-Louis regards her with some curiosity now.

"This power I have," she says, gulping air, trying to calm down, "is not a power I want. I'm trying to get rid of it. And I know how. When I was sixteen, I was pregnant—the mother of the boy who knocked me up, she . . . she came at me, attacked me in a bathroom. I had internal bleeding. Lost the baby. And when I did, *something* slipped in. A demon. A ghost."

Not-Louis gets it now. His face tightens with growing rage.

"Shut up, Miriam," Not-Louis hisses at her, though only she can hear.

"This thing, it's called the Ghost of All-Dead. I don't know what that means. But I know that if I have this baby, I break the curse. But before that happens, I can bring the demon to you."

"You fucking *scab*," Not-Louis roars.

"How exactly will you manage this?" Emerson asks her.

"Emerson," Alejandro begins, "surely you're not—"

"Shh. Step back, Alejandro. I am curious."

"I know a medium," she explains. It's a lie, somewhat. She knows *of* a medium, and presently she is hoping like hell that Gabby managed to find him and secure his help, or that means she's even further out on the edge of this cliff than she knows. "He's going to help me."

At this, Not-Louis storms over to her, curling himself around Alejandro like a snake around a tree. The entity's flesh stretches and distorts. His jaw cracks open, and his throat bulges like a hammerstruck thumb—something moves up through his chest, his throat, like a blob of water pushing through a garden hose, and then it comes out of a mouth that is open wide, *too* wide—locusts pour out, wings stuttering like playing cards in the spokes of a child's bike, a thousand children, a thousand bikes, *fddddt*, and they rush past her in a flensing swarm—

She winces.

They're gone.

Because they were never here.

The Trespasser—the Ghost of All-Dead—is gone too.

Alejandro hovers. He is eager. His knife is hungry.

"Release her," Emerson says. "Let's bring her upstairs, get a bandage on that wound. Though," he says, throwing a passing glance to her arm, where a bullet once dug its way through the meat of her bicep, "perhaps she won't require the bandage for long."

"Emerson, you old fuck," Alejandro snarls. "This is a mistake."

"Perhaps. But as I grow older, I find mistakes interesting. All that we do, all that we are, is a mistake. We must see them and make them in order to learn from them, so let us learn from this one. No more arguments, Alejandro. You've already gone and killed two of my field hands. Your judgment in this is no longer trustworthy."

Alejandro turns toward her, his eyes flashing.

He's going to kill me anyway, she realizes.

But he advances with the blade only to cut her hands and legs free. As she falls off the bed, her legs and arms gone totally numb, she collapses against the mat. She tries not to cry as the slow river of blood reluctantly fills her limbs once more.

SIXTY-SIX

ROSES ARE RED, VIOLENCE IS BLUE

Once again, Miriam finds herself upstairs in this house, sitting on a stool at a kitchen counter. They have given her a bandage, which she has applied to the knife slash in her side—already the bandage has filled up with blood and started to soak through, but already too she can *feel* the itch of the injury mending with the supernatural stitch of her newfound power.

It's evening. The moon shines big and bright, beating the sun back behind the horizon. The sky purple as a crushed toe.

In front of her sits a cup of steaming tea.

"Thank you for the tea," she says, coldly.

"It's not tea," Emerson says, "it's a dandelion tisane."

"It's fucking tea," Alejandro says. He stands where Miriam once stood, by the large window looking out over the driveway. Except he doesn't stare out the glass. He stares at her. He has a pistol in his hand—not the same pistol as Emerson held on her before. This one is longer, with a vented barrel at the top. Big barrel. High-caliber. Slick-shit hand-cannon.

"Tea," Emerson says, with no small condescension, "is specifically from the plant *Camellia sinensis*. Only tea is tea. What people call an 'herbal tea' is a decoction from a plant that is not *Camellia sinensis*—chamomile, for instance, or hibiscus, or licorice root—"

Miriam says, "You said *decoction*."

They both look at her.

"Isn't that what you do when you castrate somebody?" she asks. "De-cock-tion? Right? No? Just me? Okay."

Alejandro gently eases the barrel to point toward her. "Are you threatening us?"

"The point is," Emerson says, talking over them. "We must define our terms and use them correctly. Wine, for instance, is defined in Europe as being made exclusively from fermented grape juice, not like some of that . . . so-called 'fruit wine' you can buy. I like it when we allow things to remain what they are, and not let that definition drift. *Terroir* means that champagne is really only that when it comes from Champagne. Elsewise, it's cava, or prosecco, or spumante—viticulture is still culture."

"The roses," Miriam asks, keeping a steady eye on the barrel of that pistol. *Just keep them talking. You may get out of this yet.* "I wanted to ask. Why are there planters of roses at the end of every row of grapevines?"

Emerson smiles. "Very perceptive, Miriam. You seem like a common girl, but you're anything but—even on the run from a madman in a strange mask, you pick up on things." He leans forward, seemingly pleased with the chance to explain something. "Roses are our canary in the coalmine. They are susceptible to many of the same diseases that plague our grapes, certain blights and rusts. But they suffer it first. So, if the roses begin to die, we know to begin a regimen of aggressive defense with the grapes."

"You learn something new every day," Miriam says.

"That is my goal," Emerson says. "But it's not only about learning something new, is it? It's about contextualizing that— about finding the place of the new information in context with old, known information." He stands up straight once more and reaches toward a wine rack. The corks face outward, and he wraps his long fingers around the neck of one bottle, withdrawing it and gently setting it down before her. "Wine, you see, is

the product of learning new things, trying new things, but never
ignoring what came before, either. It's about using the past to
build to the future."

And with that, he gently gives the wine bottle a half-turn.

Its label now stands exposed to Miriam.

Pinot Noir.

Monterey County, California.

Made and produced by—

It feels like the stool has been kicked out from under her.

It can't be.

Caldecott Vineyards.

Emerson smiles a stiff little smile. "Have you had our wine
before? It looks as if you might."

"Caldecott," she says, her voice barely above a hoarse whisper.
"Yes."

"Eleanor Caldecott."

"My sister."

She stares nails up at him. "She didn't have any brothers or
sisters. That's what she told me."

"She lied. We have a very large family, I'm afraid. Eleanor was
a bit of a . . . black sheep. What with the Carl Keener problem."

Eleanor Caldecott: head nurse at the Caldecott School, a
girls' school. Mother to the headmaster of that school, Edwin.
Both of them, part of a family of serial killers that murdered
dozens and dozens of girls under the auspices of that school.

Eleanor and her family were the Mockingbird killer.
Together. As one. And she had considerable feelings about fate,
did she not?

The woman told Miriam:

*Fate has a path. You step in. You change lives by ending
lives. Don't you? That's what I do. What we do. As a family. We
see those girls twisting in the wind—poisoned girls, damaged
girls, ruined girls. Girls who will themselves become ruiners.*

Their lives are hurricanes and tornadoes, sweeping up every-thing in their paths and throwing them back to earth so hard, they shatter.

Of one of their victims, Annie Valentine, Eleanor said:

Annie Valentine's death is a pure thing. A good thing. And good things, truly good things, don't come without sacrifice. Hers is a garden of hate: leave the ground barren and only bar-ren things grow. A dead child. A dead mother. So many others. Remove her from the timeline . . .

And the garden grows.

It was then that Eleanor mimed a pair of scissors with her two fingers, just as Emerson had. *Emerson and Eleanor Caldecott.* Alike in ways she didn't even realize. Alike in ways she's only just realizing now: Eleanor and the Mockingbird burned herbs in the beaked nose of the plague doctor mask they wore when they killed—*burning roses and carnation*—and further, she too had something of a green thumb. Miriam remembers the Caldecotts' greenhouse. Verdant. Overgrown. The soil beneath each plant was dark and rich, because it was compost made from the corpses of their victims.

Dead girls.

Dozens of dead girls. Girls who were ruiners, just as Miriam was a ruiner. Girls who were damaging some kind of timeline, who were infecting fate, who were breaking the pattern.

"And we come full circle," Emerson says.

"Your sister. She had . . . abilities."

"Yes." Even as he's saying that word, he's biting the finger of one of his gloves and pulling it off. His hand grabs her wrist forcefully—

Noise. Howling wind. A keening frequency. Void and snow and—

He lets go.

"You're cursed like me," she says. She looks to Alejandro.

The gun still points in her direction. He's faking an easy, languid pose, but she sees that he's coiled and ready to react. "Him too, I bet."

"Smart money," Alejandro says, smirking.

"Explain that." Miriam quakes with quiet rage. "Explain how you do what you do, hunting and killing people like me even though *you're* just like *us*. Does the hypocrisy of it get you off? Does it get you high?"

"We have made a choice," Emerson says, plainly. "We have chosen to reinforce the pattern. To salvage it. And that's what you'll do for us, Miriam. You have made your offer but I haven't quite accepted it—let me give you the terms of the deal, and if we both agree, then we can celebrate our partnership. You will remain here. In this house. A guest, though admittedly one that is under careful watch and who cannot leave. We will see you through to the birth of your child—you've got, what, another twelve or thirteen weeks to go, I'd estimate? During those weeks, we will find this medium friend of yours and he or she will cooperate accordingly. And since you seem to know others of your kind, you'll help us find them, too. You will rehabilitate yourself and pay for your ruinous ways by helping us find and eliminate others like you. And, ideally, helping us find this . . . demon of which you speak. This Ghost of the All-Dead. If it's real, if it's not just the delusion of some diseased mind, we will eliminate it as well."

Her hand twitches.

She envisions the next act will come quickly. He leans in as he tells her this, and she knows it's a condescending move—he likes to be heard, to be seen, and so he gets closer to her as he does it. And when he does, she'll wrap her hands around the neck of that bottle and smash it against his head.

But then what?

Miriam doesn't need to be a psychic to know that she will

have dispatched the older man only to be left with the capable cartel assassin.

There will be a bullet. Probably several. They will kill her child and maybe her before she has a chance to do anything else.

Her hand coils into a fist.

That means Alejandro has to go first.

Even as she nods along to Emerson's words, feigning some manner of agreement, she reaches out, and she finds what she needs to find—

A turkey vulture, circling. Riding the heat, looking for death.

She'd rather a hawk or a falcon, but the buzzard will do. It's a big enough bird. *I'll give you death*, she thinks to the bird—a bird she knows is about to be a sacrifice. Miriam slips into its mind easily enough. She stretches out through its black feathers, its bald head, its hooked beak. Its eyes—her eyes now—look down to see the house there, bathed in the bone-white light of the nearly full moon. She angles her wings for the dive—

Wham.

Back in her body. Sun glare behind her eyes. Light bleeding in dull, distant fireworks. Fingers are wound around her hair at the back of her skull. She's staring down at the counter. The tea has spilled over its rim. Her skull pounds. Alejandro stands behind her—*he slammed my head into the quartz countertop*, she thinks—and presses the gun to her temple.

"I saw that," he says, chuckling darkly. "You threw out a tether—a thread to catch something. What were you fishing for out there?" The gun barrel digs into the meat of her temple and she winces, tears at the corners of her eyes. "A bird, wasn't it? That's how you fucked up my car with those ugly little black bastards. You little fucking *bitch*."

Emerson clucks his tongue. "Avian control. That's something else, isn't it? Your powers aren't going away, Miss Black. They're evolving."

Alejandro yanks her up off the stool—she feels the cut on her side reopen. His gun presses under her chin. His face is alive with excitement; he's into it, and she can feel his erection pressing into her leg.

Murder gets this guy off.

Any bullshit about patterns and tapestries and preserving some kind of balance is exactly that: bullshit.

He's got a fetish, and it's exactly this.

Emerson walks around the counter, standing on the other side of her.

"Disappointing," he says. "I thought we could take you in, but now I fear you'll just be a feral housecat. Clawing up the furniture. Alejandro, you're right; I don't think we can really contain this one."

"Wait," she pleads, "I wasn't—"

"Take her back downstairs. I don't want to clean blood out of my kitchen; it'll stain the grout."

Alejandro wheels her around. She grunts, lashing out with a hard kick that lands square between his legs—he cries out, shoving her forward hard enough that her ass slams against the Spanish tile.

"Your kitchen is getting bloody," he seethes, his once-perfect black hair gone out of place, matted now against his forehead.

He raises the gun.

Kssht.

His head shakes, like he was slapped by an invisible hand.

Blood drools down a pair of new holes in each side of his head. Some oleaginous glob trickles out the far side—a bit of brain.

The assassin looks at her one last time, then topples backward. The gun drops from his hand. It clatters against the tile.

Miriam's eyes dart to see—

—the hole in the window, cracks spider-webbing out—

—Alejandro's left hand shaking, flopping against the tile like a dying fish ripped from the sea and chucked into an empty cooler—

—Emerson Caldecott, staring not at her but at *the gun*.

Miriam lunges for it.

So does he.

Her hand gets it first, and she wrestles it from his grip—

Realizing the weapon is lost, he backpedals as she brings the gun up. His hand fishhooks, sweeping across the white counter—

A teacup crashes against the tile as she tracks him with the pistol.

It's followed by a wave of scalding hot tea—

(*a dandelion tisane*)

She cries out, pulling the trigger. The shot goes wide. Splinters of wood kick up off a mantle shelf.

Kssht.

The window shatters.

The wine bottle on the counter shatters too—jumping straight up like a rabbit that just got bit in the ass by a rat. Wine splashes. Green glass crackles and rains down upon her.

Through a blur of tea and a haze of pain, Miriam grabs a stool and hauls herself to standing, nearly slipping on wine and glass.

But Emerson Caldecott is gone.

Time to hunt.

SIXTY-SEVEN

TALONS OUT

It's suddenly, eerily familiar.

Winding through a rich fucker's house, gun up and out, hunting a Caldecott through the space. Last time was Eleanor's home—a sprawling estate where she ultimately ended the lives of Eleanor's vicious, murderous children. The matriarch herself did not die there, no—she met her end drowning in a river, clutching Wren, trying to drown her, too. Miriam saved Wren and then was lost to the rapids. It was Louis who came up and saved them both. Louis, who died six months ago—

At Wren's hand.

As she stalks through the house, past a tall white-stone fireplace that seems to go on forever, past a massive television whose curved screen is nearly as big as the wall on which it hangs, past a sleek black-stone bar and toward a back patio and deck that overlook a backlit pool and Jacuzzi, she realizes what a trail of tragedy has been left in her wake. A recursive series of repeated beats, lives saved, lives ended, vengeances and vindications visited again and again, blood for blood, eyes for eyes. Miriam, hunted. Miriam, hunting. All of it circling an invisible axis like vultures in the sky.

The back patio is open. Night has finally sunk its fangs in. A faint breeze, oddly warm, washes into the empty room. She listens. She hears nothing. Except—

She wheels with the pistol.

And points it right at David Guerrero.

His gun, too, is pointed at her.

"Miriam," he says, gingerly. "Put the gun down."

"You first."

"It doesn't work like that."

"It's going to have to work like that."

She can see him working through it. Like someone trying to calculate the amount of the tip for a dining bill. He's trying to see if he can do it. If he can win this against her.

If the juice, as the saying goes, is worth the squeeze.

He does the calculus. He lowers his pistol.

She lowers hers, too.

"Emerson Caldecott is here somewhere. Or—" She points to the door. "Out there."

"Are you okay? You're bleeding."

She glances down. It's true; she is. Blood soaks her side. And then there's the old blood, gone black and brown, that soaks the other side of her shirt. Her face tingles, too, from where the tea burned her.

It'll heal, she thinks. *Sooner than later*.

"I'm fine. You need to find him."

"We will."

The two of them stare at each other.

"So, what happens now?" she asks. "Am I under arrest? Should I make a run for it? Are we gonna duel it out, see who's faster on the trigger? It's probably you, but I'll warn you, I'm a tricky one."

"I have firsthand situational awareness of your trickiness, Miriam." He holds up both hands in a supplicating gesture. "We're square."

"So, you know you just killed the Starfucker?"

"I am aware."

"Then I suspect we've both got some explaining to do."

"I suspect you're right."

SIXTY-EIGHT

SEVERANCE PACKAGE

Something about it all makes her want a cigarette so bad, she's ready to chew the bumper off Guerrero's car even as she leans against it. That's part of it: the lean. She wants to lean here, craning her head back, sucking on a cancer stick, letting it fill her lungs and saturate her with a buzz like from a hive that's lost its queen—then she'd fill the darkness with the smoke, like a ghost at the moment it is banished from the corporeal plane.

But she doesn't have a cigarette.

She can't even go back in that house and slurp the wine off the floor.

Best she could do is go make more tea.

Sorry, a *tisane*.

Fuck.

She's tired. Tired from today, and yesterday, and from all the yesterdays before it. She's ready to have this be over. In a perfect world, she'd be out there right now with Guerrero and Anaya, searching for Emerson Caldecott. But she's bloody and bewildered, and still reeling from all that's happened already. And, again: she's tired.

Tired to the marrow. Tired to the core. Tired to the soul.

Inside the house, other FBI agents crawl. Guerrero's car here is no longer the only one: three others showed up. A forensics team and some other on-duty agents in the area, all sweeping the house, all looking for clues to the location of Emerson Caldecott.

Soon, a sound: the crackle of brush. Miriam flinches with the sound of coming footsteps, because at this point, would it be a surprise to see Emerson Caldecott show up, holding a bloody knife? Or Harriet Adams, now just a gory automaton held up by stiff ligaments and rubbery tendons, shuffling her way toward Miriam with renewed murderous intent?

But it's no foe. It's just David and Julie. She has a rifle slung over her shoulder—Miriam learned that it was she who shot Alejandro through the window. Sitting out here in the vineyard, parked between rows, lying on the roof of the car with the rifle out, bipod down, and scope to her eye.

They came because of Steve Wiebe.

Or that's what they tell her.

But Miriam's been sitting here on the hood of this car, leaning and sometimes reclining against the hood, and she wonders if that really lines up.

Time-wise, she can't say exactly how long has passed since she got here. But was it enough time for Wiebe to get the message, to contact them, to get them here and . . . what, track the cell phone in the vines? That's their story. But does it add up? Maybe if they're really *that* good . . .

"We didn't find him," Julie Anaya says.

"But we will," Guerrero answers hastily—whether meaning to give Miriam some comfort or to salve his own ego, she can't say.

Miriam tries not to twitch at the news, but she does. She tenses up, knowing that there's a Caldecott still out there, and that he will be none too happy to have lost one from his so-called Organization—at her hand, no less. She, who killed his sister already.

But maybe that's a problem now for Guerrero.

She tells him as much: "Caldecott is yours," Miriam says,

though there's a part of her that wants, as with everything, to handle this herself. Leaving another Caldecott in the world burns her up. But she has bigger beasts to slay. "I need to call Gabby, let her know I'm okay."

"I already called her," Guerrero says. "Though you should probably call her yourself, too."

"Thanks for saving my ass," Miriam mutters, reluctantly, still wishing like hell she had a cigarette, because right now, she'd do a cool exhale of smoke in his direction—just to make it clear that her gratitude was disaffected, detached, with a little bit of *thank you, but also fuck you* in there. Instead she just has to look gracious, and really, yuck, *ptoo*, ew.

"We're sorry things went south for all of us," Guerrero says. "You know, if you had just trusted me to begin with—"

"Fuck you," Miriam says. "Fuck you and your trust. You were using me. You know it and I know it. You pissed all over my trust and strung me along."

She can see Guerrero's starting to get mad, and is about to issue his heady retort—

But Julie interrupts him. "You're right, Miriam," Julie says. "We did not treat you like an equal partner and so, here we all are. Hoisted by our own petards, as the saying goes." The woman forces a smile. "We're just glad it all worked out."

At that, Miriam leans forward. She narrows her stare to suspicious arrow slits. "Yeaaaah. I wanted to ask you about that."

"Go ahead," David says, suspiciously.

"How *did* it all work out?" Before they say anything, she stands up and pushes on with the brief inquisition. "We're in, what, Monterey? Five, six hours north of Los Angeles—assuming no traffic, which is like assuming the sun won't rise or men won't suddenly become shitheads. I called Wiebe, what, earlier today? It must've taken time for him to tell you, then for you to try to track the phone—and to get here. And it's not like you took a helicopter because"—she gestures behind her—"this is your car, Guerrero."

He laughs softly. "Miriam, we're the FBI, we are a well-oiled machine that has long been trained on maximum efficiency—"

"Except you work out of a trailer. You're exiles from the Bureau, more or less. But you know who *is* efficient?"

They stare at her, expectantly.

"Psychics," she says.

Julie and Guerrero share a look.

"Miriam, you're mistaken—"

Julie interrupts him. "Just tell her."

He runs his fingers through his hair, then sighs.

"The day you stole Lukauskis's name from my computer, I was . . . incensed, honestly. I felt betrayed. That was real. And what Julie did was real too. She stopped me, as you well remember. Because Julie has a gift—"

"Clairsentience," Miriam says. "I saw it on the list, but I confess, I don't know what the fuck it means."

Julie shrugs. "I don't know what it means either. My ability is not so clear-cut. I have instincts. I call them *gut checks*. I receive . . . flashes; they don't tell me anything, really. They're not epiphanies with information; they're just feelings. So, I act on them."

"I've learned to listen to her feelings," Guerrero says. "And when she said to let you go, I regrettably did. But that night, I couldn't sleep—I wrestled with why I should've let you go and why I should let you stay gone. And I realized it: you're like me. You said I'm an exile. You're an exile too. Like it or not, who we are puts us outside the margin. But you working for me brought you in, and it . . . hamstrung you. Hobbled you like a captive. You needed to be out here in the world to do your magic. And you did. You did it. You found the killer. And you led us to him."

Miriam forces a bitter smile. "Cool story, bro. Still doesn't explain how you got here." She takes a step closer to Guerrero and in a smaller, steelier voice says, "What's your power, Guerrero?"

He hesitates.

"You weren't on the list. I didn't see how you categorized yourself."

But finally, he says:

"Officially? It's categorized as *biokinetic psychic-focused psychometry*."

"Speak human, please."

"It means I can find people. Particularly other psychics."

She crosses her arms over her chest. "So, go back out there and find Emerson Fucking Caldecott, *David*. Why are we just standing here?"

"I can only find those I've met."

"Shit." She blinks. "Wait, so you've been able to find me this whole time?" And suddenly, it makes sense. "You knew where I was. You knew what I was doing. You believed I'd go after Taylor Bowman and the Starfucker on my own, and when I did, you'd go where I went. You're telling me I was fucking *bait*."

"Not bait," Julie says.

"Think of us," David says, "as wolves following the trail of a fellow wolf. Maybe a lone wolf, but still a wolf. You have a track record, and a good one, of finding these monsters. We knew to rely on that."

"Jesus." Miriam rubs her eyes. Her side begins to itch intensely all of a sudden: she knows the injury is on the mend underneath the blood-soaked bandage. And, on cue, the baby kicks too. "So where does this leave us?"

"As I said, we're square. Your record is clear. You're of course free to continue to work with us. Even as a consultant. You wouldn't need to come in every day, you'd just be on call—"

"No," she says abruptly. Too abruptly, probably. "I'm a feral cat, and I don't do well with being kept. I'd love to be domesticated, but I've been out here in the wild too long, Guerrero."

"Fair enough."

"So, that means, for the record, there's no money, no healthcare, nothing like that."

"After six months, that's correct."

"Wait, what?"

"There's a severance package, obviously. You work for the government, and we take care of our own. You'll get a small stipend, weekly, and six months of COBRA healthcare coverage. Plus your apartment. After that, you are entirely on your own."

In more ways than you know, Guerrero.

"We're not square, though," she says with no small bitterness. "Not for one hot fuck of a second. You owe me. I have the name: Abraham Lukauskis. Now I need—"

"You want to know where he is."

"Damn right I do."

And then he tells her.

"Holy shit," she says, because that's not what she expected.

PART NINE

BLACK STAR CANYON

SIXTY-NINE

THE DISRUPTION

The next day, Guerrero drops Miriam off at their condo, where Gabby awaits. Soon as Miriam walks in the door, their reunion is cataclysmic. They embrace each other with sudden ferocity, like a pair of tidal waves crashing together, like one tectonic plate crushing into the next, like two hawks slamming into one another with talons intertwined as they tumble fruitlessly and happily toward the surface of the Earth.

Miriam *oofs* as she and Gabby swallow one another in their embrace. "Ow," she says.

"Sorry," Gabby says, kissing her on the cheek, then the mouth, then going in for another trash compactor hug. Miriam, for her part, is not a passive participant. She's not trapped in the hug like a guy caught under a vending machine he rocked back and forth in order to get the bag of Hot Cheetos that he was owed by the wretched snack box. She's into it. It just hurts because right now, everything hurts. And itches.

Someone else clears their throat in the apartment—

Miriam turns and sees that Steve Wiebe is here.

"I got your voicemail," he says, the words babbling out of him, "and I about pissed my pants because, like, holy fuck, what? You were in trouble, so I did like you said, I got in touch with Guerrero—I didn't even hesitate, I knew they might want to arrest me, but I had to do something and—"

"You saved me," Miriam says. It's partly true. Guerrero knew where she was, but only Wiebe told them she was in trouble and needed their intervention. "Thanks."

"Life's short, right?" he says, a nervous chord plucked in those three words. Because she knows, and *he* knows, that his life is shorter now than he'd like. "But it's long enough for a hug."

He opens his arms.

"I don't usually do this," she says. "Hugging people."

"You just hugged Gabby."

"Gabby and I *embraced*. Because we fuck each other and love one another. That said, you did good, Underwear Man."

And she hugs him.

It doesn't even hurt.

It even feels a little bit nice.

A little bit.

But all this is distraction. Miriam knows that. She has to get to the heart of the matter—forget the Starfucker, forget David Guerrero, to hell with Emerson Caldecott. He is a problem for Future Miriam.

Present Miriam has a different problem.

As she pulls away from Steve Wiebe, she says to Gabby, "Tell me it's true. Tell me Guerrero didn't lie to me." She draws a deep breath. "Tell me you found Abraham Lukauskis."

"I . . . ," Gabby starts.

And with that, someone comes shambling out of the bathroom. He wears a ragtag mess of clothes: a black T-shirt over his sallow frame, then a ratty gray hoodie over the T-shirt, then a rat-chewed black bathrobe over the hoodie. His salt-and-pepper hair is long and matted, and barely seems separate from the similarly long and matted beard, which drapes down over his chest because he has the posture of a broken coatrack. He grunts as he shuffles out.

"You," he says, his voice deep and full-throated, growling like an ancient tomb being opened. He looks at Miriam. "*You* are the disruption."

Gabby whispers in her ear: "I found him."

"Where?" she faux-whispers back. "In Hell?"

"Basically."

SEVENTY

THE MEDIUM

Lukauskis messily eats SpaghettiOs. They stick in his beard, little life preservers of pasta trapped in blobby suspensions of bright orange sauce. He's noisy at it, too. Slurping and chewing. Smacking and humming to himself. He stares into the bowl as he eats, a prophet looking for secret truths in the configuration of carbohydrate zeroes.

He sits at one side of their little nook table. Everybody else—Miriam, Gabby, Steve—stands at the other side, watching him.

Miriam leans into Gabby: "Did we have a can of SpaghettiOs? I would've eaten that."

"He brought his own," she says, horrified.

"I brought my own," he reiterates.

"He brought his own!" Steve Wiebe chimes in, his voice sounding like it's nearing the edge of madness, like he's not really sure if he should stay for whatever it is that's happening here.

"So," Miriam says, loudly, too loudly. "You're the medium."

"I'm the medium." His voice is a curious combination of California Stoner and Eastern European Pierogi-Maker. He comes from somewhere else, but he's clearly been *here* a while. "And you're the disruption."

"You keep saying that, but I don't know what it means."

He mumbles to himself, then shoves another spoonful of

canned pasta into his beard-cave. "I don't know what it means either."

"And yet maybe you could try to explain it? Pretty please?"

"Hnnh. Hngh. Fine. Fine." He takes a napkin—translation: his own hoodie sweatshirt—and wipes his mouth with it. He licks his lips and sucks gnarly curls of his own beard into his mouth, siphoning food off of them. "You are haunted. You are broken. And you are breaking things by being haunted. I see—" He stands up now and gestures, not toward Miriam but toward the space all around her. "A disruption. I had seen it before. Heard it whispered on the wind, heard it bubbled up through sewer slots. Bad energy flowing toward a vulnerable point, like water leaking through a *crack* in the *bathroom tile*. The dead are dying. The spirits are losing themselves. Disruption. You're it."

Miriam looks to Gabby.

Then to Steve.

They look back at her.

"None of that made a lick of fucking sense," Miriam says.

"Doesn't have to," Lukauskis says. "Monkeys don't understand gravity, but gravity is still gravity."

"I think he just called us monkeys," Gabby says.

"Kinda rude, to be honest," Steve says.

"*Kinda rude, to be honest,*" Lukauskis says, in a mocking tone.

"You know," Steve Wiebe begins, like he's about to go on a tirade, but Miriam has no time for any of this. He sees her look and clamps up.

"I *am* haunted," Miriam says, suddenly.

The room falls quiet.

"I have a Trespasser. I don't know if it—or he, or she—gave me this power or what. I don't even know what *it* is. For a long time, I thought it was just in my head. And maybe it was, once. But now it's getting out. If I am its prison, it's figured out how to escape—it's not out, not all the way, but this thing is testing its routes, its pathways, and it knows where to go even if it doesn't have the tunnel dug all the way out yet. My mother called this thing by a different name. She said it was the Ghost of All-Dead."

"Your mother?" Gabby asks in a low voice.

"My mother."

"Miriam, your mom is—"

"Yes, yeah, I know, she's dead. But she came to me in a . . . dream or something, and told me this thing's name, and now I'm telling all of you."

"The Ghost of All-Dead," Lukauskis says.

His voice, too, is small.

It is, if Miriam reads it right, afraid.

Which makes *her* afraid. If something scares *this* guy—

Then it ought to scare them all.

"You know what it is?" she asks him.

"I do."

And then he tells them.

THE GHOST OF ALL-DEAD

Once upon a time, things were as things were.

People died. They left a piece of themselves behind. Some-times, that piece was more powerful than whatever part of them moved on to the next world, and if that piece was powerful enough, it could affect our world.

A ghost, a spirit. Wraith, specter, haunt, haint, apparition. Sometimes, these entities are peaceful. Many times, they are lost and confused. Other times, they are angry, vengeful things, because the piece that stayed behind is the worst piece: a part of the soul broken off, forcefully, painfully, with great trauma and consequence.

This is the cycle of things. It sounds unnatural but it is the way. Death happens. Death cleaves off a little bitty piece. That piece remains.

On and on. On and on.

I can see the pieces that remain. I can speak to them.

I have been with the spirits for most of my life. Or perhaps they have been with me. They are with me now. Like a cloud of flies.

But this cloud of flies has dimmed. Thinned out. Those who remain have dwindled—and some of those who remain have gone from peaceful to angry. This was not always the case. Angry spirits could be made passive, but passive spirits were never turned the other way. Trauma could be resolved in the truly dead, but not reinstituted.

A darkness is thrust through the lingering dead. A shadow cast upon them. A disruption. They are agitated. They speak of it in babbled songs and lunatic monologues. They do not understand it or know what it is.

Sometimes, I see them moving together, like a herd of the spectral dead. Moving down streets or through fields. Whistling through the grass toward something. The anger is plain on their faces, and they are always committed; they cannot be swayed. They will not even speak to me. Their anger, their grief, it's thick around them like a miasma. I can feel it clinging to me like grease. It makes me angry. It makes me sad. I come away from it feeling rage and sorrow in equal portion.

I thought one day to discover what this was, this mad migration. So, I went to places with a great deal of death energy. Places where I have more power, though places where the dead have more power too. I can trap the spirits there. I can stick them to this world, temporarily—like a thumb pressing down on the head of the snake. The tail whips, but the snake cannot move. I found one apparition: a young man, a hiker, killed in the woods by a hunter of men. Chased, tormented, shot through the neck. I trapped him inside a coyote. I asked him, why do you do this? Why do you flee, and where do you go? And he said, I go to be with the Ghost of All-Dead. I go to join with the others and break the cycle.

Then the coyote's jaws cracked wide open. Impossibly wide. It broke out of my trap. It came for me, eyes the color of fire and blood, ribs breaking free of its skin like the tiny bones broken in a man's crushed foot. It tore into me. Ripped up my side. Clawed at my breastbone like a dog trying to dig up a toy it had buried, but my heart was the toy it sought. I did not manage to fight it off but was lucky simply because the body could no longer hold the spirit. It split like the skin of a kidney bean. All of what was inside the animal came spilling out. Including the spirit, who fled.

I did not want to go to the hospital, but on the way back to my house, on the bus, I lost consciousness and awakened in a hospital.

I hate hospitals. Many dead are trapped there. Lost and looking for a way back. They came to my bedside every night. Some of them pleaded with me to help them, to give them resolution. Others harangued me, called me terrible names, told me I would be punished for meddling. That the Ghost of All-Dead would one day see me, and then it would be over.

SEVENTY-ONE

DEATH THAT FEEDS ON DEATH

"That was two years ago," he says, standing there, swaying back and forth gently like a sapling in a strong breeze.

"Where was this?" Miriam asks.

"Same place your friend here found me."

"Black Star Canyon," Gabby says. Way she says it, her words are shot through with a frequency of real fear. "That place . . . Something's not right about it, Miriam. It's wrong. Like a painting on the wall you know is hung wrong, at a funny angle, but you just can't seem to fix it."

Abraham nods. "It's the energy of death there. It feeds on itself, creates the condition of death—like a fire that needs no fuel to thrive but for the presence of *more fire*. Some say the place was marked first with the slaughter of Indian horse thieves by American trappers who were hired as mercenaries to reclaim the stolen horses. It continued with the death of James Gregg at the hands of Henry Hungerford—once again, a dispute over a horse, this time a fight over a price that turned deadly. Squatters hide there and have shot at hikers and bikers. Killed two. Some say there have been sacrifices there of animal and human, and I can confirm the former—not only because I sacrificed that coyote, though I did not mean to. Others claim Satanist cults operate there, which is true, though far less sinister than others imagine: Satanists, I've found, are really quite nice people."

"I can confirm this," Steve Wiebe says. "I've driven a few to their meetings. They're pretty rad."

"Great," Miriam says, poorly hiding her irritation. "So, the spirits of the dead are . . . joining with the Ghost of All-Dead. I still don't understand."

He shrugs. "I don't understand it either, except that if this is the thing that haunts you, you're neck-deep in particularly foul shit."

"Kind of you to say."

"The Ghost of All-Dead is a consumptive thing. Greedy. It is gathering souls to it. Why, I cannot say."

"Maybe it's not one thing. Maybe it's a collective of them," she says. "It would explain a few things. How it seems to take different shapes and voices. It isn't the same every time."

"Perhaps. Perhaps it is a catalog of the dead. A hive mind of specters, a colony of the killed. But why?"

A chill passes through Miriam. "Cycles. You talk about cycles. It's the way of things: people die, they leave bits behind. I've also heard talk of . . . patterns. Tapestries. All of it being a part of something greater. Things were what things were." Suddenly, her mother's voice echoes in her ear: *It is what it is, Miriam.* "Maybe it's trying to break that cycle. Life and death and whatever is left between them. It's angry. It wants . . . vengeance. It believes death isn't fair and so it wants to break it all apart." Her knees start to buckle. "It's trying to use *me* to break it all apart."

"You might be right.'

Miriam barely stifles a small gasp. She has to sit down or fall down, so she roughly drags a chair over to collapse onto. Her eyes focus on a point in space a million miles away. Through everything. Away from here.

No, fuck this. She stands back up so suddenly, she nearly knocks over the chair. Miriam paces, then takes a hard turn and veers pointedly toward the bathroom. She spies herself in the mirror looking tired, lost, wayward—her eyes look puffy, like she's ready to cry. Fuck *this*, too. No mirror. Into the bedroom, then, there she goes, into the dark of that room, the blinds down, and she thinks the darkness should be comforting and quiet but it's not, because *she's* still there, herself, no matter where she goes—

There she is.

"Fuck," she says, a strangled word.

Gabby enters in behind her. A gentle hand on her shoulder. "You okay?"

"I'm fine *wait no* I'm not fucking fine. Fuck. Fuck! I'm a dupe, Gabby. It's all a ruse and I'm just the mark. Dog on a leash. Puppet on a fucking hand. I haven't done any good. I've just . . . fucked up. I've fucked up on behalf of some kind of pissed-off ghost—this thing isn't even some nightmare hallucination I conjured, it's real, and it's been pushing me down this path for so long, I came to believe that what I've been doing is somehow the right thing. But I'm not a hero. I'm a villain. I'm a goddamn *tragedy*."

"Miriam, whatever that thing wanted from you, you did what you did because you felt it was right. We're all here because of you."

"Yeah. *Exactly*."

"I don't mean it like that. I mean . . . we're here because we love you and we trust you. And we're here to help. To do whatever you need us to do. Okay? Don't focus on the past. Don't focus on what that thing wanted from you. You were in control. You did the best you could. It's okay."

It's okay.

On the one hand, she needs to hear that.

On the other hand, to hell with that.

It isn't okay.

None of this is okay.

But she can still make it okay.

"Gabby, it's not long now. Not long before . . . before the doctor dies. Beagle. Before you kill him. You realize that, don't you? The clock is counting down. Days now. But maybe we can fix it."

She kisses Gabby hard, leaving the other woman stunned and bewildered. Miriam whirls past her, past Steve, who stands in the hallway and says as she passes, "You left me in there with the crazy man. Please don't leave me alone with the crazy man—"

But she's already moving toward Lukauskis. The medium stares at her with strange, hound-dog eyes. His eyes are intense, and sad, too. Beneath those eyes hang piles of skin, bags of them, bags so heavy, he probably has to pay a shitload of extra fees to get on a fucking airplane. He stares at her.

"What do you want to do, Miriam?" he asks.

"I want this thing gone. I want to find it. I want to trap it. I want to kill it, or whatever it means to destroy something that's already dead. And I want you to help me, Lukauskis. You're *going* to help me."

He nods. "Yes, I will. But it will not be easy. Go, eat, rest, do what you need to do. We will leave here soon. We must be there at midnight, for that is when the wall between worlds is thin."

"Where is there?"

"Where else? Black Star Canyon."

SEVENTY-TWO

THE TRUTH ABOUT OCTOPUSES, PISS-JARS, AND TSARIST MYSTICS

They leave long after dark, 10 PM. Steve drives. Gabby in the front seat. Miriam in the back with the shambling pile of darkness called "Abraham Lukauskis." The car swims through the garish lights and neon sea of Los Angeles at night: the smear of fast-food signs, tattoo parlors, movie theaters. The dull thud of bass rises up under the road to meet them as they pass the hip-hop car, then a dubstep car, then a heavy metal car. Through the city, to I-5, to 91, the highway stop-and-go even now, even at night. The Los Angeles highway system, Miriam thinks, is a special kind of purgatory, and she idly wonders if these drivers never leave it. They eat here, sleep here, work here. Fast food and audiobooks and conference calls and pissing out the window, maybe shitting in the fast-food bag. Consigned to the occult hell of the endless, deadlocked highways.

Miriam thinks about this because it's easier than thinking about how Abraham Lukauskis smells. It's not that he smells as expected: it's not body odor, or trash, or piss. He smells strongly like an autumnal pinecone. Cinnamon and clove. Like he's just come from an orgy with Father Christmas and Pumpkin Spice. Was Pumpkin Spice a Spice Girl? Miriam can't remember. She should've been, at any rate.

He's got a bag of stuff between his legs. More of the same shit they found in his apartment, and at the run-down gas station in Halloran Springs: saint candles, votives, bird skeletons, chalk, crystals.

(Thankfully, no piss-jars or cat mummies.)

"That stuff," Miriam says. "We found it at your apartment."

"Sorry about shooting you in the chest," he mumbles.

"It's fine. I'm alive." She glances down at the bag. "What's the deal with all that shit, anyway? What do they do?"

"They don't do squat."

"What?"

"I said, they don't do squat."

"No, I *heard* you; I was doing a reflexive *what*, more like a *what the fuck do you mean, they don't do squat, so why do you have them, then?*"

"Because they make me feel better."

"They're just a crutch?"

"Everything is just a crutch. We all have little rituals. Knocking on wood, salt over the shoulder, rub the rabbit's foot. We like things a certain way even when it doesn't matter. We pretend the crisper drawer in our refrigerator does what it says. We make believe that the knob on the toaster actually makes the toast darker. We take herbal supplements and vitamins even though they don't do anything for us, and we just"—he mimes a stream of motion coming from his crotch—"*whoosh*, pee them out. We like what we like and we do what we do and it helps us get through the day. It is these idiosyncrasies"—that word, he pronounces each syllable distinct and separate from the next, overenunciating it—"that make us human."

"Does it help you with your power, though?"

He shrugs. "I don't know. Doesn't hurt."

"Must be weird."

"All things are weird. What weird thing do you speak of?"

"Being you. Having a power talking to . . . invisible dead people."

"I was always weird."

"Were you born with it? The curse."

He strokes his long black-and-white beard. "No. I died. And when I died, it opened this *conduit* inside me, and it has been open ever since."

Miriam wrinkles up her brow. "You died?"

"Yes. I stole a man's dog. He beat the dog and I did not want him to beat the dog anymore. So, as a boy, I went to his house at night, in winter, every night, to tame the dog he kept chained up under the porch. I fed it bread and warm water. I earned its trust, and when I did, I freed it. Me and the dog, a red hound, ran away, but the man heard the clatter of chains. He pursued us with a rifle. I took a shortcut to my house, across a frozen lake. The dog ran beside me, slipping on the lake. A shot rang out. The dog tumbled forward. Blood bounced on the ice. I collapsed atop the dog to try to save it. And then the ice broke and the two of us fell through."

Steve leans around the headrest in the front seat. "The dog saved you, right? Pulled you out of the ice? Hero Dog?"

"Yes."

He exhales sweet relief. "Thank God."

"Then the dog died."

"Oh, goddamnit."

"It was the man who shot the dog who dragged me off the lake, called the ambulance. I was dead but then came back to life. The dog was dead too, but I could see it still. It was with me then. I see him still, some days."

Miriam arches a brow. "The dog was a ghost?"

"Correct."

"Dogs have ghosts."

"Correct."

"Do all animals have ghosts?"

"No. Only smart animals. Dogs, cats, octopuses, ravens."

"Is that it? Is that the list of animals who get ghosts?"

"I cannot say. Maybe parrots."

"Maybe parrots?"

"Maybe parrots."

It's fucked-up, but it's helping. Talking to him. It's absurd, this conversation, but it calms her a little. She's a bustling cluster of nerves, like a sack of sea urchins stabbing each other, a bag of bees, a satchel of starving snakes. But this really, weirdly helps. *Crutches, indeed.*

"I'm sorry you died," she says.

"I've grown used to it."

"Used to dying?"

He nods. "I have died six times."

It's Gabby's turn to lean back. "Who are you, Rasputin?"

"I am," he says plainly, as if, duh, yes, obviously.

"Who the fuck is Rasputin?" Miriam asks.

Steve jumps in: "Grigori Rasputin. An old Russian dude—"

"Mystic," Gabby says. "Mystic, and advisor to the tsar." She beholds the looks that angle her way and she hastily explains: "I took a lot of weird classes in community college."

"I just read *Hellboy*," Steve says.

"He died a bunch of times," Gabby says. "Well, sort of. They tried to *kill* him a bunch of times, and he just kept not dying."

"I am the reincarnation of Rasputin," Lukauskis says. "Yes."

And nobody really knows what to say to that.

"This is probably the strangest car ride I have ever been on," Miriam says. "And I've been in an SUV when a guy got his foot cut off."

SEVENTY-THREE
DEAD ENERGY

The quiet lunacy of the car ride goes sour as they get closer to the Black Star Canyon. Miriam can feel it—she wants to chalk it up to just the anxiety of ants breeding in her gut, but she also can't deny it feels more palpable than that. Her skin tingles. She can feel her pulsebeat in strange places: her fingertips, her eyeballs, the backs of her calves. The baby, too, seems to shift again and again, like the little girl can't get comfortable, like she knows something is up, something is wrong. For Miriam, it's like hearing a dead frequency, or being in a place that's eerily, improperly quiet.

And it only gets worse as Steve pulls off to the side of the road at Lukauskis's command. "This is where we go," the medium says.

He points to a berm over the side of the road, thick with scrub and shrub—it rises up and then past that, sinks down once more into the darkness. Miriam can't see much beyond that, though the light of the moon draws the line over the top of what looks to be an old metal fence.

"Are you sure about this?" she asks Lukauskis.

"I am sure of nothing. But this is where we go."

He leads. They follow. Steve starts to come too, but Miriam says, "No. You wait here. Stay by the car. We might need you."

"Are you sure?"

"No. I'm not sure of anything. But this is like something out of a horror movie, and the fewer of us we have to keep track of out here in the dark, the better." And she thinks to herself, *Honestly, dude, you're too good for whatever's about to happen out there.*

He nods. He remains.

She and Gabby follow the mad mystic.

Brush crackles as they climb the berm and meet the fence. But Lukauskis is right: this *is* where they go. The chain link is pulled up, away from the ground, with enough room that they can crawl under.

One by one, they do. Miriam is last. She shimmies on her back, because of the roundness of her pregnant belly. But as she scooches forward, inch by inch, she feels the teeth of the metal fence dig into her shirt, then her skin, drawing three slow claw-marks across the pale expanse of her flesh.

She winces as she pulls through.

Blood drizzles from the rake marks. It soaks her shirt.

"Shit," Gabby says, suddenly worried. She tends to Miriam quickly, saying that they might need to turn around, go back, get a bandage.

"I'll heal, remember?" she says. "It's fine."

"Miriam, I don't know—"

Lukauskis interrupts: "The blood is good. Like chum in the water, it summons the shark. Let's keep moving. Midnight is coming."

He shambles off through the scrub, toward a small dusty trail. They follow after, and Miriam wonders: can they really trust him? Certainly, Guerrero seems to have. And though Lukauskis seems like a straight-up moonbat, Miriam tends to like moonbats. They're nuts. But they're honest. They're authentic. And in her experience, they're better people than most.

Still, something about this place . . .

It's *sour*. Her guts curdle like she just drank a glass of vinegar. The air is like air gone bad from disease. It doesn't *smell* that way. It just *feels* like it. Like it's turned, somehow. Gone rancid, gone rotten.

They wind their way over one hill, down another.

Miriam pulls the mini-Maglite that Gabby usually keeps in her purse, and flicks it on. Lukauskis turns to her, gives her an irritated look—his black eyes flashing above the thorny expanse of his tangled beard. But he keeps going on, and she leaves the light shining.

They pass a sign framed by thick vegetation:

THIS TRAIL IS NOT MAINTAINED.

ORANGE COUNTY IS NOT RESPONSIBLE FOR ANY LOSS OR INJURY SUFFERED BY REASON OF ITS USE.

The sign is pocked with bullet holes.

Further down, they find an old tent—months, maybe years, past. It's been slashed to hell. All around are cinder blocks, campfire ash, empty and rusted cans. There's a half-wall nearby, in the scrub, and several someones have spray-painted various symbols on it. The anarchy symbol, a pentagram, that fucked-up heavy metal S that Miriam used to write on her high school notebook for reasons that remain to this day unknown.

Ahead, another wall—the rocks in it bulging and uneven. Written on that is a message: WE ALL FALL. Past that, an overturned VW Bus, and on its roof someone has tagged a message in big, puffy letters: FUCK YOU.

Succinct, she thinks.

They keep walking. Miriam's circle of vision is just what the little light affords her: a halo of illumination, beyond which everything else is just creeping shadow. Trees like hands reaching for the stars. Boulders like the heads of skulking, sleeping giants.

Ahead, they cross under what looks like a fallen telephone

pole—it lies angled over the path, and they have to duck beneath it.

Spray-painted upon it is the direst warning yet:

GO BACK

NOT WORTH IT

She likes to think it's just a fucked-up hiker version of a Yelp review: *Meh, shitty trail, turn back, one star, would give it zero stars if I could*. But her gut tells her it's more a warning about what you pay by going forward, and how nothing that happens from this point will be worth that price.

She clears her throat, catching up to Lukauskis with Gabby.

"What's the plan?" she asks. "How deep do we have to go?"

"I don't know."

"You don't know what? I asked you two questions."

He grunts. "And with one stone I slay two birds. *I do not know* is a sufficient answer for both of your queries, Miriam Black."

"You have no plan? I kinda think—" She grits her teeth, biting back anger. "I kinda think we need a plan."

"This sort of thing is not a typical thing. What we do here is not math or science. It is art. Art has no plan. But if I had to guess—"

"Yeah, fucking guess, please."

"We do as I have done before. We summon your ghost. We bind it to this place by trapping it in an animal. A coyote, most likely. Then we seek answers from it. And if we must, we kill the beast."

It's Gabby's turn to ask: "And that'll do what, exactly? Miriam already said this thing is happy to kill its . . . hosts, or whatever. Didn't seem to affect it at all."

"That was elsewhere. This is Black Star Canyon. The dead energy here will create a kinship with the entity. It will trap it here."

"That sounds like a temporary solution," she growls.

"The existence of ghosts should tell you that all solutions are temporary solutions. Even death is not a permanent condition."

Fuck.

"And you're sure you can trap it in a coyote?"

"Yes."

"You've always been able to bind spirits to animals?"

He shakes his head and holds up a dissenting finger. "No. My power has evolved. As yours has, has it not? First, I could only see the dead. Then I could speak to them. Then I could . . . move them around, bind them to things, to beasts. Which makes them vulnerable, likelier to tell me the truth when they are in this plane, trapped here, with me."

Gabby interjects: "Last time, you said trapping it into a coyote didn't work out so well. That thing nearly killed you. This spirit, Miriam's Trespasser—it's more powerful. *Too* powerful just to be bound."

Shame casts a sudden and unexpected shadow across his face. That cuts him. He has not until this point seemed vulnerable to anything; he's mostly been a shambling mound of uncaring ambiguity. *Maybe this will work, maybe it won't, I died six times.* But now he looks disappointed. Worried. Injured. A little part of him seems to crumple inward. "You may be right. I failed the last time. I could fail now, too." He draws a deep breath through flaring nostrils. "Perhaps we should go. This was a mistake."

He turns to head back the other way. Miriam catches him by—well, she's not sure what piece of clothing she's holding on to, and she half-expects him to slip out of it like a lizard dropping its tail, but he's hooked.

"Whoa, whoa, whoa," she says. "You told me you could do this. You were all *full steam ahead* and now you're not sure?"

"I . . . I can be overconfident. Foolish. I've made mistakes before. When I do, I put myself on the line, and that is an acceptable loss. But now it could hurt you, and her, and your unborn child. I cannot accept that loss."

Miriam nearly bites her own lip off. "We need to do this. Now."

"It's too dangerous. Your friend is right. I have only heard of this Ghost of All-Dead in whispers, but what remains clear is that it's powerful. And I am not up to the task. I may not be able to hold it in the beast for long, if at all, and if the beast attacks . . . Those teeth, those claws. Empowered by a vengeful, angry entity? Who knows what damage it could do?"

"So, we put it in something that won't attack."

"Miriam," Gabby says.

"What is it?"

"I have an idea."

"I don't, so let's hear it."

"Forget the coyote." To Lukauskis, Gabby asks, "Can you bind the spirit into a bird? A vulture, a raven, something."

He hmms, and nods. "I could."

Miriam understands.

"Oh. Oh, fuck. If it's in a bird—I can get into its head. You trap the spirit in the bird, and I enter the bird's mind. I control the bird, which means maybe I control the Trespasser. And *that* gives you time to kill it."

She's nearly dizzy with both the fear and the possibility of it: being trapped inside an animal's mind with the Trespasser—the Ghost of All-Dead—is a horror for which she is not prepared. But it's also how she gets answers to her questions. If she can at least find a place and exert her will over it, maybe they have a shot. Maybe it's how she holds it accountable. Maybe it's how they end the Trespasser.

"A bird is perfect," he says. "A psychopomp is already a soul's vessel. Filling it with the Trespasser has . . . a kind of cosmic parity." But he shakes his head again. "It could still be dangerous. Are you sure about this?"

"No," Miriam says. "But it's the best we have. I want to do it."

"All right," Lukauskis says. "Then we need to move. Because midnight is nearly upon us, and we have a bit more walking to do."

SEVENTY-FOUR

FORGIVE US OUR TRESPASSES

They come to a clearing in the scrub and the trees, a low place peppered with massive rust-red pipe pieces laying about—pieces big enough, you could walk through them if you ducked your head—some on their side, some facing toward the night-time sky like one of Hell's own chimneys. Boulders ring the area, and some of them have boreholes drilled through them: holes big enough for rebar or a stick of dynamite. And in the center of the clearing: a crater where nothing grows, where the dirt is black and unforgiving, thrust through with a tangle of dead roots and runners.

Lukauskis tells them that the dead call this the *place of portals*.

"They gather here," he says, "like water rushing to a sunken place." But then he looks around, glaring past them with such a faraway stare that it appears he's looking *through* the world rather than at it. "But none are here. This place is dead of the dead. Devoid of all but the void."

Miriam wants to act like she doesn't understand—but she does. She can feel it. It's like being in a house when the electricity goes out. It goes beyond just a sudden silence: it's like she can't feel the frequency of life and energy all around. The air is still and momentarily cold.

And then—

A grave wind rushes in, hot and breathy, the Devil's own exhalation—and with it, the faint stink of something burning, the underlayment of rot and sulfur. Then it's gone again and the air goes dead.

Lukauskis hisses, "Something is coming. Your spirit has found us. It is attracted to your presence here in this place, a confluence it cannot ignore." He hurries around, dropping candles around the portals and quickly hanging dangling bird bones from nearby branches like ornaments from a particularly fucked-up Christmas tree. Gabby hurries alongside him, helping him set up his ritual items. To Miriam he says with a bluster of impatient irritation, "You should find your bird *now*."

She lets her senses radiate outward—though she's never before thought of it this way, she realizes now it's not unlike what Alejandro told her, throwing out a tether in the hopes of catching something—but she finds nothing, no birds, for this place is truly a dead zone. *No, no, no.* How is that possible? There are birds everywhere. But this place is a special hell, and birds, she realizes, have no interest in coming here—

Her breath is robbed from her.

Time seems to slow.

Lukauskis and Gabby continue to orbit the area, setting up the items he brought with him.

But someone else is here too.

Just as it was there in Emerson Caldecott's dungeon—

The Trespasser has arrived.

They cannot see him. They move in slow motion, but the Ghost of All-Dead appears with terrifying swiftness, rushing up on her in a blur of shadow. It has little shape; it has no face. It is like a roiling thundercloud, limbs and tendrils birthing from its center and then turning to a cloud of flies that go to vapor. The entity roars, deafening her with its wrath:

"*What are you doing?*"

She swallows hard and lashes out again with her senses—a tether cast farther and wider—but then the formless thing takes shape. Louis. His one gone-eye same as the crater here in this space: a divot of black dirt and dead roots. From within emerges a bouquet of spider legs—legs as thick as a crab's claw—that thrust up and clamp down on the Trespasser's face. Those pointed arachnid legs rip the Trespasser's facial skin into ribbons, and as that face falls away, peeling off like steamed wallpaper, a new face is revealed: Eleanor Caldecott, her face slick with algae and striated with death-marks. Then her skin is ripped off too, revealing a new face: Alejandro the killer, his eyes as dead as pennies. Each face is ripped clean from the skull, revealing a new face underneath, like calendar pages torn hastily from their binding, one after the next, face after face: the boy with the red balloon, Wren's face as she kills Louis, Gabby's face before it was scarred up, Ashley Gaynes leering and licking his lips, Harriet showing teeth red and gummy with heart's viscera, Ingersoll's hairless porcelain visage—

"You think you can trick me?" the Trespasser cries, its words spoken by a half-dozen different mouths.

Miriam realizes now, too late, that it's too powerful. *We fucked up. This is a mistake. We can't contain it. . . .*

She backpedals, tripping on something. Tumbling backward. Ass hitting ground. Head hitting a rock. Starburst behind the eyes. A ringing in her ear as her coconut is rattled—

Now the face is Louis's again.

"One. Broken. Cookie."

Now it's Ethan Key.

Now it's someone in the Mockingbird plague doctor's mask.

Now it's Ben Hodge, the boy who impregnated her the first time—

Now it's his mother, her face twisted up in sour, mindless rage, her purple lips flecked with spit, the capillaries in her eyes busting so fast, the whites of her eyes go as red as crushed cherries—

Lukauskis has noticed now that something has happened—

Can he see it? Can he see the Ghost of All-Dead? Does he know that the Trespasser is here? She doesn't know.

He's rushing over, waving his arms—

"Find the bird! *Find the bird*—"

She cries out, closes her eyes, and *reaches*—

ONCE UPON A MIDNIGHT DREARY

A mile away, a raven sits alone in a dark tree.

It is a common raven, though ravens are only common in the sense that they are plentiful, especially out here in the American West. But they are uncommon in their intelligence.

Crows, too, are intelligent, but not quite as much as the raven—and so, it is vital to note that a crow is not a raven and a raven is not a crow. (Nor are they blackbirds, jackdaws, jays, or magpies.) Crows caw. Ravens croak and scream. Crows are small, but ravens are large—as big as some hawks. The myths of the raven are many: in Sweden, for instance, a raven that calls after midnight is said to be the call of a murder victim, one who was not given a proper Christian burial and who has been made to linger. Ravens are adaptable. They have empathy. They remember faces. They can be scavengers, but they can be predators, too: hunting eggs and chicks, and swarming them in a way so that their parents cannot mount a proper defense. Ravens too have few natural predators—humans being their greatest foe in this regard. When they gather together, they are sometimes called an "unkindness" or a "conspiracy."

They are, simply put, not fools.

And so this raven, not a fool, has long stayed away from the dead place at the center of its territory. It does not know what this place is, but it knows that it is wrong, that it is *off*, and so it and its mate and its fellow ravens do not go there. They remember this.

But then, like that, in the time it would take for the bird to open its beak and snap it shut—*clack!*—the raven is lost within itself.

The bird is pushed out of its considerable mind.

(Considerable for a bird, anyhow.)

And a new mind replaces it.

This mind is not that of another raven, no—though this new mind *thinks* like a raven in many ways, and there is a kinship there in its brutal, feral intelligence and its predatory ardor. And in this, the transition from one mind to the next is easy. The raven has lost control of itself.

Its wings extend. It leaps off its branch and takes flight.

And it flies toward the dead place, even though it knows in the deep of its mind, in the back of its consciousness, that one should never go to the dead place, presumably because—

Well, that is where you die.

Through the dark it soars, a night-black bird on the night-black sky. It flies over dead trees and dry scrub. It flies over bent signs and a wrecked truck. It flies over old, blood-soaked ground—the blood is mostly long gone, but there has been enough of it spilled in this place that the bird knows it's there, layers of it under the dirt and the stone. This place has seen blood for longer than humans have been here. It has long been a place where beasts tear apart other beasts. Where their hungers are paramount. That is bad for many beasts. But for ravens, it's opportunity. (As long as they stay away from the dead place, of course.)

Soon, the raven hears the cries. *People.* It knows to be wary, but interested—humans kill ravens, sometimes, but people are useful to ravens, too. Just as a raven might use a twig as a tool to get at ants, a raven is happy to use humans as a tool, too. Humans hunt. They hit animals with their cars. They litter. They kill one another. And when they do, ravens will be there.

Ready to eat.

Now, though, the bird feels fear, but it can do nothing to assuage it. It cannot stop what it is. It cannot stop where it's going. It is going to the dead place. And soon the sounds of screams and the gabbled words of humans are given shape and form to the noise—

It flies lower, toward them. Toward the woman with the dyed-red hair on the ground, her eyes rolled back in her head. Toward the strange man who looks less like a man and more like a human-shaped termite mound. Toward the other woman with the broken-glass face.

But it's toward something else, too.

The raven cannot see it, but it can feel it. A presence. An embodiment of the dead place. This invisible *thing* is very, very mad. It hums in the air like a swarm of locusts. It carries with it the torment and anarchy of a windstorm whirling about: worse, a tornado, a hurricane.

The raven tries very hard to reclaim itself.

But it cannot. Its destiny is, at least temporarily, writ.

It flies. It lands on a pipe.

And something fixes its feet there, as if they are stuck to the pipe with little nails. It cannot move. It cannot cry out.

Something is coming.

This is the end, the raven knows.

But the end of what?

Itself, or something greater?

Something stranger?

SEVENTY-FIVE

SLIPPING

Miriam is within the raven now. She found the bird and she brought it. It took all of her concentration to bring it and keep it, because through the bird she can hear and see all of what's transpiring. She knows that she is flat on her back, and that she cannot move. She knows that the Trespasser—which the bird cannot see but can sense—has left Miriam and is now over Gabby, its tendrils of shadow pushing her to the ground, probing for a way in. She knows that Lukauskis stands there, waving his arms about like he's trying to command the wind—like he's performing a madman's variant of tai chi, stirring spiritual currents that only he can see. Gabby screams. Lukauskis bellows. Miriam cries out too, but it's not her human body that makes the sound but rather the raven's: it shrieks and shrieks and shrieks, wings flapping in panic and fear, because nothing is happening, nothing is working, and she knows full well that the Trespasser is taking Gabby—

Then, a feeling like a thunderclap, but without sound. A vast pressure change closes in on her. Gabby lurches upward, standing, gasping. Lukauskis staggers forward, nearly falling, as if he had been leaning on a chair that was yanked from his grip. And Miriam, inside the bird, feels a great darkness encroaching upon her. The mind of the bird gets paradoxically larger and smaller at the same time: as if Miriam is trapped in a vacuum-sealed plastic bag even as the world explodes around her in a great and terrible void. She manages one last look at herself there in the world, in the dead place—her back stiffens and arches into an arthritic bridge, and blood erupts from her nose like ketchup from a stepped-on sauce packet.

And then she can no longer see herself. She's gasping and—

SEVENTY-SIX

WAKING UP

She flails at herself in the hospital bed. Crying, bleating, Miriam rips the tubes out of her nose. She grabs the IV out of her arm— blood squirts across the white wall in a little red line, as if drawn by a leaky pen. Tearing off the little discs from her chest makes all the machines around her beep and shriek, and then she staggers off the hospital bed, but her legs can't support her, so she goes down to the ground, onto her knees, hard.

Her hands move to her middle.

Her thin, *too-thin*, middle.

The baby is gone.

It's soft and sunken, her belly. She cries out. "No, no, no. Not again, not again." Her lips are dry and her tongue slides across them, and it's like licking sandpaper. Even her teeth feel sandy and desiccated. She tries to stand again to find someone, anyone, but then her legs are wobbly, and her body feels like it's made of rubber bands. . . .

Darkness grabs hold of Miriam once more and embraces her.

PART TEN

THE BIRD OF PARADISE

SEVENTY-SEVEN

ONE BROKEN COOKIE

This isn't real.

This isn't real.

This isn't real.

As they talk to her, that's what Miriam tells herself again and again, over and over, repeated so often inside the chamber of her own mind that it begins to lose meaning. Three words that lose sense and shape. More noise than anything. Comforting, buzzing noise.

The doctor, a round man with hair that seems to have left the top of his head and migrated to his eyebrows and the inside of his nose, is explaining the coma to her and saying, "Waking up from a coma is not an immediate thing, Miriam. The movies always show someone waking right up out of that inert state, but it's not always like that. Over the last week, you moved into a minimally conscious state. Your body responded to pain stimuli. Your eyes began to move behind their lids. But you weren't yet conscious. You scored well on the coma scale, so we could see that there was a good chance you'd recover, and you have."

"This isn't real," she says, mirroring the phrase going around and around inside her head. It sounds just as gobbledygook out loud as the thought does, but she says it anyway.

Her mother, sitting on the other side of the bed, recoils just slightly—a small, strange moment of revulsion. Like she doesn't

353

recognize her daughter, or that she fears she's lost her mind. "Doctor, that can't be right," Evelyn Black says. "She can't mean that."

The doctor now pivots and speaks more to Evelyn than to Miriam.

"It's somewhat normal," he says, his voice with a dog's gruffness, ruff-ruff, "that a coma patient awakens with an uncertain sense of reality. They were in a vegetative dream state. The trauma suffered—"

"When she was attacked," Evelyn says, coldly.

"Yes, yes," he says, still not looking at Miriam, not talking to her, either. "That attack caused her body and brain some considerable damage. There's the Asherman's Syndrome, like we talked about. And of course the brain bleeding. As I said, the damage was considerable, enough to put her in that coma for three weeks, and it will be difficult to know how considerable until her body and mind set into . . . more predictable, stable rhythms. The good news is, she's awake—"

"I'm awake; you can talk to me," Miriam says in a small voice. All of this feels intimately familiar. *This has happened before.*

This was real.

But it isn't real now.

He turns halfway toward her. "*You're* awake now, Miriam, and we'll get you right as rain. Some light physical therapy will get you back on your feet, and with a psychological evaluation and subsequent sessions, you'll be back to work at school and . . ."
And he goes on and on and Miriam tunes out, withdrawing into herself, reaching for Gabby, for Louis, for someone or anyone who can pull her out of this nightmare. Eventually, the doctor says, "You were one broken cookie, young lady, but we will make you whole again. Don't you trouble yourself. The worst of it has passed."

SEVENTY-EIGHT

THE WORST IS YET TO COME

The therapist is a woman with small shoulders and big hips, stuffed into an itchy-looking sweater. She wears a dour face. Her eyeglasses are too big, like she's staring through a pair of Sherlock Holmes magnifying glasses.

"It's normal to feel this way," she says to Miriam, sitting across from her. Miriam is curled up into herself in a large, brown leather chair. Her arms are around her knees, hugging them tight to her chest.

"I don't believe that I'm really here."

"That dissociative feeling is normal and should pass."

"It's not a *feeling*," Miriam growls. "I'm certain of it."

The therapist—Dr. Sharpe-with-an-e—asks, "Miriam, do you know how I die?"

She hesitates.

"No," she says, finally.

It's not a lie.

"In your fantasy—"

"Trust me, it wasn't a fantasy."

"In your *vision*," Sharpe says, forcing a butt-pucker smile, "you had that power, didn't you? See how people were going to die?"

"I did."

"You can see now though that this was just a . . . delusion, right? A power fantasy, of sorts. Let's lay it all out there. You were pregnant. You . . . lost your boyfriend, the father of that child, to suicide. Then his mother attacks you in a bathroom in an act of brutal, irrational anger, and that causes you to miscarry the child and end up in a weeks-long coma. In your head, while vegetative, you create a world where you have the ability to stop death, but only by expressing your rage at that death—and by causing another. In this world, you're very special. You're at the center of things. You were— How did you describe it? 'Breaking the pattern.' Sometimes, the power you have is a gift, other times a curse, but then how do you get past that power, Miriam? Tell me."

"I don't have to tell you shit."

"Would you, please? For me?"

She sighs. "*Fine*. I . . . got pregnant again. And having the baby would fix me. It would end the curse. It would make things *normal* again."

There.

She said it.

The therapist watches her. That fake-ass tight-ass little smile of hers doesn't waver. "Now that you've said that out loud, doesn't it feel a little . . . convenient? A little pat? Isn't it *possible* that it sounds like a story that your mind made up to . . . soften the blow?"

"No," Miriam lies. She unfolds herself out of the chair and then stands up to thrust a finger in the therapist's face. "Explain *this*, though: I knew that what I had was called Asherman's Syndrome. I'd never heard that before that night in the hospital. But I already knew it. When the doctor told me, said those words, I'd already experienced that—years, *years* ago."

"You likely overheard him explaining it to your mother."

"Yeah, but—"

And then Miriam sits back down.

She feels suddenly like a doll with the stuffing ripped out.

Her memory of that day has the doctor talking to her mother, and not to her. Almost like she wasn't in the room. *Almost like you were only partially conscious and they were talking over you.*

Sharpe keeps twisting the knife. "And, Miriam, some of the names you mention . . . Louis, Harriet, Gabby, these . . . I checked. These are the names of your nurses. Louis in particular was there fairly often, though he was recently transferred to another floor."

Miriam blinks away tears. "So, this is just some *Wizard of Oz* shit."

"I wouldn't put it so glibly. You experienced something most never do—a comatose period where your mind concocted a protective fantasy, and now you are free from both the coma *and* the need for this fantasy. I urge you to view it that way. In your dream, you sought normalcy, but now . . . here it is. Here is your chance."

Now she's actually crying. She can't help it. She sniffs, wipes tears with the back of her hand. "You don't get it. I had people. I loved people. I had a daughter coming and . . . I was going to save her, I was going . . ."

The way Sharpe hands her the tissue box feels very condescending. Less like *Here, you need this*, and more like *Here, clean yourself up*. Like a prostitute handing her john a moist towelette. *Do I really know what that means? A prostitute? A john? Did I really live that life on the street, on the highway, or is that really part of my delusion?*

"You can love people again," Sharpe says.

"I don't know."

"Our time is up."

SEVENTY-NINE

BREAKING THE PATTERN

Some nights, she sleeps like she's back in the coma. Other nights, she stays awake all night, suffocated by the constricting snake of her bedsheets, tossing and rolling and sometimes sobbing so hard, her pillow is still wet by morning. Her mother, too, treats her inconsistently: sometimes, she acts like Miriam is a little porcelain doll, capable of breaking at the slightest provocation. Other times, she treats her daughter like a stranger, like she's nothing more than a ghost haunting the halls of the old house, irritating her mother with her spectral bumps and phantasmal thumps.

"You'll be fine," Evelyn always says. "You've got that Black spirit." That meant to be an evocation of their bloodline, somehow, but also in it Miriam finds a troubling echo: *that black spirit*.

The Trespasser.

She looks for the Trespasser.

In mirrors, in window reflections. She looks outside in the woods, expecting to see him standing there in the trees, along the road, one eye gone, worms squirming in the hole.

When she goes back to school, she looks for him there, too. In lockers. Behind the teacher. In the bathroom, listening to the sink to see if she'll ever hear a whisper come up through the drain. There in the bathroom, too, she finds the place where she was attacked. Where she almost died. The floor is clean. Her blood is gone. No sign of the incident remains. At least, no physical sign. She still isn't walking quite right. And the kids at school don't wanna talk to her at all. It's like she's cursed in a whole new way—a pariah, an exile, flung to the margins because of what happened to her.

She visits places where she remembers things happening.

The living room where Bird of Doom broke through the window.

The bedroom where she found Grosky's severed head.

The road outside their house where she walked, taking a bus on a journey away from the Mockingbird killer, to a house she had vacated.

She tries sometimes to contact birds with her mind. To control them. They don't care. They fly away, *tweet-tweet-tweet*.

She uses the Internet to look up things:

The Mockingbird killer.

Louis Darling.

Ingersoll, Ashley Gaynes, something, anything.

Nothing. Nothing meaningful, anyhow.

Miriam sinks into a bleak depression. She begins to accept that none of what she remembers is real. It was just a delusion. Could be that it was her mind protecting her from the truth. Or maybe it was just a chemical by-product of her then-dying brain. A brain that came back from the dead.

(*Six times*, she thinks in a voice that does not belong to her but rather to a madman mystic that is likely not real.)

Eventually, she floats through life, day in, day out. Her depression is a functional one; she isn't buried underneath it, but she recognizes it as the real Trespasser here, a black spirit that accompanies her wherever she goes.

Soon, school is over. She graduates.

Her mother takes her out to a dinner. Garibaldi's, an Italian place about ten minutes from their house.

It's there that Miriam makes an important decision.

EIGHTY

THE IMPORTANT DECISION

Miriam decides that after this—soon after this, maybe as soon as tonight after dinner—she's going to leave. That's it. She's done. She has no idea if that will fix the way she feels or not, but what she knows is that the life she lived while inside the coma was a far more interesting one than she is about to live here. Life in this space will be normal. It will be peaceful. And it will be as dull as a butter knife, and just as useful.

She wants a sharper, meaner life. Something with teeth.

Something that can cut.

And so she decides, that's it.

She's leaving, just as the Miriam inside her head had done. She's going to run away from home just as that Miriam did. That Miriam was way more fucked up. But that Miriam was way cooler.

Off she goes. But first, this dinner.

She and her mother eat in relative silence. Evelyn seems distant. And Miriam is certainly distant. Both have drifted so far apart from one another that they might as well be on different continents at this point.

Miriam eats spaghetti with meatballs. Comfort food.

Evelyn eats a salad.

They get the garlic knots, because the garlic knots are one of the few truly good things in this world. Her mother, despite the salad, taught Miriam to put butter on them. They're already soaked in olive oil, but the butter makes it fattier, tastier, and somehow even more garlicky. So, they both do that, taking their butter knives and spreading butter in there.

Evelyn orders an iced tea. A rare thing for her: caffeine.

Miriam remembers briefly a version of her mother down in Florida, in beachwear, smoking and drinking. And now Miriam decides she's going to do those things. Once she's on the road, she's going to smoke and drink.

Maybe she'll go to Florida.

She hated Florida in her dream, but she wants the chance to hate it all over again. It only seems fair.

"Did you ever smoke a cigarette?" Miriam asks her mother.

"What?" Evelyn asks. "No. No, of course not. Don't be stupid."

"Did you drink?"

"Miriam, no."

"Not even a little? Margarita. Mai-tai. Something like that."

Evelyn eyes her up. "Good girls don't drink."

"Were you always a good girl?"

"Of course I was." Then her mother's mouth fishhooks a little, itty-bitty smile. The *hint* of a smile. The *ghost* of a smile. "Usually."

Then her mother takes her straw, unwraps the paper wrapping halfway, and blows into the one end of the straw. The paper wrapping around the straw fires off like a crinkly rocket and strikes Miriam dead in the center of her forehead. *Ptoo. Fwhick.*

"Mom!"

Evelyn smiles. "What?"

"Mom, I didn't know you had it in you."

"What can I say? I have a few tricks left."

Miriam freezes, mid-laugh.

What can I say? I have a few tricks left.

Me too, she yells.

Wanna see one of mine? he asks.

Bring it on.

Then, lickety-quick, Not-Louis is gone. One minute, she's face-to-face with him, smelling his sour stink, and the next— he's vapor. The shadow tendrils disappear too. The shaking has ended. The road behind is whole once more, as are the trees all around. None are broken. None have fallen.

Once more, all is silent and still.

A few lone flurries fall.

The silence ends as a gunshot fills the night.

"Miriam?" Evelyn asks.

Miriam unfreezes. She palms a garlic knot. Idly, unconsciously, she spreads a little butter onto it.

Then she takes her butter knife and jams it into her mother's eye.

It buries deep. Miriam lends it extra strength as she uses the heel of her palm to really cram it in there good. Evelyn screams bloody murder, backpedaling out of her chair, the iced tea spilling, and Miriam realizes she's made a terrible mistake. The vision of her in the coma felt so real, so true, that she thought maybe this was it, this was the moment—

Evelyn turns and looks at her. The knife sticking out of the one eye like a shining lever.

"I pushed it too far," Evelyn says.

"What?"

"I couldn't help myself. I thought I would be funny. I wanted to amuse myself. But I broke the wall. I disrupted the illusion."

Ocular fluid oozes off the knife blade like jelly. Clear jelly. Like the kind you'd spread on a pregnant woman's belly before the ultrasound.

Evelyn takes a plop of it and pops it in her mouth. Suckle, suckle.

"You," Miriam says.

Worms squirm through the ruptured eyeball, curling around the butter knife's handle like ivy around a flagpole.

"Gotcha," the Trespasser says, showing a pair of jazz hands. It's Louis's voice, out of Evelyn's mouth. "I guess the cat's out of the bag, huh?"

EIGHTY-ONE

SHOW'S OVER FOLKS, THIS WAY TO THE GREAT EGRESS

"You fucker," Miriam says. She looks down at herself: she is the teen version of herself no more. She's back to the Miriam who came to Black Star Canyon, with the vented knife-slash jeans and the white T-shirt and hair dyed the color of monster blood.

Her mother, now with a clot of maggots pushing out of the socket, the larvae plopping to the floor in wet clumps, chuckles a deep, rheumy chuckle. Again, Louis's voice comes from her twisted lips: "I had you. I had you going, but I went and *ruined* it, didn't I? I just had to get greedy, get tricky, say a little thing— *What can I say? I have a few tricks left.* Well. Shucks. We all play with fire sometimes, don't we, Miriam? But this time, I got burned. It doesn't matter. Not like I could keep it up forever, anyway. The illusion must end eventually."

All around, the walls of the little Italian joint are beginning to rot—decaying as if in fast-forward. Moldering. Cracking. Water stains spreading across the ceiling like a growing darkness.

Miriam is pissed.

Inside her is a pyroclastic channel of magma-like rage.

But with it comes clarity.

And triumph.

"I've got you," she says, grinning wickedly. "I saw through your bullshit. And now here we are." She holds up her arms, and now the walls are crumbling apart. Beyond them: black feathers. Shifting, flexing, like a blackbird, breathing. They are night-touched and moon-slick. Soon, the restaurant is gone entirely, and they're standing there on nothing—no, floating there in the feather-bounded black.

"So sure, are you?" the Ghost of All-Dead asks.

"You're mine now. I control this space. I control this animal. And all I have to do is—" She holds up her hand, fingers and thumb just apart, poised to *snap*. "Kill the bird. Then I'm out. And you're dead."

"I'm already dead, precious girl."

"The dead can die."

"The dead *cannot* die. It is perhaps the one bonus we get." Her mother floats around Miriam in a wobbly orbit, her arms extended out to the sides as if demanding for all to see this place. She never turns her one-eyed gaze from Miriam. "Whatever that fuckhead urban shaman told you was a lie. He . . . misunderstood the situation. And now he's dead."

Blood begins to ooze in through the feathers all around them. It pushes up around them, threads of red like hungry nightcrawlers. It dribbles and runs in crooked rivulets, saturating the void.

"He's not dead," Miriam says. "Another trick of yours."

"Whose blood do you think that *is*?" Not-Evelyn says, using Not-Louis's voice. With every word she speaks, the entity's voice grows louder, and the body swells and distorts, growing larger. "It's his. I've killed him. While you sat trapped in this animal, lost to the illusion I've given you, I've been busy. I am the Ghost of All-Dead. I am not one spirit but hundreds. You cannot summon me and trap me in this sorry animal. *I am legion. For we are many*. And we're hungry, Miriam. Hungry for justice. Hungry for some fucking *recompense*. Lives, stolen, ended without thought by a callous, uncaring universe.

You were our way back in. You helped us. You saw the depredations of fate; you felt in your bones that what happened to you wasn't fair, *wasn't right*, and it wasn't. You wanted to fix it. To conquer it. Just as we want to conquer life. We want to end death. Is that such a terrible thing? Would it be so bad, to shatter that cycle and let all live, endlessly, eternally, on and on and on? No more death. No more lives cut short just because that's the way it must be. I see a better world."

By now, the Trespasser is consuming the voice—the skin of her mother's body has split like the skin of a steamed tomato, showing a glistening tangle of tendons braided with eels braided with fraying rope. The flesh of the face is in tatters, revealing a black, oily skull underneath, and the dead, dread eyes of a raven. The teeth are not teeth but individual beaks, dozens of them, hundreds, lining up like the pickets of a fence, clattering like hungry little baby birds, *clack-clack tick-tack*.

"No," Miriam says. "Death is a balance. That's why when I saved a life, I also took one. That's how it works."

"It works like I say it works," echoes the spirit's shrieking voice, but in that voice, Miriam hears something: desperation. And stranger still: uncertainty. It doesn't *know* that Miriam is helping to break a cycle. It believes it, yes. It has faith. But that faith isn't unshakeable. And now Miriam wonders: how much of what Emerson Caldecott told her is true? How much of what the Trespasser says is true? What if they're wrong? What if they believe a thing, a false thing, just as most people do? People are fallible. And the Trespasser, the Ghost of All-Dead, is no alien, no demon. It's human too. And humans are fucked up.

Not that any of it matters now.

Whatever this thing is, whatever it believes, it has to go.

Miriam reaches into the bird's mind, finding it somewhere beyond all of this—it's a pulsing, nervous thing. It's scared. It's hurt.

It wants to die.
Miriam feels sad for it.
And, in a way, she feels sad for the Trespasser, too.
But all this must end.
"It is what it is," she says.
And she snaps her fingers.
And breaks the bird's neck.

EIGHTY-TWO

THE ERROR OF YOUR WAYS

Back to herself she goes. Like being thrown from one temperature extreme to the next: like jumping from a pot of boiling
water into the depths of a frozen lake. It's bracing. She leaps
to her feet like she's been given an electric shock. She feels for
her stomach: she's still pregnant, and she can feel her daughter
tumbling around in there. Agitated. Upset. *Same here, kid. Same
here.* Miriam stops, looks around—

Carnage. All around.

All of Abraham Lukauskis's icons and objects have been
destroyed. Little bird bones scattered. Candles, shattered. A
saltcellar, broken open, the salt scattered on the ground like
snow—

(*Snow from a broken snow globe*)

And in the middle of it is a body.

Gabby . . .

No. It's him. It's Lukauskis.

He lies slumped in one of the big, rusted pipes, propped up
against its inner curve. His right eye is wide open. His left eye
has been replaced.

It has been replaced by the raven.

It is an impossible, unpleasant fit—the bird, too big for the
socket, has still somehow been pushed halfway into his skull. Its
little legs hang out the back, curled up into arthritic hooks. His

skull is swollen, as if to accommodate its too-big raven's body. His mouth hangs open. The lips are ashen, and his tongue lies out on the lower lip like the head of a resting snake. Abraham Lukauskis is indeed dead.

Gabby is nowhere to be found.

Miriam spins around, looking. She hopes like hell she'll see Gabby there, coming back through the brush, dazed and dizzied— but she knows what she'll see instead. She'll see Gabby's body, broken and ruined, hanging in a tree like a broken, captured kite.

But that, she does not see, either.

Miriam calls for her. "Gabby! *Gabby*."

Nothing.

But she hears *something*.

A gassy hiss. A wet, gabbling murmur.

She turns slowly to see that Abraham's jaw is opening and closing, creaking and grinding in crass cavitation as it does. The hiss emitting from his throat becomes words, even as his one dead eye stares up at nothing.

"*We are kinnnn, you and I. . . .*" the voice says. It's Lukauskis's voice, but she knows to whom it truly belongs: *The Trespasser.* "*Abraaaham is with us now. He has seen the p-p-power of the All-Dead. And soon Gabby will joiiiiin usssss too—you muuuust be shown the error of your ways. You mussst be punished. Her t-t-time hasss c-c-come. . . .*"

Miriam picks up a rock and throws it at Lukauskis. It thuds dully off his forehead, then *clong*s as it lands in the pipe.

The jaw stops moving.

The words cease.

Miriam cries out. She sees now that the sky is starting to brighten just a little—the faint promise of sunrise. But with it comes no hope and, instead, the realization that she's been out here for hours. *Hours* trapped in the mind of a bird, lost to the illusion the Trespasser gave her.

The trap wasn't for the Trespasser. It was for her.

And now, she fears, it has Gabby. It's taken her.

Nearby, she hears the crackle of brush. Someone's coming.

"Gabby?" she says in a smaller voice, then again, louder: "Gabby!"

The brush parts, and Steve Wiebe staggers out. The side of his face is crusted with a half-mask of blood. "Miriam," he says. "Gabby . . ."

"Is she all right?"

"She . . . hit me with a rock." He reaches for the top of his head with a ginger touch and winces. "Last thing I saw before passing out was the taillights of my car as it drove away."

It feels now like she's in free fall. She let this happen. As with so much, when Miriam intervenes against fate, it only lets fate sink its teeth in deeper. Over time, she learned to change that by killing those who would rob others of life—that seemed to break the circuit. But the Trespasser was right. You couldn't kill it. You can't kill the dead. So, what, then?

The realization hits her like a bullet to the head.

They're nearly there—it's nearly to Richard Beagle's death. Never-Dick dies by Gabby's hand. His time is almost up.

Gabby kills him. So, that's where she's going.

"I need you to go," she tells Steve.

"Go where? We can go together, Miriam—"

"Not yet. Go, get a signal, use your phone—you still have it?"

He nods and holds it up.

"Good," she says. "Go, get a signal, and call Guerrero. He'll help us."

"And what are you going to do?" he asks her.

She surveys the scene.

"I'm going to clean this up," she lies.

EIGHTY-THREE

COUNTING WORMS

Once again, time is the enemy. Fate as the end, time as the road that leads there. All efforts to intervene have failed, and now Miriam sits, ten hours after waking up next to Abraham Lukauskis's body—ten hours after losing Gabby to the very spirit she hoped to forbid from taking her—waiting for this fucking plane to take off.

Waiting for it to take her to Miami, Florida.

The countdown is: eighteen hours. She has eighteen hours to get there, and to get to the office of Dr. Richard Never-Dick Beagle in order to stop Gabby from killing him. It happens tomorrow.

Except she's on the West Coast.

Traveling to the East Coast.

Which means she already *loses* three hours. Gone. Gobbled up by the time-zone monster. Eighteen hours have lost a vital limb to the amputation, a leg bitten off, and now it's just fifteen hours.

The flight is six hours.

Which slices it down to nine hours.

Then she needs time to rent a car. Less than an hour, she hopes.

Time to drive south to Tavernier, which is an hour and a half in easy traffic, maybe two in bad traffic. Doable, because it's 2 PM now, and that means landing in Florida at 8 PM—no! Fuck. At 11PM.

Traffic should be light.

Hit the road at midnight.

Get to his "office" in the Keys by 2 AM.

He dies at 6 AM.

That leaves her with a four-hour cushion.

It isn't much of a cushion. It's uncomfortable as fuck, that cushion. It's a cushion filled with jagged rocks and sharp knives, but it's better than nothing, and it would be fine *if only this fucking plane would take off*.

She doesn't know what they're doing. They're all strapped down, buckled in, all their dumb shit in the overhead compartments. They taxied out to the runway and now they're just sitting here. Sometimes, the engines rev up and play this game, *oh oh we're gonna go*, but then they wind right back down again.

Next to her, the seat in the middle is empty. Miriam's at the window. She looks out over the wing and the ground. She should be seeing sky and clouds, but they're still bound to the earth like a dumb fucking ostrich.

A quick glance at her phone shows her the last text message she received: this one from Guerrero.

Too slow on the stick; she already made it to Miami.

Guerrero tried to intervene, trying to get them to stop her flight, or stop her from boarding—but by the time they even knew what was happening, it was too late. She'd already boarded the plane. Surveillance showed them that soon as she left Black Star, she must've gone right to the airport. She drained their account of what little money they had, bought the first flight, and got on it without a single bag.

No, Miriam thinks. *Not she.*

Not Gabby.

It.

The Trespasser.
The Ghost of All-Dead.

It doesn't matter. She told Guerrero it wouldn't work. It's why she said no to his offer to have the police or local Federal agents intervene. "They'd only get dead," she told him. "Fate gets what fate wants." She knew it sounded narcissistic as fuck, but truth was, she was the only one who could break this chain. Fate's Foe. The Riverbreaker.

I can break the pattern.

She is the Ruiner.

Right now, she's ready to ruin this fucking plane. She thrusts an angry finger up to summon the flight attendant, *bing bing bing*, and the woman hurries over, the attendant's face puckered up like she's been sucking on a vinegar-soaked tampon.

"What is it?" she says, trying to sound friendly but failing. "Ma'am."

"We need to take off."

"We will be, very shortly."

"We need to take off *now*. I need to—" Miriam taps her calculator watch. "I need to be somewhere. I need to *get there*."

"Ma'am—"

"Don't call me *ma'am*, that's fucked up, I'm not a *ma'am*, if anything, I'm a *miss*, okay?" She feels her words laced with venom.

A shadow passes over the attendant's face. Her voice is a day darkened by a sudden storm cloud. "We have a number of planes ahead of us for takeoff. Are you going to be a problem, *miss*?"

Are you going to be a problem?

That more or less defines Miriam.

And she wants to say, *Yes, yes, I'm going to be a problem, I am the problem. Someone has already decided that things are the way they are and I don't like it, so I am the problem that screws up the status quo.*

But she can't do that. Not here. Not now.

She grits her teeth and says, "No, ma'am."

"Good. Now *sit tight*."

The flight attendant hurries back to her seat, checking the overhead bins with the flat of her hand slid along their margins.

Fuck fuck fuck, take off take off take off take off.

She can feel the time slipping through her hands like so much burning rope. Steve offered to come, and now she wishes like hell he would've; then, she told him no, because honestly, his life was short enough as it was. She said to him, "Go and get on a different plane. Pick a place you've always wanted to visit and visit the hell out of it. And then the next place and the next place after that, and do all the things you've wanted to do—zipline over a volcano, jump out of a helicopter, ride a giraffe in Kenya, doesn't matter, because none of those things are the things that kill you." She told him that he only had three years, which was a curse, but it was a gift, too—because during those three years, he could do whatever he wanted. He had license to ill, as the Beastie Boys once said.

And he said, "What if what I want to do is come with you? You've given me a gift, and I can pay you back."

Miriam told him to fuck off. She said it as sweetly as she could, and she said it while giving him another hug. But she meant it.

Now she wishes she hadn't said it at all.

She wishes he was here next to her.

Because she's not ready for this.

She loves Gabby. Just as she loved Louis. And the Trespasser pulled all the strings and got Louis killed, and now that ghost-fucked motherfucker has even more power. It's possessing the person she loves, she person she wants to spend her life with, and if she doesn't get there soon—

Not soon, but now now now.

Then Gabby was going to kill someone.

You're not taking her away from me, she thinks.

She can almost hear the Trespasser's laugh in the back of her head.

Over the plane's intercom: "Folks, we are next in line for takeoff. Please make sure your seatbelts are buckled and your seat backs are in the upright position. We'll be in the air in a few minutes. Enjoy the ride."

EIGHTY-FOUR

TIME, BLEEDING OUT ON THE FLOOR

It's delay after delay after delay. They get in the air, but then there's a storm system over Texas, so that adds time. They land a half-hour late, but then taxi around the runway again and again because somehow, they don't have a gate anymore, so it's like some secret circle of Dante's Inferno. Then they get a gate and it's past midnight and all the rental car places are *closed* even though they're supposed to be *open*, so she's gotta use some emergency red phone and get someone to the desk. That takes an hour.

All the while, she feels the baby kicking.

And worse, she feels like she needs to puke—not from being pregnant, but because she can't *change time*.

(And her last . . . meal didn't exactly help.)

Then she's in a Nissan Something-or-Other, hard-charging it south, praying to all the gods and all the devils that there's no cops, no construction, no weaponized bullshit to deal with.

The car carves a line through the Keys. Dark water on both sides. The morning moon oozing toward the horizon.

The clock ticks down.

She's got two hours to make the hour-and-a-half drive.

I can do this, I can do this.

Long as nothing gets in my way, I can do this.

Just to be sure, she presses a little harder on the accelerator.

The rental car moves. Her knuckles are bloodless around the wheel. Her heart is alive in her wrists, her neck, her temples, thudding there like a woodpecker pecking at a dead tree. *Go, go, go.*

Miami to Kendall to Homestead to Key Largo.

60 MPH.

70 MPH.

80 MPH.

No cops, no cops, Jesus fuck, no cops.

And then—

There. Ahead. That's it. Off Overseas Highway. She almost missed it here in the smeary dark of the predawn morning. She slams the brakes and cuts the wheel, hard-charging into the lot outside the rat-trap office building he calls both a home and a place of dubious business.

She has a half-hour to spare.

I did it.

Gabby, though, might be here, might she not? Miriam glances around; she sees no other cars. She's alone but for the sound of the water lapping at the shore a hundred yards away.

Just to be sure, she reaches for her knife—

Only to remember she doesn't fucking have it. No way to bring the knife with her on a plane. She's without any weapons.

Not that she wants to use them. The Trespasser is a spirit, and the only thing she can stab is Gabby. Still. A blade would make her feel better.

It is what it is.

Into the office she goes.

EIGHTY-FIVE

And Out She Comes Again

The sun burns the edges of the horizon as it rises.

Miriam stands outside once again, in the ocean breeze, shivering as she leans against her car. Her body finally gives up, and she turns and throws up all over the Nissan's tire. What she throws up is rust-red and frothy, with . . . bits in it. She shudders and turns away from it.

Richard Never-Dick Beagle is already dead.

He has been dead for hours.

She got here before his time, before the date was due, but it didn't matter. Gabby beat her here—no, the *Trespasser* beat her here in Gabby's body—and with its increasing power broke the shackles of fate just as Miriam herself can do. And it killed Beagle before his time.

The presiding question now is *Where is Gabby?*

But that answer is already known, isn't it? If it's true that the Trespasser can do as it wants, when it wants—if it can truly overwrite one's destiny—then it has gone farther south. It has taken Gabby home.

And there, it will kill her.

If it hasn't already.

For so long, Miriam was sure that Gabby's fate was sealed—because who exactly do you kill in a suicide to stop the suicide? The killer in that scenario is the one who is also killed, as if in some mad riddle. The scales cannot be balanced, because in that strange, cosmic way, the scales balance themselves. But then, over time, Miriam became fooled by the idea that Gabby's suicide could be stopped. . . .

Now the memory of that vision replays in her head—

the air feels like the breath from a panting dog and she tosses and turns but her skin crawls and her heart is a jumpy mouse

another panic attack where she feels oh so small in a world so big, like she's nothing at all, just a bug under a boot

Gabby gets up and goes to the bathroom and turns on the light and the scars that crisscross her face like the clumsy lacing of a crooked boot are puffy and pink and long-healed but still horrible, Xs and dashes of ruined skin

lines cut into her cheeks

her face is monstrous like when a child breaks a vase, then sloppily glues it back together again

she's ugly, mauled, nobody will love her, nobody could love her

her breathing goes shallow, she feels woozy, sick with self-hatred

flings open the medicine cabinet

oxycodone, old prescription

and Ambien, her sleeping pills

and Ativan for the anxiety

she puts a bunch into her mouth, not even sure how much

she scoops water into her mouth from the faucet

the pills go down, and she goes back to bed

soon she stops crying

and shaking

and sweating

and breathing—

Miriam thought, *I can love her. I can show her that I love her. She won't end up there. Won't end up in Florida, swallowing a fistful of strange pills because she is unloved and ugly—no, she'll turn from that, because she is loved, and she is beautiful*, but now Miriam is reminded of that tenet:

What fate wants, fate gets.

It will take its pound of flesh.

And the Trespasser will help it.

What grim fucking irony that is.

As the sun lights the sky above, Miriam sees it—a black cloud moving this way and that. Another murmuration: a flock of birds, hundreds of them, maybe thousands, moving in unison, one never far from the next. For a moment, just one, she closes her eyes and slips into them, ducking, diving, swooping, spiraling. These aren't starlings like she saw in California, but rather tree swallows. The weather is growing warmer here and soon they'll migrate north. And they've formed this blob—and then a funnel cloud, and then a reaper's cloak—to protect themselves from the predators here. Predators like peregrine falcons. The birds, thousands of them, form together to save themselves from a single bird.

Miriam blinks, and she's back in her body.

Gabby may be dead.

Maybe she's not.

But she has to go. She has to try. She has to see.

And Miriam has an idea.

EIGHTY-SIX

THE REAPER'S CLOAK

The house is quiet, the sun is up, and Miriam finds Gabby in her bed, curled up. Pill bottles lay on the floor; one has rolled into a gummy pile of vomit. A single shaft of sunlight shines through the broken blinds over the window, illuminating Gabby's broken-mirror face.

Miriam blinks back tears. She kneels down by the bed.

She doesn't think twice about reaching down and touching the puke.

It's still warm.

"You're still in there," she says, quietly.

Gabby's eyes ease open. Half-lidded. Her lips twist into something resembling a smile. "Hello, Miriam."

The voice is Gabby's, but it isn't. Miriam can hear other voices behind it, too, like a locust song sung somewhere else, somewhere distant. Those two words, *Hello, Miriam*, thrum and hum and teem with that fly-wing buzz. Miriam takes Gabby's hand. Gabby—the Trespasser—pulls it away. But the movement is slow and sluggish, so Miriam grabs the hand again and holds it.

"It's interesting to be in a dying body," the Trespasser says, words slurring. "Last time, it was fast, one shot to the head, but *this* is . . . something special, Miriam. Really something ssssspecial."

"I'm going to get you out of there."

"No, don't. It's *warm* in here. And when Gabby dies, I'll . . . take her with me. Her spirit will be part of my spirit. And that way, she'll always be a part of you. This is a gift for you, Miriam. A gift from me to you."

Miriam strokes the back of Gabby's hand. "You don't need me anymore, Trespasser. You can break the river all on your own now. You have the ability to change fate. So, leave her. Go do what you will."

"*Nnnno,*" the spirit says, bitterly, not at all in Gabby's voice but rather in Louis's voice. Then Gabby's is back as she starts to sit up, vomit slicking her chin. "You don't understand. It takes a lot . . . for me to do this. I still need you. You're still my *Number One Gal*. Bes . . . besides, who am I without you? And who are you without me?"

Miriam takes Gabby's face. Hands to cheeks. She presses her forehead against Gabby's—the Trespasser tries to wriggle away, but she's weak, too weak to resist.

"Gabby," Miriam says, whispering into the other woman's ear. "I know you're in there. And I want you to try now, try very hard, to hear me. This thing can only be in you because it thinks you have no purpose. You have holes in your soul. But I need you. Let me be your purpose. Let me be the reason you're here. The reason you *stay* here. I'm alone. I'm going to have a baby and it's going to live—I'll make sure of it. But I need you here to help me. Without you, I'm lost. You're my wings. Help me fly."

The Trespasser pulls away, backing into the corner, holding a pillow up as a shield. Gabby's eyes blink furiously, as if irritated. When she speaks, it's in a discordant hum, the voice warbling from one to the next with each syllable: "What are you doing? She can't kick me out now that I'm in—*you* can't do *shit* to me, Miriam. I'm roaches in the wall. Only way I get out is to . . ." Her chin dips, her eyelids flutter. "*Burn the whole house down.*"

Then Gabby's body ratchets tight. Like all her muscles have

gone paralytic. Her teeth grind. She moans through clenched jaws.

"*No*," the Trespasser says. "*Stay. In. Here.*"

Miriam says, "Gabby. You don't need to push it all the way out. Just a little further. Just close to the surface. That's all I need."

Then she stands up and walks to the window.

The Trespasser: "Where are *you* going?"

"I brought friends," Miriam answers.

The bit of sunlight through the broken blinds is obscured for a moment by a flitting shadow. Then another, and another. Dark spots dapple the wall. Miriam opens the window.

A tree swallow alights upon the mangle. This little songbird is a male: its face a black-and-white mask, its back an iridescent blue.

A second lands next to it.

Those two come into the room. And then, it's like uncorking a bottle—a swarm of them floods into the room, a cacophony of fluttering wings brushing past Miriam like bats out of a cave-mouth. They alight upon the lamp, the dresser, the headboard of the bed, the bookshelf.

More wait outside. In the trees. On the roof. Hopping about on the ground, hop, hop, hop.

Gabby laughs. But Miriam can see the look there.

"What is this?" the Trespasser asks. "What are you doing?"

Miriam shrugs. "What can I say? I have a few tricks left."

"You have no tricks I don't already know."

The birds trill and chatter.

"I'm going to take you out of Gabby and put you in these birds."

"Fuck you," the Trespasser seethes, leaning forward on all fours like a wolf sitting on its haunches. Her chin thrusts out, tongue bitten between teeth so hard, it bleeds. "You're no mystic. Lukauskis is *dead*."

"I know he's dead. You killed him. If he wasn't dead, he probably would've objected to me eating his heart."

Gabby's eyes go wide.

The Trespasser freezes.

"*What?*"

"I learned from Harriet where our power lies." She thumps her chest. "I can taste her heart. And now I can taste his. I'm not . . . very good at this yet but . . . Gabby, help, keep pushing—"

She can feel it now. The Trespasser, drawn to the surface of Gabby's soul like an infection, like a parasitic worm summoned to the site of an injury—it is a black, vicious thing, roiling and diseased, angrier than any rage Miriam has ever felt. It nearly overwhelms her. Darkness grabs for her but she shoves it out even as sweat beads on her brow. Tears sting the corners of her eyes. She feels her bladder give out. It's resisting her but she pulls harder, and harder, and harder—

"Nnngh," the Trespasser hisses, and then Gabby's head snaps forward sharply. In Gabby's voice she yells, "Get it out of me *get it out of me*—"

I'm trying, Gabby, I'm trying.

Her own body tightens. Her skin feels like it wants to split. It hits her that this was too much, a task too great—eating Lukauskis's heart was no easy task after she sent Steve away. She had to break one of his candles and use the glass shard to dig through his soft middle, under his ribcage, like a dog hunting for a bone, and his heart was tough and foul. She could feel his power surge through her but didn't know what to do with it—and now she knows she's not ready. *He* wasn't ready either, and it's going to rip her apart. A mad thought careens through her head like a ricocheting bullet: *This is what kills my baby. I have made a choice to save Gabby, and in trying to save her, I'm going to kill my daughter*, and worse, maybe she won't even save Gabby at all, the price paid for nothing made—

Her fingers stiffen and splay out.

They begin to break one by one. Cracking and snapping.

Miriam tries not to throw up. She can see now the spiritual infection inside Gabby is surging out in oleaginous threads—like black oil in zero gravity floating in serpentine threads—

The tendons in her ankles, her Achilles tendons, snap like broken piano strings, and she falls to her knees. Blood trickles from her nose and she can taste it. Something wet trickles from her earholes, too. Blood. *Maybe brains, ha ha ha, guess I can't get any smarter now.*

And then her arms bend back, the bones snapping, spearing through the skin, she cries out, and exerts every last bit of will she has—

A sound like firecrackers crackling, the air gone suddenly alive, popping, snapping, a deafening machine gun crackle.

Miriam slumps forward—

The Trespasser, a broken mirror—

A mind cast into a thousand pieces, each specter ripped from its brothers and sisters, torn from its flock—

Each inside a single tree swallow.

And all the birds take flight.

They turn into a seething, roiling funnel—whipping about like a downed power line—and this living conduit of swallows flies out the window once again, disappearing up into the sky. Miriam thinks for a moment to take them, to carry them to the sea and drown them. But you cannot kill the dead, she knows. And she hopes that the Trespasser is gone, torn from its mooring, its identity lost as each of its constituent souls has been given new, if temporary, life inside the flock of birds.

Psychopomps. Ferrying souls from the land of the living to the land of the dead. And perhaps back again.

Miriam collapses onto the floor.

She is broken all over.

Gabby slides down off the bed and curls up next to her. "I'm still dying," Gabby says. "I'm still poisoned."

"I'm pretty fucked up, too," Miriam says.

Outside, a distant siren. Growing louder.

"Good thing," Miriam says, "I called an ambulance before I got here."

Then she and Gabby slump against one another.

EIGHTY-SEVEN

SIGNS OF LABOR

Time passes, as it must. As it wants. For time knows no other desire than to move ineluctably forward, and for Miriam, the fear is that it is moving forward to a place she doesn't understand, to something that is far more mystery than clue, written as a sentence that does not end with period or an exclamation point but rather a tremendous question mark.

Today is her due date.

It is both the day her baby will be born and the day that fate has told her the baby will die. She can say with no certainty that she has changed that scenario at all. She *feels* like she has. She has great hope that the Trespasser was the one who was going to end the child's life to save Miriam's gift, and in casting the Trespasser to the wind—literally by throwing that fucker into a bunch of birds—she has saved her daughter's life.

That's the theory.

She knew then, that day in Gabby's house, that the Trespasser was no more. Just as she has lost herself many times inside a flock of birds, so too has the Trespasser now lost itself. The spirits inside it have gone from one flock to another. She felt from those spirits a sense of satisfaction.

And loss.

And not just a sadness but a literal loss of self—who they were in life, and in death, and with the Trespasser, subsumed **397** under the will of the flock. The ebb and flow of life. The migration and movement.

Again, that's the theory.

"You okay?" Gabby asks her. She's sitting by the hospital bed, reading a Kindle. She grabs Miriam's hand and gives it a squeeze.

"Just fucking peachy." They've told her she's in the stages of early labor. Her water broke, which sent her here—despite it happening in all the movies, it's apparently not a thing that happens in most pregnancies. And in fact, they told her they'll have to break it again, because the kid's head has since closed up the breach.

Everything hurts.

Her body still aches from that day at Gabby's house. The ambulance came, pumped Gabby's stomach, gave her some kind of charcoal shit to purge the remaining medications. And Miriam they said would be in traction and physical therapy for a long, long time.

She wasn't.

She was on her feet the next day. She was eating a Five Guys hamburger the day after that with arms that had been broken only two days before. She mended. They called it a miracle. They wanted to put her on TV, but she told them to fuck off, please and thank you. Then it was back to Los Angeles, where she and Gabby resumed a normal life, the end.

Okay, not so normal, maybe. They had a lot to deal with, regarding the deaths of Richard Beagle and Abraham Lukauskis. Guerrero helped them through it, made sure they weren't attached to any of it—but he said, given the pervasive nature of surveillance and broken privacy in this country, he couldn't guarantee it wouldn't ever come up again. Their best insulation from that was the fact that both deaths happened relatively off the grid, far away from prying eyes. Fingers and toes crossed, it

was never exposed.

Steve Wiebe did as Miriam said.

He's already in Iceland.

Sometimes, he sends them pictures of him climbing around these big-ass black rocks and taking selfies in bubbling hot springs. Living his best life. His only life. A too-short life.

Now, here they are, in the hospital.

Miriam is trying very hard not to act worried.

But she is worried. *I don't want my daughter to die.* They keep coming in, checking her cervix for dilation, which is about as fun as it sounds. (And none of the nurses seem to respond well to the *Buy a lady a drink first, wouldja?* jokes.) They tell her that once it dilates to a certain point, she'll be in the active labor stage and then the transition phase, which leads to, well, a baby popping out of her. Except it won't just pop out—she has to *push* it out, which sounds awful. And then if that doesn't happen, they'll have to do a C-section, which she damn sure doesn't want. She's not even sure if that'll work, given her ability to, well, *heal* like she can.

Gabby says, "You're worried."

"Nope, I'm good," she lies. "My asshole hurts, though. My literal butthole hurts really bad. And my back hurts. Can you rub it?"

"The back, not the butthole, right?"

"No kinky shit today, Gabs, just the back, yeah."

She rolls over on her side, and Gabby brings out this dolphin-shaped back massager—she holds the dolphin and presses its smooth plastic fins and tail over Miriam's back. It hurts. And it feels amazing. In part *because* it hurts.

"It's okay to be worried," Gabby says.

"I'm not—I'm not worried, it's fine, I'm sure it'll all be fine." But she feels queasy with anxiety. "The baby will be okay."

"The baby *will* be okay. You did it. You . . . saved me, and you will have saved your daughter, too. Okay?"

"Okay."

But she doesn't believe it.

Hours disappear under the weight of other hours. She knows the time is coming. She has that clock in her guts, in her blood. Time is ticking down. Gabby meanwhile wants to talk about it all—the birthing process, especially, which Miriam doesn't want to hear about *at all*. Soon as Gabby starts talking about "mucus plugs" and "placentae," she's way the fuck out.

"I don't wanna talk about the horrible thing that's going to happen because I can't change it. The fact that childbirth is a gory, grotesque purging of a human being is one fate I cannot change." She winces. "Plus, I'm probably going to poop the bed. A lot of ladies giving birth poop the bed. That's fucked up. We're all born into shit, Gabby. And then when we die, a lot of us also shit again. It's just a . . . a circular log-flume ride of shit."

"It's not . . ." Gabby sighs. "It's not a log flume ride of shit. Life is good and wonderful and we are here, living it. You've literally created life with your body, and that's some truly amazing shit, Miriam."

That's the other thing with Gabby—she's really got a new lease on life. She's almost disgustingly upbeat. Miriam hates it, or that's what she tells herself. Truth is, she loves it. Or, at least, she needs it. It is the perfect counterbalance to her . . . well, *usual* attitude.

Like now.

The nurse comes in.

"Ready for your epidural?"

"Do you want the epidural?" Gabby asks. "You don't have to—"

"Fuck that, I *want* it. We're talking high-class drugs. I haven't been able to have a drink or a smoke in nine months. God, they tell you not to eat *lunch meat*, Gabby. Ham! I can't eat ham." To the nurse she says, "Can you put ham in the epidural? I could

really go for some ham. Or a hamburger. Oh, god, a hamburger."
She can't eat during this entire labor process, nor does she really *want* to, because eating means making poop, and making poop means shitting during birth, which she decidedly doesn't want to do.

"Speaking of that, I haven't had lunch," Gabby says.

"You're leaving me?"

"Just for a few. Just while you get your epidural."

"Bring me a hamburger."

"I can't, but I'll eat one for you."

"You're a monster."

"A wonderful, loving monster," Gabby says, and kisses her on the forehead before fucking off out of the room.

The nurse, a white lady with a snarl of orange hair, hooks up IV fluids and then sends out for the anesthesiologist. He's a chubby black dude with a big face and a big smile, and he hums and whistles as he gets her to lie on her left side. He says, "You know this goes into your spine, right? Spinal cord, specifically."

"I don't care if it goes up my ass, just get me some drugs."

"Done and done," he says.

And the needle goes in.

EIGHTY-EIGHT

LIGHT AS A FEATHER, STIFF AS A BOARD

She lies there for a while, waiting for them to come back and check on her. Waiting for Gabby to come back (her breath smelling like food, which will be the closet Miriam gets to actual food until this baby is out of her). Waiting for Dr. Shahini to check in—Guerrero made sure she was still on their health plan, which means she's still with Shahini for the delivery. Waiting too for the pain to fade into the background, along with, she hopes, her anxieties. *The baby will be fine. The baby will be fine. The baby will*—if she says it enough times, maybe it'll be okay—*be fine.*

She naps for a little while. Then she's up again, her bladder suddenly sending off alarm klaxons. Her eyes pop open and she sees the bathroom door just a few feet away—she gets her own bathroom, la-dee-da, common to the birthing suites, not shared with some other rando. She notices too that the TV in the corner of the room is on: it's showing some weird nature documentary about the Humboldt squid. All red tentacles and angry beaks. Teeming and seething in the Vantablack sea. She thinks, *Okay, turn off the TV, go to the bathroom, then back in bed.*

She reaches for the remote control.

Or, rather, she tries to. But she can't do it.

She can't move at all.

She's breathing.

She can look around.

She tries to call out for the nurse—

But the only sound that comes out of her mouth is a dull, muted cry. A low, banshee whine. *No, no, no, something's going wrong.*

Fuck.

This.

Whatever this is, it could be it. It could be what's going to kill the baby. The epidural, it always had a risk—paralysis, right?— and now it might be affecting the baby. What if that's what does it? Her stupid, simple primate desire for drugs in her system . . .

But it's supposed to be safe. This is a hospital.

Oh, god, please don't let this be the mistake . . .

The door to her room opens up, thank god, and in comes the doctor—not Shahini but a man, tall, thin but for his paunch, balding—

She makes the sound again, *nnnngh*, and he turns toward her.

"Miriam," he says.

Emerson Caldecott.

He closes the door and locks it. He carries with him a small black case, which he sets at the edge of her bed. From it he withdraws a very familiar knife: the same hooked hunting knife used by Alejandro.

She wants to scream at him, *You fuck, you fucker, get the fuck away from me*, and what comes out of her is a desperate, piggish squeal.

He takes the knife and pokes the bottom of her foot with it.

"Good," he says. "I snuck a little *paralytic* into your drugs— just to keep you nice and docile for this next part. Let me explain what happens next, Miriam Black. I'm going to reach in. I'm going to pull that child out. And then I'm going to cut its throat. You're going to watch. You will watch the life come into this world and then go right back out. It will be recompense for my sister. It will be for Alejandro. Most of all, it's because I want to do it. Because I enjoy it. Because you are a ruinous little slag. You will not be allowed to have a child. I will let you live a little while longer, though. I'm curious to see what happens to you after this."

She tries to thrash, tries to will her body to do something, anything.

It fails.

He holds up the knife and then pushes her ankles apart forcefully.

"*Mmmngh*," she says—not in a pleading way but in a warning, a dire warning that she wants to take that knife and use it to cut him into cubes.

"Are you wondering how I got in here? Did you not realize I was a doctor? I'm a surgeon, Miriam. I get to be the arbiter of life and death. Not you. You called me a common criminal back in my own home. . . ." He shakes his head, pulling up her gown, exposing her to him. "I am an upstanding citizen in the medical community. And then you show up, and you accuse me of things? You ruin my life, set the FBI on me? I save lives when I need to, and I take them when I need to. And if I happen to sell the organs here and there on the red market . . ." He reaches for her, then stops. "My god, that TV is so loud. Rudely loud. We can't have a nice talk with that. And I want you to really *hear* the sound of the knife taking your child's life. You won't hear the thing cry. They don't cry when they come right out; that takes a moment. But I'll kill it before it happens; you'll see."

He moves around the side of the bed to find the remote.

And as he does, the bathroom door clicks.

It gently drifts open.

A small, person-shaped shadow waits inside.

He turns to point the remote at the TV—

And Miriam Black steps out of the bathroom.

Miriam blinks—no. Not her. It looks like Miriam from days

past: hair longer, still dyed jet black, the vented jeans, the white T-shirt. A doppelganger. A clone. Or just a wayward sister.

It's Wren.

Caldecott freezes upon seeing her.

She has a gun in her hand. A large pistol—a .45 ACP, old, half-rusty, dinged-up. Caldecott looks from her to the gun and back again.

"Who might you be?"

"Someone here to square the circle."

Then she shoots him in the head. The back of his skull paints the wall. Outside the room, screams rise up. Someone is already at the door, trying to open it. It shudders against the frame. Keys rattle.

Miriam can't speak. She can't move.

Wren steps over to her. She says, "I'm sorry. I know I can't fix what I did. But at least I could fix this."

Then she walks to the window and empties her clip into the glass, firing all over it so that no glass remains. Then she climbs out onto the hospital roof and is gone. Finally, the door pops open with the rattle of keys, and two police officers storm into the room, followed quickly by nurses and Dr. Shahini. Miriam doesn't know where Gabby is. She can't move.

But something inside her does move.

The baby.

EIGHTY-NINE

GONE GABBY GONE

For a long time, nothing makes sense. She's wheeled away to another room. Shahini and nurses hover over her like a cloud of agitated flies. Blood tests come and they say she's going to be okay, but the baby is coming. She starts to get her voice back and she asks them in slurred speech, "Where's Gabby? I need Gabby," but she knows what happened. Gabby is gone. Emerson's first act was to find her. To kill her. To make sure he could do what he wanted to do and nobody would bother him. And she starts to cry even as they gather around and start to prep the room for the birth of the child. And she looks around at the nurses and—

Gabby is there. Holding her hand. Telling her not to worry, just to breathe, just to go with it.

Not to worry.

Just to breathe.

Just go with it.

"You're here," Miriam says.

"You said I'm your wings, so let's fly."

"Yeah. Okay. *Okay*. Let's fucking fly."

NINETY

THE NAMING

The baby is a rubbery, purple thing. She has hair on her head and little fists that punch the air. They suction something from her mouth, and then she's crying. Squalling like she was just taken from a very safe, very warm place—which, Miriam supposes, she was. They towel her off, plant her against Miriam's chest, and Miriam holds her there.

She names the baby Louisa.

Lulu for short.

THE END OF THE WORLD

The truck is a piece-of-shit 1997 white Datsun, though it's more red rust and spattered mud than white paint anymore. Miriam guns it down Uakea Road, past the Hana Cultural Center, toward the little schoolhouse—the Hana Arts Academy, where Lulu goes to Kindergarten.

In her gut is a breeding ball of snakes.

She doesn't want to do this.

She doesn't want to have this conversation.

It's nothing, she thinks. *It's just bullshit. She heard you talking. Or she . . . she's just being a silly little girl playing silly girl games.*

It's end of day, but before school lets out proper. She pulls up into the little parking lot by the school, a lot ringed by palm trees and black porous volcanic rock, and she sees Lulu standing there under the bamboo overhang. Mrs. Lee stands there with her, not much taller than the five-year-old. Lulu's got her yellow galoshes on—not because she needs them but because she is obsessed with them, won't take the damn things off except for bedtime—and her way-too-large R2-D2 backpack. It nearly dwarfs her, poor kid.

But she loves it, and it's stuffed with art supplies and books and papercraft and also snacks. So many snacks. The kid is a snack addict.

Miriam pulls up, leaves the engine running. She gets out, hurries to meet Mrs. Lee. "I'm sorry I'm late—class ran long," Miriam says. "You know how it is with the tourists."

"Like chatty fucking magpies!" Lulu says in a cheerful, chipper voice. Mrs. Lee blanches, as she always does, and Miriam winces. But this is part of their arrangement: Lulu says naughty words because Miriam says naughty words, and as long as Lulu doesn't say the naughty words *in school*, it's fine. And now she's technically *out* of school—if only by a few feet—so, the bad language is fair game.

Mrs. Lee sighs. "It's fine, Miriam. Thanks for coming."

Miriam gives the little girl a quick, eyebrow-arching look. "You okay, kid?"

"I'm okay, Mama."

"You're going to talk to her?" Mrs. Lee asks.

"I'm going to talk to her."

"Because this . . . it isn't okay."

That, said with the direst tone.

"I know. It's just . . . a phase. Kids are kids. *Keiki* gonna *keiki*," she says, using the Hawaiian word for children. Mrs. Lee isn't Hawaiian, she's Chinese-American, but she's been here for long enough to go with it.

"It better be."

"It is."

Mrs. Lee bends down and gives Lulu a small hug. "See you Monday, Lulu Black."

"Bye, Missa Lee," and then she bounds into the truck. There's no child safety seat—frankly, the truck isn't safe for adults, either—and occasionally someone gives her shit about it. She just says her own mother's words back to them: *It is what it is*. And then she drives off.

With Lulu in the car, Mrs. Lee says again, "It's really not okay. She scared the other girl, you know."

"Who was it?"

"Daphne."

Daphne Stevens. New girl. Her mother owns the little bed-and-breakfast north of here on Kalo Road. *The mom's kind of a bitch*, Miriam thinks but does not say. The kid's all right, though.

Shit.

"I'll handle it."

"Good. And I'll see you at yoga tomorrow?"

"See you at yoga tomorrow. Practice your crescent pose, all right?"

"All right."

"I'll see you, Mrs. Lee, and thanks again."

And then she's back in the truck and pulling out of the lot.

She chews her lip as she drives north, toward the little bungalow they call home. At the last second, she takes turn off a side road—Keawa Place—to the beach park there. "Where we going, Mama?" Lulu asks.

"Just to park. And to talk."

"Talk about what, Mama?"

She thinks, *You know what*, but maybe she doesn't. Five-year-olds sometimes have the memory of a goldfish. Worse, a goldfish you hit with a spoon to knock the sense of out of him, *whack*.

She pulls alongside the little park. Not far beyond it is a strip of white crystal sand and the sapphire sea beyond it.

Miriam tries to center herself. *Be mindful*, she thinks. It's some bullshit she tells the men and women at her yoga class up at the Hana Honu Resort—she never in a million years thought she would teach yoga, but it helped her get past both the nightmares *and* the arthritis that's plagued her since Lulu was born. So, much as she tells herself it's bullshit, it's really not. It helps her. Mind and body. (And all that shit.)

"I know what we're gonna talk about," Lulu says, and she

says it in that very special Lulu way, which is *I know something you don't*.

"Oh?"

"Uhhhh-huh."

"And what's that, Lulubear?"

The little girl reaches for the dashboard of the truck, past a busted clay pot and over a pile of receipts and drink cups—

She pops the ashtray.

Inside, a single wrinkled cigarette butt. Crushed like a crinkle fry.

"Busted," Lulu says.

"It was just one."

"Mama, you said you're quitting."

"And I am quitting. It's a process."

"Is not a negotiation." That is a thing Miriam says to Lulu all the time when she doesn't want to eat food or take a bath or literally do anything she's ever told, so it's not a surprise she's learned to say it back to Miriam like a damn little parrot.

"Fine, yes, it's not, and I'm quitting. I quit. It's done. I already threw the pack away," she lies. (Spoiler warning: it's under her seat, and Miriam smokes one cigarette every week. Which she feels bad about. But it's so, so, so good.) "We need to talk about what you said to Daphne."

"Ohhh."

Lulu gets quiet.

"Yeah, ohhh."

"I didn't mean to tell her that; I just told her because . . . I dunno."

Ah, the logic of a five-year-old.

"Shit," the little girl says.

"It's okay."

"Mama, are you mad?"

"I'm not mad, no, not at all, Lulubear." She wishes she could have a cigarette *right fucking now*, though. She puts her hand on the little girl's hand. "I just need to know: is what you told her . . . true?"

"I dunno."

"You don't know?"

"Okay, I maybe know." In a quiet voice she says, "I think it's true, Mama. I'm sorry."

She tries to walk the line between serious and softly sweet when she asks Lulu, "Tell me how you know, and tell me what you saw."

Lulu puckers her lips and pops them—*pop, plop, plorp*—and then says, "We were painting turtle shells and then she bumped into me and I saw it. I saw her in the pool. I saw a . . . I saw a scary man in a jacket like my yellow boots push her in. And then he went in with her and held her there. And then she . . . she stopped moving."

Outside, birds call and squawk. Miriam can do nothing with them. She cannot know what they are or see what they see. Just as she does not know how Mrs. Lee dies. Just as she will not heal a cut, or a broken bone, or a pulled muscle any faster than anybody else.

But now . . .

Lulu . . .

Her heart drums with the surf.

"Lulu, are you sure about this?"

"I'm sure, Mama."

"When does it happen?"

"Soon. A week is seven days?"

"A week is seven days."

"Then it's . . ." She holds up her fingers. "Three weeks, Mama."

She tries not to look upset. She needs to keep it together, because if she doesn't keep it together, Lulu won't keep it together. "Is this the first time you've seen something like this?"

Lulu is quiet. Doesn't answer. Shit.

"Lulu . . ."

"No, Mama. I seen it before."

"With a lot of people?"

"Just some."

She winces. "Me?"

Again, Lulu descends into silence. She stares, unblinking, not at her mother but at her boots, which she kicks into the glovebox. *Whump whump*.

Finally, Lulu says, "Yes. Do you want to know?"

Does she?

All this time, the one death she hasn't been able to see is that one.

Her own.

Now all those doors are closed except one. Lulu can give it to her. Her little girl can open that door and show Miriam what she has never seen: how she bites it, sucks the pipe, takes the eternal dirt-nap.

"No," she says, finally. "I'm okay, Lulubear, thanks."

"Okay, Mama."

Miriam swallows. "Daphne. Your new friend. She's nice?"

"She's real nice, Mama. She shares her smelly markers and I think that's pretty fucking okay."

"Pretty fucking okay, indeed. You want her to be okay?"

Lulu nods as serious a nod as a child can nod.

"Okay," Miriam says. She thinks to the pistol in the finger-printed safe under her bed back at the bungalow. She thinks about the man who cleans the pool at the Kalo Road B&B, and about his yellow rainslicker, and how he's never seemed quite right to Miriam. White guy, pale, too pale for Hawaii, where everyone is tan like an oiled Bronze Age shield. (Everyone except Miriam, who goes from butt-white to lobster-red.) She doesn't know his name, but she's seen him around. And now, she thinks, he's going to hurt a little girl. Drown her in the pool. That before doing who knows what else.

It kills her that this is happening.

Five years now away from all of it.

Here in Hana, on Maui, in Hawaii. End of the world. Away from it all. Like Guerrero said.

She can't think too long about it or she'll cry.

Instead, she forces a smile. "We'll make sure Daphne is okay," she says. "Mamabird has it covered."

"Thanks, Mama."

"Now let's get you back to the house, little girl. Gotta get you cleaned up—it's not a negotiation; don't make that face at me—because Mama Gabby will be off her shift at the restaurant and we're going to go out to dinner tonight for her birthday." She leans over and kisses Lulu on the temple, then pulls her close as she wheels the truck back around the other way and heads back home. "I love you, Lulu."

"Love you too, Mama. Is Daphne gonna be okay?"

"She'll be okay," Miriam promised. "We'll make sure of it."

ACKNOWLEDGMENTS

This is it.

Six books. A journey of many years and a great many vulgarities.

I have to thank you, the readers, first and foremost, because without you, these books don't get to be here. You didn't give me the first one, but you earned me the five that came after, and it's only because of readers—fans and audience members who are willing to try out a new series before it's finished—that penmonkeys like me can keep on keepin' on.

Thanks to my agent, Stacia Decker, for believing in this character from the beginning, and keeping the series and its characters authentic and true. It was *Blackbirds* that got me in the door with her as an agent and so thanks to her for giving Miriam that chance—where a lot of other agents wouldn't.

Thanks to Lee Harris at Angry Robot (now at Tor-dot-com) for bringing Miriam to life there, and then to Joe Monti for resurrecting her at Saga/S&S. When the first book went out on submission, we got the nicest possible rejections: "We love it, but we don't know what to do with it." So it's great to be in the hands of publishers who want the books *and* who know what to do with Miriam. Thanks to Richard Shealy for being Miriam's copy editor along the way, across all the books. Thanks also to Kevin Hearne and Delilah S. Dawson for letting Miriam play along in the Three Slices and Death & Honey collections.

Thanks finally to my wife, who believed in the first book enough to say that yes, we could take the chance on me trying my hand at this whole silly *novel-writin' gig*, and as it turns out, her faith in me and in the first Miriam book were (thankfully) not misplaced. I've done all right, and she's been my first reader on the Miriam Black novels since the first. People think someone like Miriam, with her foulest of mouths, could not exist . . . but they have not met my wife.

I'll note this, too, as a final endnote to the series: we live in a particularly stupid-ass timeline, and I assume at this point that the Hadron Collider went awry and fucked shit up, and now we're paying some kind of cosmic debt. We're a country perched precariously on a needlepoint of a pin, and I don't know what way we'll fall, but I know a lot of us are mad as hell, as we should be. As such, there exists a current debate as to whether or not the resistance against the current administrative regime should dare to be (*gasp*) uncivil. Should we use naughty words in our criticism? Should we dare to stand up and stand in the way of our political foes? And the Miriam Black that lives in my heart says that fuck yeah, we should. Fuck the fucking fuckers. Fuck the fucking lot of them, and fuck them if they think they can shame us for our incivility while trying to bring a hammer of sexism and racism and ableism down on our democracy. Fuck that noise. Evil people want you to be nice, because when you're nice, it's nearly impossible to point out the evil that they're doing. Fuck nice. Be more like Miriam. Speak truth to power, with as many nasty words as you can muster.

Thank you, you foul-mouthed, venom-hearted souls, you. Keep on keeping on.

Miriam would thank you, but she's too busy giving everyone the middle finger.